# ANATOMY OF EVIL

Also by Will Thomas

*Some Danger Involved*

*To Kingdom Come*

*The Limehouse Text*

*The Hellfire Conspiracy*

*The Black Hand*

*Fatal Enquiry*

# ANATOMY OF EVIL

WILL THOMAS

MINOTAUR BOOKS ❧ NEW YORK

ANATOMY OF EVIL. Copyright © 2015 by Will Thomas. All rights reserved. Printed in the United States of America. For information, address St. Martin's Press, 175 Fifth Avenue, New York, N.Y. 10010.

www.minotaurbooks.com

The Library of Congress Cataloging-in-Publication Data is available upon request

ISBN 978-1-250-04105-0 (hardcover)
ISBN 978-1-4668-3720-1 (e-book)

Minotaur books may be purchased for educational, business, or promotional use. For information on bulk purchases, please contact the Macmillan Corporate and Premium Sales Department at 1-800-221-7945, extension 5442, or write to specialmarkets@macmillan.com.

First Edition: May 2015

10  9  8  7  6  5  4  3  2  1

# ANATOMY OF EVIL

# CHAPTER ONE

I understand it is said in scientific circles that if one attempts to boil a frog it will jump out of the pot, but if one raises the temperature of the water slowly it will never notice the difference until it is too late. That analogy comes to mind whenever anyone mentions 1888. We were not aware, my employer, Cyrus Barker, and I, that events of historic significance were happening around us. As usual, I was merely trying to get from point A, January 1, to point B, December 31, in one solid and very much living piece.

At that time I'd like to think I finally knew what I was about as an enquiry agent; that I was prepared for whatever might come through the door. I'd risked life and limb and had the wounds to prove it, and had contributed in my own way to one case or another. Even Barker would admit I wasn't a complete tyro, though occasionally I'd make a boneheaded mistake and he would look at me the way a hand plane regards a stubborn knot in a sheet of pine. We had made it through the summer months of that fateful year, the "far turn" as it were, and had rounded into the homestretch, but if I thought we had the track all to ourselves and the course was easy, I was very much mistaken.

"I've got to admit," I said to my employer, Cyrus Barker, one night in early September, "that I don't understand what all the fuss is about. It's just a couple of unfortunates."

Cyrus Barker looked up from the table, which held a scrapbook, a pot of paste, and a pair of scissors. He doesn't normally keep files catalogued this way, but when several articles appear in the newspapers on a particular subject that interests him, he sets them in order by cutting them out and pasting them in a scrapbook.

"Thomas Llewelyn, an unfortunate deserves as much justice under the law as a baroness," he said, regarding me gravely. We were at home, in his library in Newington, the unfashionable side of London. It was that time in the evening when one suddenly realizes there is a bed waiting, and wouldn't it be nice to crawl into it?

"You know that's not what I mean, sir. Of course they deserve justice. I'm not saying they don't, merely that theirs is a dangerous profession. They meet all kinds of men; sailors from every nation, criminals, even the odd maniac, I'm sure. I just don't see how their deaths merit so much public attention."

"By those standards we ourselves, when the time comes, should be relegated to the back pages with the agony columns, for our occupation is easily more dangerous than theirs and only slightly more socially acceptable."

Barker had finished covering the back of the article with glue, and had set it in place, smoothing it down with hands the size of small hams. The coal fire in the grate was reflected in his dark-lensed spectacles. He seemed determined to misunderstand me, but I was not done yet.

"The newspapers of London have gone out of their way to declare the town does not have a prostitution problem. One would think it does not exist here, but now two dollymops are dead within a month and it becomes a major crisis. The *Police News* I can understand, or the *Star,* but even the *Times* has begun devoting space to it."

"The women were savaged. Not merely were their throats cut, but they were disemboweled afterward. At least, I hope for their sakes it was afterward," he said.

"That makes it more sensational, but not more important," I

said. "I, for one, have little interest in the matter. It is a Scotland Yard case, with all their resources, and frankly, they are welcome to it."

"It is just as well," the Guv said. "They are not likely to consult us over it."

"I'm glad to hear it," I replied. "I doubt I shall have anything to contribute."

"An enterprising young man such as yourself? I would think you'd be a font of suggestions for Scotland Yard."

"No doubt," I said. "But would they listen? When last I checked, they weren't hanging on my opinions."

"You're still young. Perhaps one day they shall," the Guv said. He was just past forty, and could still outrun me on a track, but he always spoke as if he'd lived for many decades and I should benefit from his sage advice.

"The odds on that are rather long, I'm afraid. But as far as these murders are concerned, how do we know they were done by the same fellow?"

"We don't. I suppose they could easily be random killings, but two murders of women of the same profession within a fortnight or so in the same district, by the same method?"

"It's some lunatic, like as not, escaped from an asylum. The human equivalent of a mad dog. Your skills are best served against intelligent criminals trying to fatten their bank accounts by trying something audacious. Something in the West End."

"Close to fashionable restaurants and shops?" Barker asked, raising his brows above the rims of his spectacles.

"Precisely."

"It is awfully inconsiderate of this fellow to commit murders in unfashionable Whitechapel."

"True, but what does one expect from a madman?"

Barker picked up the scissors and began to cut around an article from the *Daily Telegraph*. I wasn't going to convince him to take my advice.

"I'll leave you to it, then. I'm for bed. Good night, sir."

"Good night, Thomas. Sleep well."

I stepped into the hall and trudged up the staircase to my

bedroom. It was a small, monastic room with a bed, a desk and chair, and a bookcase full of my favorite books. An armoire held my clothes. My every possession on earth was in that one small room. I slid off my elastic-sided boots and wrapped my suit jacket around the back of the chair. I unknotted my tie and removed my collar, then doffed my waistcoat and slid down my braces. Then I lay down upon the bed fully clothed and prepared to wait. It was two hours until midnight, or as I preferred to think of it, the hunting hour.

Around half past ten, I heard Barker climb the stair to his garret overhead. It was a spacious room with sloping walls running the length of the house. From time to time, I heard him walk about above my head, preparing to retire. Within another half hour, he was snoring in his bed. His nose had been broken several times, and I had grown accustomed to the sound over the years.

*Not much longer now,* I told myself. Harm, Barker's prized Pekingese, waddled in according to his internal timetable and curled up at the foot of my bed. Soon, he too would begin to snore. The household began to settle. I heard the standing clock in the hall toll the quarter-hour chime. Outside, crickets formed a chorus in the nearby marshes.

I tried to distract myself. I thought about a girl, a particular girl, named Rebecca Mocatta. That summer she had married a rising young politician named Asher Cowen. I'd have preferred her to have a different last name entirely, but that's the way life is. Some people receive all the advantage, while others receive a good boot in the ribs for our troubles. Sometimes right over the heart.

No doubt there would be children soon. A rising young family and a credit to Bevis Marks Synagogue. Her parents would think her well shed of a young Welshman who had acted as *shabbes goy* in their home one Sabbath if they gave him any thought at all. We'd been alone for no more than a few minutes, but those moments had haunted me ever since.

Did she ever think of me? I supposed I wouldn't, if I were her. Still, it would be nice if she regretted never speaking to me again, if only for one minute, for sixty seconds together. That's all I would ask for, and no more.

Slowly, carefully I slid out of bed, pulled up my braces and donned my jacket. There was no need for a collar or waistcoat where I was going. Picking up my boots, I slithered fluidly out into the hall, and crept to the top of the stair. There was a creaking board a quarter of the way down, but by staying to the inside, I was able to reach the ground floor without making a sound. I turned the key in the lock and slid the bolt back slowly, knowing our butler, Mac, is a light sleeper. Stepping outside, I wriggled into my boots. I was free.

Jumping across the stream in Barker's garden, I skirted the stone lantern until I reached the moon gate, which I unlatched. In the lane, I took one last look back at the house, expecting to see an electric light go on somewhere. Nothing. I had successfully broken out of my own home. The night air was chilly and I put my hands in my pockets as I walked down the narrow alley behind the house. Somewhere a cat yowled, but otherwise, the neighborhood of Newington was as quiet as a tomb.

A half mile away was the stable where my horse, Juno, was boarded. It had been Barker's horse to begin with, but Juno and I had bonded so closely that when I finally had the money, I made him an offer on her, promising she would still be at his disposal when needed. He accepted, and it was done. The stable boy slept within the building itself, and he knew that we kept strange hours in our profession and to expect me at any time. He came out of a stall when I entered. There was straw in his hair and he was wiping his eye.

"Ho, Albert," I said.

"Evening, Mr. Llewelyn. Shall I saddle Juno for you?"

"If you would, please. I've got a late errand to run."

I reached into my pocket and handed him a shilling. Albert came instantly awake. I made my arrival worth his while. He led me to Juno's stall. The bay mare had been asleep as well, and did not take kindly to having her warm blanket removed in order to be sent into the cold September night. She squealed in protest, which woke the other horses, who answered her in sympathy. I went to my locker and found the box of sugar lumps I kept there. She needed a bribe, as well. She curled her lips in anticipation and stuck out her tongue to receive two lumps. Then she masticated them so long I began to wonder if she was indulging in sarcasm at my expense.

Returning to the locker while Albert haltered and saddled her, I took out a heavy Ulster greatcoat and a bowler hat. The coat was made of thick wool so full of lanolin that it repelled all moisture. I dug my toe into the waiting stirrup, grasped the reins and the side of the saddle, and drew myself up. Juno gave a final snort in protest. Albert offered me a riding crop, but I shook my head. Once I'm in the saddle, Juno and I become one. Her shod hooves clicked on the flagstones between the two rows of stalls. The boy opened the door wider and the two of us, horse and rider, rode out into the night. Within a few minutes, we were in Newington Causeway, heading north, toward the river and Tower Bridge. The south side of Whitechapel was on the other side.

A fog was rising, if one could call the mixture of soot and factory chimney effluvia a fog. It would be the perfect night to stalk prostitutes, dark and wet. The fog stung the eyes and settled in the back of the throat, leaving a bitter taste on the tongue. Building eaves began to weep as I passed and moisture trickled down sooty windows. My body was plenty warm in my coat, but my nose was cold. Juno's nostrils blew out plumes of white mist ahead of me and I felt as if I were riding a dragon.

I crossed the new bridge into Whitechapel, passing the Tower of London. Southwark and Lambeth had already gone to bed, but the 'Chapel is always awake. Men stood in front of public houses with glasses in hand, or staggered down the streets, supporting each other to keep from falling down. As I passed, women of all sorts leaned eagerly forward from the alleyways into the light, displaying themselves for my benefit. It had been a while since anyone here had seen a horse of Juno's caliber. This fellow, whoever he was, had a horse for riding. He must be a gentleman.

In Minories Street there was a stable with which I was acquainted that was still open though it was nearly midnight. I paid the men handsomely to brush and blanket Juno and I gave her a feed bag of oats. I headed north on foot, watching the faces of the few people who moved furtively along, heads down and hands in pockets or clutching their clothes around them. Like Cassius, they had a lean and hungry look. The thought penetrated my mind that I had no business being here. I was courting disaster. My bed awaited me a few miles south, yet stubbornly I refused to return there. I would see this through.

The Britannia was a shabby-looking public house at the corner of Dorset and Commercial Streets. A concertina was being played inexpertly within. When I entered, I could smell stale beer, rank cigars, and the odor of unwashed humanity. It made me want to gag, but in the past year or two I had learned to suppress such impulses. It was a natural part of life, a smell common to thousands of public houses. I tried to keep my emotions in check and not let my imagination get the best of me.

I spotted my quarry at a table near the far back. A homburg hat was pulled low over his eyes. He looked simultaneously nervous and dispirited. If I hadn't known better I might have thought he didn't want to be there. I ordered two half pints of bitter and carried them through to him at the table.

"Thomas!" he cried.

"Israel," I replied. "Are you ready? It seems a perfect night for it."

Israel Zangwill was my closest friend. When we had first met he was a teacher at the Jews Free School. Now he had become a reporter for the *Jewish Chronicle*. Israel was Whitechapel born and bred. He knew it better than anyone: its history, its cartography, and every crime ever perpetrated here. But there was something more. A year before, a girl he loved, the talented but melancholy poetess Amy Levy, had killed herself by putting her head in a gas oven. It had pushed his gentle soul to the edge.

Taking a gulp of beer, I made a face and set it down again. It had been watered down and probably given a jolt of opium to pep it up as well. I should have expected no less from such an establishment. Zangwill did not seem to notice and drank half the glass in one pull. He belched and excused himself.

"Made in Whitechapel, you know," he said. "Not three minutes away. You can't beat Albion Brown Ale."

"If they can't kill you one way, they'll do it another."

"Have you ever had that feeling as if you are children playing at being adults? I feel as if my father is going to catch me and tan my hide for being out so late."

"That's odd," I replied. "Sometimes I feel as if I'm a hundred years old."

Israel is not what one might call a handsome man. He is hatchet-faced and thin, and his eyes are bulbous, but those eyes see everything and the information he takes in is strained through his volatile brain, down his arm and into his pen. He is like a Jewish Dickens, combing the streets in the odd hours, taking impressions, crusading for better conditions, and occasionally getting himself in trouble.

"Have you got it?" Israel asked in too loud a voice, as if we were on stage and he wanted the audience to know he was Conspirator Number One.

I opened my coat and let him spy the Webley Mark III whose handle was sticking out of my breast pocket. "You?"

Zangwill reached down between his ankles and lifted a bull's-eye lantern. As I watched, he opened the hatch and lit the candle with the help of a box of vestas. His long fingers shook. He was clearly nervous.

"We could still call this off, you know," I said. "Be sensible, go home to bed, and never speak of this again."

"We've never been sensible before," he replied. "I see no reason to start now."

"That's the spirit," I said, slapping him on the shoulder. "Can you feel it? I think no woman in Whitechapel is safe tonight."

"Then let us get started," he replied.

I tossed a few pence on the table more from habit than thankfulness, and we left. We moved easily through the district with the tails of our coats flapping behind us. Pasting articles into scrapbooks might be good for some, and I'm sure it was a sensible and sagacious pastime, but we were young and needed to *do* something. I had seen my share of death in the past, occasionally in these very streets, but this was different. A lunatic was on the loose and would likely be killed or captured by the police within a day or two. Why should they get all the credit? If we could track the killer down ourselves, hold him at gunpoint, and deliver him to the police, we'd be heroes. People would pay to read Israel's account of it in the *Chron-*

*icle*. I planned to confess all to the Guv the following morning, but of course, as the saying goes, it is easier to get forgiveness than permission.

"Buck's Row School is up ahead there," Israel said, pointing down the street. "That's where the first woman, Mary Nichols, was found. By the wall there, against the playground."

Reaching our destination, he opened the shutter on the dark lantern in his hand and a small circle of yellow light splashed onto the cobblestones. The soil left by dozens of horses over the summer had filled the spaces in between the cobbles and it was this soil which had absorbed and still held the blood from the first victim. Cynic that I was, I reasoned that since then the ground had probably been salted with fresh blood—pig's blood—by guides hoping to make some money. Since the first murder, it should have been washed away by the rain.

I had only the vaguest idea how the poor woman had been savaged. That news had been kept back from the newspapers, and one had to attend the inquest to hear the full details read aloud. In print, having been so bold as to state that the unfortunate's dress had been lifted over her waist, a newspaper could be no more explicit without risking censure for indecency. Of course, there were other ways to sell copy. As I recall, one industrious journal said that the first victim's head had been sawn clean off, hanging by a mere flap of skin.

It was Death, you see, which had brought us out here in the middle of the night. The Age Old Mystery. Nothing makes us so alive as seeing that another has died while we yet live. After five or six millennia to deal with the matter, we still had come no closer to understanding or accepting it, that we too are mere mortals and sometime our own number will come, and after . . . what?

"Are there many unfortunates along this street, so close to a school?" I asked.

"They don't ply their wares during daylight, if that's what you mean."

"But they actually perform their business right here in the street?"

"In the alleyways nearby, where it is dark as pitch," Israel said, pointing toward a narrow court.

"Without a bed, or walls, or privacy?"

"This isn't Claridge's, Thomas. Privacy is expensive and a bed is what these women are attempting to make the money to afford. It's fourpence for a bed in the tenements around here. Well, not a bed, per se. A blanket on a hard floor in a doss-house, more like."

"These women lead very pathetic lives," I said.

"Until they meet very pathetic ends. But most of them are drinkers, you see. If they didn't need the drink to begin with, they'd have stayed with their husbands and been respectable. The need made them go out in the streets after midnight and ply their foul trade."

"What about their fancy men? What do you call them? Pimps?"

"This type of woman wouldn't have any. No pimp would waste his time on a woman past forty on her way out of this world. Too much trouble keeping them sober, you see. And it's no use trying to extort them for money because this kind rarely has a penny. When they do, it's right into the nearest establishment, like the Britannia, for a glass o' gin, please. Their only purpose in life is to get drunk as swiftly as possible. Their only solace is oblivion."

"And there are hundreds of such women in Whitechapel?"

Israel nodded. "Perhaps thousands. Odd women. That is, without a mate to care for them, on their own, forced to fend for themselves any way they can. Living in the city without a skill to fall back on. They haven't the talent of a Bernhardt, or the beauty of a Langtry. When they finally struck the ground, it was a hard fall, I'm sure."

Suddenly, this didn't seem as much a lark as I had hoped it would be. It was tragic. "So, have you ever . . . ?"

"No!" he said, shaking his head at the idea. "The Torah forbids it. And what if you catch a dose? Who wants to end one's days in a madhouse because of a few moments' pleasure? No, no, believe me, these women, worn out and unappealing, and half inebriated as they are, could only attract a certain sort of man. Someone who, like themselves, has fallen in life to a state of brutality. A man just holding on to his life, perhaps already a victim of vices and diseases that have softened his brain. A brute with a fierce temper, or as you said already, a lunatic."

"This district looks to me like a prime example of natural selection. The weak, the aged, the infirmed, all fall prey to the wolf culling the herd."

"You had better not let your Baptist employer hear you quoting Darwin."

"And you, I suppose, believe the best solution against the fate of such women is socialism."

"Of course!" he cried. "Decent housing and regular food. An occupation, leading to pride in work. A spirit of community here in Whitechapel, providing improvements such as regular street lamps. Did you know, Thomas, that there are streets in Whitechapel so dark and dangerous that even the police travel in pairs? In this, the most modern city in the world!"

"It's a pretty speech," I said. "Unfortunately, our theoretical drab will throw over her decent housing and free food in order to step into a pitch-dark alleyway with a perfect stranger to make enough money to get herself roaring drunk. Until such time as there is a cure for John Barleycorn, all the speeches by the Worker's Union won't make a bit of difference."

"You're a harsh critic, Thomas Llewelyn."

"Perhaps, but then I don't see General Booth's Salvation Army turning the East End into a Paradise with fountains and swans, either."

"There it is, just up ahead," he said, opening the lantern again. He was out of breath, though only twenty-four. He spent much of the day seated in a chair and never took exercise, save when I dragged him out on an errand. "We are in Spitalfields now."

"I don't know how you keep these districts straight," I said.

"You're one to talk. Is your office in Whitehall, Charing Cross, or St. Martin-in-the-Fields?"

"All of them, I think."

"Tut-tut. Rozzers. We'd better go this way."

I looked ahead and saw two constables waving people away from a doorway. I feared we wouldn't get to see where the second victim was slain that very morning.

"Come with me," Israel whispered.

He led me down a series of alleyways until we found ourselves in a dead end.

"Help me up," he said.

I cupped my hands and lifted him against a fence. After a moment, he tapped me on the shoulder.

"Right. The victim was found on the other side of this fence, between the steps and the fence itself. Let me help you."

Eagerly, I peered over. The blood was still fresh, dark and slick as ink, for the murder was less than a day old. It was a deserted stoop in a back yard connecting several buildings together. Until that morning it had been an anonymous spot people passed without thought. Now the police had to keep people away from it.

"Oy! You lot! Get down from there!" a constable cried, and Israel and I beat a hasty retreat. We ran through a warren of streets in the north of Whitechapel, an area known as Mile End New Town. If the police had pursued us, they gave up rather easily. Eventually, we collapsed against a brick wall in Underwood Street, huffing and puffing, with sore feet and stitches in our sides. We had the street all to ourselves.

"My word," I said, when I caught my breath, "what is that stink?"

"What do you think? No one has an extra penny for the street sweeper here. Anyone with a proper broom goes into the City and tries to take over a corner there."

"Is it all as bad as this?"

"No, some of it is just neglected. Sort of shabby-genteel, you know. It's mostly our crowd here, the Jews. The Ashkenazi from the Jewish Pale in Warsaw, or Moscow, or Berlin, chased out by the pogroms of the tsar and the kaiser. We are struggling, but give us time. Some of us will rise, and when we do, we'll put a fresh coat of paint on these buildings and mend the fences and sweep these odiferous streets. There is no more gentrifying power than a synagogue full of worshipers."

"Israel, I came here to catch a killer. If you're going to start preaching, I'd rather be sleeping at home in my nice, cozy bed."

"I'm sorry, Thomas, but the Whitechapel Killer is not a jack-in-the-box, to pop out of his hole at command."

Just then I sensed that we were not alone in the darkness. The street was empty, and I heard no sound that suggested someone was there. It was more a feeling. The hackles on the back of my neck rose. Had Mary Nichols had such a feeling before the blade cut into her throat? Did Annie Chapman realize she was not alone right before her life was snuffed like a candle?

Israel suddenly lifted his dark lantern in my face, blinding me with the light.

"Thomas, look out!" he cried.

A crushing hand seized my neck in a viselike grip, cutting off all air to my lungs. The last thing I saw was the lantern falling to the ground, as my friend fought off the figure in black that was choking the life from him.

# CHAPTER TWO

W e were lifted bodily, both of us, and shaken like rats in a terrier's jaws. Granted, neither of us is over nine stone, but still, we were two grown men. He was real, I told myself; the Whitechapel Killer is real! We had come in search of him, but he had found us instead! He carried us, still hanging by the collars of our jackets, into the light provided by a sputtering gaslight from a nearby tenement.

"And what are you rascals up to, capering about in the middle of the night?" Cyrus Barker demanded in his low Scots accent.

If it is possible to collapse without actually touching the ground, then we did. I went limp with relief, and would have spoken if he didn't actually have me by the neck.

"Well?" he demanded. "What have ye to say for yourselves?"

"Sorry, sir," I squeaked.

He set us both down. I leaned against a wall and coughed, but Israel actually sat down upon the pavement. He is terrified of my employer, and I supposed I could see why. Emerging suddenly from a dark alley in the middle of the night, Barker was terrifying.

"Explain," said the Guv.

The words tumbled out of my mouth, which was just as well, since Israel was still speechless. I told Barker about the article my friend was writing for the *Jewish Chronicle* and how I had offered to help him since it was dangerous to travel Whitechapel alone. Most of it was true.

"Why the subterfuge?" he asked. "Why feign a lack of interest in a case you intended to investigate within an hour or two?"

"I thought you might not let me go out," I admitted.

The Guv broke into a smile, albeit a chilly one. He shook his head. "Thomas, you are an adult, not that you're acting like one. You may come and go as you like. My only concern would be if you investigated a case we are working on together without my presence. This, however, is not my case, as much as it pains me to admit it, and probably never shall be. I followed you because I had no idea where you were going. Now that I am here, allow me to warn you. These are dangerous streets, gentlemen. Be careful where you go and don't be afraid to use your Webley if you need to, though only as a last resort."

I had not mentioned the pistol, so either he inferred that I would bring it or he noticed that I carried it under my coat. To ask him which would only give him satisfaction.

"You really think the killer would dare attack us in the street? We are full-grown men, not soiled doves," Israel said. It would have sounded better if his voice hadn't cracked.

"No, Mr. Zangwill, I am referring to the street gang members and disgruntled workers who have lost their situations recently to Jewish immigrants. I understand there is a so-called vigilance committee afoot in the area. My associate is as Welsh as Tintagel Castle, but he could be mistaken for a Jew while in your company."

"You don't think I can handle myself?" I asked.

"I do, but it would be folly to attempt to find out either way without a better reason than an assigned article in the *Chronicle*. No insult to your esteemed journal intended."

"But we Jews have nothing to do with these murders," Israel continued.

"Perhaps, but one cannot rely on vigilantes to use logic or accept your assurances at face value. Would they sympathize with your people's history of ill-treatment?"

Barker was referring, of course, to the pogroms which had occurred in Russia, Poland, and Germany, which had sent tens of thousands of Jews fleeing to England and the United States.

"How would I know?" Zangwill asked. "You create a straw man and warn us against it. Have you witnessed this committee you speak of? Do you know what kind of men it comprises, or how many? For all I know, it may be a figment of your imagination."

My employer stared at him blankly. That is, I could not read his expression behind the thick mustache and black spectacles he wore at all hours of the day or night, even in darkest Whitechapel. He might be ready to throttle Israel again for having the gall to question his veracity. Barker seemed to grow taller then, and more menacing, like some sort of ogre or troll from a Norwegian storybook. Just as quickly, he receded back to his normal size, which is formidable enough at any time.

"You did not tell me," the Guv said to me, "that your friend is educated in the debating arts, but then I would suspect such nimbleness of mind from a socialist. 'Straw man,' indeed. Very well, Mr. Zangwill, I admit the existence of such a committee is only hearsay, and I have not spoken to any of its members. Well argued, sir."

My jaw must have dropped. Israel arguing with Barker and besting him? Barker humbly accepting that he had been beaten? We had fallen down the rabbit hole.

"Were it not past midnight I would treat you both to a pint of stout," the Guv said.

Israel arched his brows in my direction. "I have a better suggestion, if Thomas will approve."

I understood what he meant. He was speaking of the Barbados Coffeehouse, where the two of us met frequently. I was not certain how I felt about having my public and private worlds collide, as it were. Offhand, however, I could think of no reason why we should not invite him.

"There is a coffeehouse in Cornhill Street, sir, called the Barbados. Have you heard of it?"

"Is that in St. Michael's Alley?" he asked. "I believe I've seen it, but I've never been inside. Is it fine?"

"You may see for yourself, sir. They stay open late on nights when the Yiddish Theater is performing, if you are interested. We could just as easily try another time."

"None like the present," Barker said. "Lead the way, gentlemen."

It was a walk of close to a good mile, through many streets and neighborhoods, from where we stood to the relative harbor of the City and Cornhill Street, but I felt safer with my employer, and he set a brisk pace. There is nothing he enjoys so much as a good walk, which he calls "the most social of exercises." No one ever got to know a street from the perch of a hansom.

The Barbados had been around for two hundred years, tucked among the warehouses where coffee is unloaded from ships in the Caribbean. It was a way, as I recall, for the West India Company to take money away from their rival, the East India Company, who was making a fortune importing tea from China and exporting opium. Coffee has never found a toehold here the way tea has, but it developed a following that has never gone away among the law clerks, civil servants, and intellectuals. Many government decisions have been made in coffeehouses, and inquests and other minor bits of business are still performed there. I have been in many of them, but none are a patch on the old Barbados, in my humble opinion.

It's not much to look at from the outside, its windows dark, its walls a faded terra-cotta. Once inside, however, you immediately step back two centuries. The floors, ceilings, and tall booths are carved out of black maple. The ceiling is low, and it bristles with mismatched tankards hanging down like fringe. Each table has a hollow in the center where pure Virginia Cavendish is kept for the visitor's pleasure. When we were seated, Barker naturally reached for the traveling pipe he kept in his pocket. We both stopped him.

"How is this?" he asked. "Tobacco, but no smoking?"

Just in time, the proprietor arrived. His name was Frobisher, and his family had run the place for nine generations. Frobisher was entirely bald, not so much as an eyelash, and he and I had had our skirmishes at one time or another.

"We would like to recommend this gentleman for membership," I said.

"On what grounds?" Frobisher asked, eyeing Barker with something approaching concern. There is a Magwitch-like element to his appearance that I suppose I've grown accustomed to over the years.

"On the grounds that if you do not consider his membership, he might reduce this building to rubble within the hour," Zangwill said.

"He's joking," I assured Frobisher. "Mr. Barker is well known among the law courts and is well spoken of in government circles. I can offer references. In fact, I have one here."

So saying, I pulled out my watch, which was actually given to Barker by the Prince of Wales, after we stopped an assault on his life by the Irish Republican Brotherhood. There aren't many references better than the Prince of Wales in London. Offhand, I could only think of one.

A form was brought forward, Barker dipped a quill in the inkwell, and he gave his signature which never varied: a capital *C* followed by a squiggle, like a man's scrawl left when dying, followed by a capital *B* without flourish, and a similar scrawl. In his defense, I have heard that his Chinese is practically legible, but only to the Chinese.

"What's going on?" Barker asked.

I handed a pound note to Frobisher and I explained to my employer that he had just joined the club, where for one pound a year they kept a churchwarden on the premises for his exclusive use. He would get a plum pudding at Christmastime, and should he ever pass away, his pipe would be ceremonially broken and hung overhead in his memory. There was something Pickwickian about it; it simply could not be passed over.

Soon his pipe was brought out and Barker charged and lit it. Then a cup followed and he dutifully took the first sip. Zangwill leaned forward. It was true; there was no better coffee in all the British Isles than in this place. However, if he was awaiting a reaction from Barker, he would be disappointed. My employer has no taste buds to speak of. One could put a hornet in his mouth and he would not give the satisfaction of a reaction. He'll eat anything placed in front of him and never knew the good from the bad. In restaurants I've known him to order the oddest things, like a stranger who doesn't speak English. I suspect the stronger something tastes, the better he likes it.

"Mmmph," he said, which was the closest Zangwill would get to a compliment. It was like a verbal writ, acknowledging flavor. I'll give Israel this: he recovers well and he knows what questions to ask, a fine quality for any reporter.

"What do you make of these murders, Mr. Barker?"

*Fine thing,* I thought. *Get someone else to do your thinking for you, Israel.*

"I would say that this killer is enacting some sort of ritual. The cutting of the throat, possibly after near strangulation, followed by the second cut of the abdomen. The exact moves both times. This was not a frenzied attack, but carefully planned out and possibly rehearsed."

"Was it some sort of pagan ritual done by followers of Satan?"

"As I recall, the ritual you mention requires some sort of altar. I meant it was a personal ritual to the killer. For whatever reason known only to him, he is going through the steps in a process."

"Could the murders have been some sort of punishment for their wicked lifestyles? The stabbing of the abdomen was so close to the child-bearing organs. Could the murders have been intended to kill a child within them?"

"They were past childbearing years, for the most part," Barker said, puffing on his pipe placidly as Frobisher recharged his cup.

"Oh, yes, I suppose they were. Could it be possible that the killer meant to kill Annie Chapman the first time, but in the dark mistook Mary Nichols for her? Then he'd have to kill her all over again."

"That is possible. In fact, all of your theories are possible, and a thousand theories besides. It is better, however, to gather more facts before trying to test a theory. Chances are, one of them might be correct, but it will get buried under another more sensational and grotesque one. I suspect at the end of the day, the killer will be revealed to not be the monster we all think and even hope he will be, because he will be revealed not to be a monster at all, but a man, a man like you and me. This is reality, you see, and not high opera."

"Of course," Israel said. "That makes perfect sense."

That was Israel's way of interviewing people, to slap them with a blunt or fantastical question, followed by a soothing pat on the back, as if to say, "We're mates, you and me." Questioning was akin to riding an unbroken horse; the trick was to not be thrown off. To do so, one has to be able to discern what the animal is thinking.

The problem with Barker, however, is that he knows what the other man is thinking. He doesn't fidget, he never seems hurried, and he's rarely out of control. Only by watching Barker day in and day out for years can you deduce—no, can you *guess*—what he may be thinking or may be about to do next, and even then you are often wrong. For example, he often approaches our offices by different routes, crossing Westminster or Waterloo, alighting on a different corner each day, sometimes as far away as Downing Street. But then, I have seen him in the bathhouse in his garden, covered with scars, studded with bullet pocks, burn marks, charred flesh, and tattoos from a dozen secret societies. He came by his methods the hard way. As good as Israel was, well, he may think he was riding the steed, but I suspected that crafty old steed was in fact riding him.

"One idea put forth is that the Whitechapel Killer hates women," Zangwill pontificated. "Such men are the worst examples of their sex. The killer not only cuts their throats, which of course silences them—the original Silent Woman, eh? But then he cuts them open down there, you know. There is an unconfirmed rumor he removes the organs. Surely this is the work of a virulent woman hater."

Barker gently knocked his pipe into the depression in the table. The clay churchwarden looked extremely fragile in his blunt hands. Then he drained his cup, which must have been cold by then, but when the Guv starts something, he always finishes it. He set the cup back in the saucer with a click.

"He could just as easily be a medical student who desperately wants to find a body to vivisect. In that case, he goes for such women because they are easily accessible most of the time, and for no other reason."

"But then he'd have to be sane."

My employer smiled again. "My good sir, make no mistake. The last I heard, only insane people run about slicing women from the very bottom of society's underbelly. I don't believe you can sustain a logical and cogent reason why a normal person would kill two women in this manner."

"But there still may be one," I said.

"Yes. Unfortunately, the only way to test a new rope is still to swing from it. That's where the Metropolitan Police come in."

"They do?" I asked. "What do you mean?"

Barker lifted his hand, palm up, in my direction. "There are a thousand theories and we are only two agents. I could enlist and organize every private detective in London and still not match the number of constables and inspectors of the Met. They are men seasoned by working with murderers, confidence tricksters, thieves, and harlots. They can generally tell when someone is lying."

"You've got an excellent perspective, Mr. Barker. What if we gave you a column in the *Chronicle:* 'Thoughts of a Private Enquiry Agent,'" Israel said. "We could do all we can to gather clues for you and open doors. All the information we find will come by you first. I'm sure we could pay you pretty well."

That was when I knew Israel had lost the fish off his line, if it were ever on. He forgot Barker is a rich man by East End standards. By West End standards, as well, I supposed. He's got an office in the center of London and a home which, while Newington might not be Park Lane, is half an acre of some of the most beautiful land in England. When Kew Gardens comes to your door asking for cuttings, you know you're doing something right.

"Thank you for thinking of me, Mr. Zangwill, but I'm afraid I must refuse. There may come a time when I sit back and deduce from the safety of an armchair, but I have no wish to start that career prematurely."

"Ah," said Israel, realizing his mistake. "I hope I have not offended you."

"Not at all."

"We Jews have much to thank you for. You saved us from a pogrom in London."

He was referring to my first case with Barker, in which we were hired by the Jewish Board of Deputies, led by Sir Moses Montefiore himself. A Jew had been crucified in Petticoat Lane and it was hoped we would stop a pogrom from occurring there. Barker did, by finding the killer who fanned the flames of hatred, and by organizing a golem squad of able-bodied men to combat a possible mob.

"You are not out of the woods, yet, laddie. There are many that still want to see your people gone, but with the help of the Lord we both worship, we won't let that happen."

My friend nodded solemnly. I realized for the first time how much he had at stake. Though an Ashkenazi Jew, he was no import from a Warsaw ghetto. His people had been here for generations. If London became unsafe, and I could not imagine what London would be like then, he could find no haven in Europe. He would have to start again somewhere in the colonies.

I don't make friends easily. Who would I drink coffee with at the Barbados if he were gone? Could I ever go there again if his people were driven out of a place they had inhabited for two centuries? I couldn't name the number of times he'd made me laugh so hard I almost fell out of the booth, laughed until the tears streamed down my face. Israel was not only my jester, but my father confessor, as well. He knew all my secrets, mundane as they were, and I knew helping him through Amy Levy's death may have been the best thing I had ever done.

"I hope I haven't alarmed you," Barker said, and for a moment, I thought he was speaking to me.

"No, sir," Israel answered. "I understand what difficulties a Jew faces here. I've known it all my life. Thank you for talking to me."

"May I request that my name not be mentioned in relation to what we've said here tonight?"

"Of course, sir."

Barker slid out of the booth and was gone in a second, leaving his pipe behind still cooling. He had not asked me to go home with him or even offered me a ride, but then, I'd ridden Juno, and she was stabled not far away. I wondered how Barker had made his way here, to have suddenly jumped out of an alleyway in Underwood Street.

"You work for the strangest man I've ever met," Israel remarked. "He's going to get you killed one of these days. Surely there is a safer occupation in London."

"This from a man who coaxed me out of a comfortable bed to hunt monsters at midnight."

"I thought you were the one who coaxed me."

"Don't change the subject," I said. "I have to go, too. I must be up and ready to leave the house by seven."

"You and me both, Thomas," he said, handing all our pipes carefully into Frobisher's hands. "Thanks for coming out."

"My pleasure. You acquitted yourself rather well with the Guv."

"Did I really? I was terrified. It was like sharing a booth with a live tiger. He could have so easily reached over and gobbled me up."

I mulled over what he said as we stepped out into St. Michael's Alley. A mist too fine to be considered rain had begun to fall.

"Don't think he wouldn't," I told him, slapping him on the back.

# CHAPTER THREE

The morning after the events I've just recorded arrived mercilessly early, but we went to work anyway and returned home again after a busy day. Barker's back garden was beginning to change with the seasons, the Japanese maples turning a fiery red. We'd had our dinner and a steaming bath in the bathhouse, and I sat in the back garden enjoying the cool air in the shaded gazebo by the back gate as the sun set over Barker's house. His dog, Harm, lay at my feet with his head up but his eyes closed, enjoying the ending of the day as much as I. Etienne, Barker's chef, had made an apple pie laced with kirsch and caramel, and under my employer's sardonic scrutiny, I had enjoyed a second slice. I was twenty-four years of age and I felt my constitution could withstand it. Momentarily, all seemed right with the world. However, as we know, Nature abhors two things: a vacuum, and Thomas Llewelyn having too easy a time of it. From the back garden I heard the electric bell on the front door ring. Harm was off the mark, sprinting toward the bridge. I followed at a more sedate pace. I knew our butler, Mac, would answer it, but it was best to be prepared for anything.

Mac was talking to our visitor by the time we entered the back hall. There is a straight passage from the front hall to the back, and from where I stood I recognized Robert Anderson, an old friend of Barker's who holds a position that sounds Cromwellian when I say it: he was England's spymaster general. Mostly his work involved tracking anarchists, Irish bombers, and secret societies. In his spare time, he argued numismatics and the eschatological End of the World. Anderson's position was that despite the verse that says "but of that day and hour knoweth no man," when Jesus would return to collect his flock, Anderson very well could and did, thank you. However, being the keen observer that I was, I noticed he did not carry his worn and heavily annotated Bible with him that day. This was a professional visit.

"Mr. Anderson," I said in greeting. Anderson was approaching sixty, I supposed, and was a spare man with a beard and salt-and-pepper hair. He was an Irishman but we did our best not to hold it against him, being a household of outsiders ourselves.

"Thomas," he said, looking haggard and preoccupied. He bent and scratched the top of Harm's head. "Is your master in?"

"Up on his perch, as usual."

"Good. I need to speak to him. You had better come, too."

That settled that. Something had happened, something that required Cyrus Barker's unorthodox methods. Whatever it was, I'm sure he would kick in the door, illuminate it, and shake it until its bones rattled. My employer could be subtle when he wished, but so far, this had not been a subtle year.

We climbed the two flights to Barker's aerie. I noticed the short climb seemed to exhaust Anderson. When we reached the top, he collapsed into a chair and the Guv poured water for him from a pitcher into a tumbler. Barker was in his Asian smoking gown over shirtsleeves. His hair and thick mustache were still as black as the lenses of his spectacles. He seemed ageless, timeless, as solid a sentinel as Stonehenge.

"Robert," he rumbled in his basso voice. "What brings you here at such an hour?"

Anderson drank off half the glass and coughed twice. "I have some news."

"Pray tell us then. What has happened?"

"I have been given a new position. As of this morning, I am assistant commissioner of Scotland Yard, in charge of the Criminal Investigation Department."

"Then I suppose congratulations are in order. Lad, bring the sherry."

Anderson waved me down again. "There is more. Much more, in fact. I've been chosen over the heads of several qualified detective inspectors, so my arrival will not be greeted with wholesale enthusiasm, as I'm sure you'll understand. Besides that, I am overworked and in poor health. The hours have been long and I've had to beg the government for every farthing. I'm afraid I've used up all my reserves. My doctor and my wife have ordered me to Switzerland for six weeks' recovery and for once I am too weak to argue."

Anderson definitely looked ill. His skin looked ashen and his lips almost bluish. I hoped that it was a rest cure he was being sent to and not his final journey. I liked the old gentleman, and more importantly, Barker did. It seemed a shame if he missed hearing the last trumpet he'd been heralding all these years.

"I'm sorry to hear it, Robert," Barker said, going so far as to lean forward and pat him on the back of the hand, a rare gesture of affection for so undemonstrative a man.

"Would you consider working for Scotland Yard temporarily? I know it isn't your cup of tea and you value your independence, but I could really use someone to safeguard my interests while I am gone."

"In what capacity would I be working there?" Barker asked.

"As my assistant, nominally."

"They'll try to push me out," Barker warned, leaning back in his leather chair and crossing his ankles on a horsehair hassock.

"Then push back. That's your nickname in the Underworld, isn't it, 'Push'? I could find a dozen men to act as a kind of bookmark while I'm gone, but I believe you might actually get something done. Have you read about a couple of murders in Whitechapel, unfortunates who had their throats cut?"

"Aye, there was one named Nichols, I believe. Do you recall the other, lad?"

"Annie Chapman, I think, sir."

"Detective Chief Inspector Swanson has been tracking the case since the first murder in August. I'd like you to keep an eye on it for me. The newspapers are starting to print speculative articles about it. We need to solve it quickly."

"Whitechapel's a nasty little place, full of foreign sailors and the most desperate poor," I said. "I'm surprised this sort of thing doesn't happen more often."

"We are under the assumption," Anderson went on, "that it is the work of one man, a multiple murderer. There is no incentive for him to stop until we catch him."

"Did the second murder occur in the street, like the first?"

"Yes, in Hanbury Street. She was a common prostitute. We assume she was plying her trade and the murderer was a client."

"I understand they were savaged. Was there any apparent reason for stabbing their abdomens?"

"None that we can fathom. They were both women in the lowest rung of their profession. On their way out, if you know what I mean." He sat back in his chair. "Before you accept, I must warn you, there is a cost. Before I came to ask you, I had to get Commissioner Warren's permission to bring you in as special agents. I'm afraid he had conditions."

My employer tented his fingers. Personally, I think he was enjoying himself. "Which are?"

"That you temporarily close the doors of your agency and take down your hoardings. If you work for Scotland Yard, you cannot work private cases as well. Also, all deductions you make in this case become the property of the Metropolitan Police. Warren doesn't want to pick up the *Pall Mall Gazette* and read 'Cyrus Barker Apprehends Suspect.' Do you understand?"

"Of course. I assume I may still keep my chambers as a base of operations? Or am I to be given an old, battered desk within the CID?"

Anderson gave a dry chuckle. "I'm not certain one can be found. We are at full capacity, I'm afraid. Will you agree to these terms?"

Barker considered them for a moment. "Will I be given full

access to the files? The lad and I don't have time to repeat someone else's work."

"The files are currently spread out all over London, but I'll write
an order demanding that they be returned to 'A' Division."

"Is there a chief suspect as yet?"

"A few fellows have been arrested, but there is little to hold them
on. Each inspector has his own theory, but there is no consensus.
Whitechapel is like a bad haircut. We've combed it backward and
forward and still can't do anything with it. It has begun affecting
our duties in the West End. If our constables are patrolling Flower
and Dean Street in pairs, who is watching the jewelry stores in
Kensington? This fellow must be apprehended quickly."

"Even if it means bringing in 'amateurs'?"

Anderson crossed his arms and tried to suppress a smile.
"True, Commissioner Warren dislikes private detectives."

"Private enquiry agents," I corrected.

"You see?" he said, poking a thumb in my direction. "Now
you've got him doing it."

"It sounds to me," Barker said, "that you'll be well out of there
and Thomas and I shall be taking the blame for your appointment."

"I don't claim this is going to be all beer and skittles, but I believe your shoulders are wide enough to carry a few remarks at my
expense."

"What rank am I to hold?"

"I've been considering this since this morning. You will be
given a rank equal to inspector. However, you are to liaise with the
Queen's secretary at Buckingham Palace. Her Majesty is very interested in the case. I thought you might make use of that royal connection to anyone short of a detective inspector."

"Any handle will do to turn a pot," Barker remarked. "Are you
well, Robert?"

Anderson grimaced. "I had pains in my arm last week," he said.
"My doctor told me I am ripe for apoplexy. He enlisted my wife's
aid."

"A formidable woman."

"I can argue with one of them, but not both. It is deucedly incon-
venient, and will not do my career any good, but I have no choice.

I need you there, Cyrus. Scotland Yard has some good officers: Abberline, Swanson, and the others are all fine investigators, but as I told Warren, for my money you're the best man hunter in London. You'll crawl down a hole after a wounded badger, if need be."

Barker said nothing but gave a nod at the compliment.

"And you, Thomas," Anderson said, turning to me. "This will be harder for you. Most men will not dare confront Cyrus openly, but they will have no problem confronting you. You'll be in for some ribbing."

"I'm paid handsomely, sir," I said. "And I don't really give a damn what they say or think about me."

"That's the spirit," Anderson said, regarding me with his blue-green eyes like aquamarine stones. He ran a hand over the top of his head. Out of vanity, his own or his wife's, he had begun combing hair from the side of his head over the top to cover a pinkish scalp. *He's nervous,* I told myself. He doesn't want to go, and he needs this Whitechapel fellow trapped quickly.

"How long do I have to consider?" Barker asked.

"Oh, buckets of time. Bushels full. Five minutes, perhaps?"

Barker gave a grim smile. I wondered what was going on in his head. There were several elements to this offer that Barker might find unpalatable. He would have to work with others, many of whom he did not trust. We would have to shut our agency's doors, which Barker had never done before, and we had no idea how long it would take to track down the killer once we began. The more I thought about it, the more absurd the offer began to sound.

"I'll do it," Barker growled from the confines of his chair.

"Perhaps you should—" I began, but Barker reached across and shook Anderson's hand. The die was cast. It was on his head now.

I felt I was the only one who realized our world was about to be turned upside down. The worst part was that most of the work would fall on me. The Guv was like a forward in a football match. He could be relied upon to kick the ball into the net, but he expected others to get the ball to him, and woe to us if we disappointed him.

"I really must get home to pack," Anderson said, rising. "If I leave it to my wife, she'll make sure all my favorite articles are left behind and take only the suits she prefers me to wear."

Barker's old friend reached into his coat pocket and handed him an envelope with a wax seal. Buckingham Palace. Had we been finessed? I hated for our services to be a foregone conclusion.

Anderson shook our hands again and took his leave. He was on the stair when Barker suddenly waved me after him.

"See him to a hansom cab," he murmured. "In fact, bring one here to him."

I was up in a flash and running down the staircase. Anderson was descending with an unsteady hand on the wall. He is normally a gaunt but vigorous fellow, but with this stress and overwork, he looked frail. I did not try to help him, but hovered nearby in case he needed help. He reached the bottom of the stair without incident, and a minute or two later the ground floor. We proceeded out the front door, but there he stopped and put his hands on his knees and stooped.

I found a cab for him in Newington Causeway and brought it back to our door. Helping him in, I thumped on the side of the cab and it jingled away. Then I went back upstairs to Barker's rooftop nest.

"Did you see him off safely?" Barker asked.

"Safe enough. His face was rather pale. The man needs a rest."

"Thank you, Thomas. I'm sure you spared him his dignity."

I nodded and sniffed. It is a funny little country in which we live. Criticisms are taken to heart, but any compliment is quickly brushed away.

The Guv had moved to his rack of meerschaums by the window. He selected his largest pipe, tiny white hounds cornering a ghostly stag at bay, and began shoveling tobacco into the bowl.

"You wanted in on this case from the start," I said.

He acted as if I'd said nothing and snapped a vesta alive on a French porcelain striker. One puff, two puffs. Three. He blew out the match and tossed it into an ashtray by his chair.

"You will not vouchsafe an opinion," I said.

"There is no possible opinion to give," he answered, blowing a gust of smoke toward the fireplace. "I have not seen a shred of evidence or read a single report, or even spoken to a constable."

"Yet you jumped at the chance to take the case. Why?"

"Because Anderson asked me to, and he is a friend. Because he needs me, too, so he can recover from overwork. And because it might return us to Scotland Yard's good graces. Are those good enough reasons for you, or shall I continue?"

He just wanted in on an interesting case, I thought, the first to come along in a while. Frankly, I felt the same way.

"It is your agency, sir. You may run it as you see fit."

"See if I don't!" he said.

"I hope he isn't correct about the Yard holding us responsible for Anderson being hired."

"Either way, Thomas, you may rest assured of one thing."

"And what is that, sir?"

"As you so eloquently told Robert, you will be paid handsomely."

I nodded. "There is that."

"You should go to bed. You were up late last night, and we have a busy day in the morning."

"Doing what, exactly?" I asked. "What's going to happen when we walk through the doors of Scotland Yard?"

"I have no idea," he said. "But I've pledged to Robert that we will do our best for him, and so we shall."

# CHAPTER FOUR

Barker was up at his usual time the next morning, shortly after five. By the time I was shaven and dressed it was six-thirty and I barely had time to eat and to drink a cup of pressed coffee before the Guv came in from the garden. He had been issuing instructions to the gardeners: more mulch for this plant, and less nitrate for that. The garden was to look austere, as all Asian gardens do, so the trick was to keep the plants alive without actually letting them flourish. I suspected he felt the same way about his assistants.

"Come along, lad. We mustn't be late for our first day," he said, waving me out the door. I was certain no one would miss us, or even notice if we failed to show up at all. No sooner did we find a cab in Newington Causeway than it began to rain, a thin, silvery drizzle which would keep on for hours. It pattered lightly on the top of the cab, but inside we were snug and dry. I wouldn't have been a cabman, perched on the back of a moving hansom cab, exposed to all weathers, for all the tea in Canton.

We reached our offices and there had our first conflict of the day, mild as it was.

"Jeremy," Barker said. "We are shutting the offices."

I watched the information sink in. It always takes our clerk a few moments to process information. Slowly, his eyes grew to the size of a penny.

"Sir?"

"We have taken a case with Scotland Yard. It requires us to shut our doors. You shall continue to keep the offices, but you must turn away anyone who wishes to hire our services. I imagine one could put a sign in the window, saying we are no longer taking clients. You may lock the door, if you wish. Thomas and I both have keys. Unless, of course, you prefer to stay home until I call again."

"For how long, sir?" the clerk asked, looking slightly distraught.

"A month or so, I should think."

"But sir, there will be telephone calls and messages and telegrams. There are all manner of people coming and going."

"You must tell them our services are fully engaged at the moment, and we are not taking clients. It will be good for the agency's reputation."

"What shall I do in the meantime, Mr. B? I'm staying, if that's all right with you. Regular hours for me. But how will I fill them?"

"You might have the floors polished and the furniture redone. Inspect the ceiling for cracks and have the doors repainted. Keep all the receipts, as per usual."

"You're to pay me for doing nothing?"

"Well, not nothing," the Guv said.

"Full wages?" Jenkins asked.

"Of course."

"Hallelujah!"

"Indeed."

Cyrus Barker rooted through his mahogany desk until he found a screwdriver. Then he stepped out into the steady downpour and unscrewed the brass plaque advertising his name and occupation which was attached to the railing. His suit grew wet as he worked and Jenkins jumped up and seized an umbrella, leaning out to hold it over him. I couldn't think of anything to do beyond moving to the door, ready to take the wet plaque from his hands when it was finally free. The last screw always gives the most trouble. He tugged it free and handed it into my care.

"There ye are," he said. "Jenkins, have a man in and take down the hoarding above the door."

"Yes, Mr. B," Jenkins said. I had not been with the agency long enough to take such liberties with his name, only four years to date. But then, Jenkins was a character, while I was expected to toe the line.

"Do you need anything from your desk, Thomas?"

"Just my notebook and my revolver," I said, turning a key in the lock and sliding up the rolltop desk.

"No pistol, lad," Barker said, shaking his head. "Too many questions. Are you ready?"

I retrieved my notebook, feeling momentarily naked without my Webley, and locked the desk again.

"Yes, sir."

"Jeremy, if we are not back here by five-thirty, lock up and be on your way."

"That I will, sir, to the letter."

It was but a few dozen steps between Craig's Court and Great Scotland Yard Street. Cox's and Co., Ltd, stood beside us and Barker kept an account therein. Between our offices and Scotland Yard, there was a row of public houses, which fed the clerks and officials of Whitehall, and then there stood a wrought-iron gate, guarded by a constable.

"State your name and business," demanded an older-looking officer with a ginger beard shot with gray.

"Cyrus Barker and Thomas Llewelyn," the Guv said. "We start work here today."

"You'd best come in, then. Tell the desk sergeant in the second building on the right."

He stepped back and let us through. We passed the first building, which housed the Criminal Investigation Department where Barker had taught a class in antagonistics until a bomb went off nearby in a public lavatory. When it was rebuilt, there was no room for the kind of classes we taught, and since then we had opened a school to the public in Soho. The thinking was that if Scotland Yard did not appreciate us, the public would. So far, this theory had proven to be correct.

Behind it was the Metropolitan Police Headquarters, or "A" Division, as it was known to much of the Yard. It was a jumble of mismatched four-storied buildings connected by interior halls; no two alike in color, shape, or type of brickwork. As many as there were, the place was packed to the rafters. There were too many officers because there was too much crime in the Empire's capital city. To house them all, a new building was being built on the Embankment just behind.

We passed under the familiar blue globe and stepped inside. The hall was full of citizens seeking redress. One man held a bloody cloth to his forehead. It was half past eight and he had already had a memorable morning. Barker did not step to the front of the line, so instead, we waited in a queue for a quarter hour, watching people come and go. The men I recognized as officials all looked tense. Two women had been slaughtered, who would ordinarily be considered as inconsequential, and yet the Metropolitan Police were already feeling the pressure of their deaths.

"What can I do for you, gentlemen?" the sergeant asked. His dark hair was greased into a swirl on top of his head and his mustache was waxed to points. A typical desk sergeant, to be found at every station in the City.

"Cyrus Barker and Thomas Llewelyn, signing in," my employer said. "I am the new assistant to Robert Anderson."

"Ah!" the sergeant said, as if Barker was a peg for which he had just found the proper hole. "The commissioner has been awaiting your arrival."

"We had no appointment. Are we late?" Barker asked.

"Right on time, more like. He has his hands full with this new killing. He's up on the third floor. Closer to heaven, you might say."

The desk sergeant pointed toward a stairwell with the nib of his pen. We climbed three flights of stairs to a row of offices culminating in a secretary and a desk blocking a door painted with Sir Charles Warren's name in gold letters. We gave our name to the secretary and he directed us to sit before stepping inside. He came back a few seconds later.

"The commissioner will get to you as soon as he possibly can."

With those comforting words, we sat, and were still sitting an hour and a half later. Now Barker had achieved his objective for the morning: he had arrived within the walls of "A" Division. He had nowhere he needed to be, and he is a patient man. Exceedingly patient. He did not fidget, or scratch his nose, or move a muscle. He merely sat in the chair like a wooden figure facing the commissioner's door. Rather, it was I who grew indignant at our being kept waiting and became stiff and sore in the hard wooden chair, and sighed and coughed and changed positions every few minutes, and paced and asked the secretary how much longer it would take, and was assured the commissioner would see us very soon indeed. *This is a punishment,* I told myself, *for being Anderson's men, and not rank and file, and Cyrus Barker not getting along with Warren in the past.* This sort of pettiness just gets right up my nose.

So, as I said, an hour and a half ticked by very slowly. Ninety minutes, five thousand and four hundred seconds subtracted from my life. Shakespeare could have perfected a sonnet in that time, and Mozart a short libretto, if not a full score. Not that Thomas Llewelyn could have written a sonnet or libretto, but I might have at least enjoyed the chance. Finally, a voice within made a short cough, causing the secretary to finally sit up.

"You may go in now," he said.

We stood and went inside. Warren sat behind a large desk, looking much as I had seen him a year or two before. He is a good-looking man, military straight, with a face dominated by a mustache shaped like an inverted *V.*

I could not help but compare Warren's office to Barker's. The latter was airy, spacious, and lined with bookshelves. He did not collect art in a great way, but there was a Ming vase and a Constable in the waiting room. Behind his desk was a faded coat of arms on a wood panel, and under the desk a Persian rug. Warren's walls were lined in framed articles from the *Times* that praised the Met, and photographs of squads of constables seated in rows like footballers. His desk was impressive for its size and fineness of carving, but it had not been refinished in the last eighty years. Where Barker had books, Warren had files. He did not strike me as the kind who spent his evenings reading, unless it was military history. Papers lay loose in a tray, something the Guv would never allow on his glass-topped desk, and there were rings in the red oak. All the same, it was the best Scotland Yard had to offer, with a green baize carpet and matching captain's chairs for us to sit in. I assumed either that the commissioner was unmarried or that his wife never visited his offices.

"Barker," he growled, like a cat who had finally latched a claw onto a tail.

"Commissioner."

"Come begging for a job, have you? Is the enquiry business not lucrative enough for a gentleman's tastes?"

"You know why I am here, sir," Barker said.

"I do, or so I've heard. Anderson requested you. You must be chomping at the bit to get at the Whitechapel murderer."

"It is certainly an interesting case."

"Anderson claims you are one half bloodhound and the other half saint. What stories have you been running on him?"

"None at all. I have been busy with cases and haven't seen him in six months."

Warren leaned forward and placed his hands on the desk in front of him. "Perhaps the two of you could explain to me why I should ignore my natural inclinations and accept you into the fold, so to speak?"

I dared speak up, for the Guv is not one to trumpet his own successes. "It appears," I said, "that you require the services of an experienced tracker and investigator."

"When I want your opinion, Mr. Whatever-the-hell-your-name-is, I'll ask for it. But don't hold your breath."

I tend to work by instinct as an enquiry agent, and it seemed to me that he was testing me to see if I would break and run to hide behind my employer. I wasn't going to give him the satisfaction. "I work half a dozen buildings away from this one, and am a convicted felon. If you don't know my name by now, Commissioner, then perhaps you need all the help you can get."

Warren inhaled and for a moment I thought he was going to pounce on me. Instead, he merely blew the air out again. "Very well, Mr. Llewelyn, since you wish to offer yourself as an advocate for Mr. Barker, tell me why I should hire him."

"Because he is relentless. Once he starts a case, he won't give it up until it is finished. Once begun, he will go at it with all he has, tooth and nail, never backing down, never compromising his principles, barely eating and sleeping, giving all that he can until the client is satisfied. No one can threaten him away, cajole him, trick him, or beat him. And he doesn't do it for the money, I can attest to that. I've tried to convince him to raise his enquiry rates for years, but no. For some reason, he cares about this city he has come to adopt far more than it deserves and even cares that women of a low reputation cannot walk the streets without being cut up like cadavers."

Warren sat back for a moment and then leaned forward and jotted something in a memorandum book on his desk. He was giving us only half his attention. "Is that the best you can do?" he asked.

"If you're looking for superlatives, Commissioner, I suggest you read our advertisements in the *Times*. I'm merely telling the unvarnished truth."

"Mr. Barker," he said, turning to regard him directly. "You have a reputation for appearing in the newspapers, frequently, and at our expense. The Met's reputation is such that I will not allow it to suffer any more than it already has."

Barker leaned forward. "I admit, sir, that it is normally my policy to seek publicity where I can; however, I would not do so for an agency which is currently closed. I would promise not to seek out the newspapers in order to improve my reputation."

"You do realize that the way Anderson was chosen did not sit well with this department. Swanson was the most satisfactory man for the position. Your presence here as Anderson's assistant might ruffle some feathers among the ranks."

"I'm liable to ruffle plenty of feathers by the time this case is over."

Warren frowned and crossed his arms. "Now you see, those are the kinds of things you say that make me worry this will not work out. We are a team here, Barker. We must help each other. One detective discovers something and he passes it on to others, who work on it together. You may have been on your own too long."

"Commissioner, I am a blunt man. I want to work on this case, and I'm willing to work under any constraints you give me in order to see it through."

"If you go to Whitechapel, I expect you to get down in the muck with the rest of us. None of your manservants bringing you a hamper from Fortnum and Mason."

It was the word "us" that had me biting my lip. I doubted Warren went to Whitechapel very often himself.

"I rose from the muck, Commissioner," my employer said. "I am quite comfortable there."

"Good. Now I spoke to Anderson before he left last night and we agreed that you are to come in as a special inspector. Mr. Llewelyn will be a special constable. This means that while he is working for you he is also subordinate to any sergeant, inspector, or official in the building. You yourself are subordinate to the detective chief inspectors. It is necessary to have order here, a chain of command. Can you work within this framework?"

"Yes, sir, I believe I can."

"And what about you, Mr. Llewelyn? What have you to say for yourself?"

"I will endeavor to bring favor upon these hallowed walls, sir."

"Oh, yes, a university man. I forgot. Perhaps you can help some of your new comrades with their spelling. And their manners."

"Yes, sir."

"Gentlemen, I don't particularly want you here, but Anderson insisted that I give you a try. That is what I shall give you. One try. If you speak to the press, you are out. If you do not treat your superiors correctly, you are out. If I find you sitting about doing nothing, you are out. We run a tight ship here and we have a multiple murderer to catch. We do not have time to nursemaid a pair of tyro officers. Don't put your head up because as God is my witness, I will hammer it down again!"

Barker looked at him steadily, and for a moment I thought he might kick against the goads. He does not respond well to threats. However, all he did was nod his head.

"As you say, sir."

Charles Warren looked disappointed. Perhaps he had thought to draw Barker out to discredit him.

"You will be paid, but on a temporary basis. You will work under Assistant Commissioner Anderson when he returns. Until then, keep your noses clean, and if you turn up something in this investigation, tell Detective Chief Inspector Swanson or one of his men. Don't keep it to yourself. Understood?"

We both agreed that we did.

"Raise your right hand. 'I state-your-name do solemnly and sincerely declare . . .'"

And so he administered the Police Oath to us. We promised to serve the Queen and protect the peace and that was that. When a man is young, he dreams of all sorts of occupations he might venture, but not once in my life did I ever consider becoming a peeler. I made a note to myself to duck all my known friends. I couldn't face the humiliation.

Things only got worse after that. A constable took me to the equipment room where the sergeant there made much of the fact that I was three inches below regulation height.

"We don't have a children's size, Constable Llewelyn," he informed me as I tried on helmets.

"That's very funny, Sergeant. I shall have to remember that one."

"This patch here will go on your shoulder. It denotes you as a special constable. We call you 'specials.' You'll have to get your mum to sew it on."

"I'm perfectly capable of sewing it on myself," I told him.

"Oh, you can sew, can you? Izzat why you was brought in, to make repairs on uniforms? That's good to know."

Eventually, after more remarks at my expense, I was given a tunic and a pair of trousers that were rather roomy for my taste. The material for both was a heavy and uncomfortable blue wool that smelled as if it were not long off the sheep. I was responsible for providing my own boots, but they gave me a thick black belt and a truncheon. When I was fully dressed the sergeant pointed to a long mirror by the door. I walked over and stood in front of it, staring at someone I never suspected existed before, Special Constable Thomas Llewelyn.

"Look at that," the sergeant said. "He looks just like a proper constable, only smaller."

I stepped into the corridor again, to find Barker talking with a sergeant there about the case. He had a cup of tea in his hand and had taken off his jacket. Now, Barker rarely takes off his jacket save when he works in his garden. It can be the hottest day in July and he'll wear his jacket in the office. Most of the inspectors in "A" Division took off their jackets, however, and he was doing what he could to fit in. Still, with his maroon tie, black waistcoat, arm garters, and Windsor collar, his clothes were a cut above theirs.

He finished the conversation he was having with the constable and came forward to inspect my appearance.

"You look smart," he said, looking me over.

"There's a first time for everything, I suppose. What next?"

"We shall have to purchase a pair of boots for you."

"Yes, sir."

"Are you ready to begin, PC Llewelyn?"

I stood as tall and straight as my five-foot-four-inch frame would allow. I nearly clicked my heels.

"Yes, sir!"

"Come along, then. Let's see what sort of trouble we can get ourselves into."

I don't believe he listened to a word Warren said.

# CHAPTER FIVE

On first sight, Scotland Yard was an ugly building, with scraped paint in the halls, jackknife carvings in every seat or bench, and floors rubbed down to the bare wood. The building exhaled a sweet smell of damp rot. That being said, it was a hive of activity. Every room and hallway was packed with men, and all of them seemed to be discussing the same subject: the death of two prostitutes.

I stood in the hall for a moment, dazed by the babel of conversations and arguments going on around us, when a sergeant put his head out of a door and pointed a thick finger in my direction.

"You, there, with your hands in your pockets," he said. "Two cuppas, and be smart about it!"

I glanced at the Guv, who gave me a shrug, and then I said, "Yes, sir."

The sergeant pulled his head back into the room.

"Where do you suppose the kettle is?" I asked my employer.

"I have no idea. You find it and I'll meet you later in the Records Room."

I asked several constables, who seemed too busy to answer, and finally stumbled upon a sort of small kitchen. Now, I don't rate that I have many good qualities but I can brew a fine cup of tea, or so I've been told. Personally, I won't touch the weed, but I have received enough compliments from those who claim to favor it. The tea in the canister was of the poorest quality, mostly stems and base leaves; I assumed it was purchased for the Yard by the bundle. I picked out the worst offenders and put the rest in the pot before pumping water into it from the basin. I lit the gas with a box of matches I routinely carry for Barker, settled the old, black cast-iron kettle on it, and then began searching through the cupboards. No sugar, lemon, or cream to go into it, nor any sort of biscuit. Savages. I'll bet they took it strong and hot.

Five minutes later the pot came to a rapid boil and began to shriek. I poured it into cracked cups and saucers with the aid of an unused strainer I found in one of the drawers. Then I attempted to carry them back to the waiting sergeant.

Suddenly, the hall was full of constables and sergeants hurrying to get wherever they were going. I was jostled and bumped and knocked about as I balanced the cups as best I could. Just when I thought I was going to make it, and could actually see the sergeant's room in sight, someone came out of a side room and knocked one of the cups over. The second spilled as well, but I deftly poured the dregs from both saucers into one cup and pocketed the other before entering the room.

The sergeant was talking to a delicate-looking old woman. I set the cup at her elbow. She looked at me doubtfully, but murmured her thanks. No doubt she assumed I had been there for years rather than minutes. I turned and addressed the sergeant.

"I only brought the one cup, sir. I'll get the second one now."

"Don't bother. I only needed the one. I assumed you would spill one, at least."

"Yes, sir," I said, saluting.

"No need for that. This isn't the bloomin' army. On your way, Constable."

I stepped out and immediately found Barker waiting for me as if he'd never left. He led me through the labyrinth of halls and down a set of steps to the basement. Then he opened a door and ushered me into a room. There were several long tables and the walls were lined with shelves containing tall boxes bound in marbled paste-board covers with ends of imitation leather and brass. Like the rest of the building, it was packed from floor to ceiling.

There was a constable in the room whose duty it was to make inspectors sign in and out for specific files, so they did not disappear for good. One might think all constables want to go out in the field and investigate or walk a beat, but there one would be wrong. Some stay close to the nest and never fly away, never rising to sergeant, content to stay the course and collect a regular paycheck. This constable was just such a person.

"Have the files from Mary Nichols been returned?" Barker asked.

"Oh, yes, sir," the constable said. "They was turnt in this morning, sir, at the order of Assistant Commissioner Anderson."

"May we see them? We will not leave the room."

"'Oo are you, sir, if I might ask?"

"I am Cyrus Barker, assistant to Mr. Anderson. And you?"

The constable snapped to attention, or as close to it as one could get sitting down. "I'm PC Kirkwood, sir."

"Pleased to meet you, Constable. This is my assistant, PC Llewelyn."

"Pleased to meet you," I said, shaking his hand. Kirkwood had gray muttonchop side whiskers cut short, which covered most of his cheeks. He wore small bifocal spectacles set far down on his nose.

"They only created this room in July," Kirkwood explained. "It has been my duty to hunt down every file in this building, not to mention in the officers' homes, and have them brought to this room to be inventoried, classified, and filed away. Then I had to teach everyone to sign them in and out. Now if you need a file and it isn't here, I can direct you to whoever has it."

"That's brilliant," I said.

"It's efficient," he corrected. "Some inspector laying hands on a file a half hour early may mean the difference between catching a criminal and letting him skip off on a steamer to Nova Scotia."

"Has a file been started for Annie Chapman yet?"

"Just arrived, sir. At the moment, Chief Detective Inspector

Donald Swanson has part of it on his desk. Postmortem results aren't in."

"No doubt he's in Whitechapel this morning."

"At 'H' Division, conferring with Inspector Abberline. He's pretty well moved in there for a while."

The Guv nodded, a sign that he had heard and was turning something over in his mind.

"Sign here, if you will, your names and the file number," Kirkwood said. " 'Time in' is 11:31."

I signed for us and received the Nichols file. We pulled out a couple of noisy chairs and removed the top of the box. Inside were manila folders and one of green pasteboard which proved to contain the postmortem. I'd have looked at that first, but understood my employer should have the choice. Luckily, he picked up the initial report, leaving the green folder for me.

Mary Nichols, or "Polly," was a forty-three-year-old prostitute who was murdered in Buck's Row on August 31, scarcely a week ago. Her body was found at 3:40 A.M. by a pair of carters: Charles Cross and Robert Paul. At first they thought her only passed out drunk in the street, for the body was still warm, but when the police were brought and a bull's-eye lantern shone upon her face, one could see that her throat had been cut and her clothing soaked through with blood. Worse yet, when the body was taken to the mortuary in Old Montague Street and her body stripped and examined, they discovered she had been disemboweled as well.

The Yard had been caught out in many ways during this first case. The locale of the murder had been washed clean of blood by the time the first inspector arrived. The body, once it had arrived at the mortuary, was cleaned by attendants and the clothing thrown into a pile. There was so little blood splattered on the cobbles, it was possible she was cut while lying down, and her eyes were wide open upon death, as if disbelieving this cruel trick of fate.

The author of the file could not say with any degree of certainty whether the victim's name was Mary or Polly. She was an unfortunate, a prostitute, and like other members of the criminal classes had found the need to occasionally change her name for various reasons. If her name was Polly, she might have chosen Mary because it made her sound more virtuous, like the Virgin Mary, or otherwise, like Mary Magdalene. It was a common Irish name, so common as to be practically anonymous. Whitechapel was full of Marys. If her name really was Mary, it was possible she chose Polly because it made her stand out from among the Marys. "Polly" sounded fun-loving and gay. A man seeking female companionship might have chosen her over her companions simply because her name was Polly.

In the photograph affixed to the file, she lay in a box made of what looked to be galvanized tin. One hesitated to call it a coffin. A coffin was made for one person, and it was buried with them. This contained someone else's remains a half hour before, and probably someone else's a half hour later. The galvanizing process involved submerging the tin in molten zinc for durability. That box must have held hundreds of bodies. For all I knew, both victims had used the same one. There was no way to differentiate one box from another. There was no shroud, nor any form of lining; merely bare metal. No dignity, no personality, merely anonymity. *How did you end here, Mary?* I wondered. *You were once so full of life and promise.*

In fact, she was full of life an hour before her death, witnesses claimed. She'd been sitting in the Frying Pan public house, having a glass of gin, making jokes with her friend, and bemoaning the fact that she didn't have enough money for a bed for the night. She did have a new bonnet, however, and on the strength of that she was certain to make up the money she needed. Mary was not beautiful, but she was presentable enough. She was in her forties in a profession whose members rarely reached fifty and lived in a district in which the average age of death was around thirty-five, yet she still lived. She was resilient. She knew the cruelty of life, but she was optimistic. She knew the dangers, or at least, she thought she did. She wasn't prepared for her killer, but then who would be?

A friend, whose statement was in the file, had met up with her later in the evening, sometime around two in the morning. Mary had already served several clients on the strength of that new bonnet, but had just as quickly drunk the money away again. She was drunk and still hadn't the ready for a bed. She was a confirmed drinker, an "alcoholic," to use the fancy new professional term. She could not quit. Given the choice, she had chosen a drink over even a place to sleep several times that evening. She lived to drink and had died because of it. Had she spent the few pennies she made on her bed the first time she earned it, she'd have been safely tucked away when the Whitechapel Killer chose his first victim.

I put down the file and picked up another.

Annie Chapman, the second victim, was what is known as a casual prostitute. She made her living as a worker in crochet and by making and selling paper flowers, but in order to pay for the drink to which she had become addicted, she occasionally stepped out with men. She was a sad case. Annie was forty-seven, plump and consumptive, but well liked at her boardinghouse, where she was known as Dark Annie. In fact, one of the men she stepped out with was considering making the arrangement more permanent. The reputation left behind by both victims was that neither of them would be missed, but the truth was that Annie would be missed by many tenants and even by the landlords where she stayed. The sermons that preached that such a wicked life inevitably turns a woman into a shrill harridan were not strictly true.

Annie had found herself in a rare argument a few days before with another local woman which came to blows, leaving her bruised and feeling low. She had considered going to a casual ward on September seventh until she recovered. Three days later she was still feeling ill when the owner of her lodging house came asking for rent. He claimed she was drunk and told her to pay him if she intended to sleep there that night. She went out to make the few pence for her bed the only way she could. Unverified claims put her at the Ten Bells Pub on Church Street early the next morning, probably having spent the rent on drink like Nichols. An hour later, she was found nearby in Hanbury Street between a set of steps and a wooden fence. Her face and hands were covered in blood, and her hands raised as if vainly trying to ward off the relentless steel of the knife that killed her. The tip of her tongue protruded between her teeth and the cut in her throat had sliced the neckerchief she wore in two. When she was taken to the mortuary, the postmortem revealed that her entire womb had been removed and was nowhere to be found. Like Mary Nichols, her sister in death, Annie was placed in a battered tin coffin and photographed, pale from consumption, her tongue still visible between her lips.

As luck would have it, and one must remember in the East End most all luck is bad luck, there was a folded apron found beside the corpse, a leather apron as might be used by a butcher or tanner. If it was a clue, the Whitechapel Killer had been conspicuously forgetful to leave behind so well tended an article of clothing. If not, he either intentionally left it behind or it was already there when he killed her. Why did he not take it with him, while carrying away the portion he had cut from her body?

I knew these streets now, or was getting to know them. Nothing worth so much as a farthing was left on the streets. Even an orange peel tossed to the ground would be picked up by someone else and eaten. These people were on the verge of starvation. A leather apron, even a used one, was worth sixpence or more. There was the cost of a bed and a meal right there.

I flipped out my notebook and wrote the first of what would eventually be hundreds of questions: does the killer bring a candle or some kind of lantern, or does he perform such skillful surgery by touch only, in total darkness?

I looked over at my employer. The file was on the table in front of him and he was sitting back with his legs crossed and his arms clasped about his chest. He looked low, as anyone who had just read what he did should look.

"What do you think?" I asked.

"I think sometimes I want to buy a croft on an island in the farthest Hebrides and not see a single human being from one year to the next. I have been negligent, lad. The money that sits in my accounts could have been put to use and done some good there."

"You already contribute to several programs there, sir," I reminded him. "Besides, no amount of money is going to help women like Mary and Annie. They need the drink. They wouldn't say thank you for a home and steady employment if it meant they couldn't have several glasses of gin per day."

The Guv relaxed his grip on himself. "I suppose you are correct, but I cannot abide it. We are given a paradise on Earth, and yet we make it over into the very picture of hell. I wonder if this killer feels that he is releasing these women to a better life than they have been living. I've been guilty, lad, of forgetting. I stand in my garden and tend to my plants, while scarcely a mile away women like this, who should be grandmothers and pillars of their neighborhood, offer themselves in the street to strangers for the price of a bed."

# CHAPTER SIX

That afternoon, while I was busy carrying messages to various departments for the desk sergeant, and a few to various buildings nearby in Whitehall Street, Cyrus Barker stepped out for an hour or two. He didn't say where he went, but then I had grown used to such behavior. He certainly didn't need my permission to do what he thought best.

Six o'clock finally arrived according to the booming of Big Ben, and I went downstairs to the room full of lockers and changed into my regular clothing while the Guv spent the time chatting up anyone who would speak to him. He would take in information and opinions piecemeal, making no judgments as yet, merely asking questions. I'd seen him do it a thousand times. He would start with no opinion, consider that of whomever he was speaking to and then squeeze them as if they were a sponge. Later, when he had put together all the various accounts and formed a possible theory, he might come back and question them again, asking still more probing questions. Sometimes he would bark at them, threaten them in order to shake them up. When he was done questioning a witness, he either had all the information they could give or he could estimate their opinion. That being said, he approached them according to his personal instinct, never two people the same way twice. I suppose that is what Scotland Yard meant when they said that his methods were "irregular." They were not, nor could not be, successfully codified. They were uniquely his.

I met him in the hall by the front entrance. He's not an expressive man, but I could tell he was pleased with his first day at the Yard. By the creases at the corners of his spectacles, I deduced his eyes were half open with satisfaction.

"A good day?" I asked.

"Well enough for our first."

I cautioned myself not to ask where he had disappeared to during the afternoon. He would reveal it in what he liked to call "the fullness of time." That's the way he actually spoke, a farrago of quaint phrases, Scottish axioms, and things he'd picked up in books. Autodidacts are always unique. Couple that with an early life spent among the Chinese as an orphan, hiding his race in order to survive, and you have not merely unique but remarkable. Travel does not merely broaden the mind, it deepens it as well.

We climbed into a hansom cab and Barker told the cabman to take us to Whitechapel. I suppressed a sigh. Here I was thinking my day was over. Obviously, the Guv wanted to tour the streets a second time. My duty was to see that he stopped to eat something, otherwise he'd be so caught up in his work that he might not stop for hours. I speculated that at some point he would eventually run out of energy, but that would be hours beyond what I could endure.

If I had known we would be walking Whitechapel officially within a few days, I'd have had no reason to sneak out of the house under cover of darkness with Israel to search for the killer. Our vehicle crossed through the Strand, into Fleet Street, through the City, and finally into Whitechapel, a matter of about half an hour during the busiest time of the day. Traffic was very slow around Aldgate, but Barker did not seem inclined to get out and walk. I theorized he must have a particular destination.

"Here we are," he finally said, leaning forward to get out as we drew to the curb. We were at the corner of Thrawl Street and Brick Lane. It was not a prepossessing address. I stepped down and regarded one building in particular. Certain public houses call attention to themselves by having a door on the diagonal at a corner. This one did, as well as a stone emblem over the lintel, illustrating the name for the illiterate masses.

"The Frying Pan?" I asked.

"It's not merely a public house, it is also an inn. Rooms are available by the week. I have let it for the month."

"The month?" I asked. "You mean we'll be staying here for an entire month?"

"Or until we find the Whitechapel Killer. I want to be here when he kills again. No news is worthwhile that is learned secondhand."

As stoic as my room in Newington is, I'd grown accustomed to it. My books are there and my clothes, and Mac sees to my every need, if begrudgingly. Etienne Dummolard makes my coffee and my breakfast, and Harm and I tolerate one another. To give all that up to live over a raucous public house for a solid month seemed too great a sacrifice just to capture a murderer. On the other hand, it was no use saying no to Barker. One might as well try saying it to a wall. The results are the same.

"Let's go in, then," I said.

The proprietor, when we met him, looked like a partially shaved bear. He must have weighed twenty stone, and had the circumference of a barrel. He gave us a key and we climbed a very narrow staircase to the first floor. It made me wonder how the proprietor squeezed up the stair. I hazarded a guess that the place had been built during George III's reign, when this street was the very edge of town and green fields were all one saw to the east. No sooner were we in the room than my employer handed me a tin and a spoon.

"Keating's Bug Powder?" I asked, reading the label.

"It's mostly boric acid. I bought it earlier. Spoon it along the walls and a little between the sheets of the beds. I have no wish to share mine with bedbugs and cockroaches."

"As long as we're going first class," I said.

"That's the pity of it, lad. In Whitechapel, this *is* first class."

I looked about. The wallpaper was old and yellowed, unless that was their original color, and there were two single beds, a desk, and a large chest of drawers that might be as old as the building. A window faced the dreary street, but it was better than no window at all. When I first came to London, I had stayed in worse than this. I set to work, armed with my trusty spoon. It felt like I was preparing for some sort of unholy ritual: stay inside the circle and you will be safe.

"So, this is where you went today," I said by way of conversation.

"Aye," he growled. "One cannot catch criminals from an armchair in Charing Cross. We shall spend the next few hours observing where the people congregate at night, what they do, and how they live. I'm given to understand that Mary Nichols drank in the room below us just prior to getting her throat cut."

"So you did not simply pull the name out of a hat."

"A hat?"

Having spent half his life in China, Cyrus Barker sometimes misses common idioms.

"A conjurer's trick," I explained.

"Ah. No, if you recall, this was mentioned in her report."

I tried to recall the mention, but I had read a lot of information that day.

"Are you finished?"

"Almost."

I pulled back the covers of the first bed and sprinkled more Keating's Bug Powder onto the sheets. I did the same with the second.

"What about a change of clothes, sir? Should I call Mac on the telephone set in the morning and have him bring a steamer trunk?"

"No, in the morning, we shall purchase clothing in Petticoat Lane."

"The booths won't be set up until Sunday, sir."

"No, but the permanent shops will still be open. A half-dozen boiled shirts and some twice-turned trousers should allow us to blend into this crowd without being noticed."

"If you say so."

Between the bed and the bug powder and the thought of wearing someone else's trousers, my limbs were beginning to itch.

"How long will we be out, would you say? A couple of hours?"

"Oh, Thomas, the district doesn't fully waken until after midnight."

"But I have work in the morning!"

"That cannot be helped. Strong tea must stand in place of a few hours' rest."

"What about washing?"

"There is a public bath a few streets away."

At least I could take comfort in the knowledge that his needs were taken care of.

"What will Etienne say?" I asked. "You know how he gets."

Etienne Dummolard used Barker's kitchen to prepare our breakfast and experiment on recipes for his restaurant, Le Toison d'Or. He was temperamental and would pack his equipment and leave at the slightest provocation, such as our disappearing without notice and interrupting his routine.

"Coddling only makes him worse. He should relish not having us underfoot and catering to our needs."

"Oh, come," I said. "Etienne hasn't catered to a need in his life."

"Just so," Barker muttered.

"What about the W.C.? I don't suppose—"

"There is a privy out back."

"Wonderful. Have you tried the food here?"

"I thought it best to wait until you arrived. Your palate is more sensitive than mine. Shall we go downstairs and try it now?"

As it turned out, there was a red-faced cook in her sixties who ran the kitchen and was known in the East End as an excellent cook. True to the name of the establishment, she had a half-dozen seasoned frying pans on the old Aga that continually fried potatoes, mushrooms, cutlets, tomatoes, fish, and vegetables. It was solid English food in which black pepper was considered an exotic spice, but there was plenty of it, to be washed down with ale or tea. I would have dearly liked something to complain about, but could find nothing. The poor old thing stood on her pins and cooked for sixteen hours straight every day without complaint. Those pans were well seasoned, indeed. I bet they stayed red hot for hours.

After we ate, we began our second foray into the streets of Whitechapel. My first surprise was that at least half of it was as clean, well settled, and orderly as the City of London a few streets away. This, most likely, was the Jewish influence. Wherever they went on the earth, they brought with them civilization, orthodoxy, cleanliness, and order. Despite the fact that they were packed like sardines in a can, they worked hard to prosper and move out of the area, leaving it in far better condition than when they found it.

"Do you see that church there?" the Guv asked, indicating a spire that stood tall in the night. "That is St. Mary Matfelon. It is the original white chapel from which the district gets its name."

"What are all those funnels, putting out black fumes?" I asked, pointing to a row of chimneys to the north.

"Sugar refineries. The tall one there belongs to a match manufacturer, which gives the area its sulphurous odor. Then there's a lot of tanning that goes on by the stockyards, and the fish markets over at Billingsgate."

"No wonder the place smells the way it does. What are the more dangerous sections of Whitechapel, the ones we'll be interesting ourselves in?"

"You've already seen Buck's Row and Hanbury Street. There's Flower and Dean Street, the worst row of tenements in all Britain; and Fashion Street, where even the most hale of police constables will not tread alone, and Wentworth Street, which flows into Petticoat Lane. The navy warns their sailors to avoid that street, and that is saying something. It isn't merely the brothels and fallen women. There are sellers of pornography, counterfeiters, pickpockets, white slavers, gamblers, and rampsmen. Why break your back for twelve hours a day, the residents reason, when you can beat a man into unconsciousness in five minutes and steal his watch and wallet? They seek to avoid Adam's Curse, laboring with the sweat of one's brow."

"Sir, what sort of man consorts with prostitutes? I mean, are they local or do they travel here from other districts?"

"I would imagine most would be local, with the occasional wealthy man who comes to take in the prurient sights of the East End. There are brothels all over London, even in respectable streets, and those who would temporarily leave their wife's side to indulge in depravity must surely know where they are. To come here may be the most dangerous gamble of all. Women like the two who died, those who only occasionally walk the streets, are not examined for the diseases spread by their occupation, which I'm sure you know are untreatable and end horrifically. One is truly gambling with one's own life. But then, that might be part of the attraction."

"Do you think the killer's presence will curtail some of the activity in the area?"

"Not in the least. Do you think you and Israel were the only ones to take in the sights last night? I imagine that most men who came to Whitechapel were not as particular as the two of you, and ended the evening in the pubs and brothels. I should warn you, however, that those who come exploring without truly knowing what they're getting themselves into frequently wake up in an alleyway clad in their underdrawers, their possessions gone in six directions. Don't bring anything that cannot be easily replaced. In fact, I think it best if I carry the wallet while we are in Whitechapel. Not because you are incapable of defending yourself, but rather because if someone sees you with it, there will be several attempts to liberate it from you simply because you do not appear to be a threat. Few would dare approach me."

I was loath to part with the wallet because with it came a certain amount of independence. Now I would have to ask permission for every purchase I made. However, I saw the sense in what he was saying and reluctantly tendered it into his care.

A game of rounder was taking place in a dead-end alley, its young players paying little heed that catching the ball required running into traffic. It was already growing dark here, but what else did the youth have to do at night? They made paper flowers their mothers sold the next day or practiced picking pockets or worked at situations that children should not in order to feed their families.

"Look at them," Barker said. "They are already seasoned by hardship and cynical. The adult men are either feverish for making money or have given up and only care for their personal pleasures. Their wives—common law only, you understand—are either bowed down by woe and strife, or have become harridans, fighting to survive. Either way, they look ten years older than their husbands."

As we walked we came upon a group of young people walking, perhaps five years younger than I. One of the girls upended a bottle of what I took to be gin down her throat, finishing it before simply letting it shatter on the curb. This was no place to take pride in, so there was no attempt to keep it clean.

Nearby, there was a group of women sitting in the gutter, having a discussion. They weren't drunken or of low repute, they were what passed for respectable women here, but with no money for tea rooms and no parks in which to sit, they stooped in their cobblestone gardens and mended their husbands' shirts or darned his socks while passing the time of day. Perhaps for five minutes they could forget that they lived in the worst part of London.

"I'm very lucky," I told my employer. "If you hadn't hired me, I'd be living in streets like this. Thank you for taking a chance on a failed scholar with a record. Most wouldn't."

Barker nodded. He's not an emotional man, or if he is, he controls it tightly within himself. He, too, had seen hardship and loss and like the people here had learned hard lessons: no one will show you sympathy. Keep yourself in check. Don't display emotion, it will only get you in trouble. Don't speak until spoken to. Think before you speak. Keep a constant vigil in every direction for danger. This is the catechism of Whitechapel.

East London was much darker than West London. The gaslights were farther apart, and many shops shut down early and were locked tight. The darkness was palpable. I could stand in front of an alleyway and not see a man standing therein, though he be but three feet away from me. It made the streets seem ever more dangerous. A hand could come out of the darkness, armed with a razor, and one would be cut before one even knew what was happening.

"This isn't the lark you had with your friend the other night, is it?" my employer asked.

"No, sir."

"Where are we?" he asked. He knew, but was testing me.

"Dorset Street." We had just passed under the sign.

"Come with me."

He seized me by the arm and let me into one of the tenements. Inside, the halls smelled of cabbage and mold. Somewhere above us a couple was having a row and a child was crying. We passed down the hall and turned into another, parallel with the street. We were heading east. I like knowing my bearings and what direction I'm facing at all times. The Guv kicked open a sprung door and we passed across a small court with raw sewage running down the middle, until we passed under an arch and were in Dorset Street again.

"I'd like to obtain a map, sir, so I can memorize the streets," I said.

"I'll get one for you tomorrow. There is a test that all London cabmen must undertake before receiving his badge. He must know every street in London. It would not harm you to study for such a test yourself."

"Yes, sir," I replied.

It was an unusual occupation in which I found myself employed. Some information is generally helpful, such as how to shoot a gun, or defend oneself, to know the streets, and the signs about a person that reveal criminal activity, or to understand the cant, which is criminal slang. I now knew dozens of things that were only useful in our work, or perhaps that of a barrister.

We had just stepped into Dorset Street when we were accosted. A constable noticed us and without a word laid a hand on Barker's shoulder and jabbed the tip of his truncheon into the Guv's side, where it thumped against the gun and holster there. He was a gray-mustached veteran and must have noticed the telltale bulge in my employer's coat.

"What's this, then?" the officer demanded.

"What you think it is," Barker replied.

"None of your lip, you. Open your coat slowly."

Barker complied. He was carrying two revolvers in holsters under his arms. They were .44 Colts, manufactured for the American firm right there in London.

"We are special officers, working for Robert Anderson," he explained.

"Got any proof of that, sir?"

"I do, but isn't 'H' Division a few streets away? We're heading there now. Have you time to accompany us?"

"I believe I will. Do you mind if I ask you to give me those barking irons you're carrying?"

"No, Constable, I don't mind at all."

"Will you surrender them to me, sir?"

"No, Constable, I will not."

"I see. Might I have your name, please?"

"Certainly. It is Barker," the Guv said. "Special Inspector Cyrus Barker."

# CHAPTER SEVEN

We were marched down to the Commercial Road Station, "H" Division, and questioned thoroughly. It was just the sort of situation that would have made me anxious in my younger days as an enquiry agent. They read our papers and then asked us a battery of questions, first separately, then together. Any discrepancies were gone over numerous times, trying to break us down, and there was the obvious suggestion that we be placed in the cells overnight until our bona fides could be established. At one point the head inspector demanded to know why Anderson was sending hired spies into his district. It was bad enough with the City Police and the Home Office trying to take a slice of the pie. I'd have felt sorry for him if he hadn't been so difficult about it. An hour later, he had finally tired of toying with us and let us go. We had successfully introduced ourselves at "H" Division. Barker and I shrugged our shoulders and went on about our business. It's best to be philosophical about these things, I've found.

We trudged over the cobblestones of Whitechapel on the way back to the Frying Pan. Actually, the Guv informed me, they were limestone setts, not cobbles. Cobbles were round, flat stones brought here by glaciers a few millennia ago. The setts were cut into brick-bat shapes and set on top of a layer of sand. There hadn't been true cobbles in centuries, though some still existed in remote corners of the country and in graveyards. Most cobbles were now used to make buildings. I had worked all day and now was being given a history lesson about stones. It was starting to feel like the longest day of my life.

Finally, we stepped into the Frying Pan, and the Guv bought us each a half pint of stout for a nightcap while the publican announced that the final drinks would be served. I was no longer green and understood that drinks would still be served for a few hours, only money would change hands a bit more surreptitiously. Barker raised the tankard to his lips, then wiped the foam off his black mustache with a finger before smacking his lips.

"Better than the Britannia's," I said. "They dose the ale with laudanum."

"We'll avoid that one if we can," he said.

"A word with you, gentlemen," a man said from a nearby table. He was in his forties, sturdily built, with his hair parted in the middle. He could have done with a shave, and his clothing needed pressing. There was an open bottle of rye and a tumbler in front of him. Barker turned and looked at him. I could picture him sifting through files of cards in his head.

"Tom Bulling," the Guv finally said. "What do you want?"

"Now, Push, don't be that way! I just had a question or two."

"Such as?" Barker growled.

"Oh, you know. Why, for example, you closed your doors on a very popular enquiry agency. Or why you have been seen going into Scotland Yard. And why exactly you've decided to hire a room here. This isn't your average holiday spot. Taking the waters here will pro'bly kill you."

"How did you come by this information?" my employer asked, leaning over the table on the knuckles of one hand.

"I'm a friendly bloke," Bulling replied. "Got friends here in the Chapel, friends in Scotland Yard. At the Syndicate, we're up on the latest information. We have to be."

"Syndicate?" I asked.

"Central News Syndicate," he replied. "We provide the news for several newspapers."

Barker crossed his arms. "Why should my situation be of any concern to you?"

"Oh, Push," he said. "You're well known about this town and everything you do is of interest. Have a story for me? Doesn't have to be a new one, you understand."

This was exactly what Warren had warned us about, having our names in the newspaper. It was enough to cost us our positions at Scotland Yard. A reporter dogging our steps was all we needed.

"Nothing at the moment, sir," the Guv replied.

"That's strange," Bulling said. He had a rough voice and a Cockney accent. "You look like a busy man. P'raps you're involved in a certain case in the district. There have been a few murders here lately, in case you hadn't heard."

"Pray tell," Barker said, giving a ghost of a smile.

"I wouldn't have to use your name. In fact, you could write it yourself if you'd prefer. 'Recollections of a Private Enquiry Agent,' or such like."

"Thank you, no."

"A comment, then. How do you think the Yard is handling the Whitechapel Killer case? What would you have done instead? Your take on who the killer might be."

"Whom," Barker corrected.

"Well, la-di-da. Come on, Push. You're always good for a story to help a working man earn a living. I'm working to a deadline."

"I'm sorry, Mr. Bulling, I cannot help you."

Bulling replenished his tumbler and tossed it down.

"Wouldn't it be better if I used real facts rather than conjecture? The public don't much care which, after all. They'd believe either, but it might matter to you. I hear Warren has it in for you. Sent your friend Inspector Poole out to Bayswater, where he's collecting dust from inactivity, just for working with you. What's going on there?"

"You'll have to ask Scotland Yard."

"Don't think I won't. I thought we was mates, Barker. You was the one man in London that money couldn't buy, nor power corrupt.

Maybe I was wrong about you. Never thought I'd see the day you and Warren was thick as thieves."

"You must write as you please," the Guv said. He showed no anger at being questioned, but he was adamant in his refusal. "You shall, anyway."

"I can make it easy for you, or I can make it difficult. This is my mansion here, so to speak. I was born two streets away. I'm known here. They'll talk to you if I say talk, and they'll dummy up if I tell them to. I know all the gangs. Grew up with some of them. You been hangin' 'round Whitehall too long. You've grown a heart cold as Portland granite."

"I'm sorry, Mr. Bulling, I cannot—"

"Fine, then. Join the hexstablishment, for all I care. I try to do you a favor and get me fingers bit off for my troubles. But I'm a patient man. I'll assume you've had a bad day. You might change your mind. I've got what you call a soft heart. Pass me a word, a clue, a lead, and we'll let bygones be bygones. No use hendangering a friendship, says I. But I can't go carrying it round all by myself forever. There's give and there's take. Lad, talk some sense into your master."

"He is perfectly capable of making up his own mind, I'm sure," I said.

Bulling's face took on a nasty grin. He leaned back and crossed his boots. "Ah, the honeyed tones of Oxford. Mr. Butter-don't-melt-on-the-table hisself. You're a bad influence on him, boy. He used to be a man of the people. Now he's just another toff."

"Hoy! Bulling!" the publican roared from the back. "Get your blooming daisies off my table."

Reluctantly, the reporter removed the offending boots.

"The people of London would like to know why a prominent enquiry agent should suddenly hang up his shingle and start lurking in a bog hole like this one. Has a dip in the Exchange caused a crisis in your finances?"

The Guv made no response.

"Quiet as the sepulchral tomb," Bulling said. "No telling tales out of school, I reckon."

"Tell me," I dared ask. "Have you cadged this out on your own, or has someone tipped you off?"

"Industry!" he replied. "My industry is my byword. When all my competitors are three pints in, I'm out tracking a story. Never say die. You gentlemen ruminate about that. Ta for now. Ta for nuffink!"

He picked up the bottle and tumbler and left, or tried to. The publican met him at the door and took the glass out of his hand. The bottle had been paid for. Meanwhile, Barker went silent. I'm a talkative man, and I say five times the number of words Barker does on any normal day, but I knew when not to ask a question.

"Bullings may once have been a fine reporter," Barker finally said, setting his bowler hat on the table. "But John Barleycorn has him in his grips. Now he relies upon informants and begging. Or rather, wheedling."

"How do you suppose he knew what we've been up to?"

"Information is worth money, even a penny or two. Someone passed the word of our closing on to him. He probably has many informants at Scotland Yard. Constables aren't paid well. He was likely informed about our staying here from the hour we arrived. It wasn't hard for him to put it all together that something's going on. If he presses hard enough, he'll learn that I've become a special inspector."

"Do you suppose he'll write something, as he threatened?"

"Probably not, but if he does, so be it. We'll always have enquiry work."

"Now that we're here, I'd like to work on this case," I said.

"I'm glad to hear it, Thomas. I was worried you might find making tea beneath you."

"No work is beneath me, sir, that is honest work. And who knows? The tea I made today might give just the lift a constable needs to catch a criminal, or an inspector to track down a murderer."

"The wisest words I heard all day," he said.

Not long after, Barker ordered two dozen oysters and another round of stout. After a long day in my new position I was famished and this part of the East End had the freshest oysters to be had in all London. When the tray arrived, we set to, squirting lemon juice into each shell and swallowing the salty bivalves. I've heard the flavor described as coppery and iodine, but those of us who grew up on them think them delicious.

"You're not just here for the oysters," I said. "We're here because of Mary Nichols, are we not?"

"This pub is a favorite among the local unfortunates. I'd like to speak to them when they are not working."

Within the hour, the door opened and four women entered, all in the early stages of middle age, in tatty hats and darned shawls. Unfortunates. I saw them in the streets, making bold and suggestive stares at passersby, but here we were seated with a pint in hand and it was as if they'd been trotted out for our observation.

"Pink 'ot, my good man," one said to the owner, who seemed unconcerned that low women had invaded his establishment.

"Gimme some sherry, barman," the second said regally, a gap-toothed woman in a straw boater.

"Oh, la," said the third. "H'aint she smart? A pint's enough for the likes o' me."

I didn't hear the fourth one speak, because the first suddenly brayed over something the publican had said. The foursome was making a spectacle and seemed to enjoy doing so.

"Gwen," one said, "Lend me that wool scarf o' yours this Saturday. Jim's back in town from Liverpool Docks and if I 'ad it he might tike me to the music halls, I reckon."

"Not till you pay back the sixpence you borreyed last week!"

The woman broke out in language fitting for a sailor, but then she tipped her companion a wink as if to say all was forgiven.

"Why is the Whitechapel Killer murdering women like these?" I murmured to my employer. "Does he think he's doing a public service?"

"Lad," he admonished in a low voice, "there is no such thing as an ugly woman."

He was accusing me of being ungallant, of being quicker to give up my seat on the omnibus to an attractive woman than to one who is old or spotted or in some way imperfect. The Guv treated the old and young, the beautiful and the not so beautiful alike. He opened doors for crones as if they were duchesses. As rough as his manner was, I must admit his behavior was sometimes better than mine.

"That's not what I meant," I said, defending my statement. "If one came into Whitechapel for . . . certain services, surely such women would not be one's first choice. There are younger women here, prettier women, even more demure women. Is the killer so poor that he can only approach such women as these?"

"No. I suspect the women probably never saw a penny of it."

"Then I don't understand, unless the man himself is hideous, and any woman looks fetching to him."

Barker shrugged. "Perhaps some men might prefer a woman who is more experienced in such matters, compared to an ingénue."

I was about to make a remark when one of the women we were discussing invited herself unbidden to our table, taking a seat in front of us.

"'Ello, gentlemen. 'Aven't seen you here before. Jules, at the bar, don't 'low no solicitin' 'ere, so I'm just informing you gents that I'm frequently found along Commercial Road most nights and I could show you a jolly time, rilly."

Now that she was closer to us I could see that her teeth were stained and her skin coarse. Her clothing was mismatched, a dark green cloak over a blue skirt. The toes of her boots were cracked.

"Thank you, madam, for the kindness of your offer," Barker said, "but we've had a long day and must be up again in a few hours."

"Suit yourself, dearies. If you change your mind, ask for Sadie."

Barker actually raised his hat. I did likewise, if for no reason than I didn't like being shown up by my employer.

"We'll keep that in mind, madam."

"Did you know Dark Annie?" I asked, referring to Annie Chapman. It was her nickname from the files.

She hesitated for a moment. "By sight, yes. Pasty-faced, she was; consumptive. My cousin had it, so I know. Don't see why anyone would go with such as her and risk getting it, too, but I'm sure she had to eat, same as you and me. Poor old thing. She chose the wrong fellow and the wrong alleyway together. She never was very lucky. What happened to her, I wouldn't wish on me worst enemy."

She threw back the last of her drink, which was pink gin that had been heated with a poker. She looked regretfully at the bottom of her glass and then up at Barker. It occurred to me then they must have been of like age, though she looked years older than Mrs. Philippa Ashleigh, the widow with whom my employer had an understanding.

"Come, lad, let us be going," Barker said, rising. "It was charming to meet you, Miss Sadie. I hope you have a pleasant evening."

The unfortunate let us pass without comment or ridicule. It might have been the most polite refusal she'd received in a very long time. We climbed the narrow stair to our room. Once inside, a problem occurred to me.

"Sir," I said. "We still have no change of clothes in the morning. I mean, I can change into my uniform, but you have no other suit."

"As I said, we'll pick up a few boiled shirts at Petticoat Lane in the morning," he replied. "We shall fit in better both here and at Scotland Yard in such attire, and after this case is over, we'll hang them in the changing room in our office. That way, you'll have a change of clothes handy whenever you have to investigate the East End."

We crawled into our beds. I was exhausted, having worked from seven until midnight. The bed was hard and smelled of bug powder, but I was beyond caring. At that moment, the room might just as well have been a suite at Claridge's.

# CHAPTER EIGHT

The next I knew, I was being shaken awake by Barker's rough hand. There was no gentle, tony voice from Mac urging me to wake as he gradually drew open the curtain. In fact, there was no gentle anything.

"What o'clock is it?" I asked.

"Half past five."

"And why are we rising so early, may I ask?"

"You may. You might not receive an answer."

My employer sometimes works under the misguided assumption that he possesses a sense of humor. I pushed myself up to a seated position, and began rooting about for my shoes.

Downstairs, breakfast was served promptly at six. The sun was just peeking over Whitechapel steeple. There were eggs and bacon and kippers, as well as toast and fried tomatoes.

"What time is the lane open?" I asked.

"Seven or so, but if we mill about and look interested, they might open their shops for us."

"You do realize we'll be paying the most we could pay," I said, cutting my bacon. "The prices fall steadily throughout the day."

"Do I look as if I am in need of a bargain?"

"No," I admitted. "I suppose not."

We ate and then went to the lane, where Israel says all good clothes go to die and then be sewn together and resurrected like Frankenstein's monster. It is a street, Middlesex Street, actually, and several others that branch from it, full of used-clothing dealers and vestments of all sorts, from ecclesiastical raiment to military garb. I don't know why a person who is not a member of Her Majesty's Guard would need a busby hat, but it can be purchased there all the same.

When Barker makes a purchase, which is rare, he tends to do too much rather than too little. He bought us three suits, half a dozen shirts, and two pairs of boots each. The clothing was plain, functional, and unmemorable, but then we were trying to blend in with the crowd, not stand out. He also bought us both an overcoat and a bowler. I suspected we were wearing kosher clothing.

"Was yesterday an example of what we'll be doing today?" I asked. "Research, working in 'A' Division, then walking Whitechapel?"

"I'm not merely having you work at Scotland Yard to give you something to do. We are working our way slowly through both Scotland Yard and Whitechapel, the way a worm burrows into an apple. If done well, we will not be noticed. Or at least, you won't, which is the intent. I'll be the one calling attention to myself from time to time. Keep your eyes and ears open and pay attention. I hope that you can collect information quickly."

Back in our room, we changed into our not-so-new clothing and then walked to Commercial Street to find a hansom cab. When we arrived, I changed into my uniform and took my purchases into the kitchen to begin my first pot of the day while Barker went down to the Records Room to consult with PC Kirkwood. Every minute or so, a shoulder appeared in the hall, or an ear listened for the tea to be ready. I opened the shortbread tins and filled the tea ball with loose black tea before letting it steep. I was experimenting to make the perfect pot.

When it was ready, I made two cups and put a biscuit on each saucer and brought them to Barker and PC Kirkwood, whom I thought we should cultivate. As I left, the queue began forming quickly for the tea.

"Thank you, PC Llewelyn," PC Kirkwood said when I put a cup on his desk.

"You are entirely welcome." I turned and regarded my employer.

It was Tuesday, the eleventh of September. We had acquainted ourselves with the victims, and now it was time to look at the suspects. I had expected close to a dozen, so when the constable placed just three folders in front of us, we both eyed him scathingly. These were the detritus. All the important suspects' files were still in the hands of our superiors, in spite of Anderson's warnings.

"Tell me, Constable, do you know who currently has which file?" Barker asked.

"No, sir, I'm sorry," Kirkwood said. "Whoever checks out a file, his name is confidential."

"I see. Are you at least able to tell me which files are still outstanding?"

Kirkwood pushed back his helmet and scratched his forehead. Now that I wore one I understood how hot and uncomfortable they could be.

"I don't see why not, Inspector Barker. They are a matter of public record for all inspectors. Allow me to consult my book."

Kirkwood pulled a ring of keys from his belt and unlocked his desk. He lifted a small black notebook from inside and began to consult it, making sure we did not catch a glimpse of the writing therein. When he was done, he carefully locked the book back in the desk.

"Three suspect files have been borrowed. They are for James K. Stephen, Montague Druitt, and Francis Tumblety."

"Have you got that, lad?"

"Yes, sir. Tumblety. Should we speak with the other inspectors?"

Barker shook his head. "There is no need. We have these other files in front of us. Let us examine them first, while we wait for the others to be returned."

He picked up one, seemingly at random, and handed the other two to me. I followed his example, if for no other reason than to prove that I, too, could have boundless patience. Actually, I had little to none, but the Guv had once suggested that by feigning patience one might eventually acquire it in some measure. I thought I would put that theory to the test.

"Ostrog," I said aloud. "Odd name."

I opened the file and began to read. Michael Ostrog was a Russian Jew and a doctor whose career was cut short by mental illness. He was placed in the Surrey Pauper Lunatic Asylum the previous September for what was considered homicidal mania, but was released as recently as March. He also was a thief and confidence trickster, with a career going back to 1863. Ostrog was about fifty years of age and seemed to combine bouts of great cunning with mental confusion. Once in the middle of a trial, for example, he stood and told the judge he must leave for France immediately.

Dr. Ostrog was known to have both a hatred for women and a habit of filling his pockets with medical scalpels and other equipment. Since his release he had disappeared. The report made the inference that his fellow Jews were hiding him. Ostrog was tall and thin with a short beard. Apparently he went by dozens of aliases in order to make money and retain his freedom. No record of him receiving an actual license to practice medicine or a diploma either in England or Russia had been found. Though released as "cured," he had failed to report for his monthly inspection since March and was considered a dangerous man at large. A note in the file suggested the police keep an eye on the book stalls in the City and Whitechapel for him. He had a habit of stealing books from stalls and libraries.

I could not count him out as a suspect. He was a homicidal maniac with a scalpel in his pocket. He hated women and he may have lived in the area. However, according to the file, no one had seen him for at least a month. He could be in Rio de Janeiro or the Congo, for all Scotland Yard knew. For that matter, he could be in Hanbury Street hunting for another unfortunate to slay.

The next file had the name Ludwig Schloski written on it. Apparently, the suspect had recently arrived from Poland, and according to his common-law wife, Lucie Badewski, he was a violent man who enjoyed mistreating women. She had called the police after he had attempted to strangle her. He kept a knife under his pillow and routinely disappeared most nights during the killings, not returning until the morning. Searching through his private papers, she found his true name was Seweryn Klosowski of Kolo, Poland. Schloski was a good-looking fellow with a handlebar mustache and a swooping forelock of hair he combed high on his head, but he was a cold-blooded fellow who had an interest in poisons. He had earned a minor medical certificate from the Warsaw Hospital in practical surgery and worked as a nurse in various hospitals in London. If that wasn't bad enough for Lucie Badewski, his wife arrived from Poland, and he attempted to move her in with them. It was enough and to spare as far as Lucie was concerned. Potential murder was one thing, but bigamy was out of the question. She moved out.

The case against Schloski seemed to hang on the testimony of the one woman who had reason to hate him. There was no damning evidence from neighbors, for example, or arrests by the police. She had not pursued charges against him for the attempted strangulation. The poisons he carried could be explained by his continued studies in medicine, and if a fellow could be made a suspect for staying out late, most of Whitechapel would be kept under watch. That said, I'm sure he was no saint. Chances are he was aggressive, manipulative, and controlling, not to mention a bigamist. However, none of those things seemed to go with cutting up a woman on the street and removing her organs. This fellow was a charmer, who like as not would prefer to work inside. I had no doubt under the right circumstances he might kill, but not in the manner of the Whitechapel Killer. If Lucie Badewski were smart, she would be on a ship bound for America by now, well shed of him.

I put down the second file and looked at my employer. He read more slowly than I, but that was because he tended to ponder between sentences. Nevertheless, he soon finished the first file and closed it in front of him before pushing it over to me.

"If that's another Polish Jew," I said, pointing to the folder, "I'm going to suspect the government is looking for a scapegoat."

I took the file. It was another Polish Jew, this one named Aaron Kosminski.

"Crikey," I said. "I suppose they don't believe an Englishman capable of such aberrant behavior. They're all pure as Galahad."

I wiped my eyes, which were growing weary from all the reading, and began again. I picked up the third file. Kosminski was a young man of diminished mental ability. That's my term; the file said he was a dummy. He was twenty-five years old and lived with his family who owned a factory. They watched over him during the day and apparently locked him in at night. Kosminski spoke a garbled form of Yiddish and according to the investigating officers sometimes sat and stared at nothing for hours on end. Recently he had been placed in an asylum temporarily while his brother's wife gave birth, because there was no one to watch him closely. Shortly after he returned to the residence, the police were called, because he had threatened his sister-in-law with a pair of scissors. He was not arrested. The eldest brother explained that he occasionally had manic episodes and had been upset at being incarcerated and by the arrival of a new member of the family who cried and required constant attention.

The constable who recorded the incident described him as extremely thin, though the family seemed well-off by East End standards. He was also what the constable called "malodorous." I pitied the family that had to deal with an adult sibling with little hygiene and subject to maniacal episodes, who had to be locked in at night. I suspected Kosminski was off in his own world most of the time.

"Why do you suppose," I asked Barker, interrupting his reading, "that they didn't leave this chap in the asylum? I mean, he did prove to be a danger and they seem wealthy enough by Whitechapel standards to keep him there."

"You're thinking like a Western European, not an Eastern one," the Guv replied. "The only law they've seen is the Cossacks who kick in their doors in the middle of the night and seize a family member who is never heard from again. It is very difficult for them to trust authorities. Besides, in their culture, one takes care of one's own family, especially incapable members like Aaron Kosminski. To put him in an asylum would be considered a betrayal. The fact that Kosminski's family put him away even temporarily is proof that they have been influenced by Western culture."

"I don't think much of any of these suspects," I said. "The first one, Ostrog, seems a little more promising than the other two."

"Allow me to make my own decisions," Barker said.

He was sitting back with the files in front of him, tapping on his lower teeth with a pencil and reading the other two files. He looked miles away.

"Let's take a walk," he said, when he was finished.

He stood and left the room. I glanced down at the table. He hadn't touched his tea or the shortbread. He really was starting to act like an inspector. I shook my head and hurried out the door after him.

Once out the door, he turned east toward the Embankment and began to walk with his chin sunk on his breast and his hands behind him. When he reached Northumberland Street, he turned again and began heading north.

"Do you not trust PC Kirkwood?" I asked.

"It is best to discuss theories outside of the Yard as much as possible. You were correct about the three suspects. There was a reason why the files were there. Ostrog has probably left the country; Schloski is probably romancing a barmaid; and Kosminski was safely locked inside for the night under the scrutiny of his brothers. That being said, we must investigate each one, and not get in the habit of relying on others whom we neither know nor trust."

"'Trust, but be careful in whom,'" I quoted, which was his family motto and used to appear in his advertisements in the *Times*.

"Precisely."

"We have three different types of suspects," I went on. "We've got a mental imbecile, a doctor who has gone homicidally mad, and an intelligent medical man with brutish tendencies."

"That is a good analysis," Barker said.

"Thank you, sir. But why is it good, exactly?"

"Because the killer himself must be one of the three types. Either he is an imbecile who doesn't understand what he is doing, or a man who is slowly losing a battle to insanity, or he is completely sane, but calloused toward women."

"I thought you said none of these men was the killer," I said.

"I'm not talking about individuals, lad. I'm talking about types."

"Is it possible for a sane man to commit murder?" I asked.

"I would think it likely that most murders are done by sane

people. They have merely convinced themselves that a person or persons must die. Then they plan how to go about it. It is morally evil, but they are legally sane."

"So, which is he?" I asked.

"There you go again, lad, trying to put a label on him. Let it develop in the course of the investigation. One should not force these things."

"I would remind you that some of the best police officers in London are trying to solve this case as quickly as possible in order to prove we special constables are not needed. Men like Swanson and Abberline."

"They are welcome to it," the Guv said.

"I know even if we track down this fellow ourselves, Scotland Yard will get the credit," I said. "You do intend to try, don't you, sir?"

"Of course," he answered, "because the people in charge and the men investigating the case will know. They are the ones I'm trying to prove myself against. I wonder if you realize how many organizations will be trying to horn in on this case in order to solve it and get the credit."

"What do you mean?"

"You tell me. With whom are we in direct competition?"

"Scotland Yard," I answered.

"Who consists of—"

"The Criminal Investigation Department."

"And?"

"The Met. That is, the regular police. I'm sure they'd like to solve it and be able to lord it over the CID."

"Who else?"

"Special Branch. They're devious and not above breaking the law to get what they want."

"Very good. Continue."

"Uh . . ."

"Don't stand there blowing bubbles like a goldfish, Thomas. Who else?"

"I'm sorry, sir. I can't think of anyone."

Barker snorted. "Oh, come now, lad, show some imagination.

What about the Plainclothes Division? Surely they'll be out hunting the killer. Don't you suppose the Thames Police hope a murder happens close to the river? There is the Home Office, responsible for domestic affairs, and the Foreign Office, who might decide to step in if they suspect the killer came recently from Poland or Russia. Consider 'H' Division itself, the Whitechapel Police. They'll consider the murders to be within their jurisdiction, and might not be likely to share their theories with the Met. Even the Yeomen Guard of the Tower Hamlets considers that area of London their responsibility, and might withhold facts in order to investigate for themselves."

"When you put it that way, sir, it sounds like a jurisdictional nightmare."

"That's exactly what it is. I understand even the coroners and medical practitioners are fighting over the chance to examine the bodies. Their reports will be read widely and could be the making of a career."

"You make it sound like a foxhunt," I said.

"A foxhunt! Aye, Thomas, that's what it is, everyone after one little creature. And the hounds are the newspapers baying on every street corner, 'Another Horrible Murder!'"

"With so many hounds and hunters, it should be an easy matter to bring this murderer to book."

"Perhaps," Barker said, "even probably, given ideal circumstances. But if each of us insists on grasping his few facts and not sharing them with the others, I suspect several more women will be killed before this case is over."

# CHAPTER NINE

W hat next, sir?" I asked Cyrus Barker. That is, Special
Inspector Barker of the Yard. I don't believe either of us
would get used to that any time soon.

"I believe it is time to speak with the real heads of the investigation, Swanson and Abberline. I would prefer to take them on one at a time."

If anyone knew exactly how matters stood with the Whitechapel Killer, it would be they. We had met each of them in the course of previous enquiries, and I must admit they were highly competent as far as I could tell. Swanson was nearly as good a tracker of men as my employer and I wondered why he did not go into private work where he could make more money. Abberline was innovative, always trying to bring in science to aid in his cases. Both were well respected within Scotland Yard; I'd even go so far as to say some constables would march through a fire barefoot at their request. If we could get their backing, even their approval, it would certainly make our being there much easier.

We tracked Detective Inspector Donald Swanson to a classroom similar to an operating theater, containing fixed semicircles of benches around an open hub. The hub contained two standing chalkboards, one with a hand-drawn map of Whitechapel on it and the other listing facts about both of the victims. Swanson was alone in the room, adding comments to the second board, when Barker knocked on the door frame. He turned in our direction.

"Barker," he said. "How are you settling in?"

"Well enough," the Guv replied. "No one has been conspicuously rude to me, though Llewelyn here has been thumped once or twice in the halls. Still, Anderson warned us this wouldn't be easy."

"No, it won't be," Swanson replied.

He was about Barker's height, but at least three stone heavier. I couldn't fathom how many yards went into the making of his gray suit, but above his walrus mustache was a hawkish nose and even more raptorlike blue eyes. His bulk did not extend above the neck, though I suspect his top hat would have swallowed my head without touching an ear on either side. I had seen him work, and he carried that bulk as if it were mere pillows. He was quick off the mark when it counted.

"What have you done so far?" the chief inspector continued.

"We have reviewed the files of the victims and some of the suspects, the ones still in the Records Room. Also, we've walked around Whitechapel viewing the spots where the victims were found and taking in the local color, so to speak."

"You know as much as I, then," Swanson said.

"I find that hard to believe. I understand a few of the suspect files are missing."

"What files would those be, gentlemen?"

"The files concerning Mr. Druitt, Mr. Stephen, and Dr. Tumblety to be precise. I believe Assistant Commissioner Anderson requested that all files be returned."

"So he did, so he did," Swanson said. "I admit that the file for Montague Druitt is on my desk. I had returned it on Anderson's orders, but some fresh information came in and I retrieved it again. I am actively investigating this suspect and would like to keep this file at least temporarily."

"What became of the files for Stephen and Tumblety?"

"Ah! Yes, of course. Inspector Abberline has been pursuing leads in the Tumblety matter."

"And Stephen?"

Swanson opened his mouth to speak, then seemed to notice me.

"Is he privy to such information?" he asked, looking at me.

"Anything you say to me you may say to him," Barker answered.

"Very well. The Stephen file was supposed to come to you. If it is missing, it can only be in the hands of Inspector Littlechild."

"I thought I knew everyone in the Yard, but I'm not familiar with the name. Who is he?"

"He was an inspector with the Special Irish Branch, but during the last attempt on Her Majesty's life, he was assigned to guard the royal family, and he took the opportunity to ingratiate himself at Sandringham. Since then, he's managed to recruit a half-dozen men to his detail, forming an unofficial Special Royal Branch, if you will."

"I was under the impression I was given free rein here, and the meetings at the palace were merely to give me more authority," Barker said.

"I'm sure that was what you were intended to think, but it's complicated. If you were under the impression that Anderson asked you to come in merely as a friend, and because his health is broken down, I suspect you came under false pretenses. There's more to it than that. A lot more. You are in intrigue here up to your ears. As much or more so than when Great Scotland Yard was for the Scots kings come down south to visit their Sassenach neighbors."

"Who is this fellow Stephen?"

"He is the Duke of Clarence's tutor."

"And he is considered a suspect?" I asked.

Swanson turned and regarded me appraisingly. "He's got a file and is being actively investigated. Of course, that doesn't necessarily mean he's the Whitechapel Killer."

The Guv held up a hand, to stop Swanson from going on.

"Pray do not tell us any more regarding Mr. Stephen. We would prefer to read the report for ourselves and question witnesses."

"I would like to have your notes transcripted and added to the general files, in that case."

"Certainly," Barker replied.

They both nodded as if coming to an unspoken agreement to work together.

"Now, what is this business about Robert Anderson bringing me in under false pretenses?" the Guv asked.

"I am not the one to ask. It's Freddy Abberline you should speak to."

Cyrus Barker leaned his head to the side until I heard his vertebrae crack. "Thank you, I shall, then. Come, Constable Llewelyn."

The Guv passed down the hall until he came to a door and gave it a thump that shook it in its frame.

"Come in," a voice said from within.

Barker pushed his way inside. Abberline was as thin as Swanson was stocky. He was perhaps a year beyond thirty but rapidly losing his hair. What he lacked above, he made up for below, with Dundreary whiskers and a mustache. His office was full of apparatus for the Bertillon system of criminal investigation, and there was a microscope on his desk. Years later, when men like Warren and Barker and Swanson had retired from the force, men like Abberline would be in charge, the scientific investigator.

"Cyrus Barker," he said. "I was wondering when you would arrive. Have you come to take over? Shall I move out and give you my office?"

"What are you talking about?" Barker grumbled.

"As if you didn't know. So, as they say, a new broom sweeps clean, eh? I just want to know why Anderson couldn't tell us to our face. Where's he hiding, in a hotel in Brighton?"

"He is in Switzerland, recovering his health. Why, have you heard otherwise?"

"Yes, and you're the hammer he's decided to use."

"Inspector," he said, "I give you my word that I have no idea of a plot against the Yard hatched by Robert Anderson. He looked genuinely ill when I spoke to him and he asked me to come here and work in his stead, collecting information. I have no proof. It was an oral agreement. I didn't think I'd need it."

"You nonconformists all work together," Abberline said with a sneer. "You expect me to believe you're not working for him?"

"What do you mean? I just told you I am working for him."

"No, not bloody Anderson. I could care less about that jackanapes. I'm talking about Munro!"

Barker's brows suddenly sank behind his dark spectacles in a frown.

"Munro? James Munro? What does he have to do with this?"

"Only everything. He's trying to start a coup right here at the Yard, but he'll have to get by me to do it, and that goes for you if you're part of it!"

Barker dropped into a chair in front of Abberline's desk and rubbed his face with his hand. He had crossed swords with Munro in the past, when he was head of the Special Irish Branch. Munro had held the assistant commissioner position before Anderson, but he and Commissioner Warren had not gotten along. Also, though he and Barker did not like each other, both were Scots nonconformists, who took their religion seriously. One would think, and obviously Abberline did, that their similar backgrounds would make them friends, but such was not the case.

"Mr. Anderson made no mention of Mr. Munro. I was not aware they were acquainted."

"More than acquainted. Thick as thieves, more like," Abberline said.

"You say that Munro is trying to take over Warren's position and that Anderson is helping him. Can you substantiate that?"

"Of course not. Munro's too clever a fox for that. It's as you say, an 'oral agreement.'"

"Then permit me to doubt Robert Anderson's part in a coup d'état. Where is Munro these days? I haven't heard of him since he quit the Yard in protest at the start of the year."

"It's not like you to be behind, Barker. The Home Office has given him a fancy chamber down the street and a salary, for no other purpose than to be a thorn in our side."

"What was the cause of the enmity between Munro and the commissioner?" I asked.

Inspector Abberline took a deep breath and blew it out slowly before answering. "Munro expected to be made commissioner. He knew that the city board in charge of filling the position usually brought in men from the army, but he believed he had influenced enough important people in the City to change the policy. He nearly blew a hole in the roof when Warren was chosen over him, and then he had to sit by and watch Warren make the usual mistakes a tyro makes, such as the Trafalgar incident. Munro wouldn't get over the slight, and began intriguing and blackening Warren's name all over town. Finally, Warren went to the board and threatened to resign. Naturally, they talked him out of it. Then Munro charged in and threatened the same thing. They accepted his resignation."

"Are you telling me you are against the board hiring someone who had risen through the ranks?" Barker asked him.

"No, I'm not, actually. I believe they should do away with the policy of hiring from outside of the department. It ruins morale. A commissioner should come to the position already knowing everything there is to know about the work. The army and the Met are two different institutions entirely."

"Then why throw in your lot against Munro?"

Barker and the detective chief inspector eyed each other levelly. Without speaking, Barker nodded.

"Your allegiance does you credit," my employer said. "Warren approved the rise to your current position."

"He's a good man, if a trifle naïve. He tends to see things simplistically, but he works hard and he's not a bad chap when you get to know him, but it's been all swords and daggers at him since the very first day. Munro can be quite Machiavellian when it suits him."

I had to smile a little. It was probably the first time the word "Machiavellian" had been used in conversation at Scotland Yard.

"Why did Swanson send us to you, rather than tell us this himself?" Barker asked.

"He has no respect for Warren, and he thinks Munro's rise to the commissioner's chair is inevitable. He's not going to cross him. Swanson is playing a larger game. He always takes the practical approach. He accuses me of being hotheaded. I suppose I am. You'd better not be trying to trick me, Barker. If you are working for Munro and I find out about it, I'll have your license. I won't hesitate for a second."

"Thomas." Barker turned and looked at me. "Would you be so kind as to tell Inspector Abberline how I feel about Mr. Munro?"

"I suspect, Inspector, that if Munro were on fire, Mr. Barker would not cross the street, even for the pleasure of stamping him out. Is that close enough, sir?"

I saw Abberline actually crack a smile.

"Aye, Thomas, very apt. Very descriptive. There is no love lost between us, countrymen or no. Inspector, do you feel this new case will be used by Munro to discredit the commissioner?"

"That's exactly what I feel. It's all over the press, and now the royal family is interested. There is a very good chance for Warren to get a black eye over this, and I want to avoid that."

Barker sat back in the chair, which groaned under his weight, and did not speak for half a minute.

"Inspector," he finally said. "I do not believe that Robert Anderson knowingly intrigued with Munro against the commissioner, but when he returns, I shall call him to task. In the meanwhile, I will work to help the Yard in any way I can to bring this killer to justice."

"Then you should know that a suspect has been apprehended. We just got a telegram in. He's being brought in now for questioning."

"Why wasn't I informed?"

"I'm informing you now. With any luck we'll have this case over and done with before it does any damage to Warren's reputation."

"Who is the fellow? What is his name?"

"Pizer. They call him the 'Leather Apron'."

# CHAPTER TEN

Pizer was being held in a temporary cell within the crowded building. Abberline gave us permission to see him as if the building and everything in it were his to parcel out as he saw fit. Unctuous, is what he was. Or bumptious. Possibly both at once.

We were still trying to fit in to our new surroundings and the quickest way there was to ask directions. Barker reasoned that if the commissioner's office was called "Heaven," then Hell must be in the basement. We worked our way down as far as we could go, then passed down a hall to a circular stairwell and descended into the basement. His deduction was correct, and we asked for Pizer's cell, assuring the guard that we had Abberline's permission, galling as it was, to see his prisoner.

The turnkey unlocked the cell and I filed in behind my employer. Pizer, the so-called Leather Apron, was a short, stockily built man with a wispy mustache and a full beard thick as a beaver pelt. It made him look like a character from a Yiddish play, a shtetl farmer somehow transported to modern London. He spoke with a heavy accent that for the sake of clarity I shall omit.

"What? More of you? Can't you leave a man in peace?"

"We are sorry to be a nuisance, sir," Barker said. "The sooner we establish your movements on the night of the various murders, the closer we may come to freeing you."

"Freeing me? You jest. I shall never be free, sir. I am a Jew, despised of all the world, forced to wander ever west and west. All life is a trial."

"Then you must bear up and do so with a smile."

"Ha! You sound like my rabbi. At least you haven't started kicking me like the last few fellows that were in here."

"You must find yourself a proper barrister."

"A barrister," he cried, gesturing with his hands. "Do I look like the kind of person who frequents barristers? Very well. Unlock the cell. I'll walk down to the Middle Temple myself."

"I understand you make boots. What think you of the pair I am wearing?"

So saying, Barker raised a limb and rested his heel on the berth Pizer was sitting on.

"They are obviously secondhand. They weren't made for you. You need to have a new heel put on both boots, and some of the nails should be tightened. Actually, I do not make boots. They are a luxury in Whitechapel. More often I repair them. Sometimes I make opera slippers I can peddle to a few dealers in the West End, but I never get a good price, no matter how perfect they are. My looks are against me, you see. One could no more mistake me for an Englishman than one could a giraffe. And when some crime occurs, by all means, blame a Jew! He's as good a suspect as anyone."

"Where were you on the eighth of September? Do you recall?"

"Recall! They won't let me forget! I'll tell you what I told your predecessors: I was with my brother at my flat in Mulberry Street all night. He told me to lie low, because they don't like me there. Some people have got it in their minds that I am the Whitechapel murderer, though during the first murder I was at the Crossman's Lodging House, and even spoke to a policeman while a fire occurred at the docks. I was with my brother the second time. It is the old Blood Libel legend they fear, but I am no Levite. I'm not even permitted to touch blood."

I recalled my first case with Barker among the Jews. They feared the English public would be swayed by a legend now centuries old, that the Jews needed human blood for their sacrifices. It was gross ignorance of the lowest sort, but every few decades the story surfaced again and Jews found brickbats thrown through their windows, and foul words painted on the doors. Christians make bad neighbors, I have heard it said, which is far from what we have been taught.

"I assume they have taken your knife."

"Of course. They are welcome to inspect it closely. I purchase my leather already tanned. They'll find no blood on it unless they put it there themselves."

"How came you to go by the name 'Leather Apron'?"

"The Gentiles cannot remember my name. Apparently it is too foreign for them, though it is only five letters. Somebody came one day looking for Leather Apron, for the article I wore in my line of work, so I thought, 'If they remember that, it's better than nothing' So, I go by 'Leather Apron.' It actually brings me work."

"I understand you got in a little trouble last month—a gross indecency charge?"

"Yah, yah, that is typical. I see a woman walking with a fancy man one day, and another one another day, and I assume she is a prostitute. I approach her, and we start talking, trading banter as is the custom. I thought we had decided upon a reasonable transaction and began opening my trousers and then she starts to scream. The next thing I know I am arrested. It seems she is only a casual prostitute and won't take Jews, those awful disgusting Jews who killed her savior. I know I am not an attractive man, but my money is good and I am clean and healthy. She could do worse. May the next Gentile she meets give her a pox!"

"And that's all?" Barker asked, as my pen transcribed quickly in my notebook.

"It is, except that your inspectors believe I am a piece of challah dough that needs to be pummeled and kneaded every few hours. I expect the newspapers will call me a monster and a mob will form outside every night hoping to hang me. The police will bring them to a fever pitch and then innocently release me into their loving arms, without even a knife to protect myself. Then good-bye, John Pizer, and good riddance to another Jew. It was a mistake to come here. The Cossacks are brutal, but at least they were honest about it. The British hate us, while trying to appear pious and fair-minded. It is a farce."

"I will check into your alibis on the dates in question."

"Does it matter? If my alibis are proven, will I be protected? It will do me no good to be found innocent by the police if I am killed."

"If need be, I will see you to a place of safety myself, Mr. Pizer."

"What is your name, sir? You are different from the others I have spoken with."

"I am Special Inspector Barker."

The man leaned forward and suddenly clasped the Guv's hand. "Thank you, sir," he said, trying to quell the raw emotion in his voice. "I wish you luck in your search."

I called the jailer and we were let out again. I had done eight months in a cell that size for a crime I did not commit and it felt wonderful every time I was able to leave one.

"Opinions?" Barker asked as we walked down the hall from the cells.

"Pizer's a toad, but he doesn't deserve to be in there, nor should he be beaten and hung by a mob. It's one thing to be a Jew and look like Mac, but it's another thing to be built like a blancmange. He's a pathetic figure. Do you really plan to take him to safety while a mob cries for his blood?"

"I'm sure we can get him out of there during the day and away to someplace out of town."

"Inspector!" Barker called, once we'd reached the first floor. He's got a voice that rattles windows. Ahead of us I saw Abberline turn on his heels at his approach.

"Inspector, have you made any progress establishing Mr. Pizer's alibi?"

"His brother vouches for him on the night of Annie Chapman's murder, but so far we have no nonrelative witnesses on the night in question. We're still searching for the constable he claims to have spoken to during the fire that evening of Nichol's murder."

"Are you overtaxed due to the patrols in Whitechapel?"

"Yes, we are, rather."

"Would it be amenable if I attempt to establish his alibi myself?"

Abberline shrugged his shoulders and looked at him as if he were mad. "If you like."

"Capital. Special Constable Llewelyn and I shall get right on it. Thank you, Inspector."

Abberline's eyes swept mine as if to ascertain whether Barker was having him on, rather than volunteering to take on a duty. I nodded solemnly, if for no other reason than to assure him that both of us were on the level. It is one of my unwritten duties to assure others that Barker truly means what he says. Luckily, there is never any doubt on that score.

The name of the sergeant at "A" Division was Meadows. I doubt he appreciated the irony of his own name. There, with nothing but brick and cobble in any direction, he stood behind the desk in Lemon Street, a man whose name conjured wildflowers, and maidens making daisy chains. From him we were able to list the constables who had been abroad the night of Mary Nichol's murder, and might remember speaking to Pizer during the fire. Later that evening, after eating our dinner at the Frying Pan, we set out for our nightly walk, intent on finding our witness. Barker walked up to the first constable we saw. We identified ourselves and questioned him.

"Constable, were you on patrol the night of the London Docks fire, the same night as Mary Nichol's murder?"

"Aye, sir, I was."

"Do you recall speaking to a man named Pizer that night, a Jew who was a resident of the tenement? He says he spoke to a constable who can establish his alibi."

"Pizer? Nay, I cannot recall speaking to such a man, but I was busy with the fire, sir, and I didn't speak to anyone much beyond yelling for them to stay back."

"Thank you, Officer. What is your name?"

"Thatchwick, Inspector."

"Found it," I said, consulting my list.

"Well, thank you, PC Thatchwick. Stay vigilant and perhaps we shall catch the rascal tonight."

"I hope so, sir."

That was one conversation, verbatim, according to my notes, but it might as well have been a boilerplate for every one that came after. The names were changed, of course, and where they had been on the night in question. It had been a busy night for the blues of Lemon Street Constabulary.

I expected the Guv to go by a certain routine each night, but he purposely avoided it, so that we went a different route and thus came upon new vistas and never repeated ourselves as we explored Whitechapel. He also quizzed me, asking me which street we were approaching or what this one led to. If he recognized a person there, he'd tip his hat, then ask who that was, and when we had spoken to them last. He never allowed me to fall into slack habits or take a street or neighborhood for granted.

Sometimes he would plunge into a tenement, take the stairs to the roof, cross over to the next one and go down that stairwell to the street. The squalor in some places was appalling, but in others, someone took as much pride in their rooms as if they were in Fitzrovia. There was fresh paint on some walls, and the floors, though bare, were washed regularly. Certain streets such as Flower and Dean were infamous, but others, especially those close to the synagogue, might have been mistaken for the City.

Naturally, I was tired, and grew morose over this steady tramping night after night. In my more philosophical moments, however, I reasoned that I was getting an education of sorts. I now knew the East End backward and forward, all the major buildings, the churches and synagogues, the graveyards and monuments. I knew when businesses closed and when workers got off their shifts, which restaurants served proper food and which to avoid. The names of some of the unfortunates became known to me and the bawdy houses where they plied their illicit trade.

So far, we had three quarters of the names marked off the list of constables on duty that night. If I've given the impression we find our man every time we step out of our door, such was not the case. Enquiries often led us nowhere. People forget. They lie. They bear false witness out of some sort of duty to a friend. They make up things. But every now and then they tell the truth and we catch a break.

"Your name, Constable?"

"Newbrough, sir."

PC Newbrough was as shiny as a freshly minted farthing. He was young, adenoidal, and if he were fortunate, his chin would grow in or he'd be able eventually to grow a beard.

"Constable, do you recall a fire on the night of Mary Nichols's murder? According to our records, you were on duty that night."

"Yes, sir," he replied. "A fire on the docks, it was. Lamp knocked over. Couldn't say for certain it was arson. Everything that might have been called evidence burned. Still, it was contained by the Whitechapel Fire Brigade well enough, without too much damage. If it was set for a claim, it didn't do enough damage to make anyone any money."

"Do you recall speaking to a man that evening named John Pizer?"

"No, sorry. Can't say as I do. What did he look like?"

"Five foot four, stocky, bull-necked—"

"Has a beard that looks like a dead badger," I said.

Newbrough pointed a finger at me. "Leather Apron!" he cried. "Why didn't you say so? Everyone knows Leather Apron. He's a perpetual nuisance there. Always bothering the whores, wanting something for free. He'll call it flirting but I call it making an affray. We arrested him for public lewdness recently."

"Mr. Pizer claimed that was a misunderstanding. He also said he was being hounded by locals for being a Jew."

Newbrough snorted, then turned it into a cough. It was not good to act informally around an inspector you did not know.

"The whole neighborhood is Jewish, sir. They don't like him because he's odd, like. Maybe not threatening but sinister. He's a peeper, looking at women and girls, staring at them boldly, trying to start conversations with them. A woman bends over and he's looking at her cleavage. One of those types. Lonely, and not likely to ever be unlonely, if you take my meaning."

"DCI Abberline has been looking for you. Pizer claims he spoke to a constable on the docks the same hour that Nichols was killed. He'll want your testimony in writing tomorrow."

PC Newbrough saluted. "Yes, sir. I'll stop by 'A' Division and make a statement first thing."

"Excellent. I won't hold up your rounds any longer. Thank you, Constable."

"'Night, sir."

"Are you certain Pizer is innocent, sir?" I asked, when we walked around the next corner. "He was very close to the murder scene. Just because he was seen by PC Newbrough within the hour is not proof that he didn't do it."

"That is true," Barker said, walking with his coat open and his hands clasped behind him. "However, the fact that he frequents the unfortunates in the area is to my mind evidence of his innocence, in this matter at least. I suspect that the Whitechapel Killer kills because he cannot gratify his lusts any other way, though I admit I don't yet know how or why."

"This fellow's psyche is warped, no mistake."

"Aye. Probably more than we can fathom."

"Pizer lied," I said.

"Did you expect otherwise? He's got no reason to trust us, and if he paints himself in a good light it might get him released earlier."

"I suppose you're right."

"You can't expect every suspect or witness to think and act like a middle-class Englishman."

"Will you help him get released?"

"I told PC Newbrough to report. I shall let the wheels of justice turn on their own."

# CHAPTER ELEVEN

I was at my post the next morning, waiting for the early messages to pile up at the front desk so I could deliver them. I had last seen Barker at his desk, but I doubted he was there; he had metamorphosed into the Scotland Yard version of a social butterfly, talking to everyone, introducing himself, and asking questions in such a way that even experienced men didn't realize their pockets were being picked for facts.

I turned, realizing there was someone at my elbow. Jeremy Jenkins was standing beside me. Granted, he was no more than twenty meters from his favorite spot on earth, the Rising Sun, but it had never occurred to me that the man was capable of coming this far south. It was like seeing a tram car coming down a country lane, or Her Majesty out for a constitutional alone in Hampstead Heath.

"Jenkins! What has happened?"

"Message for Mr. B. Very important. Thought he should see it right away, like."

"Fine. Come along, then. We'll see if we can track him down."

We finally found him on the second floor, toward the back, with a good view of the new construction on the Embankment, talking to a sergeant I hadn't seen before. By that time, Jenkins was about played out. I realized then I should have taken the note and sent him on his way. Thin as he is, Jeremy could not in any way be considered athletic. Under normal conditions he shuffled about like an octogenarian.

"What's this?" Barker asked when Jenkins handed him the note.

"Message for you, Mr. B," our clerk wheezed, then leaned against a wall for support.

"'N. M. Rothschild and Sons, London Branch,'" Barker read.

*Rothschild*, I told myself. Only the largest private fortune in the world. They gave loans not to individuals, but to entire countries, like Russia or the United States. Or England, for that matter. They were all descendants of one family of Jewish moneylenders, who now between them financed much that occurred throughout the world, from municipal projects to wars.

Barker slid a thick finger into the corner of the envelope, and ripped through the top of the vellum like a plough in a field. He retrieved a business card therein, and read the printed side. From where I stood I could see there was writing on the back. He flipped the card and glared at the scrawl. He did not change expression, which is to say he did not show one, but he grunted to himself. Then he handed the card to me.

"'The Right Honorable the Lord Rothschild,'" I read. "'St. Swithin's Lane, the City. No number.'"

"I believe we may assume he owns all of it."

"Today at two o'clock, it says."

"We are moving in exalted circles. Thank you, Jeremy. If you would be so kind, please send a note confirming the appointment."

"Something stylish, sir?" our clerk asked. He was a forger before he became Barker's clerk.

"Nothing too flamboyant," our employer replied. "Businesslike, but elegant."

"Right you are, Mr. B. Consider it done."

Having gained his wind, our clerk turned and shuffled away, gripping the stair rail unsteadily as he went through the door.

"I wonder what the baron wants," I said.

"I wonder," Barker countered, "what the chances are that we will give it to him. In any case, we can only speculate until this afternoon."

At one forty-five, we found ourselves in St. Swithin's Lane, a narrow alleyway in the City that, while prosperous, looked like it hadn't changed a jot since Elizabeth was on the throne. Finding the correct entrance, we passed inside and made our identities known to his private secretary. In a few moments, we were shown into Rothschild's chamber.

Young and impressionable persons such as myself should not be allowed to see such opulence. It only arouses covetousness and envy. Unlike the current fashion toward bric-a-brac on every wall and rooms full of heavy furniture, his was understated and uncrowded. What there was in the way of furnishings was exquisite and antique. His desk was French Louis XV on a fine Turkish rug. The wood was old, but rich and warm-looking, possibly due to tending with beeswax. The walls had glass cases which held both books and curios, many having to do with the ancient Rothschild family and Judaica. A menorah of silver, according to a small plaque, was from the synagogue in Warsaw, fashioned in the days of Rabbi Ben Judah.

In the center of the room, standing behind the desk, was the baron himself in his shirtsleeves, looking decidedly not ancient. His hair and beard were black, his skin sallow but healthy, and his eyes gleamed with vitality and interest.

"Gentlemen," he said, shaking his hands. "Thank you for answering my summons. At this time of the day I generally take some light exercise. Would you have any objection? Mine is a sedate profession, and I must exercise when I can."

"By all means," the Guv said. "My colleague, Mr. Llewelyn, can testify that I am a great believer in exercise. I have a small courtyard attached to my chambers to which I can retire after sitting all morning."

"Fortunate man!" he said, lifting a pair of Indian pins. He began swinging them about, first high, then low, left and right, over his head and down at his ankles. I had used such clubs myself enough times to recognize by the sound as he swung them that they were heavy ones, though they looked no different than the regular kind. It took a man in excellent shape not to be pulled off his feet as he swung them about.

"I recall your dealings with my uncle Sir Moses Montefiore," he said as he flexed the pins over our heads. "You worked for him, did you not, when there was a near pogrom here a few years ago?"

"I did."

"He trusted you. He needed you. I need you, as well. May I trust you?"

"That would depend on what precisely you need me to do. I currently have a client and am working with Scotland Yard. What would you ask of me?"

"I understand one theory concerning this killer is that he is a Jew. A man named Pizer was arrested."

"He is one of several suspects. Several of them are of the Hebrew race."

"Ah!" Rothschild said. "Then you believe he is a Jew."

"I'm dealing in probabilities. Most of the population in Whitechapel now are foreign-born Jews. There is a prejudice against them at Scotland Yard. I'll admit that, or at least I assume it. However, the suspects whose files we have read warranted looking into. Pizer, for example, was not arrested randomly. He called attention to himself. Once we had established his alibi yesterday, he was released. In fact, it was in the afternoon, since Pizer claimed some citizens have come to 'A' Division at night hoping to cause him mischief or worse.

"Encourage your people to keep a low profile until this fellow is caught. We hope to catch him by the high holy days, if not sooner. Suspend public demonstrations and socialist gatherings, which would foment unrest among the uneducated Gentile population."

"I do not know if I can do that," Rothschild admitted.

"Then meet in secret. Don't draw attention to yourselves."

The banker nodded. "That I can do. I'll suggest it in the synagogue. Some will recall you and shall do what you suggest. Not all, of course. Is there anything else?"

"Some charity would not come amiss. Free soup and bread.

Convince the mothers and children you are benign and you go a long way toward convincing their husbands."

"Vegetables and flour are cheap, and our women are always looking for something to do. Consider it done."

"Are you hearing of any incidents of anti-Semitism?" I asked.

Rothschild turned in my direction. "A few, but that is normal. A broken window here, a goldsmith shop broken into there. Not everything is about race. We came here to prosper. This sort of thing is a consequence of that prosperity."

I looked over at my employer and saw he had become immobile and silent. Nathan Rothschild looked at him, waiting for him to move or speak, and then looked at me again. I shrugged my shoulders. The Guv was prompting him to fill the void with a fact or opinion, even if it were a good-bye.

"If this fellow is a Gentile, I wish he would have chosen another district to do his killing. If he is a Jew, he has no business endangering his own people in this manner. All I want is safety for our district. If a Jew is implicated, or arrested the way Mr. Pizer was last week, it could be exceedingly dangerous. Might you consider warning me before arresting a Jew for these crimes, if it should come to that?"

"That would depend. What will you do if you learn that it is true? Will you spirit him away to a place of safety? That you must not do. You cannot interfere in our investigation."

"That is hard," Rothschild admitted.

"It is. Your first impulse, to help your brother Jew, does you credit. But not this time. Let us do what we can to safeguard the Jewish population, regardless of whether the killer is Jewish or not."

"Do you think he is?"

"I have no way of knowing. The inspectors in 'A' Division have examined every Jew with a criminal record hoping to incriminate him, but so far they have been unable to build a satisfactory case. That doesn't mean they won't, nor does it guarantee that the killer is not of the Chosen People."

Rothschild rubbed his beard in thought. "I'm afraid I am guilty of thinking that this monster could not be a Jew, but I suppose I could be wrong. Though the numbers are small, we have our criminals, our madmen, like any other race. I see that now, but forgive me for hoping you are wrong."

He opened the bottom drawer of his desk and slid the weighted clubs into it. Then he donned his coat again and straightened his tie.

"How can I help?" he asked. "Do you need money?"

"No. This is one case where money is not an issue. There are several rewards being offered for whoever finds the Whitechapel murderer. Likewise, I do not think encouraging your people to search their neighborhoods will do much good. There are dozens of officers circling it in pairs and countless others hoping to collect the reward money. I suppose I don't need anything."

"You are the first man to come into this office in a twelvemonth and not ask for some sort of remuneration. Isn't there anything I could do for you?"

"I covet your prayers. We could use as much wisdom as possible."

"I will go to Bevis Marks on my way home from work tonight."

The two men came together and shook hands again.

"Come, Thomas," Barker said. "Let us examine the district by day."

We left the building and made our way down that narrow but very expensive alley that housed Rothschild's offices, heading south. In a few minutes we were in Middlesex Street, in what was popularly known as Petticoat Lane. The booths were full of men intent on selling clothing items that should have been broken down and used to make paper long ago. There were ties that went around a fashionable man's neck when Dickens and Carlyle were young men.

"We're not buying again, are we?" I asked.

"No," Barker said. "I'm trying to see the area through new eyes."

We watched for several minutes while the vendors called out about the quality of their products. Most of them were ignored. The makeshift tents and buildings were full on Sunday afternoon, but now there were few customers. We passed along Wentworth Street and soon found ourselves in Goulston Street.

It was made up of mixed buildings: shops, private flats, warehouses, and vacant structures. It was seedy and down-at-heel, but not especially different from its neighbors. There was a knife sharpener, a kosher butcher, a woman's mantle factory, a seller of used orchestra instruments, and a bookstall on the street. Most of the buildings were vacant or had been turned into tenements. There were always more coming here, hoping for a better life, but not finding it. I didn't see how anyone here could prosper.

"Have you your notebook, Thomas?" Barker asked.

"Always," I told him.

"Find me the address that Aaron Kosminski was released to."

I flipped through many pages before I finally discovered the answer.

"Twenty-two Goulston Street, sir."

"That would be . . . the mantle factory," he said, pointing to a small building.

"What is a mantle, exactly?" I asked.

"I was going to ask you. I'm not well versed in feminine fashion."

"Nor am I, sir. I suspect it is some sort of small cape. There was a scandal about them recently, as I recall."

"What sort of scandal?" the Guv asked.

"Underpaying their employees or making them work too many hours. Something like that. It was in the newspapers this month. Not quite as exciting as murder, is it?"

We looked at the factory. It was well appointed by the standards of the area. The building had been painted in recent memory, in shades of turquoise blue. Though it claimed to be a factory, it looked to have once been a large family dwelling. Windows had been installed in the ground floor, which were covered by iron bars to discourage break-ins. People were moving about within, I could see. The door opened and a man came out with some sort of wrapped items on hangers. No doubt they were the aforementioned mantles. It seemed at once too prosperous and too busy to house a man who was insane and who attacked his sister-in-law with scissors.

"Perhaps this address is wrong," I said. "He wouldn't be the first patient with a false address."

"Perhaps," Barker answered.

That was the Guv, patient and philosophical, perfectly content to be where he was and to have something to do, even if it were simply standing about outside a shop on the worst side of town.

"Shall we go in?" I asked.

"No, I don't think so. We have no reason to go in yet. I wonder if Jenkins might have that article on mantle factories," he said.

"Let us go and see if we can find a cab in Commercial Street, sir. You can ask him yourself."

Cyrus Barker stood on the paving stones with his hands behind his back, one fist wrapped in his empty palm, no expression readable on his face. His attention appeared to have been drawn by a small handwritten sign in the window.

"Lad," he asked, "by any chance do you know how to sew?"

I looked over his shoulder. The sign read: *SITUATION AVAILABLE IMMEDIATELY FOR SEAMSTER AND MANTLE-MAKER. MALE ONLY, EXPERIENCE PREFERRED. APPLY WITHIN.*

"As a matter of fact, I do."

"How did you acquire this skill?"

"Well, sir, my mother was determined that I would not go down in the mines like my brothers. At one time, I suspect she considered apprenticing me to a tailor, it being, as far as she was concerned, a 'clean' profession. My father and brothers came home every day with ripped shirts and trousers and my sisters were never fair hands when it came to sewing. The upshot was that the work fell to me. In my family, everyone must contribute, you see."

"I never get your limits, Thomas. You do not cease to surprise me."

"Shall I apply, sir?"

"No, but we shall hold it in reserve if other roads fail to bring us up against the Whitechapel Killer."

# CHAPTER TWELVE

We were coming down Fairclough Street that afternoon when we became witnesses and then participants in another aspect of the case. It was unseasonably dry and warm for September, and only a few tumbling leaves were necessary to convince one it was not August. Cyrus Barker and I had shed our coats at the Frying Pan and were now walking the district unencumbered by anything heavier than a bowler hat. I wouldn't claim I actually enjoyed spending my evening hours endlessly circling the area with my employer, but I had grown accustomed to it. We walked and talked to people who lived there and meanwhile kept an ear out for the hue and cry that the Killer had struck again. Then this night, we heard it.

The Guv heard the cry before I did, of course. He put his head down and listened for a direction or repetition of the call. It came again. I heard it now, though not clearly, several voices calling out at once in a muddle until I heard the word "Killer." It stopped us where we stood, waiting for the rabble to come to us, or to head it off if they passed us by.

We glanced at each other, wondering if this was it, would we finally confront the man we had been following for two weeks? Then a gaggle of people squeezed out of an alleyway, surrounding one figure the way army ants attack a grasshopper.

The man in the middle, batting at the people trying to subdue him, was a well-dressed fellow in a swallowtail coat and a top hat. He had pince-nez spectacles, which were swinging about him on a chain, and he held a small Gladstone bag in his hand, which he was using to defend himself. He looked in a panic, as he should, considering that the crowd that followed him were baying for his blood. He wore white patent-leather gaiters on his shoes, and with his snowy shirtfront looked as much like the Whitechapel Killer as Mr. Pickwick.

"I'm not!" I heard the man cry as he came closer, dodging the people who were plucking at the ends of his collar and anything else they could lay hands upon. Barker stepped out into the middle of the street to intercept him and I joined him there. The man at the center of the mob's attention did not notice our presence until he blundered into us and fell back when we did not give way. Barker's hands were in his pockets, but they emerged, holding his temporary badge in one hand and a pair of police regulation bracelets in the other.

"I am an inspector with Scotland Yard!" my employer bellowed over the voices of the crowd. "I am taking this fellow into custody! Anyone who is willing to speak in evidence against this man may follow us to 'H' Division!"

"Here, now," one man spoke up, a sturdy-looking fellow in his forties with an authoritative manner. "We are making a citizen's arrest of this person."

"Duly noted," Barker said. "Follow us to the constabulary and make a statement."

"But I didn't do anything!" the man said. "I'm not the person he claims I am. I'm just a cigarette salesman!"

"He keeps his sharp knives in that case!" a woman in the crowd cried, pointing to the bag which even now he held clutched to his chest. "Make him open it! You'll see!"

Barker clapped the darbies about his wrists, which elicited a cheer from the crowd.

"I didn't do it, I tell you," the man whimpered.

"Do you want to be safe as houses in 'H' Division," I whispered in his ear, "or torn limb from limb out here?"

"If my employers find out I'm arrested, I shall lose my position!" the suspect cried.

Barker took one of his elbows and I the other, and began the long walk to the constabulary on Lemon Street. I'll grant you that the Whitechapel Killer probably looked like a normal fellow and not an inhuman monster, repellent to the eye, but even so, this crowd could not convince me that the miserable person we were hustling along was the man responsible for two or more deaths. We had no more pressing matter, however, and the man appeared to need our help. The Guv had never denied this fellow was the Killer, and as far as the mob was concerned, he was helping them by arresting their subject. One man in the crowd even carried a makeshift torch, as if we were going to burn a witch.

A man with the look of a sailor pushed his way to the front with long loops of hemp wound loosely about his arm.

"Borrowed this bit of rope from a dry-goods store," he said, not to us, but to the crowd. "Why don't we see if this fellow can dance a jig about our heads?"

"This man is now our prisoner," Barker said.

"So he can sit in a safe cell and get three meals a day until some barrister gets him off? They all work together. I want to see his punishment now!"

The man turned and smacked a fist into the suspect's kidneys. The poor man staggered and cried out, but we held him tightly between us. Barker spun us around behind him and confronted the man who had struck our prisoner. He lashed out and kicked the fellow in the stomach, knocking him over onto the cobblestones. The man fell with a groan.

"We'll have none of that," Barker called out. He did not sound angry or concerned. If anything, he sounded almost bored, as if this sort of situation happened all the time and he was just keeping order. He sounded, in fact, like a Scotland Yard inspector.

Before the crowd could make a decision or argue about what had been done to one of their own, we turned and moved the suspect along again.

Being harried and punched and seeing a man struck down had been enough for our mild-mannered suspect. He stopped protesting his innocence. His cheeks, which were red when we first saw him, had gone pale, and he was bathed in sweat. Finally, the station was in sight, and we mobbed the entrance. As soon as we entered, the salesman collapsed on a bench and did a very good impersonation of a puffer fish lying in the sand.

"Get a cell ready!" Barker called to the desk sergeant. "We need to take some statements."

Abberline stepped out of an office. As part of the investigation, he had begun to spend part of every day here.

"What's all this, then?" he asked.

"The good folk of Whitechapel claim this gentleman is the Whitechapel Killer," Barker said. "Some are prepared to give evidence. One of them was too expedient and I had to give him a kick."

"I'll just bet you did. All right, Constable, get this fellow in a cell, and muster all hands for some statements."

Just then, the sailor came in, still holding his stomach.

"Clancy, is this the man?" the inspector asked. Obviously he knew him.

"It is," the sailor said.

"Not much of a catch you've brought us today. More minnow than shark. Are you sure you've captured the right man?"

"He was talking to one of our girls and reaching into his bag, ready to slit her throat!"

"I never!" the man spoke up from his bench. "It's a damnable lie."

"You never what? Caught you red-handed, we did."

"I suppose there is one way to end this argument. Your name, sir?"

"I am Leon Goldstein."

"Mr. Goldstein, have you any objection to us opening the contents of your bag?"

"None at all."

Barker took the bag from his hand, brought it to a nearby table and opened it. He peered into the interior and a droll smile played on his lips. Then he upended the bag and poured its contents onto the table. Empty cigarette boxes poured out, in various sizes. But no knife.

"Look in the lining," Abberline said. "Perhaps one is secreted inside."

"Why has it suddenly become necessary for the Whitechapel Killer to carry a bag?" Barker asked. "One blade is enough. He needn't carry hatchets and saws as well for his grisly operations. I would think he'd prefer to have his hand free to seize his victims by the throat."

The sailor slapped at the pile of boxes in disgust, scattering them across the room.

"Careful!" Goldstein cried. "That is expensive merchandise!"

"Why were you speaking to the whores in Fairclough Street?" Clancy asked.

"What do you mean? They smoke, too, and have money that they make themselves. Why shouldn't they need my products?"

"And you weren't soliciting them for their trade?'

"I was working!" he insisted. "And I'm a married man."

"That doesn't stop most of the men here."

"I have invested a good amount of money in that satchel and its contents. Were I to avail myself of those ladies' services, which I would not, I would need to set down my bag. One cannot leave merchandise lying about where they could get stolen. It would ruin me."

"That's enough!" Abberline cried. "Show's over. He's in our custody now. We'll handle it from here."

Three constables went to remove the Whitechapel residents from the building.

"What am I going to do?" Goldstein repeated.

"Far better to come back when the workday is over and your samples are locked away," Abberline said.

"Yes. No! I don't come back," Goldstein said.

"Is your route only in Whitechapel?" Barker asked.

"I canvass all of North London. A compatriot does the south side. I walk a different district each day. That way I only return every fortnight to give people time to be in need of more cigarettes, you see. I actually roll them myself. I get the materials at wholesale prices and make a decent profit."

"Interesting," the inspector said. "You come into Whitechapel every now and again, like the Killer."

Goldstein looked at him blankly. "What killer?"

"The Whitechapel Killer. He's killed two women so far, at least. Haven't you heard of him?"

"I don't pay any attention to the newspapers. I am a busy man. I have cigarettes to sell. Will this take long?"

"Not long at all," Barker said. "You're free to go, as far as I'm concerned. You can step right out the front door this very minute a free man."

"But the crowd threatened me and punched me! They said they would hang me! Why aren't you arresting them?"

"Well, Mr. Goldstein, so far you haven't sworn out a complaint against anyone. The powers of the Metropolitan Police do not extend to mind reading."

"What am I going to do? I have a route to finish."

"You are not under arrest, Mr. Goldstein," Barker said. "You were being set upon by an angry mob. I brought you here for your own personal safety."

"Then I am free to go?"

"Unless DCI Abberline disagrees."

The inspector shrugged his shoulders. "I've spent too much time on this matter already. I've got a murderer to find. But while you are here, I want a list of the dates you have been in Whitechapel. Got that?"

"Yes, sir."

"Wait an hour for the mob to disperse," Abberline ordered, sitting Goldstein down in a chair. "And when you leave, get out of Whitechapel, you hear me?"

Goldstein blinked and put on his pince-nez, which I noticed had been cracked during the affray.

"But I have orders to make," he said.

Abberline's face turned the color of a tomato. "Are you as thick as you look? Don't you realize how narrowly you just missed hanging from a lamppost? Change your bloody schedule! Try Lime-house or Camden or Stepney. Anywhere but here."

"They don't buy cigarettes much in Limehouse," Goldstein said.

Frederick Abberline ran a hand across his face. His patience was gone. "That's it for me, Barker. He's your responsibility now. If he opens his mouth one more time, I'm going to hang him myself."

"I don't—" the salesman began, but I jabbed him in the ribs with my elbow.

"You're going to get yourself killed if you don't shut your mouth," I whispered in his ear.

The man's shoulders sagged. I believe it finally sank into his skull that he wasn't going to meet his quota of cigarettes sold in Whitechapel that day. The inspector retreated back into his office. Barker sat down at the table beside him.

"How is business in the 'Chapel these days?" he asked.

"Not good," he admitted. "The competition is undercutting my prices and sales have fallen off."

"Look," I said, "write down your name and address and schedule while I go get a cab. I'll take you out of here in bracelets, then after we get in the hansom, I'll take them off again. I'll let you off near Aldgate Station, where you can go anywhere you like. Fair enough?"

"Can I keep my samples?" he asked. "I paid a lot for that case."

"Of course you can keep your samples. Now make that schedule. Here are paper and pencil. Don't leave the room until I get back."

As I left the room, I told Barker I was collecting a cab. I went out and found one rather readily in Commercial Road. Then I returned, pocketed the list, and took Goldstein in darbies to the cab. True to my word, I let him out a free man at Aldgate Station.

"Don't come back into Whitechapel for a while," I advised. "If you are recognized, Mr. Barker and I might not be there to help you."

The last I saw him, he was trotting away with his Gladstone in his hand, ready to put this day behind him.

It was a simple matter, forgotten by everyone but me. A salesman is accused of being a killer by a crowd of residents upset by the recent deaths, simply because he was carrying a bag. I recall it as the first time in the public mind that Whitechapel's most infamous killer was said to carry a Gladstone bag. This is how legends are born.

# CHAPTER THIRTEEN

That evening Cyrus Barker and I were walking our usual beat, from Bishopsgate in the west to Brady Street in the east. I could now draw a rather faithful rendering of the entire district, with all of the streets and many of its buildings. Also, I could name at least thirty individuals in the area whose names we had reason to learn, and several dozen others whom I recognized but whose names I did not yet know. In short, I knew the area well enough to have grown tired of it, and bored with everything and everyone. I was there to help find a killer, not to be entertained; I know that, but still, I had been in Whitechapel long enough that I felt I had come to know all her secrets, save for the one we had come there to learn. I knew, for example, that there was a missing cobble in Whitechapel High Street on the left by the cotton warehouse. I knew, because I had stepped into the hole on several occasions.

All evening, men were coming off work and going home, unless they worked the overnight shift, in which case they were having their dinner with strong tea in order to stay awake the rest of the night. The evening shift was dangerous. A half-awake worker was liable to make mistakes, and mistakes in Whitechapel factories usually meant a trip to London Hospital, with mangled or missing fingers. There may have been an occupation in the East End that wasn't slowly killing the men, women, and children that worked at it, but if there was, I hadn't found it. The prostitutes were not the only unfortunates. It was said the girls in the local match factories gave off a glow at night, due to the phosphorous they handled. It was something of an education to learn that mine was not the only dangerous occupation.

As I recall, we had just come out of Jane Street, a minor passage off Commercial Road. Ahead of us a group of men were coming out of some kind of meeting hall, though it was nearly midnight. My mind automatically said socialists, for only they would debate the troubles of the world so late into the night. They appeared to take no notice of us, so I felt the safety to do likewise. They passed, we passed, and all was as it should be. That is, until the axe bit into the wood of a fence not two feet from my head.

"Oy!" I cried.

Granted, it wasn't the response of an educated man, but this was neither the time nor place to say, "I say there!" If I had, they'd have laughed in my face. Actually, I didn't need to say anything, for Barker was already answering the statement with two pocketfuls of sharpened coins. I watched them glitter as they spread across the courtyard. Most of them bounced harmlessly off the brick walls nearby, but at least a few found yielding flesh.

I pulled the axe from the fence and turned toward the half-dozen men who faced us.

"Did somebody drop this?" I asked. "You can have it back, if you like."

Then a final man came out of the building, no better dressed, but more commanding than the others. He was in his forties, with sandy hair and a clean-shaven face. Few bothered to shave often in this part of town.

"Well, well. The Governor and his Nibs," he said. "This is a pleasure. You must forgive my boys for their high spirits."

"And you are?" Barker asked.

"Lusk. George Lusk of the Mile End Vigilance Committee."

"You're a fair distance from home, I must say. What business have you here in Whitechapel?" Barker asked.

"The same as your own, I expect. Security."

"Is this security you offer free of charge, or are you collecting payment for it, one business at a time?"

"We are privately funded," Lusk said. "Some philanthropists believe that the best persons to deal with this Whitechapel Killer are the ones who live here in the district."

"So you say," Barker retorted. "But this is the Jewish quarter, and I do not see a Star of David among you."

"We're more interested in why you're here, Push, you and your man Friday. Were you hired by a client, or are you hoping to catch the killer yourselves?"

"What if we were?" the Guv asked, crossing his arms. "What would that matter to you?"

"It would matter because you're muddying the waters. We don't need professionals here trying to make a name for themselves, nor amateurs trying to become heroes so they can cadge free drinks the rest of their lives. It's our women who are dying here. We already put up with all the peelers marching around, but when we see the two of you here night after night, we have a right to ask what's going on. We want no toffs here, even ones disguised in castoffs from Petticoat Lane. So, I ask you again nicely, what brings you here?"

"I'm sorry, Mr. Lusk, but for the life of me I cannot see how my business is of any concern to you. Whitechapel is not your personal fiefdom. As far as I know, people still can come and go as they see fit without your permission. Doubtless, some are here after the reward monies offered by various organizations for the Whitechapel Killer, but you cannot convince me that you are not tempted yourself."

"Very well, Push," Lusk said. "The buzzards have been circling all month and it was only a matter of time before they alighted on the lampposts. Your reputation goes before you. I've heard you are a charitable gent. We don't have a mansion in Southwark. This may be our only chance to see this kind of money. We need it more than you. It could mean medical attention or a decent place to live, or even a full meal, for once."

"I sympathize with your plight, sir, but I already have a client. I am currently about his business. I myself have no interest in the reward."

"Easy for you to say, but if you catch the killer, we won't get paid."

"That cannot be helped."

Lusk shrugged. "I tried, Mr. Barker, really I did. But you just wouldn't listen. All right, boyos. Teach these chaps some manners!"

The men began to circle us. I knew for a fact that my employer had a Scotland Yard inspector's badge in his pocket, not to mention two Colt revolvers, any of which would have stopped the coming scuffle in a trice. However, he had few enough outlets for his own particular bloodlust to turn this one down. Who was this Lusk fellow, and under what bushel basket had he been hiding that he would challenge Cyrus Barker in the street? I could only think that his education was about to begin.

Fighting two people at once is only for the advanced pugilist, but it can be done. The first step is to move forward onto the balls of the feet and be ready to move quickly. Your hands must be up before you, ready to slap away whatever attack may be coming your way, and you must do your best to line yourself up so that one of your attackers is always in front of the other, blocking the other's movements. Never get into the situation where you have one on either side. Slip it, run, if this happens, then try again. Slap away a punch, then seize or push one man into the other. If possible, tie their limbs into knots. From time to time, it is necessary to punch or kick the one in front to pacify him, but for the most part one is attacking the man behind, using the closer opponent's body as a weapon. As much as you can, attempt to create confusion and frustration between your adversaries. And when you fight, by all means, fight dirty. Punches to the eyes, the throat, the ear. When two are attacking you, the Queensberry rules go out the window. If one of your opponents falls down, immediately attack the second man, with the momentum of the fight in your favor. Lastly, avoid high kicks, if not kicking entirely. They are powerful and effective, but slow. In a fast and close-quarter fight with two men, there is no time for beautiful, aerial kicks.

And so the two men came at me at once. The first threw a punch which I blocked, then pulled him off balance, pushing him into the second man. The first man stumbled into the second, and as he tried to get up, I gave him a good tap on the nose. I'm no natural fighter, but I do have a good right jab. Blood seeped from his nose. There is nothing more encouraging to you and discouraging to your opponent as spilling claret. The second fellow came around the first, prepared to fight, but after avoiding the first blow, I thrust him over onto his brother and began kicking them as they struggled. Not hard, you understand; but hard enough to discourage them.

"All right, lads, come on. On your feet. I haven't got all night," I said, knowing it's always a good policy to add insult to injury.

The first was getting onto his feet when I swept his front foot from under him and he fell again. Now they were angry. Is there anything more frustrating than two fellows not being able to subdue one small, harmless-looking chap? As they tried to rise again I kicked one into the other one. He trapped my foot, but I merely bore down on my front leg, and as he fell, I punched the second one in the lip just below his bloody nose.

That was it, the entire fight from start to finish. I hadn't really hurt either of them, only embarrassed them and tangled them together. The second would need to stanch the bleeding, but I hadn't actually broken his nose. I stepped back. To be more precise, I danced back, because I was feeling good about the exchange, and wanted to appear unwinded and ready for anything. Barker stood in the street with his hands in his pockets, looking at the leader. Men were sprawled in the street about him groaning. He looked disappointed the scrap was over so soon.

"You were saying?" he asked.

Lusk licked his lips. "We represent the people here, Barker. It is our duty to protect them, not swells like you. We don't need amateurs coming in and causing trouble or worse, and we don't need professionals taking money out of the district."

He tensed when Barker reached into his pocket. My employer is known for being well armed. But he only retrieved his special inspector's badge.

"We have been retained by Scotland Yard in this case," he said. "I'm sure you understand the necessity to bring as many trained men into the field as possible."

"Well, I'm blowed," Lusk said. "Sorry, Push. We've agreed not to hamper the Yard in its investigation. In fact, we hope to provide information for you as we find it. You can understand the need to tighten security around here and not let just any Dick and Tom walk the streets."

"No harm done," Barker replied, shrugging his beefy shoulders.

"Not on your side, no. I've got half my squad down. What am I gonna do now?"

"Help your men up and start again tomorrow. Come along, Thomas."

# CHAPTER FOURTEEN

There was a note awaiting us at the Yard the following morning. The paper was embossed and had originated from Buckingham Palace, from the office of the Queen's private secretary. It read: *I have an opening in my schedule at one o'clock this afternoon. We must discuss several matters concerning White-chapel. I look forward to making your acquaintance. Ponsonby.*

"The royal imperative," Barker remarked. "If I had plans or interviews today, I am to cancel them. Something has occurred at the palace."

"We can't go like this," I said. "Even just to see the Queen's private secretary. I'm a mess!"

"Agreed. A change into our best day suits is in order. We must return to Newington. If you will acquire a cab, I shall call Jacob Maccabee from our offices and let him know what we require."

I made a fresh pot of tea and put out some biscuits, then slipped outside in search of a hansom. "A" Division required a constant supply of vehicles for its inspectors coming to and from its head-quarters, so cabmen routinely slow when they pass Great Scotland Yard Street. I hailed one, clambered aboard, and told the driver to wait for my associate. After a few minutes, Barker came down Whitehall Street, and climbed aboard, calling our address in Newington. It would be good to be home again, even if only for an hour or two.

"The timing is perfect, actually," I said, trying to sound positive. "By the time we return, they will have collected new information about the victims and the killer's whereabouts."

When we arrived in Lion Street, it was almost pleasing to see Mac's face and he seemed relieved to see us. It must have been deadly dull rattling about in that big Georgian house, polishing floors and silverware to a high gloss. The man had declared an all-out war on dirt, and to him, my existence within the house was a challenge.

"I have taken the liberty of preparing a cold collation. We cannot have your stomachs gurgling in front of Her Majesty. I have brushed your best suits and they are on your beds. I shall have your boots polished by the time you are ready."

I went into the dining room with its paneled walls, hung with targes and claymores. The table held plates of cold roast beef, sliced thin, flanked by pots of mustard and horseradish sauce, an endive salad, a small wheel of sharp cheddar with biscuits, olives, and fresh bread. I was disappointed when Mac brought in tea. To tell the truth, I was getting tired of it. Then he returned from the kitchen with a French press full of coffee and set it at my chair.

"That smells wonderful, Mac," I said. "You've outdone yourself."

"Not at all, Mr. Llewelyn. Just a few things I threw together at the last minute."

I knew better. He likes a compliment from time to time and is not likely to get it from Barker, who is often turning over a case in his head.

We dined and then I took a short nap before it was time to dress. My closet, thanks to my employer, was full. There were knee-length morning coats for visiting wealthy clients before lunch, cutaway jackets and sack suits for everyday wear, and evening kit for going out at night. Then I had a suit much like my everyday one, only more formal. The buttons were silver, the waistcoat filigreed, and the lapels satin. I had only worn this suit once that I recalled, when visiting a baron.

Mac bustled in from upstairs, with his talc whisk broom in his hand. He frowned at me. Something was amiss, but then, it always was when standing next to an Adonis. I am not tall enough, my chin is not prominent enough, when compared to perfection.

"What's wrong now?" I asked.

"Your hair. It could do with a trim. I wouldn't want it to prove a distraction to Her Majesty."

"We're not going to see the Queen, Mac, merely her secretary."

"You might pass her in the halls."

"If I did, I doubt she would be concerned with my hair."

To Mac's way of thinking, Her Majesty, Victoria Regina, was the arbiter of all things and must and should think exactly like Mac himself. I, on the other hand, suspected she had more important matters to consider.

"I'm fine," I told him. "It's too much."

"Are you sure?" he asked.

"I'm sure, Mac. Thank you."

"Very well," he answered. And sniffed. I hate it when he sniffs. He took the brush to my suit a little more vigorously than I would have liked. Then he opened my wardrobe, took my top hat out of its box and set it precisely on my head, down upon my nest of curls, because of course I was incapable of setting it precisely there-upon. No one could except Mac, and perhaps Queen Victoria, but it would be beneath her.

"Choose a proper stick," he warned. "Black with a silver ball."

It occurred to me then why moving temporarily to the East End had been so liberating. I could dress as I like. In fact, at Scotland Yard, neatness was practically frowned upon.

Then Barker came down the stair from Mount Zion, shining like Moses himself. His many buttons gleamed, as did his silk top hat. He had freshly brilliantined his hair. He looked resplendent.

Afraid that too much movement might spoil the cut of our suits, Mac even went into Newington Causeway and summoned a cab. Knowing him, he probably turned down one or two before finding just the right one. One cannot be too careful in these matters.

We were on our way then, and for once I was nervous. I knew

we weren't going to visit the Queen, but who was this Ponsonby cove and what would he think of Cyrus Barker? It's a funny thing about the Guv. He's got all of us—Mac, me, Etienne, Jenkins, even Mrs. Ashleigh—fussing over him, making certain he puts his best foot forward. I don't believe he ever once worries about anything himself.

Buckingham Palace began as a town house owned by the Duke of Buckingham. Not many people know that. Then George III visited there, fancied the place, and bought it for the missus.

For a time, it was known as the Queen's Castle. It was expanded, then expanded again until it was imposing even by Westminster standards, where the Abbey and the Houses of Parliament stand. It was built to keep small Welsh coalminers' sons like me out. What if I didn't genuflect low enough? I hadn't practiced my bows. What if I said the wrong word or couldn't say anything at all? What's the worst that could happen? They didn't really behead people at the whim of the sovereign, or of her private secretary. Or did they?

After a brief discussion with the guards at the front gate, we were ushered into the grounds and bowled down the drive to the palace itself. It resembles nothing so much as a large block of marble. There's not a turret or a tower to be found. This sort of design would not do in Bavaria or Paris, but the English prefer function over form. As long as it repelled cannonballs and class insurrection, it would do fine.

We stepped through the doors and were met by a man who might have been a butler or a retainer, or even some sort of security. He looked at Barker gravely and took our hats. After the Guv explained our purpose, we were led down carpeted halls and past paintings that were larger than I. My heart began to beat in my breast. Try not to trip, Thomas, you prat.

The fellow eventually came to a door, knocked on it and entered. I would have been inclined to stay outside until invited in, but my employer went through immediately, so I followed. The room was large; part of it was given over to comfortable furnishings and a large fireplace, but part contained a large desk, a filing cabinet, and various chairs of the Chippendale variety. A man was just rising to his feet. Had this been a play and I was casting for the role of

Queen's Private Secretary, I'd have hired him on the spot. He was between fifty and sixty, with a salt-and-pepper beard, and looked thin and elegant. At first he looked taken aback, which was understandable.

"You are Cyrus Barker, whom Robert Anderson recommended?" he asked.

"I am, sir. This is my assistant, Thomas Llewelyn."

"Won't you have a seat, gentlemen? We have much to discuss."

My employer is not one to let another control the conversation. He spoke while in the act of lowering himself into the chair.

"I assume Her Majesty has been informed of the recent Whitechapel murders."

"Oh, yes, she knows. She has been beside herself over the matter. Thrice in my hearing she has used the phrase 'murdered in our beds.' She is of the opinion that Scotland Yard is sitting on its hands. I must admit I happen to agree with her."

"Of course you do, Sir Henry. You are not a police officer. But you are a military man. You understand the logistics involved in patrolling a city. These murders are occurring at night in the darkest part of Whitechapel. The darkness is so intense that a constable could pass by the killer standing in the shadow and not even see him. Had there been better lighting in the lowest sections of London, this would not have started, let alone continued. This killer works in total darkness and thrives upon it."

"But come, gentlemen. Two gruesome murders."

"I will admit that no one anticipated a second killing. All the patrols came in to Whitechapel to lend assistance. They assumed he would scurry back to his burrow, wherever it is, or that we would apprehend him. Instead, he attacked like a fox among the chickens. He is bold. By the heavens, he is bold!"

"The fact that he is bold will not assuage Her Majesty's fears. If Commissioner Warren cannot safeguard the population, it may be necessary to bring in another man. The Home Office is of the opinion that it was a mistake not to have chosen from within the ranks of the Metropolitan."

"We are well aware of the Home Office's opinions of the matter. This killer will be caught, I assure you of that. It is inevitable.

Whitechapel is flooded with officers and they are learning the streets and the people. New facts and new suspects are considered each day. We have the most modern police department in the world. They use the Bertillon system of detection. He cannot stay hidden forever. He is but one man. A madman, of course, and madmen move erratically, but one man all the same. We understand that our reputation is on the line."

"It was said in the halls of Parliament recently that perhaps they've been sinking too much money into Scotland Yard. Better to shut it down, set it up in some other part of London with new methods and better training."

A smile spread across Barker's face, the kind that goes with thoughts of vengeance.

"Led by James Munro, I'll be bound."

"The name has been suggested," Ponsonby admitted.

"No doubt. One cannot whitewash a turkey and call it a swan, Sir Henry. Munro is trained in all the same methods you now consider obsolete. Meanwhile, Commissioner Warren, who, to state the obvious, was trained in the same strategies you yourself studied, is now facing censure. It appears you are arguing on the wrong side."

"Perhaps you are right," Ponsonby said. He opened a file on the desk and closed it again. "How is it that a private enquiry agent speaks so highly of his chief rival?"

Barker leaned back and glanced at the ceiling, which was full of cherubs and heraldry. "I find it a comfort that I must scratch a living working unusual cases because most crimes are solved by the Yard. Sometimes the sheer volume they solve means they don't have much time for unusual and more cerebral crimes, which are my meat and drink, but one cannot argue with their success. The Sûreté, the New York Police Department, and the Tokyo Keishicho can only hope for such a record."

"You are being squandered, Mr. Barker. They need you in the House of Commons when an increase in funding is required. The file the Home Office provided tells me you need not scratch out a living at all, that you are a wealthy man. Why not sit back and take your ease?"

"We all must work, Sir Henry. Skills grow rusty if one doesn't use them. And even women such as Mary Nichols and Annie Chapman, living on the very edge of society, should be able to do so without being butchered."

Ponsonby nodded. "I concur, as does the Queen. Understanding that these women were forced by circumstances to go outside the law in order to make their living, they nevertheless deserved such safety as the Empire can provide."

"Is Her Majesty often concerned with being murdered in her bed?" the Guv asked.

"She has survived several attacks upon her life, as I'm sure you are aware, and the hub of the anarchist movement is currently among the Jews in the East End."

"As are the Workers' Unions, who hope to reform society by doing away with the monarchy," Barker added.

"Precisely. She is more concerned with those matters than of this Whitechapel Killer actually breaking into the palace. You must understand, she is occasionally given to hyperbole."

Sir Henry then stood and crossed the room to a window. He pushed back the tails of his coat and stared out into the grounds deep in thought. The silence seemed interminable, but was probably no more than ten seconds. I wondered for a moment if we had been dismissed. Finally, he turned about.

"I had to decide whether to bring you into my confidence, sirs, before I discussed a certain matter, which is of some delicacy. To do so, I had to convince myself that you were capable of discretion. Our normal liaison with Scotland Yard, Inspector Littlechild, I do not consider capable. I have complained on several occasions about his vulgar manner to the commissioner, but to no avail. He is not the sort of person to present to Her Majesty. This matter cannot leave this room, save when speaking to your immediate superiors, and nothing about it may be written down. There must be no file upon this subject at Scotland Yard, lest it fall into the wrong hands and become an embarrassment to the Crown. Do I make myself clear?"

"You do, sir," Barker rumbled.

"And you, young man?" he asked, turning on me. "I include you in this silence."

"You may rely upon our discretion, sir. We would do nothing to harm the monarchy."

Ponsonby stared at us momentarily, as if finally convincing himself that we were worthy of his confidences, and with good reason. We were total strangers to him, and at best, I was an addendum to his file. I imagined he had no idea I was tagging along, and if he had he'd have learned things that were not in my favor, such as the fact that before I was hired as Barker's assistant, I had done eight months in Oxford Prison for theft, or that my best friend was one of those Jewish socialist intellectuals he feared would try to bring down the government. I offered him my most trustworthy face, for all that was worth.

"Very well," he began, slowly pacing the carpet. "The matter concerns the Duke of Clarence, the royal heir but one to the throne. He has a tutor by the name of Stephen. James K. Stephen. Brilliant fellow. Came highly recommended. He and the young duke are quite close. Albert Victor is now twenty-four, and Stephen is twenty-nine. I suppose like most royals, the duke has led a very cloistered existence. Stephen proposed to take him on an outing into Whitechapel, to visit the tenements there."

"As his father did several years ago," Barker said. "If memory serves."

"Indeed, yes. His Royal Highness found it very informative. I would even say it will make him a better ruler when he ascends the throne. And though the tutor suggested the matter, it was approved by the Prince of Wales. As before, no notification would be given, and no attempt made to beautify the area or shield him from anything. He would see Whitechapel as it truly was, though I must state this was decided before the recent killings there. They went late last month. They were given no escort to draw attention to them, but they were discreetly followed by the Home Office, as a matter of course."

"He is the royal heir, after all," I said.

"Precisely. Unfortunately, the two managed to somehow evade the Home Office an hour or two later in the worst part of the district, before turning up again in Commercial Street. There was a minor flap when they returned, but they and the driver of the vehicle all claimed they had simply traveled about the streets and did nothing more dangerous than to pass through one or two of the worst tenements heavily swathed in scarves so as to not be recognized. However, the Home Office became suspicious of Stephen and looked deeply into his background, interviewing his acquaintances past and present. They came to me with what they found. I was not pleased with the information they had acquired."

"What did they find?" Barker asked.

"James Stephen is a sodomite. The Home Office now suspects that during the missing hour they were in a private residence which caters to such . . . activities. The heir is impressionable, and Stephen has very winning ways. We fear that the two have become—that Stephen has introduced the duke to these practices. The Home Office now informs us that they have gone out at least once more to Whitechapel without notifying us. In order to separate him from such influences, we have sent Albert Victor to Balmoral."

"This is all very interesting," Barker said. "And I suppose under the Labouchere Amendment, James Stephen could be prosecuted if the Home Office has enough information to make a case beyond hearsay. However, I do not believe Scotland Yard would prefer to become involved in this matter. Is there more?"

Ponsonby ran a hand across his brow. "There is. Apparently, Stephen is subject to spells. They began at university, I understand, but he was in a carriage accident recently, and the spells have become more frequent."

"You are being rather vague, Sir Henry," my employer said. "How does Mr. Stephen act during these spells?"

"His behavior has been diagnosed as a form of mania. He is highly restless, full of energy almost to a fault, argumentative, and euphoric. During these periods he is known for being markedly misogynistic, but then, I understand he is critical of the fair sex at the best of times."

"What you are implying," the Guv said, "is that the tutor of the heir to the throne is a suspect in the Whitechapel killings."

"We cannot be sure of Stephen's whereabouts on the nights in question. It appears there are other members of the staff within the palace who are sympathetic to his interests."

"And how do the duke's father and grandmother feel about the matter as it stands?"

Ponsonby, who had been standing during our conversation, suddenly collapsed into a chair. It was as if his limbs had given out. He passed a hand over his face again.

"I have not dared to tell them," he answered.

It was Barker's turn to smooth his mustache, if only to hide the smile on his face. I cleared my throat.

"Indeed?"

"We—the prime minister and I—have been considering the best time and proper method of informing them. Such news would destroy his father, and as for Her Majesty, I'm not certain she understands that such things exist. The matter would have to be explained to her."

"I do not envy you your task, Sir Henry, but I still do not know how I can help you. The Home Office is following Stephen adequately, I'm sure. If I am pulled away from the investigation to shadow one suspect, who may turn out to be innocent, I may be hampered from laying hands on the killer when he reveals himself."

"Stephen is a lot of things," Ponsonby said, "but I do not think innocent is one of them."

"Innocent of the crime of murder, at least. Is there more?"

Ponsonby nodded. "I fear so."

Barker began ticking off points on his fingers. "The royal heir may not be inclined to fulfill his duties to the monarchy, his tutor is not only a frequenter of male brothels, but might be responsible for several horrendous deaths, and the household is riddled with his supporters. What more do you fear?"

"This fellow, Littlechild. He knows everything and I am inclined to think that he will not keep silent about the matter without something in return."

"I am a plain man, Sir Henry, and I prefer plain words. Is Inspector Littlechild blackmailing you?"

"Not yet, but I'm not sure why. He's an oily fellow, but a straightforward one. I've been waiting for him to suggest some sort of payment, and then I would pounce. I could have him sacked and jailed within the afternoon. So far he has said nothing, which I find perplexing."

Barker pondered this behind those smoky quartz spectacles. He tapped his chest, or more precisely, the pocket where his tobacco was normally kept, but not in this suit. It was just as well. I doubted one could just light a pipe in Buckingham Palace without a formal censure.

"Tell me," he finally said. "Is the inspector acquainted with the Home Office agents?"

"They are thick as thieves. I understand they have even ridden together while following Stephen. Why do you ask?"

"Let me consider the matter."

"What shall I do in the meantime about the Duke of Clarence and Mr. Stephen?"

"You must inform the Prince of Wales about his son's indiscretions, and let him decide whether to tell Her Majesty. This is not a firecracker, it is a blasting cap. You do not want to be holding it when it goes off."

Barker stood. He had bustled in and now he was ready to leave. He took out one of his cards and gave it to the Queen's private secretary.

"I can be reached at Scotland yard in a matter of minutes. Pray call me if anything new occurs."

# CHAPTER FIFTEEN

I was growing accustomed to the routine, if one could call it that. Each day began with research in the Records Room, went on to making tea and delivering messages, lunch, interviewing witnesses, dinner, then walking Whitechapel. Sometimes the entire routine was overthrown, if there was a coroner's inquest or a new suspect. I felt I now knew the area better than anyone who was not raised there. I could walk down most streets and know what was around the corner, though it had taken close to a month to learn it. Even the unfortunates had begun to leave off harassing or enticing us. Now they bantered with us, assuming we were local. We had invented occupations for ourselves in case anyone asked: I was an out-of-work tailor, while Barker was an ex-miner who had received a small settlement due to black lung. We walked to help improve his health and had come to London to improve our fortunes. That was our story. The incurious believed it. As for the others, those who knew Push in the East End or recognized us from previous cases, they understood our need for partial incognito, assuming we were working with the Board of Deputies or some such organization to find the killer. The reporters, the Jews, the unfortunates, the publicans, the aid society members and socialists in Whitechapel, none of them suspected we were working with Scotland Yard. Whitechapel was the center of London's Underworld, and no matter how long the police had been there, they were still the enemy. A private agent, on the other hand, he was just a working stiff trying to make a living. There was even a chance he actually gave a tinker's damn about what happened to the people who lived there.

I was passing through the halls of Scotland Yard when I heard my name called by the desk sergeant. When I hurried up, he handed me a telegram.

"Who for, Sergeant?" I asked.

"Your master."

I took the note to my employer, who slit it open with a knife. He read the piece of yellow paper, covered in glued-on words, and folded it into his pocket with a look of intent on his face.

"Who is it from, sir?" I asked.

"Ponsonby," he answered. "He's plugged the leak in the palace staff and now has them working for him. He says Stephen is restless and shall probably go out tonight. He's been leaving through the stable entrance, Sir Henry claims, and picks up a cab a few streets away."

"Are we going to follow him?"

"Of course. The only way to tell where a fellow goes is to follow him. It is possible he commits murder on the nights when he is agitated."

"But he may be going to a brothel, sir. That is, a male brothel."

"Aye," the Guv said.

"A male brothel," I repeated.

"What concerns you, Thomas, that someone you know might spy you going in there, or that you might be approached by a male prostitute?"

"Both! Do we have to go in? Can we watch from outside?"

"Need I remind you that James Stephen just escaped from Buckingham Palace, which is surrounded by guards? How difficult do you think it would be for him to slip out a side entrance of an establishment that is designed to afford anonymity to its clients? In fact, if he is careful enough he could establish an alibi of sorts. One cannot be accused of murdering a woman in Hanbury Street at the same time one is accused of gross indecency somewhere else."

"I suppose it doesn't matter how much I protest. You're going there, anyway."

"Where the case leads, Thomas. We go where the case leads."

"That's what I'm afraid of."

The Drake Club was a residence in Halifax Street built in Regency days when the wealthy were first building outside the City, where land was cheap and plentiful. It must have been an ample mansion then, with marble columns and level steps, the pride of the neighborhood. Now it was unkempt and ramshackle, like an old widow fallen on hard times. The slate roof was sagging under its own weight. In every window, however, there was a splash of color, a vase full of peacock feathers here, or an oriental fan there. It was vulgar but it achieved its purpose. As I stood watching, two men hurried furtively inside.

"Shall we?" Barker asked, gesturing toward the front of the building.

"Isn't there a back entrance?"

Barker laughed and clapped me on the back, propelling me forward. I climbed the worn staircase, feeling as if everyone I ever knew was watching me do so. I was reminded of a paradox a math tutor had tried to drub into my head when I was young, conceived by the philosopher Zeno, that if one continually halved the distance between a point and where one stood, one could never reach it. However, the philosopher didn't have Cyrus Barker's elbow between his shoulder blades, and before I knew it, I was through the door.

Inside, the house had been given a coat of paint, a virulent shade of violet. Mismatched carpets lined the floors and the doorway to a parlor was hung with ropes of beads. There were men standing about with drinks in their hands, talking to youths who had kohl-smeared eyes and were in various stages of undress. One of the men, who might be a judge or a barrister, reached over and caressed the neck of one of the youths. I looked away.

It was so crowded inside, we had to wait in a queue. A bored-sounding young man greeted people, then directed them toward another room or an upper floor. The fellow's cheeks were rouged and he was wearing a white blouse with breeches and no hose. I had been in other establishments full of women and at least there was no attempt to show the wares therein right in the front entrance hall.

"May I help—" the young man began, then his eyes took in my employer.

There are larger men in London than Cyrus Barker. Not many, but some. He stands a little over six feet and weighs fifteen stone. There are probably stronger men, though one might be hard-pressed to find them. Also, there are more menacing-looking men than he, provided he is in a good mood. I suppose a tiger, a gorilla, or a crocodile spends the bulk of its days in sedate activity, and yet I would not want to be locked in a room with one, because of the small percentage of the time when it is not. Likewise, the youth looked cautiously at the Guv, not because of what he was doing, but because of what he was capable of doing.

"I need to speak to the Countess," Barker said.

"He's occupied," the young man answered, without conviction.

Barker leaned forward until the two of them were nearly touching foreheads. The man's eyes went wide.

"I wasn't asking."

There had been a good deal of chatter in the lobby and the adjoining rooms, but my employer's foggy voice has a way of cutting through it like it was cloud vapor. All talking ceased.

"I . . . I suppose I could see if he's through with his appointment."

"Aye, you do that, laddie."

The youth turned and scampered up the stairwell. My employer sniffed, opened his coat, planted a fist on each kidney, and looked about him, as at home there as he was anywhere.

"You certainly gave him a turn," one of the nearby youths told him.

"I intended to do so."

"I haven't seen you before. Do you come here often?"

"This isn't a social call."

Barker reached into the pocket of his waistcoat and drew out his repeater watch. He compared it with satisfaction to an ornate standing clock in the hall.

"I've given him enough time," the Guv said, and began to climb the stair. I followed behind. It was crowded there but men gave way quickly for our progress. If they hadn't, they might have found themselves acquainted with the carpet ten feet below.

Just then a man appeared at the top of the stair. He was perhaps forty years of age, thin and clean-shaven, though the skin of his jawline was nearly gray. His eyes were dark and luminous. There was nothing frivolous in his attire save for a small green carnation in his lapel. His brow rose when he saw my employer and he broke into a grin of sheer delight.

"Push, old thing! *Bonne fortune!* You've been dreadfully naughty not to visit me, but here you are, unannounced, so I suppose I must forgive you. And who is the bean cove with you, who looks as comfortable as a cat in a kennel?"

"Henry," the Guv said, "this is my assistant, Thomas Llewelyn. Thomas, Henry Inslip."

"Welcome to my humble lattie. The one rule here is that you are free to do as you please. But I know Cyrus too well to think he came here for social purposes. You're working, dear boy, aren't you?"

"You know I am," Barker said.

"An interesting case?" he asked, drawing out the middle word until it was laced with innuendo.

"Quite interesting."

"And important?" he asked, arching a brow.

"Very important."

Inslip grinned again. "We all know what little pitchers have. Follow me to my humble cell where we can dish the dirt. Would someone pass the word along to the kitchen that there are three for tea? And be certain they serve it in the best Limoges, or I'll be ever so cross! We have guests! Follow me, gentlemen!"

We followed him up the steep staircase and down a hall carpeted in a heavy Persian runner while cherubs disported themselves across the ceiling. We passed men in pairs, younger ones with older ones, the elders not acknowledging each other's existence. He led us into a room painted in gold and robin's-egg blue dominated by a painting over the fireplace of a beautiful young woman. The room seemed to be a farrago of masculine items, such as leather-lined glass ashtrays and a rococo desk, with more feminine ones: a wig on a stand and an Asian parasol propped in a corner. Inslip curled up in a chair and then eyed us speculatively.

"All right, Push, what really brings you here? Has Philippa finally tired of us and tossed you out? You know, you really must put a ring on that woman's finger, laddie boy. She won't wait forever. How is she, by the way?"

"In excellent health, when last we spoke. Now, you like games, as I recall. I propose we play one now. We shall call it 'Vague Terms.' First I shall say something vague and you shall say another, and in this manner, I hope we shall reach enlightenment without saying anything incriminating at all. How does that sound?"

Inslip clapped his hands. "Priceless, old boy. I can hardly wait. Very well, but I demand the ability to withhold a response if I feel it may be injurious to a member of my flock. N'est-ce pas?"

"Certainly," Barker said. "Allow me to begin. I understand that a certain person has been at this establishment recently."

Inslip smiled. "Certain persons come here all the time. Really, I cannot confirm or deny."

"The person I'm speaking of arrived with another person who has been here many times before and probably since. In fact, the likelihood is that the other person is here now or shall be soon."

"That is entirely possible. People come and go at all hours."

"If these visits become known to a larger number of people, there could be an unpleasantness."

"Oh, dear," the Countess said. "Is that a threat? Are you warning me?"

"No, Henry. It is more a prediction. If this, then that. I'm sure you understand."

"Oh, good. You nearly gave me a turn there. Very well. Back to the game."

"You know my profession. I am a man hunter. I am stalking someone."

"Aren't we all, Push? What sort of fellow is he? Butcher, baker, candlestick maker?"

"Oh, butcher. Decidedly a butcher."

"I believe I've read about the fellow. He certainly gets a lot of press. How does he fit into the game. Unless—"

"Let us say some of us lead double lives. And one of us might even lead a treble one."

Inslip sat back, deep in thought, and tapped his lips. "Would we be talking about the first gentleman or the second?"

"The first is out of the country. In fact, he has been this entire week."

"'While the cat's away, the mouse will play,'" Inslip quoted.

"Until he steps into a trap. Some mice are victims of their own appetites."

"Aren't we all?"

"You know, it would be a shame if this mouse, being chased by various cats, should scurry into the wrong nest and thereby endanger all the other mice."

Here Barker opened his hands, indicating the walls of the very establishment we were in.

"Very thoughtless of him," Inslip said, his brows knitting in concern. "But I know this mouse. He is very thoughtless. Also self-indulgent and outrageous."

"That is a dangerous combination," my employer said.

"How certain are you that he is the mouse you are hunting?"

"That's why we are here. We are trying to establish his movements at certain times and days. It would be helpful to know which mouse hole he was in at various times. You see, he has winning ways and people might be inclined to vouch for him under certain circumstances. In fact, some already have. This sort of thing hampers our enquiries."

"Naughty mouse," Inslip said. "He is a sore trial to his friends, I'm sure."

"On the other hand, I should hate to see an innocent mouse caught in the wrong trap, if you ken my meaning."

"Oh, we wouldn't want that."

"If only someone were able to provide either a genuine alibi for an innocent man, or the proof necessary to establish his guilt."

"A rat among the mice."

"Now, now! We don't know that," Barker said, raising a finger. "Yet, it would be good to have this information soon, before it becomes necessary to take other, more direct approaches. One that will not end well for anybody."

The tea arrived. Inslip seemed deep in thought while the manservant served the cups. The tea was expensive Assam and lightly scented with vanilla.

"Let me look into the matter," our host finally said. "You will forgive me if I cannot simply take your word for this. I must see for myself. Oh, it would kill me if this butcher were here in my very own establishment and I didn't know. Under my very nose."

"It is a predicament," Barker admitted.

"I enjoyed your game, Cyrus. You are always a refreshing fellow. 'Vague Terms.' I shall have to remember that."

"Come, Thomas. It is back into the cold streets for us."

"May I offer you any of our services tonight, Cyrus? Mum's the word, I assure you. No? How about you, my bijou friend? Can I tempt you with something?"

"No, thank you, sir," I said.

"Your young man has nice manners, Push. You've trained him well. We'll talk again soon."

We left the room, passed down the staircase, and right out the front door. I'd have preferred to slink out of there by some back alley, but such is not my employer's manner. We walked for several streets under a dull drizzle.

"You're quiet tonight, Thomas. You've said four words in the last hour."

"I scarce know how to begin. I was not aware you were acquainted with anyone of that crowd."

"I am acquainted with many members of the Underworld. I know murderers, thieves, poisoners, and opium dealers. Why should it surprise you that I know the mandrakes, as well?"

I shuffled along, trying not to slip on the wet cobbles. "I don't know. You're a Baptist, and yet you spoke to him readily. You even drank tea with him!"

"Of course I did. He would be hurt if I didn't show him the courtesy. But, why not a Baptist? Have we such a stern, unbending reputation that you think I would not talk to them? Lad, we are all of us mired in sin, but each of us is redeemable. Every last one. You must believe that, you who have attended chapel these four years."

"But what of Sodom and Gomorrah?"

Barker suddenly gave a great laugh at my expense. "Sodom and Gomorrah? Surely you haven't fallen for that old superstition! If you read your Bible closely, you would learn that the sin of Sodom and Gomorrah, for which they were destroyed by God, was not sodomy. Ezekiel clearly states that the sin of Sodom was of arrogance and for not providing help to the needy."

"But what about the men of the town crying, 'Let them come out that we may know them'?"

"That practice wasn't particular to those cities. It was common in wartime throughout the entire Middle East, a brutal punishment for strangers, not the sexual predilection of the populace. Whoever came up with that interpretation is wrong. It is not scriptural from the original Hebrew."

"I would have thought you'd believe such men worthy of damnation."

"Oh, they are. So are you. So am I. 'All have fallen short of the glory of God.' But His grace is sufficient."

"But that building is illegal," I argued.

"It is. Unfortunately, there is no other place for them to congregate. They are a consistently small percentage of the population, but they do not go away. They have remained so throughout history. Fortunately, the police generally choose to overlook the 'crime,' unless for political reasons they choose not to."

"Such as the Duke of Clarence appearing at a brothel, or the Whitechapel Killer being one of them, or both at once," I suggested.

"Precisely. I would not have made use of such information as I did unless I felt his particular group was in danger. Whitechapel is a powder keg. Its citizens are overwrought. I am concerned for Inslip's 'flock,' and for the Jewish population here, should the killer prove to be of either group. We must be careful what we say, either to Scotland Yard or the palace."

"I didn't understand a good deal of what he said."

"He speaks Polari. It is a secret language of downtrodden people: mandrakes, circus performers, sailors, Jews. You'll pick it up."

"I didn't even know such a thing existed," I admitted.

"Welcome to the Underworld, lad."

"But it must be dangerous to live this way. Why should any choose to do so?"

"I don't think one would choose to do so if one could help it. Most men with this preference choose to marry to hide what they consider a weakness, but then slip out at night to come here."

"Much like the married men who slip out to attend more conventional brothels, who have no such excuse. Such a man who sullies his marriage vows should be horsewhipped."

"You and I agree on that, yet Whitechapel teems with unfaithful husbands. They outnumber the men with no wives, who visit the district for companionship."

"Underworld," I said. "Underbelly, more like. It makes me sick."

"It should. What is the Underworld but Man's Weakness, and those who would prey upon it for profit?"

"I feel sorry for the Jews who are forced to live in such a place, amid squalor and vice."

"In their former countries, before the pogroms, they were bankers and doctors and jewelers. Now they unload barges at the docks, or collect night soil. But there is a saving grace. There is no more gentrifying influence than a synagogue full of Jews anxious to reform the neighborhood. Respectability illuminates vice better than a lantern. The bawdy houses will eventually move to some other district, along with their inhabitants."

"Unless there is a pogrom in the East End."

"We'll do our best to avoid that," the Guv said.

"There's two of us. They don't stand a chance."

Barker nodded. "That's the spirit, Thomas."

"That was sarcasm, sir."

# CHAPTER SIXTEEN

The next morning, we caught another hansom and Barker asked to be taken to Downing Street. We would not be speaking to the prime minister, but visiting the Home Office on the southern side of the street. Barker planned to beard the lion in his den.

"You're really going to drop in on Munro unannounced?" I asked.

"The better to catch him plotting his next stratagem."

I had been several times on the Foreign Office side, but not on the Home Office side. There was a clerk in an alcove, a small scattering of chairs, and a staircase. Barker did not hesitate but took the stairs. The easiest way to get around a guard is to act as if you belong there. I did not make eye contact when the clerk called out, but he did not follow us, so we were in. On the first floor, my employer passed down the hall until he came to an open door. Inside, two men were having some sort of discussion.

"Is Munro on this floor?" Barker asked, sounding put-upon, as if he'd been stalking him for a while.

"Last I saw, he was in his office on the third floor," one of them said.

"I tried there," he insisted. "He wasn't in. Oh, well, I'll try again. Thank you."

We climbed two more flights of stairs. Barker sauntered down the hall, his hands folded behind him, until we approached a door with Munro's name on it. It had no title. What did the fellow do there? Was there even a name for his position? This was a strange case, I reasoned. We spent our nights circling the lowest section of London and our days in glamorous institutions such as the Home Office and Buck House. Barker knocked, and a voice inside told him to enter.

"Barker!" Munro said as we stepped inside. "What kept you? I was expecting you days ago!" He seemed almost jovial. I had only seen him the other way before, as angry as a swarm of hornets. He is a compact man, with a bull neck, a sturdy frame, and bandy legs. His hair was plastered to his head and he had a small mustache. Like many in Scotland Yard, he was a Scot and a nonconformist, though to what denomination he belonged, I did not know. They were being polite so far, but I was certain that would not last.

"There didn't appear to be any reason to hurry," Barker replied. "And I did have a few things to occupy my time."

"Congratulations on your appointment, by the way. There was a time when I would have said Cyrus Barker would never wear regulation blue."

"That was your recommendation, anyway," my employer answered.

"Still holding that against me? Water under the bridge, old man."

"I am not concerned over that, but rather the fact that your name keeps cropping up in my work."

"I'm a popular fellow."

Munro opened a humidor and helped himself to a cigar. I didn't want one, but I noticed he didn't offer any to us.

"What is it you do here at the Home Office?" I dared asked.

Munro shrugged his burly shoulders. "I run the Special Irish Branch from here."

"And what is your relationship with Robert Anderson?" Barker enquired.

"He is my friend, just as he is yours."

"Some people at Scotland Yard are under the impression that I am working for both of you, and that collectively we are trying to remove Commissioner Warren."

"I cannot deny that I consider Warren incompetent. It is a matter of public record. In fact, I quit the Yard, something I thought I would never do, because I felt I could not work with the man any longer. He is a tin soldier. His plans for the future of the Metropolitan Police are not in line with those of other modern police forces in Vienna, Berlin, and Washington. He believes he is still a colonel and the Yard is his standing army. He is eviscerating the Criminal Investigation Department and dragging the Yard back into the Dark Ages. If his methods are adopted, we shall no longer be the leading police agency in the world." Here he tapped on the top of his desk with his finger several times. "That is what I am trying to stop."

"Through intrigue," Barker observed.

"Of course, through intrigue," he said. "If by intrigue you mean talking to everyone I know and expressing my concern over how he is ruining a fine institution."

"And spies."

"Spies?" Munro asked, looking bemused.

"Inspector Littlechild."

"Barker, if 'twill make you feel better to admit it, I have been using Littlechild to keep abreast of what is going on in the palace, but only because I fear that Warren in his heavy-handed way will cause a door to be shut in our faces that may never open again. I understand Her Majesty was extremely wroth over the killings. Were you at the palace?"

"Of course."

"Was Ponsonby concerned about security at Buckingham Palace?"

"Of course. Her Majesty has been very troubled over the situation. You're well informed in matters that don't concern you anymore. More spies."

"They are my friends, Barker. I've known some of these men for over thirty years. I could have chosen a more respectable and profitable profession, but I went against my family's wishes to become a police constable. I was treated abominably for the first few years, but gradually rose through the ranks to assistant commissioner, receiving several citations and recommendations. I was considered the obvious choice for commissioner, but at the last minute that gang of ninnies with more money than brains chose to vote along class lines and pick an officer on the basis that he looked good in a suit and was as dull as a country parson's sermon. I'm not saying Warren's a bad man or a poor husband or father, I'm merely saying he doesn't understand the first thing about running a police force. How could he? He's had no training or experience. One does not take a costermonger, even a successful one, and make him the head of a bank. Why would anyone believe a soldier would make a good commissioner?"

"That does not change the fact that you are intriguing in this case," the Guv said.

"That's correct. I am. I am using my years on the force to collect information for the Home secretary. Not to your detriment. Robert insisted upon it. Rather, you have been given the opportunity to fulfill an ambition you would not have been able to do otherwise. We, both of us, hope you solve the case. If you discover the killer's identity and communicate it to Swanson and Abberline, the public will never learn of it, but the members of the Yard will know. Warren's board members shall know, as well. I'll make certain of that."

"You seem awfully certain of my abilities, sir," Barker said coldly.

"Just because I do not gamble doesn't mean I can't recognize a fast horse when I see one. And while we're on the subject, I never thought you would make an inferior detective. I merely thought there was too little about your past in your application. Years were missing. For all I knew, you were in jail, the way this little chap was. I couldn't just accept your word on the matter."

The "little chap" remark aside, this meeting was not turning out as we hoped. Instead of denying what he had done, he was explaining everything away. The problem was we did not trust him. Were we wrong or was he trying to pull the wool over our eyes? I could not say. Even Barker was flummoxed.

"So you are the Home secretary's assistant now?"

"What of it?" Munro asked in return. "I have been hired here on a consultant basis. The work is such that I cannot discuss it. I have been lobbying for the commissioner position should it come open, since several members of the board work here in this building, but I have done so openly and aboveboard. You do not have a monopoly on honesty."

"I should like to know how one can lobby for a position that is already filled," Barker said.

"There are many politicians and citizens unhappy with how this case is being conducted by the administration. For example, when the first body was found, it was brought to the morgue, stripped of its clothes and washed down, removing any evidence of the killer."

"I heard about that," Barker admitted. "But it was a mistake. It's what is normally done with a body prior to a postmortem. That was not Commissioner Warren's fault."

"No, but the next move was. The two men who did so should have been sacked, as an example. This isn't the time to be generous. You are being very closely watched. The newspapers are starting to bay for blood. Even Her Majesty is angry. You can't have the citizens of Whitechapel thinking the Met is doing nothing to protect the women there. This is not a good time to be commissioner of police."

"What about Scotland Yard? I heard a rumor you might change it entirely, including its name and location."

"I must admit I intend to modernize the Met, and when we move east to our new premises on the Embankment, I see no reason to carry the old street name with us. I am recommending we have our own laboratory and morgue with staff on the premises. The Bertillon system is inexact and we are considering new methods for identifying criminals. And there will be accounting for employees. No dead weight, you understand. No hiring because one is a friend of a friend, and annual evaluations of one's work and attendance. Oh, and no drunkenness. I insist upon that. You would not believe the number of constables that stop in for a pint on their rounds. That day is past, or will be, if I am hired."

"What will you do if the killer is captured and Warren keeps his position?" I asked.

"I will wait. Entrench, if necessary. Oh, it was a blow when Warren was hired over me. We were at loggerheads almost immediately. If Prince Albert can wait decades to become king, however, I can wait a year or two. There is certainly enough work here to keep me occupied."

"What was Robert's place in all this, precisely?" the Guv asked.

"He believed the hiring of nonmembers of the Metropolitan Police to the highest positions to be wrong, even if it meant that he himself was brought in from the Foreign Office. To his way of thinking, I should have been commissioner and Swanson the assistant. As to intrigue, we both know he is an honorable man, but he has been a spymaster for years. No one understands intrigue as well as he, or the necessity for it. We don't do it because we like it. It is the only way to get things done. He watched the Fenians and the Irish groups alongside me. I know you, Barker. You would rather not sully your reputation, such as it is. But you work for yourself and don't need funding. The rest of us must fight for every pence. I lost my pension when I quit to save my honor. Unless I am rehired, I shall lose it permanently."

"I don't want you interfering in this case," Barker said.

"Such interfering as I intended has been already done. The die has been cast. We merely wait to see the outcome. I'm not ashamed of what I've done, and I don't need permission from a 'special inspector.' You have never been in my position before, so forgive me if I say I don't need you to act as my conscience in the matter."

"I was hired to track the Whitechapel Killer and find him. I will not be involved in any conspiracy to deprive Warren of his position."

"I'm not asking you to do so. Circumstances may force him out without any of us doing anything. I am merely trying to be the one they offer the position to, if it is vacated."

Barker nodded and rose to his feet. He bowed formally. "Thank you for talking with me," my employer said. "My apologies for arriving without an invitation."

"The door is open if you have more questions. I envy you. One of the crackingest cases ever to happen and here I am stuck at a desk. I'd give anything to be back with Special Branch again, truncheoning heads in 'H' Division. Is he really as bloodthirsty as they say?"

"Unfortunately, he is. Come, Thomas, we've got work to do."

We walked down the hall to the stairwell again. Barker looked just as confused as I.

"What just happened?" I asked.

"I have no idea," Barker admitted.

"Could it be that we are working on the wrong side?"

"Any side where we are working with Munro is the wrong side," Barker said, his voice echoing down the stairwell.

"But I don't want Warren to change Scotland Yard, either."

"Nor do I."

"So what do we do? I hate playing at politics."

Barker rested his elbows against the rails. "We continue the way we are going . . . but cautiously."

# CHAPTER SEVENTEEN

Inside Scotland Yard the following morning, I changed into my uniform, and I was soon brewing my first pot of tea. I didn't expect any reaction from switching teas, and was therefore not disappointed when I received none, though there was a certain smacking of the lips that was gratifying. It was as I was getting ready to make my second an hour later that my plan bore fruit. Two inspectors came back to where I was working and filled their cups themselves, talking all the while.

"'Yours truly,' he says. If that don't take brass, I don't know what does. Bad enough we ain't caught him yet, without him thumbin' his nose at us."

"It's a fake," the second one said. "Someone having a lark at our expense. Some crackpot, or a Home Office johnny trying to make us chase our tails. 'Jack the Ripper,' my backside."

It was just a name to me then, eliciting no automatic response as it does now. Still, it gave me a turn. I had no trouble remembering the name after the two men returned to their office. It must have been a letter, or it could not have been possibly faked, and it must have been taunting somehow in order to have been at "our expense."

Someone must have taken credit for the killings, ending with the facetious "Yours truly, Jack the Ripper." Had the killer the gall to write the Yard and chide us for not finding him yet?

My employer had not been given an office, in spite of his position. There were no offices to be had. Instead, he was given a scarred desk in the corner of a crowded room. I was insulted for him, and would have made a scene if he hadn't warned me to keep my head low.

When I entered, the room hummed with activity. A woman cried in a chair because her home had been broken into; a witness was being questioned, but his English was broken and difficult to understand; two inspectors were arguing how a theft at the docks might have begun, and a priest was assuring a constable of someone's sterling reputation. So much noise. Barker works in near silence in our chambers, and even a small cough on my part will warrant his disapproval. I bent and spoke lowly into his ear. He nodded and pulled the repeater watch from his pocket.

"It is nearly nine A.M. Let us see how quickly we shall be informed of this new development in the case. I congratulate you. The kitchen appears to be a capital location to pick up insights."

"Thank you, sir, but what do you think of the name?"

"You are the classics scholar, Thomas, not I. Extrapolate it for me, if you'd be so kind."

"Well. Jack is the diminutive of John. It's rather a jaunty name. There's Jack and the Beanstalk, Jack the Giant Killer, Little Jack Horner, Spring-Heeled Jack. It's a common name for adventurers, people who accomplish things. There's bravery to it, audacity. They don't write tales about Cyrils or Nevilles."

"But none of the people you mentioned actually lived, if I'm not mistaken," Barker said. "The first three are from fairy tales, are they not? The final is a legend: a fire-breathing man who can jump over walls. I hunted for him on his last known sighting in London, but found no evidence of his existence. That was before your time."

"I wish I'd been in on that one," I admitted.

"Don't. It was hysterical women and trampled grass, nothing else."

"Do you think he's trying to suggest the old case?"

"Perhaps. I apologize. I interrupted you. Pray continue."

"'The Ripper,'" I continued. "Not 'the Cutter,' not 'the Slasher.' Ripping is mutilation. But there was no sign of ripping on the bodies. The weapon used was extraordinarily sharp, not a dull weapon that would rend flesh. Not even the victims' clothes were ripped. Annie Chapman was wearing a kerchief and it had been sliced as neatly in twain as her throat."

"It is meant to inspire fear, then," my employer said. "As bad as being cut might be, and to be honest, all men fear the blade, having one's flesh ripped is even worse. Whoever came up with this name is to be congratulated on imagining a memorable and awe-inspiring moniker."

It took over two hours before anyone thought to inform the special officers of the news. They wouldn't go so far as to not tell us, but they might as well have. A constable came and led us to the office of Detective Chief Inspector Donald Swanson.

Swanson was seated at a desk in an office with windows of frosted glass for privacy. There was just room inside for a desk with a chair and another for a visitor. He was a DCI and yet the space he worked in was no longer than mine in Craig's Court. The walls were lined with photographs of criminals, presumably ones he had captured. I guessed they gave him incentive to go after more.

"Barker," he said, offering a hand to be shaken, which my employer accepted. "Thank you for coming."

"What can we do for you, Chief Inspector?" the Guv asked.

Swanson carefully reached into a drawer of his desk and pulled out a canceled postal card. "This arrived this morning. It has been passed around a good deal already, but I promised the commissioner that you would have your glance. Here it is."

Barker took the card eagerly. It was addressed simply to "The Boss, Central News Office, London, City." The writing was in red ink and the card had been smeared in a way that made it difficult to read. The lettering was large and clumsy.

"Read it to me, would you, lad?"

"Yes, sir."

Dear Boss,

    I keep on hearing the police have caught me but they won't fix me just yet. I have laughed when they look so clever and talk about being on the right track. That joke about Leather Apron gave me real fits. I am down on whores and I shant quit ripping them till I do get buckled. Grand work the last job was. I gave the lady no time to squeal. How can they catch me now. I love my work and want to start again. You will soon hear of me with my funny little games. I saved some of the proper <u>red</u> stuff in a ginger beer bottle over the last job to write with but it went thick like glue and I cant use it. Red ink is fit enough I hope <u>ha.ha.</u> The next job I do I shall clip the lady's ears off and send to the Police officers just for jolly wouldn't you. Keep this letter back till I do a bit more work then give it out straight. My knife's so nice and sharp I want to get to work right away if I get a chance. Good luck.

Yours truly,<br>Jack the Ripper

Don't mind me giving the trade name.
Wasn't good enough to post this before I got all the red ink off my hands curse it. No luck yet. They say I'm a doctor now. <u>ha ha</u>

Immediately, I pulled my notebook from my pocket and began to copy it with every misspelling and punctuation error. Obviously, it could be a hoax, but it could just as possibly be the genuine article. In either case, we had a small opportunity to see it, so I went to work quickly. As soon as I finished, Swanson picked up the card and put it back in the drawer.

"This goes to the commissioner now," he said. "He's taking it to the prime minister."

"Would you care to discuss this later?" Barker asked.

Swanson gave a canny smile. "You would be in your rights to kick up a fuss if I withheld this from you," the detective chief inspector said, "but I'm under no obligation to share any of my theories with you."

The Guv stood and inclined his head. "That is so. Thank you, sir, for calling us in so promptly."

Swanson narrowed his eyes to see if my employer was being ironic, but he wasn't. We left the office.

"Two hours," I muttered.

"The CID could have waited to the final moment of our shift to show us the card and still have considered it a prompt delivery. Two or three days, even a week, would not have been unheard of."

"I thought the purpose in having such a pool of detectives is to have them cooperate, not compete."

"Let us go back to our chambers," Barker muttered. "If they won't discuss theories with us, I have no wish for them to overhear ours."

It felt good to get out of the building with its stifling air, into the brisk sunshine of a London afternoon. We stepped through the gate, nodding at the constable who stood guard, and began to walk north in the direction of Craig's Court. It felt strange being out in public in my uniform, but it was stranger still how I was adapting to it. I stopped thinking about it most of the time, even wearing the helmet when I wasn't required to do so. There was often so much to do, I had no time to think about how I looked or what I was wearing.

It was good to step through the front door of number 7 Craig's Court again, even if only to see the lanky, sardonic frame of Jeremy Jenkins. He burst out laughing upon the sight of me.

"Going to a costume ball?" he asked.

"I don't need to come here to be insulted. I can do that all day over there."

Barker brushed past me and headed for his smoking cabinet and his chair. The salver on his desk contained a half-dozen messages from people wishing to hire his services, all of whom had gone away disappointed. Just because the hoarding had come down didn't mean no one knew where Barker's door was. I don't know if Jenkins had much of an opinion about what went on here on normal days, but I suspected he encouraged potential clients to leave messages, hoping our employer would change his mind and give up this folly he had undertaken.

Once my employer was in his chair, with his pipe going, his

feet up on the corner of his desk and his hands folded across his waistcoat, he spoke. "Now, read out the letter to me again slowly, lad, if you will be so kind."

I did so, even describing each misspelling and punctuation lapse. When I was done, he stared at the tin squares on the ceiling as he sent plumes of smoke their way.

"Boss. Job," he repeated. "That sounds like an American to me. Those aren't words I would ever use."

"They are English words, but out of usage here. They are probably an example of words still used in the colonies that fell out of favor a century ago here. Certainly 'grand work,' 'get buckled' and 'proper red stuff' are English enough."

"His whole manner of speaking sounds theatrical and artificial, don't you think? He strikes me as an educated man attempting to appear as an uneducated one."

"Precisely," I said, holding up my notebook. "Why use an apostrophe in 'wouldn't' but not in 'won't'? He mashes sentences together here and here, but uses grammatical sentences over here."

"You note how he is pleased when the police make statements about being on the right track? He says 'talk' as if he were present when someone from Scotland Yard spoke, but I don't believe anyone from the Yard has ever spoken openly to the public about the case. They've been ordered not to. Is it possible that this so-called Ripper has some kind of connection to the police in order to make this statement? I'll have to ponder that."

"He's so bloody gleeful. He's killing people, women, and he makes it sound like a lark, like stealing a policeman's helmet. Do you suppose he's a misogynist?"

"Perhaps he's a coward," Barker said, pushing himself out of his chair. When he is angry, he paces with his head down and his arms akimbo, fists planted firmly against his kidneys. "He's not harming men, or even strong young women like the matchstick girls. Why even bother killing Dark Annie? Her lungs were in such poor shape the winter would have probably finished her."

Beneath that rough-hewn exterior beat a soft heart. Barker cared, even about a sickly, drunken, part-time prostitute that even her husband had given up on. It angered him that the Whitechapel Killer had done in that particular woman, whom he had never even met save in a police file.

"The act was unspeakable, small wonder his English is as well," I remarked.

The Guv held up a warning finger. "No, don't fall into the assumption that the person who killed those women also wrote this letter. We have no proof of that. This could be the work of an individual claiming to be the killer, or something else. Something we haven't encountered before."

"Is it common for people to write in to the newspapers and confess to killing someone? Anonymously, I mean?"

"It is. Apparently, it happens all the time."

"There are a lot more strange people in London than I realized. Small wonder Europe considers us a nation of eccentrics. It would never occur to me to write and confess to something whether I did it or not. I happen to have a profound respect for the Metropolitan Police, having felt their truncheons against my rib cage on more than one occasion."

"Do you know how many gates there are in London? Official gates?"

I looked over at him, wondering what the relevance of his question was. "No, sir, I cannot say that I do."

"There's one at Buckingham Palace and Kensington Palace to protect the royals from harm. And there's one at Scotland Yard, which we passed through not half an hour ago. Do you know why it's there?"

"I never thought about it. I suppose I thought it for show."

"It is, in a way. When the force was first formed a half century ago, the populace resented it. They were frightened by how much power the peelers might attain. The Yard in turn feared retaliation, even armed rebellion. The gate is not merely for show. When the CID was formed and later the new Plainclothes Division, the protests occurred all over again. When the average East Ender looks at a constable walking his beat, he doesn't see the helpful officer keeping order in the town that the West Ender sees."

"Is it as bad as that? I know Israel and his band of intellectuals are trying to bring socialism to the East End, to improve conditions there, but are you implying the government itself might be in danger?"

"Not just the government, lad. The monarchy."

"Are you serious? All because a man killed two prostitutes?"

"A fire begins with a single spark."

"I don't know," I admitted. "Most of the East Enders just want a dinner and a few pints in them at the end of the day. They're not politically motivated, or at least that's what Israel tells me."

"Precisely. And what would motivate them is a sudden seeming lack of safety, like a man with a knife roaming the streets at night."

"But he only kills unfortunates."

"Say rather that he has only killed unfortunates so far. If you had a wife or daughter walking these streets, would you consider them safe?"

The thought occurred to me then that Rebecca Cowen traveled through these very streets. Her synagogue was nearby and she had friends here. Were she to leave an acquaintance's home too late one night . . . I cringed at the thought.

"No, I suppose not. So, it's on Scotland Yard's shoulders to capture this fellow for everyone's sake."

"Right. And heaven help them if they don't."

Just then light dawned in the old Llewelyn noggin. "Therefore," I said, "it is the responsibility of all men to lay aside their normal activities for a time and hunt down this killer for the good of the community."

"Aye."

"Even if it means taking down a shiny brass plaque one has had engraved at some expense."

"Sacrifices must be made."

"For the common good."

"For the common good, as you say."

I tried to cudgel my brain into more insights. "This fellow, Jack—"

"No. I will not call him that. We have no actual proof that the killer and the author of this missive are one and the same."

"Leather Apron, then?"

"That is worse. If the East End believes that the killer is a Jew, all the worst scenarios you might consider will come to pass. It could be the flashpoint for pogroms and riots that will dwarf what happened in Pall Mall last year."

He was speaking of Bloody Sunday, when troops were brought in to quell an impromptu riot of radicals on the orders of Commissioner Warren. He was still in trouble over that, politically speaking.

"How bad could it get?" I asked, as much to myself as to my employer.

"Whitechapel isn't Whitehall, Thomas. The first is plaster and wood, the second brick and marble. The entire East End could burn to the ground and countless lives lost."

"Because of one madman."

"Now you see what I fear."

"I assumed you feared nothing, sir."

Barker gave that wintry smile again. "There is paralyzing fear and there is motivational fear. It is better to do anything than nothing."

"This may sound naïve, sir, but is this rare, that a madman could kill and keep killing periodically?"

"Very rare, and I'd like to keep it that way. Of course, there are multiple murders every now and then, but they are generally all at once, a man destroying his entire family, for example. But this, a lone man, moving about, seeking whom he will devour; he is an anomaly, and we must see that he stays that way. His very presence fractures the safety of society. It is not merely the death of a few prostitutes. It is what society does afterward to compensate the citizens' fears. Imagine curfews. Imagine gates everywhere. Imagine a much larger police presence."

"Won't Warren like that?" I remarked. "Those are dire possibilities. Do you really think it might lead to that?"

"Not if we capture him in time."

"Do you think he can be captured?" I asked. "More likely, he'd end up dead."

"I would prefer he live and be locked away where he would never have the opportunity to harm another person, but if he dies I must confess I will not lose much sleep over it."

I nodded. "What do you suppose set him off?"

"You conjecture some kind of catalyst, an event in his private life? If so, it could be anything. The smallest event, even no event at all. A thought that occurred to him, or the desire to give in to the impulses in his brain."

I snapped my fingers. "There is a novel I just finished reading, sir. It is called *Crime and Punishment,* written by a Russian named Dostoyevsky. He wrote about a young intellectual who kills out of ennui, for the mere experience of doing it. Then he regrets it as he is inevitably tracked by an inspector and is finally caught and sent to Siberia. Ultimately, he finds redemption."

"Redemption is fine, Thomas, and I wish it upon him. Right now, though, forgive me if I want to get my hands about his throat."

# CHAPTER EIGHTEEN

I am a naturally curious person. Given a stick and a hornet's nest, I will inevitably poke it. We were sitting and discussing the letter when something Munro said came back to me. I spoke before the consequences of such an action occurred to me.

"So, Munro once turned down your application at Scotland Yard."

"Just so," he said coolly.

Cyrus Barker does not like to answer questions about his personal life, but if one can find him when he is feeling nostalgic or in a contemplative mood, he will discuss his past. I suspected this might be just such a time.

"That must have been shortly after you arrived in London."

"Well, to begin with," Barker said, "I had decided it was time to leave China and come to Europe again."

"Why?" I asked.

Barker looked a trifle discomfited. "After her husband's death, Philippa had tied up all the legal matters and was anxious to return to England to inter his ashes and assume the running of Tulsemore, her estate in Sussex. Her father had passed on in her absence and she had inherited it, you see."

"And you?"

"And I had intended to follow after her."

"Is that it?"

"What do you mean, is that it?"

"When you last mentioned this event, your mortal enemy Sebastian Nightwine had tricked you into going to Peking on some sort of errand for the dowager empress. The errand for which she gave you Harm."

"Let us not discuss the errand," Barker said.

"As I recall, you claimed it was 'indelicate.'"

"So it was."

"Oh, I beg your pardon," I said with excessive grace. "I didn't mean to interrupt. Continue."

"Very well. So I was sent to investigate a case in the Forbidden City, my very first, and I solved it successfully. Ho and the crew had brought the *Osprey* up the coast to Tiensen, where I met them, and we proceeded—"

"No, no, no," I interrupted, putting up my hand.

"Is there a problem?"

"There is. You've told me enough about the way things are run there to know you don't just leave the Forbidden City like that. If they like you, you stay forever. If they don't, they kill you. One doesn't simply walk out the front gates with a cordial 'Cheerio.'"

"Confound it, when did you become such an interrogator?"

"Since you taught me. Don't change the subject. How did you get out?"

"Over the wall."

"That's more likely. Why?"

"I didn't care for the positions the dowager empress offered me as her personal employee."

"Which were?"

"Eunuch was one of them."

"Well, I could see where you might have some objection to that. And the other?"

"Paramour."

"Ah, yes. Mrs. Ashleigh might have some objections. So, the decision to leave China was not in fact a decision at all."

"Very well. We were being actively pursued. Chased, if you prefer, by the Imperial Navy."

"Why?"

"The empress revealed to her soldiers that I was not, in fact, a eunuch, which in the Forbidden City is punishable by death, though all of them had been complicit in bringing me there, knowing full well that . . . Well, as I said, it was indelicate."

"You're blushing, sir."

"I do not blush. Anyway, we were pursued south along the coast, and Philippa had gone ahead by steamer packet." He stopped and stared at me as if I were going to challenge him on it.

"Proceed," I said, the Grand Inquisitor.

"We continued through the China Sea, losing the Imperial Navy completely, and into the Indian Ocean."

"Around the Cape of Good Hope?"

"No, up through the Suez Canal. I spent a few days in the Holy Land while we provisioned, then continued through the Mediterranean and around France to Britain."

"To Seaford?"

"Aye, that's where we docked. We put ourselves up at a little place nearby called the Owler's Inn and tried to get our land legs again. Philippa had just arrived and her home was still swathed in sheets. It was where my crew broke up. Some took their pay and signed on to other vessels. The rest of us went to London to seek our fortunes."

"No," I said. "You already had your fortunes."

"I suppose we did. Anyway, Ho wanted to open a tea shop, and Etienne to train as a chef in Paris. Eventually I found myself alone."

"Stop!" I cried. "That won't do at all. The fortunes! How did you make them?"

"I assumed you had worked that out by now. You often hear of men coming back from the Orient having made their fortunes."

"I have, but how? Everything's vague and nothing is explained. I've known you for years and I still don't know how you made money. For all I know, you were a pirate."

He pulled a face. It was not exactly a denial. I jumped out of my chair.

"You were! You were a pirate!"

"No, lad, not as such. What we did was illegal and very dangerous, but not exactly piracy."

He left it at that, or would have preferred to. I wouldn't.

"Well?"

He sighed. "If you must know, we were treasure hunters. A good many ships were sunk over the years, loaded with gold bound for England. Tea and opium money. I purchased a diving bell and built a hoist on the *Osprey* and we settled in Bias Bay, which I'm sure you'll be pleased to know is infamous for its piracy. We amassed enough money in six months to retire. It was then that Sebastian Nightwine informed the empress dowager that I could solve her problems for her. Is that enough for you? May we move on?"

"Sorry, sir," I said. "But what about London? There you were, a rich man. Why did you not set yourself up as a gentleman?"

"I tried it, for Philippa's sake. She wanted it very much. But I cannot do nothing. I've worked all my life. I'm unable to sit about and I bore easily. I love to read, but even books became tiresome on a continual diet of them. Then one day, I passed through Whitehall and there was the famous Scotland Yard, and I thought, 'That's for me.' I'd solved the empress dowager's problem readily enough."

"Did you go in and apply?"

"I did, right then and there. In my folly, I believed they would jump at the chance to acquire someone who had worked for the empress dowager of China."

"I take it they did not."

"They had never even heard of her, though she rules over a tenth of the earth. It hadn't occurred to me until then that I had little written proof of my claim and what I had was in Chinese. Even translated, there was no way to assure the authorities that my papers were genuine. Plus, I was over thirty, not a particularly young man to be starting as a constable. Then there was the matter of my spectacles."

"They would not accept them?"

"Against regulation. In fact, everything I did seemed to arouse the suspicion of the inspector who was put in charge of verifying my claims."

"James Munro."

"Aye."

"So that's the source of the bad blood between you."

"He would not stop provoking me to remove my spectacles. He claimed I had a secret. He claimed I was a half-breed, someone's illegitimate whelp. He accused me of being blind in one eye. Anything to force me to take them off."

Then he pulled the offending articles from his face and threw them on the desk.

I leaned forward and stared intently at him. There was a scar bisecting his right eye from the outside corner, extending nearly an inch above the brow to the inside, extending down the cheek. At one point, someone must have slashed him across the eye with a sharp blade. The cut had sliced through both eyelids, and they had been sewn together poorly. The top was creased with scar tissue. The bottom had barely been repaired at all. There was a V-shaped nick in the lower lid, through which one could see the white. A milky groove ran vertically down the eye itself, where the blade had cut it.

"Can you see through it?" I asked.

"Almost perfectly. I was wearing my spectacles at the time, and they were broken off my face. If I hadn't been wearing them, the damage would have been irreparable."

"Who did this to you?"

"An old foe from my youth. I've had it for almost decades."

I eyed the scar again. "Katana?" I asked.

"You are correct. The injury happened while I was in Japan."

"The lost years."

He smiled grimly. I don't like to use adverbs when I can help it, but he smiled, and his smile was grim.

"Did you come up with that term yourself?"

"No. As I recall, it was Mrs. Ashleigh who called it that."

"Ah."

He wouldn't put the spectacles back on. They lay there open and inverted on the table. His face looked all wrong without them, and it wasn't just because of the eye. He looked naked without the moon-shaped spheres, more vulnerable than I'd ever seen him.

"Munro suggested I wear a patch, but to do so would diminish the sight in this eye. The loss was too high a price to pay, you see. I refused. The commissioner made it a condition of my hiring, and there was an end of it."

"I see. What did you do?"

"What could I do? I marched out of there madder than—"

"A wet hen?"

"If you say so. Madder than a wet hen. I marched out the gate and down Whitehall Street. When I reached Craig's Court, there was a property for sale, and I sat down on the steps in front of it to still my anger."

"Number seven."

"Indeed. I looked down the court. Back then, there were hoardings hanging from both sides, advertising for enquiry work. *Why not?* I asked. I looked in the windows at the vacant building and took down the estate agent's address. I bought the property that day. If Scotland Yard had no use for my services, then I would make them regret that decision, in a manner they were not likely to forget."

I picked up the spectacles. They were of copper mixed with brass, and were hinged at the corners and again halfway down the earpieces. The bridge vaguely represented an undulating dragon. The lenses looked black as coal, but when I glanced through them everything took on a sepia hue.

"Here are your spectacles," I said, handing them to him. I couldn't look at that ruined eye for another moment.

He took them and put them on, first one ear, and then the other. I let out my breath. I never wanted to see behind those lenses again if I could help it.

"Well, then," I said, for want of anything else to say.

"Well, then, what?" he demanded. His ginger was up, I could see. He was going to be disputative.

"The spectacles didn't matter," I said. "Munro just didn't want to accept you into his private party. Obviously, you had abilities that he was jealous of, so he went for the spectacles. It could have been something else. You're too tall or too heavy, or they don't accept former soldiers or sailors or nonconformists, whatever was available to exclude you."

Barker stared at me and frowned. I'd seen it enough times to recognize it, spectacles or not. He was in one of his brooding moods, I could see, and there would be little reasoning with him.

"Of course, it might be helpful if you can clear up this trifling matter of tracking the Whitechapel Killer," I said.

"'Trifling matter,' indeed."

"May I assume this is just a temporary engagement with Scotland Yard?"

"Well, of course," he said, but the way he said it in no way alleviated my concerns.

# CHAPTER NINETEEN

We were on our way out the door at six, and I admit I was rather down. Somewhere, I told myself, this Whitechapel Killer was laughing at us, and he had a reason to. A comic artist had done a drawing in the newspapers of a constable in a blindfold, playing blindman's buff with a gang of criminals who were laughing at him. It had been passed about the squad room. It was a part of my new position I hadn't thought of before; public evaluation on the performance of our duties, and criticism that we were not up to scratch. We were public servants, after all, and subject to their opinions.

I looked up and realized we were going over Westminster Bridge.

"Where are we going?" I asked.

"Home," the Guv said.

"Why?" I asked. One doesn't get the rose without the thorn around here.

"I received a new file today. Swanson had been holding on to it. We're going to interview a suspect tonight."

"Why are we going home, then?"

"To change. It's an evening affair."

"Ah," I said. "I see."

It is a pity Barker doesn't understand sarcasm. Or perhaps it is a mercy.

When we arrived in Newington again, it was obvious Mac had been tipped off to our arrival. I could smell food cooking, and a brace of top hats were on the chair in the hall. Mac knew, but I didn't. At least he hadn't informed Harm, who was dancing circles in the hall and yipping with happiness. The master was home. And his appendage.

"Is she here?" Barker asked.

"She said she wanted to air the rooms in her town house, sir. She'll be along directly, in time for dinner."

"Who?" I asked Mac directly, having little success with our employer.

"Mrs. Ashleigh, of course."

"She's coming here?"

"You don't know much, do you?" he murmured, rather pleased with himself, as he went back to the kitchen.

As if on cue, Mrs. Philippa Ashleigh's carriage arrived at the curb in Lion Street. Mac stepped out and escorted her to the door. She was, as always, beautiful, ageless, cultured, and charming. She wore a cream-colored gown with a stole of ermine and a choker of diamonds that if sold could have fed all of Whitechapel.

"Thomas," she said. She had a way of making one feel she had come all the way from Sussex expressly to see you. "You look well. All in one piece?"

"For the most part. It's wonderful to see you again."

"Are you excited about this evening?"

"I might be if someone were to finally tell me where we are going."

"To the Lyceum, dear boy. Cyrus has tickets to the most successful show in town!"

"What play is Irving performing? I'm afraid I haven't kept up with the theater column."

"Not Irving, silly," she said. "Richard Mansfield. The play we're seeing tonight is *Dr. Jekyll and Mr. Hyde*."

Forgotten were the cares of the day and the opinions of the

anonymous citizens who paid our salary. We had tickets to the theater! Now, Thomas Llewelyn might have been a classics scholar, but he could still add two and two. The suspect Barker and I were seeing that evening could only be Mansfield himself. His performance was said to be so shocking that women fainted in the aisle. It was implied, if not actually said, that no fully sane actor could give such a disturbed and disturbing performance. My friend Israel had gone several times, though never in the good seats, and said that whatever trick was done to turn one title character into the other was worth the price of the ticket. And if we were to question him, obviously, we had to join him in his dressing room afterward.

The production had come into the London theaters the year before to much fanfare. The book itself, *The Strange Case of Dr. Jekyll and Mr. Hyde,* by the author Robert Louis Stevenson, now stood on my bookshelf. I had been much impressed by it. The man never wrote an imperfect sentence. Alas, the delights of the theater were generally shut to a man in my profession, and I had expected never to see the controversial actor perform his most famous role. Now, unbidden, we were going, thanks to a file at Scotland Yard. By my calculations, Barker must have decided to go to the theater the day before in order to give Mrs. Ashleigh time to prepare.

"How are the delights of an old London inn?" she asked.

"Perfect, thanks to Keating's Bug Powder. The food is good enough at the Frying Pan, but I'm afraid the fellow I'm sharing my room with snores."

She laughed. Philippa loved to get my private opinions of her permanent suitor, as if Barker were some antediluvian creature and she and I the foremost authorities upon the species, comparing notes. She carried about with her a measure of ease and bonhomie. Nothing seemed to fluster her, and nothing was so important that she could not puncture its self-esteem. As far as I was concerned, she was the epitome of grace and charm.

Theirs was a most unusual arrangement, as far as I could tell. They would not wed anytime soon, but both took it for granted that it was to happen eventually. When not engaged in a case, he would drop down to her house in Seaford on a Thursday and return on late Saturday, so as to avoid the Sunday Express, known as the "Sabbath Breaker." They were very close, but he seldom spoke of her. I got the impression that though she spoke of him to me, because of my circumstances, she did not do so to others. They were both intensely private people.

Dinner was served. The main course was coq au vin, supported by halibut in butter, roasted potatoes, lobster bisque, haricots verts, and *choufleur*. A mixed berry tart and green salad finished the meal. White wine was served, and coffee. Afterward, Mrs. Ashleigh whiled a half hour away in the library with Harm while Barker and I dressed in our evening kit, under the sober scrutiny of Jacob Maccabee. At his insistence, I tried a hair cream that he used himself, which would tame my gypsy curls for the night.

"Are you certain about this, Mac?"

"I assume you want to wear your top hat," he said, "and not have it float about your head."

When I went down to the ground floor again, Mac was helping the Guv on with his opera cape. He was wearing green-lensed spectacles, which according to his own fashion he only wore to the theater. They reminded me of jade disks. Finally, Mac opened the front door and we swept out to Mrs. Ashleigh's open carriage.

We arrived in plenty of time for the curtain and were seated in our box. I was to hold Philippa's opera glasses, a very important duty. Barker sat silently for the most part, but Philippa kept up a stream of information about the people in the theater that she knew.

"That's Lady Margaret Thurston in the third tier. She's divorcing her second husband. Beside her is her daughter, Hyacinth, who came out this year and has caught the eye of the youngest son of the Earl of Warrick. In the next box are Rabbi and Mrs. Mocatta and the Cowens."

"What?" I asked. "May I?"

I borrowed the opera glasses and looked across, adjusting the rings to bring everything into focus. I could feel my heart begin to thump against my breastbone. Rebecca Cowen was there, looking a trifle bored, but so beautiful it made my heart ache. She wore an evening gown and I stared at the delicate perfection of her shoulders.

"Do you know the Cowens?" I asked.

"By reputation only. He's very popular in his district. Popular in Poplar? She's rather shy, but then, she's young. Rather pretty, though, don't you think?"

"Is she? I hadn't noticed."

"Thomas, I hope you are a better liar while on a case."

The lights came down and the play began, and we were all drawn into the story of the ill-fated doctor and his supposed lodger. Mansfield was no Henry Irving, but the role was his and he performed it well enough. I looked over and watched my employer as Mrs. Ashleigh slid a proprietary hand under his arm.

Finally, the moment came that I had been warned about by Israel Zangwill. Jekyll was alone in his laboratory, and first drank the formula which he hoped would remove all trace of evil from his soul. He was noting facts in a notebook, and taking his own pulse at the side of his neck, when suddenly, he pitched forward in pain. The audience gave a sudden moan, perhaps in sympathy. Mansfield fell back, disarraying his hair, then slowly pulled himself up again, hunched forward upon the laboratory table. He raised his head, and he had another face! Philippa gasped beside me, and raised the glasses to her eyes, while I trained mine on the actor's features. His eyes were sunken in shadow, his nose was suddenly hawkish, and his mouth had become a rictus of teeth. It was as if his face had become a human skull. Then he began to laugh, a short, maniacal sound. There were screams in the audience. Looking over, I saw Philippa's arm latched upon Barker's. Finally, she would not look, and handed the opera glasses to me hastily.

Instantly, I turned and regarded the third tier. Rebecca had raised a gloved hand to her mouth. Her husband sat there looking bored, the lout. How hard would it be to act solicitous to his new bride?

I trained the glasses on the stage again. Gone was Jekyll entirely and in his place, this devil, Edward Hyde. *Could such a thing happen?* I wondered. Oh, not a physical transformation, of course, but a mental one? Was some fellow leaving his office at night and turning into a monster, preying upon unfortunates, becoming a completely different person in the process?

One could see why there was a file on Richard Mansfield in the

Records Room. He had just terrified a thousand people. Perhaps I had underestimated him as an actor, and he was every bit as good as Irving. Or perhaps he carried his mad performance into the streets afterward, and had been given another name in Whitechapel.

The play went on but I was preoccupied. Rebecca. Dr. Jekyll. Asher Cowen. Richard Mansfield. I fell into a reverie until suddenly the curtain was coming down and people rose to applaud. Belatedly, I did the same.

"Wasn't he terrifying?" Philippa asked. "He gave me gooseflesh."

"Indeed," I answered. Barker, on the other side of her, was gathering his hat and stick. No doubt his mind was on the case.

I turned and raised the glasses to my eyes, hoping for one more glimpse of Rebecca Cowen, but she was already leaving, with her family. The chasm between us, the space of the theater seating, seemed somehow symbolic. Symbolic, and utterly crushing.

There is no need to go through the various stages that eventually led us in front of the great actor, the cajoling, threatening, and bribes to the stage manager. Suffice it to say, we were finally shown into the actor's dressing room. Mansfield sat in a white shirt with the collar sprung, the insides stained orange with greasepaint. His hair was wet, as if he'd just been caught in a shower. He apologized to Philippa for his dishabille.

"I have lost two stone since I began this play last year. It is exhausting," he explained.

"You were marvelous," Mrs. Ashleigh said. "It was a tour de force."

"You are too kind. My word, you're a big fellow," he said to Barker. "I like those spectacles."

"Thank you. Mr. Llewelyn and I are with Scotland Yard."

"You certainly dress well for policemen. Is there a special division for theaters?" Mansfield turned toward the mirror and began to wipe at his face with a small sponge. "Is this to be an interrogation, then?"

"Certainly not, not in front of the lady. But we can chat, if that is not too disagreeable. I'm no critic, but your performance was very good, and the trick with the lighting was inspired."

"The lighting?" Mansfield asked.

"Yes, the change from full-on lighting to overhead, lengthening the shadows. I noticed it because my spectacles are sensitive to changes in light."

"You are the first person in a year to cotton to that."

"Aye, well. Mum's the word. That's the phrase, is it not, lad?"

"Yes, sir."

"I hear DCI Swanson has questioned you in this matter of the Whitechapel killings."

"Yes," the actor said, looking over his shoulder. "Have you ever heard anything more stupid? I'm an actor. I'm just playing a role. I could be Julius Caesar or Richard III and no one would suspect me of anything then. This play has been a blessing as well as a curse. It's doing very well; almost too well. I suspect this business in the East End is swelling our crowds. I've a mind to give it up, for fear that my name will be linked forever with Stevenson's creation and nothing else, but I've got rent to pay on this theater and a wife and children at home. It's taken me years to reach this level of fame."

"Then why give it up?" I asked.

"Because it's killing me. My doctor has warned me that I am endangering my health. I'm like a limp rag every night. That Swanson fellow wanted to know where I went after each performance, but the problem is that I can't go anywhere but my hotel. I'm asleep in the cab by the time we arrive. The thought of me running around the East End, it's ludicrous. I've tried cocaine to add energy to my performance, but there is a falling away after, and I can barely make it through the final curtain. My hair has begun to go gray. I've had to start dyeing it. My doctor is giving me iron tablets and vitamins. My wife says it's just a play like any other, but sometimes I feel as if I shall become Hyde's final victim. This play shall be the death of me."

"You poor man," Philippa said, actually touching his shoulder.

"My apologies, madam. It wasn't my intention to complain."

"It should be an easy matter to establish your whereabouts," Barker said. "I assume Swanson has done so."

"Of course. The management at the Carlisle were not happy about having to vouch for a guest, but I have a memorable face and no one saw me leave."

"Then we have nothing to say, save that you may add another sterling performance to your reputation. The audience was most appreciative."

"Yes, they were. I shall in no way impugn the London theater-goers. They are the best on earth."

"We shall leave you to your well-deserved rest. Good evening, sir."

"And you. My best wishes to the Yard on catching this monster."

We left the dressing room and were soon stepping out the stage door into a cool evening. Mrs. Ashleigh pulled her stole closer around her. Autumn was coming on.

"'No one saw me leave,'" she repeated.

"Very good, my dear," Barker told her. "He has just proven to us that he was capable of looking like two completely different people. Why not three or four?"

"So, he doesn't necessarily have an alibi at all. You didn't believe him when he said he dropped off?" I asked.

"Not for certain, no."

"He was very convincing. How does one know when an actor is telling the truth?"

"When he is completely silent. And not otherwise," the Guv said.

We took Mrs. Ashleigh to her pied-à-terre in Kensington. My employer climbed down and she kissed me on the cheek before alighting. I stayed in the cab to let them say their adieus. When Barker returned, he looked as if he was waiting for me to make some sort of remark. I decided to change the subject.

"You know, I rather believed Mansfield. It's at least possible he's telling the truth. Or his version of it, at least. The chances that an actor playing a monster should coincidentally be a monster are remote at best."

"We're overlooking something, lad. I don't know what, but the facts don't add up. It may be time to throw the pieces of the jigsaw back into the box and start again."

"How many times shall we have to do that, sir?"

"Until the picture makes sense."

# CHAPTER TWENTY

As humble as it was, my mattress looked inviting after a long night at the theater. I doffed my finery and folded it carefully before pulling on a shirt and trousers, in case we should have to go out again. There was nothing prophetic about this; it was just a precaution, but I was glad I did so all the same.

Later that night we were awakened by a pounding on the door. For the first few seconds I didn't know where I was. Nothing looked like my bed, or my window that faced the garden. Then I remembered where I was, just as Barker opened the door to whoever was knocking in the very middle of the night. I heard, but could not make out, a low conversation in the hall outside our doors. Something had happened. After a minute or two, I heard the man's sturdy boots going back down the hall again and Barker returned.

"Thomas," he said. "Dress yourself. There has been another murder."

"An unfortunate?" I asked, hunting for my boots.

"In Dutfield's Yard."

"That's off Berner Street."

"I'm glad all that walking has taught you something."

We dressed quickly and hurried out into the night. The sky looked blue with starlight. Orion spanned the horizon, as we jogged along swiftly. The area around Berner Street was full of people, though it was not even five o'clock. They start work early here, and somehow East Enders know when there is something nearby that would offer them a few moments' entertainment.

We pushed our way through concentric knots of people until we came upon a still form which had been tented with a large piece of canvas and an overturned cart, guarded by two constables. I attempted to get close, but was warned away. We began to try to convince them of our identity, which was not easy for there were children running about, trying to get a view of the body, and a half-dozen others who felt their status or occupation entitled them to see it, as well.

"Let them in," a gruff voice ordered. I turned and recognized Detective Chief Inspector Swanson puffing placidly on a bulldog pipe. We moved closer to hear what he had to say.

"Apparently, the victim's name is Elizabeth Stride. 'Long Liz,' they called her. She was a Swede, about forty-five. An unfortunate, obviously. That's all we have so far. We're waiting for Warren to come and take over the investigation. We've been ordered not to move the body until he arrives."

Barker and I took a moment to view the body in situ. It was in the same position as the others, with her arms down at her sides and her lower limbs drawn up and separated. The throat had been cut to the bone and a stream of blood ran like a long scarf toward the gutter. I could see bone through the gaping wound. There was no blood on her petticoats, however, to indicate she had been savaged. The victim had a long, thin face, which may have earned her the name. Like the others, she appeared to be old before her time and haggard, as if she had seen rough usage in life. Her features were almost mannish, and she looked as if she could have given anyone who tried to mistreat her a difficult time of it. I examined her hands, looking for wounds, or an attempt to ward off her attacker, but found none. There was only a little blood in the gutter by the wall near where she lay. I wanted to cover over her petticoats, but I couldn't. It was all evidence.

"I've taken a witness into custody, but only to get a full statement. He's in 'H' Division now. He saw Liz arguing with a man earlier this evening. Thought it was a couple having a row, and crossed the road to avoid getting involved. The suspect called out to a second witness whom the Jew noticed standing nearby, smoking a pipe. He called out 'Lipski,' and the second man began to follow. The witness, whose name was Schwartz, feared he would be attacked and fled."

"Was it a case of mistaken identity?" I asked.

"No," Swanson said. "They call all Jews 'Lipski' here. Both men he identified had fair complexions and brown mustaches. Proper Englishmen, according to Schwartz. That was close to midnight. She was found within the hour. She might have had time to find another client or she might have gone for a drink. That's what we're up against here. The clients won't speak, the victims can't speak, and the witnesses must be coerced or threatened. Nobody wants to help, but oh, they'll complain that we aren't doing our duty to protect them."

"Who found the body?" Barker asked.

"Another Jew, coming home a half hour later from some anarchist meeting or other. His pony shied on him as he turned into the yard. He got down to investigate and found her on her back, as you see. What do ye suppose the Ripper uses to cut a throat like this? A dirk, perhaps, or a sword?"

"That would certainly draw attention," Barker said. "I doubt a man in a full kilt and dirk is out there taking lives, or a Coldstream Guard in his best ceremonials, though I suppose militaria is available for sale in Petticoat Lane?"

"Either weapon could be hidden under a cloak, but were he to be caught, the evidence would be very damning," Swanson said. "This is not the day for a gentleman to be found with a sword case."

"Indeed not, if he expects to survive an angry mob, aristocrat or no. Fear is one attribute that cuts across all classes. How can we help, Inspector?"

"Search the yard inch by inch for anything out of the ordinary," Swanson said.

"Aye, sir," Barker answered.

"Without a lantern?" I muttered to Barker when the inspector had left.

"Dawn will be coming soon. You must accustom your eyes to the gloom."

I reasoned if he could see in the dark with his smoky quartz spectacles, I could do so without. We began to search, beginning with the area around the body and moving out in every direction, including upward where blood might have sprayed upon a wall. At the Guv's suggestion, I touched nothing, but made a notation in my book of anything that looked out of the ordinary. It was difficult and backbreaking, stooping to examine minutely every inch of the courtyard. My eyes began to blur from focusing intently and from lack of sleep. It was just a bit of ugly paving, with bits of broken brick and cobblestones and mud. Anything of value whatsoever, from bits of broken glass from ale bottles to the very night soil left behind by workhorses, would be collected and sold by someone locally to whoever could turn a profit on it. When one came to think of it, it was efficient. Everything was used, and everyone employed collecting it or coming up with ways to benefit. The night soil would fertilize someone's garden in Kent, and the broken green glass would end its days in a child's kaleidoscope in Poplar.

"Sir!" I called out a half hour later to my employer, who was on the other side of the court. "I found something!"

He came trotting over, as did some of the constables who were searching nearby. They leaned over my shoulder, as I kneeled on the small grate of the sewer. One shone his regulation bull's-eye on what I was pointing to.

"Some sort of stalk?" Barker asked.

"A grape stalk," I said. "And still green. Who could afford grapes in Whitechapel? I doubt anyone even sells such a luxury in this district. Perhaps it was brought as a favor."

"Who would buy a favor for a common streetwalker?" a voice asked behind us. It was Abberline, who had arrived from the station on Dutton Road.

"Someone who doesn't know the ways here," my employer answered.

"Like a rich man with money for fresh fruit in September."

"Why would such a man need to come all the way to Whitechapel when the unfortunates in the West End are younger and more attractive?"

"Because they don't fight back so hard here when you slit their throats, and cut out their privates for souvenirs," Abberline said. "They are beaten down by life, not like some young chippy who takes offense when you start waving a knife in her face."

"So, you're convinced the killer is from the West End," Barker said.

"I'm not convinced of anything," the inspector replied. "And won't be until I've got him jugged like a hare. Then you can ask him all the questions you like, Inspector Barker."

The way he said the word, I suspected he thought the Guv was nothing of the kind. He also wanted us to know that he considered the case his, being in his jurisdiction, and while he might be polite enough to allow us to help him, that only went so far, and not a step further.

"Why don't you hand that bit of evidence over to me?" Abberline asked me, as if it was really a question. I looked over at my employer for confirmation, not that I should give it to the inspector, for obviously it belonged to him, but that I should touch the thing at all, since we had been ordered not to. Gingerly, I picked up the fragile stalk with a handkerchief and extended it toward Abberline. Both were snatched from my hand.

"This is all you have to show so far, a stalk of grapes?"

"I found it on the cobblestones."

"Do you deduce the Ripper stopped for a nosh before cutting up his victim?"

"This one was not cut up, as you say," Barker stated. "She was murdered with one slash and then left."

That said, there was little to discover now that the grape stalk had been found. I examined the long slick of blood but found no foreign matter in it. Barker came up beside me.

We crossed the courtyard and approached the inspector, who had a dyspeptic look on his face.

"There is nothing more, Inspector," the Guv said, not adding undue stress on the last word as Abberline had done to Barker. "Dutfield's Yard has been swept thoroughly."

Just then a constable came running up so swiftly that he skittered on the traffic-polished cobblestones and fell. He was one of the younger ones, like me, really, the kind that would be used for messenger work. He was back on his feet in a trice and running toward the inspector as fast as he could.

"What is it, Parker?" Abberline demanded. "What has happened?"

"Another one, sir!" the constable cried. "Two in one night!"

# CHAPTER TWENTY-ONE

Another one. My mind could not take it in. Was there more than one Ripper? A gang of them, perhaps? How many unfortunates would be found before the day dawned? I have rarely seen Barker stunned by anything, but he was stunned now. Jaw-dropping, pale-skinned, eyebrows-rising-to-the-hairline stunned.

"Where?" Abberline shouted.

"Mitre Square, sir," the constable answered. "It's horrible. He—he carved up her face and carried away her vitals entire. I never seen anything like it!"

"I don't need your opinions, Constable!" Abberline barked. "Lead the way now!"

The young fellow stepped back and raised an arm as if to ward off an attack. I suspected his nerve had been shattered by what he'd seen. Police constables learn to see a great deal without displaying emotion, but apparently, this was something else again.

Mitre Square was several streets to the east. Abberline had no vehicle at his disposal, and at five in the morning, there were no hansoms available in Commercial Road. We were afoot, but if there is one thing men in our profession learn to do it is to walk long distances. I'm sure Abberline was accustomed to getting about his district *à pied*. There is the steady plod, learned as a constable while walking one's beat, and the trot, when an emergency was occurring. This was naturally the latter. Two murders in one night. One could barely take it in. Apparently, one had not been enough for this killer. Soon he would be killing in droves.

The Guv took running in stride. I did my best to keep up, but then my gait is not as long as his. My emotions were a mixture of anticipation and dread. Something had shocked the constable, had set him on edge, and I was anxious to see what it was and experience it for myself knowing full well there would be an emotional toll afterward.

I admit there is within me a flaw, a desire to see things that are terrible, such as railway or carriage accidents, to see how bad they can be. My senses want to be stimulated, shocked, and appalled, and then of course, my heart goes out to the victims and I want to help. I do not wish that such a fate would fall upon them, yet the next time I pass a carriage accident, I know I shall gawk again. I do not believe I am alone in this weakness. We want to see for ourselves the very worst: the compound fracture, the injured horse, the aftermath of a drunken brawl, or the politician that falls at the hand of an assassin, the street Arab run over by a cab, the cow dead on the tracks. These are things from which society has done its best to insulate us, and yet, safe in our protected sphere, we crane our necks searching for the blood.

Aye, the blood. We had just come from a woman whose life's blood had spilled out across a courtyard in a stream. There must have been a bucketful, at least. I have heard that in the body, encased within the veins, the blood is not red, that only when it comes in contact with air does it turn that particular shade of crimson that causes our heart to beat in sympathy and alarm when it splashes on the pavement. Staring down at Elizabeth Stride's corpse, I felt as if we all are merely vessels of blood, beakers, flagons, tankards. Walking wine glasses, fragile as a brandy snifter, so easily dashed to the ground, splashing our contents everywhere for all to see.

"Hurry, Thomas!" Barker called. "Don't lag behind."

Are we congratulating ourselves that it wasn't us? Is that why we stare? Do we not know that the probability that we will be next improves with every attack? Are we glad to cheat Death and Injury again? Is it bravado on our part? Do we revel in a feeling of false invincibility? I ask this because we were all running, our faces flush with exertion, and I never felt more completely alive. Then we turned the corner into Mitre Square and came up to a large group of people milling about and there we met Death. In spite of everything, I was not prepared for it.

A woman lay there, like the others, on her back, with her hands down at her sides and her limbs splayed open, resting on her outer heels, but the Ripper had not spared this one. Great gobbets of flesh had been cut from her body as if she were a pig on a butcher's block. It stained her petticoats and lay in puddles about her. Her throat had been cut and yet still these were not the worst things about this tragic death. The killer had seen fit, when going about his work, to entertain himself by carving shapes in her face. A vertical slash had been sliced in each eyeball, the ears had been nearly severed. An inverted *V* had been cut in the flesh of each cheek. Had she still been dying when her face was first incised with the blade which had killed three other women?

It was too much. That is the thing about terror. One reaches a point and it isn't academic anymore. It seizes us in its skeletal claws and shakes us by the throat. I cried out involuntarily as I saw the poor drab laying there.

"Merciful heaven," Abberline muttered under his breath. As for the constable who led us here, he stumbled to a nearby wall and became ill.

Barker squatted on his haunches and put a hand on the cooling ankle of the victim. I don't know if there is a Baptist version of last rites, but he lowered his head and prayed over her body.

"Don't touch her, sir," a man said beside us. I turned and regarded the speaker. He was sketching the body in a notebook with colored pens, every horrible and disgusting detail. It seemed an invasion of the corpse's privacy. I wanted to rip the notebook from his hand and toss him over my shoulder, using the Japanese method

Barker had taught me. My employer stood again and regarded the artist.

"Surely this is not for the newspapers," he said.

"No, sir," the man said. "For Scotland Yard. The commissioner wants an exact representation, he said. Apparently, they bundled off the first two victims too quickly. Said he wanted things done thoroughly and scientifically."

"As you were, then," Barker said.

I returned to glaring at the unfortunate again. It was another woman in her forties, this one looking a trifle underfed. A bonnet had been pushed to the back of her head. Unlike the others, this poor woman might have been handsome for her age. Her hair was chestnut and her skin was fair. The blade had cut through her eyelids and cut off the tip of her nose, but the wounds had not bled. She had been disfigured after death. The Ripper, or whatever name the Guv would call him, had become a consummate professional now at cutting throats. In every case one slash had extinguished life, or at least I hoped it had.

The body had been illuminated by a full-sized oil lantern a constable had liberated from somewhere. Barker took it by the wire and moved to the other side, near the victim's left hand. Objects that belonged to her had been spread out beside her, but not taken. There were coins, a comb, a pocket handkerchief, and a small envelope containing lozenges.

"Who spread them out like this?" he demanded. "Was it you?"

"No, the Ripper," the artist replied.

The Guv sighed. I began to think that whether the killer had sent the red-inked letter to the newspapers or not, he was going to be known by that sobriquet forever.

"Interesting."

"What is, sir?" I asked.

"How everything is spaced. There doesn't appear to be any pattern, but he set everything out deliberately. I cannot fathom why he should care to examine the contents of her pockets."

"Why should he want to carve up her face, for that matter?"

"What do you suppose he does with the parts he cuts out and takes away?" Abberline asked at my shoulder. He had an unsettling habit of moving without a sound, but perhaps my nerves were merely ajangle. "Some sort of trophy, perhaps? Does he preserve them in a jar?"

"He's mad as a hatter," I said.

"Or he wants us to think he is," Abberline answered. "Who found this body?"

Immediately one of the constables came forward. He'd been combing the street for clues. "I did, sir. That is, I was notified where she was and was the first officer on the scene."

"Who actually found her, then?"

"A couple of Jews. We questioned them and got their address before letting them go."

"More Jews! Do they own the quarter from dusk to dawn? Do they wander about looking for bodies?"

"No, sir, but they work later hours and take shifts others will not work."

"Was there any identification on this one?"

"No, sir, but I recognize her. She was just in the cells a few hours ago. If we go back, we can get her name."

"She was at 'H' Division? On what charge?"

"Drunk and disorderly. She'd sobered up enough to go back on the street."

"In other words, we sent this woman to her death. Why can't this bastard move on to another district, like Poplar or Clerkenwell? What's so bloody enticing about Whitechapel?"

Just then a medical examiner for Scotland Yard came toward us, armed with his satchel. He was a round-headed fellow with a short spade beard. He looked irritable at having been awakened to view a body in the middle of the night. Barker gave him the lantern and the surgeon looked at the body with distaste. Then he reached into his bag and took out a ruler to measure the length of the cut. I preferred not to watch this, unless I was ordered to. Barker and I stepped away and gave him room.

"Does he work in pitch darkness or did he bring his own lantern?" my employer asked.

I knew he was not referring to the medical examiner. He was still trying to figure out the modus operandi of the killer.

"There haven't been any spent vestas nearby or any drops of dried paraffin," I remarked. "It's like he can see in the dark."

"Pray don't give him demonic powers," the Guv said. "We have enough work to do tracking him without that."

Somebody suddenly cleared their throat rather loudly. I looked up from the body to see a phalanx of constables coming forward, led by an officer with elegant side whiskers and a waxed black mustache.

"Here now," he said. "You boys are off your pitch. This is a City murder. Off with you."

Abberline looked in both directions, then stomped his foot and cursed. We had strayed just a street or two out of his jurisdiction, but those few feet made all the difference in the world. We might as well have been in Glasgow for all the authority he had here.

"Oh, come on, McWilliams," the inspector nearly pleaded. "It is obvious that the two murders are connected by the same killer. Your department needs to work with Scotland Yard on this case."

"It is not obvious at all," McWilliams replied. He was a very elegant-looking man for an inspector, dressed more like a banker, down to the rolled-up umbrella. He was all patience, where Inspector Abberline had none. "This might just as easily be a new murderer working within the City, who was inspired by your Ripper killings."

"We need to investigate this crime scene!" Abberline insisted.

"Beggar off. I'm not one of your subordinates to order about."

"Look, look," Abberline said, trying to sound reasonable. "We'll share information. I'll tell you what I found in Dutfield's Yard, and you tell me what happened here."

"Why should I care what happened over in bloody Dutfield's Yard? That's your case, not mine. I've got my own work to investigate, thank you. Now if you gentlemen will kindly go back to where you came from, and be about your business, I'll be about mine."

I thought Frederick Abberline's cheeks had grown a dusky red and he looked about ready to strangle his equal from the City Police. However, just then a constable came up and whispered in his ear. He was too far away for me to hear, but Barker was nearby and he has excellent ears.

"All right, lads!" the inspector bawled. "You 'eard the man. Let's be about our business!"

He turned and began to leave. Something else must have occurred for him to give up so easily. He wasn't leaving at all, but going to another destination. McWilliams watched him through narrowed eyes. I was passing the Guv when he seized the cuff on my coat, arresting my progress. As nonchalantly as possible, I circled around him and came up on his right shoulder. I was not dressed in my uniform and there was no indication I was with Scotland Yard. We watched Abberline and his men leave.

"Cyrus," McWilliams said, coming up to us. "You're keeping low company these days."

"I go wherever the tide takes me, James. You know that. Wouldn't it be a peach if the City Police caught the Whitechapel Killer and wrapped it all up in a neat bow for Her Majesty's government?"

"You know, the thought had occurred to me, as well. It would certainly be a feather in my cap. That's how a chap gets the word 'sir' put in front of his name."

"Precisely. Do you gentlemen need any help? You look as if you have everything in order."

"We've got this locked tight, thank you," McWilliams said.

"Do you mind if we observe? We shall not disturb any evidence. Feel free to tell us to push off if you've a mind."

"I'll give you five minutes, but not six. Fair enough?"

"You are the soul of generosity, James. This gentleman is my assistant, by the way. Thomas Llewelyn. Thomas, Detective Inspector James McWilliams."

We did not shake hands, but both touched the brims of our bowlers in acknowledgment. His was beaver skin, while mine was felt, but I was trying to fit in among the men at Scotland Yard, not their more well-bred brethren in the City. Then the inspector returned to his work. Despite his air of patience, he had work to do. We all did.

The artist had been sketching the entire time. I moved behind him enough to see what he was working on without crowding him. The body was now not only fully sketched out, but nearly finished in various-colored inks. Needless to say, red was the predominating color. It was a lurid little drawing, one that no newspaper could print, but it was accurate. I could see a need for an artist at Scotland Yard itself, creating images based upon witnesses' descriptions, as well as drawings of victims and their positions. I chanced to look over at my employer. The Guv was down on the ground, resting on his haunches, examining the body as intently as the artist. He was studying the mutilations on her face. Had the killer tried to carve letters into her skin? The vertical slash could be an *I*, and the cut in each cheek a *V*, but then they could just as easily be Roman numerals. The meaning in either case was obscure, known only to the madman who dared use a woman's face for parchment. I glanced down across her form, but she had been so ferociously stabbed that all was soaked in blood. I looked away.

We turned. Another constable was running toward us.

"Now what?" Barker suddenly demanded.

The sergeant halted in front of Barker and saluted him. "Beg pardon, sir, but you're wanted in Goulston Street. The commissioner is asking for you directly."

"Commissioner Warren is here in Whitechapel?"

"Yes, sir, with Chief Inspectors Swanson and Abberline."

"Is there another body?" he asked grimly.

"No, sir. A message. A message from Jack the Ripper himself. They're arguing over what to do with it."

"That can't be good. Well, lead the way, Constable. We haven't got all night."

We were following the steady clop of the sergeant's boots ahead of us. Goulston Street looked deserted, but when we got closer a knot of people were standing about and being warned to give way by a sergeant. We were led through the crowd to a doorway. The first thing I noticed was a rag on the pavement, a bloody rag. Then someone flashed a bull's-eye at the wall by the entrance and I saw the words in a childish scrawl too high to have been written by a child. *The Juwes are the men who would not be blamed for nothing.*

I tried to work it out. It wasn't clear. If the "Juwes" were not blamed for nothing, then they must be blamed for something, if I read it right. Was he blaming the Jews for the murders? But if he were a Jew, there would be no reason for him to blame his own countrymen. Was it a false message and he was trying to blame the killings on someone else? Barker and I stood and puzzled over what the message was trying to say.

"At least wait until the photographer gets here and records the image, sir," Donald Swanson was saying to the commissioner, who had a face like thunder, as they say. Abberline seemed just as anxious to stop Charles Warren from doing something precipitate.

"I'm sure it won't be more than a couple of more minutes!"

"My mind is made up! It is too dangerous. Suppose word gets out in the district? We could have a riot on our hands, broken shop entrances, tar and feathering, even a hanging. No, gentlemen, I'm sorry. I will take full responsibility!"

So saying, he raised an arm and wiped the chalk message from the wall with his sleeve. Swanson and Abberline groaned simultaneously. The commissioner stood there, the sleeve of his black frogged jacket white with chalk, and a dazed expression on his face, as if shocked at his own audacity. Before we could even react a man appeared with the long-awaited camera. Abberline smacked his own forehead in anger.

"Sergeants, disperse this crowd!" Warren shouted at the men guarding the entrance.

"Shall I get a photograph of the entranceway?" the photographer asked.

"Why bother?" Swanson asked. "Next time, do try to run a little faster."

· I stepped forward then and was repelled by a strong odor in the entrance. It made me step back.

"Offal," Barker said in my ear. "Offal and blood on the rag. I suspect the cloth was part of the last victim's apron. He must have carried the organs away in it or used it to wipe his hands afterward."

"He's getting worse each time, sir," I said.

"Perhaps."

"Is there any chance he will stop here?"

"I wish there were, lad, but I fear it will only become worse."

# CHAPTER TWENTY-TWO

L ater that morning I arrived at my locker to find a new jacket and trousers hanging on the hook. It was new material, well stitched, and when I reached into the collar looking for some sign of its origin, I saw a label that read K & R Krause Brothers. They were Barker's personal tailors. He must have grown tired of seeing me in ill-fitting trousers and a tunic at least a decade old. I tried it on. Of course, it fit perfectly. The special constable badge was sewn on the shoulder, and there was a proper pair of boots for me to wear with them. My concern was that it all would look too new, and I'd be chaffed for looking too spotlessly neat, like a painted tin soldier, with rouge on each cheek.

I needn't have bothered worrying. As it turned out, the Yard was too dispirited to pay any attention to what I was wearing. The Ripper had struck again the night before—twice—and all the patrols in the area had done little good for the victims. Everyone looked angry, and with good reason. The newspapers were full of articles claiming we were shirking our duties, and about as effective in saving local women from harm as a knitting circle. Meadows intimated to me that he anticipated some kind of stirring speech from one of the DCIs, if not the commissioner himself. Not a public one, mind, but within the office, offering encouragement and a renewed vow to track down this killer together. I would have appreciated hearing such a message, feeling a bit dispirited myself, but as it turned out, we missed it. The palace had called for our immediate presence there.

Once we had secured a hansom and were bowling west toward Buckingham Palace, I looked over at my employer. He wasn't dressed as formally as on our first visit, but I noticed he was better dressed than on an ordinary day. He wore a blue anodyne tie in a paisley print under his wing-tipped collar and his waistcoat was of gray kid.

"You were expecting a call from the palace?"

"I anticipated it, if that's what you mean."

"I hope the Krause brothers did not work all night on my behalf."

"No, I ordered it last week, having seen the state of your uniform, and its arrival this morning was merely coincidental."

"What sort of reception do you anticipate we shall receive?"

"The message Mr. Ponsonby sent merely said, 'Come at once.' I conjecture that the royal family is in an emotional crisis over the double murder last night. Unfortunately, being the official liaison between them and Scotland Yard means that we will be held responsible for every shortcoming of the department, real or imagined."

"He's going to yell at us," I said.

"I have no doubt."

I sighed. The morale at the palace didn't look any better than that of the Met. The butler at the front door seemed preoccupied and did not speak as he led us to the Private Secretary's office. Inside, Sir Henry was in a dour mood.

"Her Majesty has been extremely upset all morning. She has received several messages from the public concerning the killings last night. We anticipate hundreds more shall be arriving in the afternoon post. The sovereign's public demands that she do something about the women being slaughtered in Whitechapel. Her first wish is to take Scotland Yard to task for doing little in the face of such horrible murders."

"It is hardly little, Sir Henry," Barker said, unperturbed by the Queen's demands. "We have denuded the West End of officers in order to send them into Whitechapel, to patrol in pairs. There are three times the number of constables walking a beat there now."

"And yet one man passed through your sieve like water and killed two women!"

"Had we caught him already, it would have been nothing but happenstance. The political and social need to catch him does not equal our ability to track him because he has no sign or mark upon his person indicating whom he is. I could have seen the Whitechapel Killer myself this morning, or have even spoken to him, without realizing his identity. We are fortunate, indeed, that a multiple or compulsive murderer such as this is exceedingly rare."

Ponsonby continued to look truculent. I wondered what browbeating he had been given that morning by the Queen, and what promises he had made to her.

"The newspapers claim you have done nothing."

"Obviously, we do not let them look over our shoulders, so they cannot see the number of suspects we have investigated and eliminated in the past month. Nor can they see the effect of having constables in nearly every street. Many criminals have moved to Poplar or Bethnal Green where there is a lower concentration of police officials, but not the Whitechapel Killer. In spite of the much greater chances of being caught, he has returned to the same area to kill unfortunates over and over. He has a mania. He cannot stop the killing, and therefore, he will inevitably be captured."

"I wish I had your confidence," Ponsonby said.

Cyrus Barker began counting on the fingers of one hand. "When Mary Ann Nichols was killed, nothing happened beyond the standard investigation, because as gruesome as her killing was, there was no sign that it was anything but an isolated incident. With Annie Chapman's death, however, we realized we had a multiple murderer on our hands, and dispatched dozens of constables into the East End. Yesterday the killer struck again, but seems to have been interrupted in the act. This might have been enough to discourage another murderer, but at that point he had to kill again, either out of a compulsion or an inflated sense of self-worth. He did so at great risk to his freedom. He was probably surrounded by officers in all directions last night."

"And yet he succeeded."

"You must understand, the Yard has never faced such an adversary before. There are no procedures on what to do, but we are adapting our methods almost daily and noting what to change afterward should this happen again. Isn't that correct, Mr. Llewelyn?"

"I'm running out of pages in my notebook, sir," I said.

"On behalf of the Met, Sir Henry, I apologize if our actions have caused you to receive any criticism that was meant for our shoulders."

"Her Majesty is a woman of strong opinions, as is fitting for a monarch of the Empire. This matter has affected her greatly, both because of her sex and the letters she has received today from her subjects in Whitechapel. She asked me to read one. I promise you that the woman who wrote that letter was actually in fear for her life."

"I have no doubt she is correct. While the killer has yet to kill a woman who is not an unfortunate, let us not forget that there are women working in factories in Whitechapel, the bakers, the sugar refinery workers, and the matchstick girls are often on the streets early, heading to work, while the killer was actually committing his acts of atrocity."

"The letter he sent certainly seems the work of a madman," the Queen's secretary said.

"Sir, we are taking the letter very seriously, but I suspect it is a forgery, either the work of the press or some solitary individual wanting to take credit for the killings."

"Credit?" Ponsonby asked. "Why should anyone want to take credit for such horrors?"

"For the power, of course, the power to frighten an entire nation, including its queen."

"What should I tell her?"

"That the public is safe. That's true to the best of our knowledge. We are trying to curtail prostitution in 'H' Division for the safety of the unfortunates who are breaking the law. We've got hundreds of officers combing the streets of Whitechapel as we speak and it is only a matter of time until he is caught."

"I should inform you that she has vowed to offer a reward for the capture of this Ripper fellow."

"That we hope she does not do," Barker said. "It only encourages unemployed young men to come into the area hoping to make their fortune, thereby diluting the number of officers among the general population."

"Her Majesty is very adamant. She even suggested viewing one of the corpses privately. She has taken this very much to heart."

"Tell her this, if it will help. As I recall, the Detective Force, which eventually became the Criminal Investigation Department, was authorized by her in 1842 under the recommendation of her husband, the Prince Consort. We only wish her to have the same confidence he placed in us."

Ponsonby raised his brow, considering the matter. "She would probably see through such a ruse, but I shall keep it in reserve if I need to use it."

"I know it may seem that the Yard is working perilously slow, but when the case is complete, I do not doubt that the record will show we worked swiftly and efficiently to capture a man whose name we do not even know."

"What say you to the argument that your purpose, the Yard's purpose, is to anticipate and prevent such murders?"

"When a murder is committed in London, Sir Henry, it is generally for financial gain or a result of domestic disturbance. The killer knows the victim, sometimes very well. These murders are unique, in that neither is the case and I doubt that the killer had ever met the victim before he killed her. His purpose for doing what he does is veiled, unless he finds some kind of emotional release by killing. He is opportunistic, which is akin to randomness. I suppose at some point he knows that he might kill again soon, but even he might not know whom or when. He might be thwarted by too many residents or constables in the area, but at some point the conditions are good and he will strike. It's like a wolf searching for food. Most of the time he is not successful, but occasionally he is."

"Well, this wolf has been too successful for my taste."

"Mine, as well, if I may state the obvious, sir. He is damaging the hard-won reputation of the Metropolitan Police Service. It sells more copies for the newspapers to complain that we are incompetent and slow."

Though he had expressed little to me before, I could hear the frustration in the Guv's voice. He hated, absolutely hated, being caught out. Generally, he could get ahead of a criminal's plans and anticipate his next move, but this time, the killer himself didn't know his next move.

"I shall try to convey your words to Her Majesty, though I'm not sure she will understand them."

"You may tell her that whenever a murder actually occurs, we learn a great deal about the killer's motives and methods. Two in one night has given us much to digest and discuss. We're that much closer to tracking him to his lair."

Ponsonby nodded, but said nothing.

"I could speak to her directly, if you require it," my employer said.

"That won't be necessary," the Private Secretary said. "I know best how to speak to her in language she will understand."

"Then I wish you good fortune."

"Thank you. Good hunting to you."

Barker stood. "Come, Thomas. Back to the Yard, to learn what has been discovered."

Meadows caught me as soon as I walked through the doors of "A" Division.

"Make tea, Constable," he said. "Then report back here. We've had two bags of post this afternoon and we'll need help sorting it."

"Aye, sir," I said, seizing the brim of my hat.

"Chop, chop, my lad. First the tea."

I went back to the kitchen where someone had tried unsuccessfully to make it in my absence. What he had created was a kind of leaf soup. They had opened a box of shortbread and it had been consumed down to the crumbs. Three things necessary to the detection of crime, in my opinion, are sugar, butter, and flour. I opened another tin, reminding myself to purchase more. Then I drained the soup and emptied the leaves into an ash can, before starting a new pot. Once it was brewing, I returned to the front desk.

"What room, Sergeant?" I asked.

"Down that hall, third door on your left."

I followed his instructions and found a kind of postal room. There were letters piled on the table, surrounded by constables opening and reading them. Perhaps the Ripper would communicate with us again and accidentally reveal something about himself. I pulled up a chair and seized a letter. I reached into my pocket and retrieved a jackknife so as not to damage potential evidence that might be inside.

The first letter was from a woman who suspected her neighbor of being the Whitechapel Killer. He kept odd hours, glowered at her in a way she found threatening, and was less than civil when speaking to her. She provided his name and address for obviously he must be the man we were looking for. The letter would probably come to naught, but on the other hand, one never knew. A woman's intuition can be quite accurate, sometimes.

The second letter was long and rambling, written in a very small but precise hand, unsigned. The killings, the author maintained, were part of a vast European conspiracy on the part of a Jewish group known as the Illuminati, to destroy England's way of life. The Rothschilds were mentioned as leaders in this organization, and the solution was to deport all persons of the Semite races back to their countries of origin, regardless of how many years their families had been in Britain. It has always been the plan of the Jews to destroy the Christian races, he wrote, etc., etc., etc.

I'd have tossed the letter away, but for all I knew this writer might actually have been the Ripper himself. Any letter arriving had to be adequately read through and evaluated. It wasn't my place to destroy it, no matter how banal and narrow-minded or insane I felt the message was.

The third letter I opened was from the sheriff in the town of Knowle, outside Bristol. He was glad to tell us that Jack the Ripper

was living in his village, and he was keeping a close eye on his movements. If the commissioner wished to travel by train to his station,
they could apprehend the man together.

A pair of hands seized my shoulders. I did not jump, but looked
up into my employer's smoky lenses.

"Come, Thomas."

"What's going on, sir?"

"The postmortem on the fourth victim is about to begin."

# CHAPTER TWENTY-THREE

Golden Lane is an optimistic-sounding street name where the City of London mortuary and coroner's court resides. I don't know if the Guv informed authorities in the City that we were working with Scotland Yard in this case, or if he kept silent about our current positions, but he had me change clothes, out of my Met uniform. We had become plainclothes detectives.

There was a small operating theater, tiled in brick, with professional medical equipment and at least three doctors present, led by Dr. Frederick Gordon Brown, the official City coroner. When I looked around at the small crowd of men attending the proceedings, I noticed no one from Scotland Yard was there, save for us. I ventured the opinion that someone in the City Police owed Barker a favor.

The postmortem chamber offered no place to sit, but there was a rail around the table on which the corpse lay, which both kept the audience from coming closer and provided a place to rest one's elbows during the proceedings.

Brown was a sturdily built man in his late forties with a curling mustache that gave him a jaunty look, belying his grim task. My attention was not on him, however, but rather on the unclothed form that lay on the table. When last I saw her, she lay in a pool of blood in Mitre Square, dressed in layers of clothing. Now she was pale and naked on a table, ready to be cut open. In spite of her occupation, I'm sure never in her life had she been so exposed in front of so many men.

Twelve hours before, this woman, Catherine Eddowes, had been walking the streets, drinking with her friends, and looking to collect enough pennies for a bed for the night. She was fully alive with no thought in her mind that she might be lying here now, a half day later. She had opinions and plans, some of which extended beyond this afternoon and into the new week.

"The victim," Dr. Brown began, "was five foot three inches tall and forty-five years of age."

He began to detail the various external wounds on her person. Part of her ear had been cut off. Her eyelids had been slit. The tip of her nose had been removed. The upside down V-shaped cut in each cheek had swollen so that it looked worse than a simple mark on her skin.

For some reason, I felt as if I would have liked Kate Eddowes alive, in a way I would not have liked the other victims. We had nothing in common, of course. I doubted she could read, and we were over twenty years apart in age. However, in spite of those horrible wounds, I could see her face in life. I suspected she laughed often, in spite of her profession. She was the kind that got on well with everyone and did her best to brighten peoples' days with a joke or a remark. She drank, it's true, and she must have been a neglectful mother while in her cups, but I felt sorry for her. She didn't deserve this. She didn't deserve *him*.

I watched Dr. Brown pick up a scalpel and, without preamble, begin to cut diagonally across her chest. Illogically, I expected the wound to bleed, but of course, all the blood in her body had begun to coagulate. The coroner made a *Y* incision which extended below her waist. With the aid of the other doctors, Brown pulled back the skin and prepared to remove the breastbone and front ribs.

No doubt, she knew the Ripper was out and about. Her sisters in the profession chaffed one another about him. Perhaps they had

considered themselves invulnerable. Reaching this age, in this profession, that was something, wasn't it? The average age of death
in Whitechapel was thirty-seven. Any more than that, and you
count yourself one of the lucky ones. And anyway, what is a woman
that age to do? Spend her fifties in bed, an invalid, being taken care
of by your overworked children? That's no kind of life.

Brown lifted a large, purplish organ he had severed from the body
and put it on the scale.

"Weight of liver, 1.3 kilograms. I suspect Bright's disease."

It was the drink. She never could put down that bottle. It was
her reward when she finished a bad client, and there were always
plenty of those. Brutes. Selfish men. Lunatics. Unwashed. She
couldn't trust anyone, but when they were gone, she owed herself
a little celebration for getting through it. A pint or a glass of gin.
Gin 'ot.

I might have seen her, I told myself. She was here in these very
streets, as I was. Leaning closer, I examined the face again, trying
to picture it whole. A small brunette in a new bonnet she was proud
of. She wasn't young, but she might have been vivacious. She'd been
pretty enough once to turn a head or two and she could still con-
jure a ghost of her former beauty. She understood the sashay and
the come-along look, and had learned a thing or two in her years.
You had to, in order to survive.

One by one, the coroner was removing organs from the body and
calling out weights and comments, which another doctor copied
down in a book. Dr. Brown was very matter-of-fact, but then he
did this sort of thing every day. He had little need for speculation,
relying instead on observation.

I, on the other hand, was a mass of speculation. Why had he cut
her earlobes? Did he think they looked pretty that way? Did he
think he had to do it before proceeding further down the body?
What was the significance of the V-shaped notch he put in each
cheek? Was he trying to beautify her again with his sharp knife?

The coroner cut the back of her head with his scalpel, from one
ear to the other. Without any change in expression, he slid his fingers into the cut and began to separate the tissues holding the
scalp to the skull. It was time consuming, but he had all the time

he needed. This was his work, after all. Perhaps he was already thinking about dinner. One flap of skin and hair lay on her forehead, and he reached for the bone saw to begin the process of sawing open the skull.

She hadn't deserved to be a casual prostitute. She might have been a respectable grandmother if only some man had successfully provided for her. Surely a chance for a real home and family might have been enough to make her quit the bottle. She might have once been very close to having everything she wanted in life. She'd stop taking clients like this. Just this final one, you know, to earn her bed. Just four pence. She'd earn that quick enough.

Funny how a saw cutting through bone sounds just like you'd expect it would. I realized I was wincing and stopped. Cyrus Barker's big arms were crossed. His brows had sunk behind his spectacles; he looked angry, or perhaps it was sheer professionalism. Was he as matter-of-fact as Brown, or more like me? What was in his mind at the moment, while a woman's skull was being opened like a walnut right in front of him? Did the man feel anything?

Dr. Brown took a small hammer and chisel to the skull and with a few taps it came free. Inside, the brain looked as pink and fresh as a rose or a carnation. It seemed impossible that it was not connected to anything living now and must inevitably decay.

The spell was broken then. This thing on the table, sans brain or organs, could no longer be considered a person. It was but clay, fodder for the yawning grave. Brown weighed the brain then and clapped the skull cap back on the empty cavity, and stretched the skin of the scalp back over it. It went back in place, and no one looking at it would think that there was no brain inside it.

*Where was her soul, exactly?* I wondered. She was a fallen woman. No doubt Spurgeon would say she was in hell right then. Another favorite of mine, George MacDonald, on the other hand, writer and mystic that he was, believed that after a time of penance, a loving God would take her to heaven. Was there such a place? I'd dearly like to think so, although my closest friend, Israel, had no need for Sheol and such things. Spurgeon or MacDonald? I had been a member of Spurgeon's flock, but just this once I hoped he was wrong. And I'd like to think he'd wish the same thing himself.

Brown had threaded a needle and was looping stitches across her mottled abdomen. Poor dear. I wondered what she would be buried in. Her clothes must be kept as evidence. I would pay for a nice, plain dress myself, if need be. Bury her like the grandmother she would have been had circumstances not been as they were. Give the old girl some proper dignity in her final departure.

Again, I had that feeling of nakedness. All these men staring solemnly at her exposure. Even death was a kind of nakedness, with no life to clothe her in. Deprived of all dignity, stripped bare of humanity, displayed like something in Madame Tussaud's Chamber of Horrors for all the world to see.

"I think I'm going to be sick," I muttered, but I wasn't. It wasn't my stomach that wanted to reject this. It was my mind.

Peeping Tom had his eyes put out with a hot poker for daring to look at Lady Godiva, or so the story goes. I understood that now. I didn't want such a punishment, but understood it nonetheless.

"Phillips," Brown said.

His assistant brought a canvas sheet stained with fluids from other postmortems and finally, finally, covered her obscene nakedness with it. Her shroud. At last she had earned it.

"I must attend her funeral," I said to Barker, as the men watching the spectacle had begun to leave.

"I was going to give you the morning off, lad," the Guv protested. "You've been working for weeks without a break."

"No, sir, I'd rather be there. I must see this thing through."

"Very well, Thomas. May I accompany you?"

"If you wish, sir. I'd appreciate it."

We stepped into the hallway and out into the clean air of the autumn afternoon.

"What thought you of your first postmortem? Was it instructional?"

I tried to say something, but three thoughts came at once, like when someone hits random keys on a typewriting machine and they all jam together in the air.

"Well, no matter," he said. "It was a rite of passage."

———

A private enquiry agent, in the course of his duties, is forced to attend a number of funerals. Many enquiries begin with a death, and it builds trust in a client to have an agent attend the service of the person who is often the victim. More than a few end with a funeral, as well, and for various reasons, difficult as it might be, one attends them as well, if for no other reason than to watch a murderer put into the ground for good. I have been to lavish funerals with dozens of carriages swathed in black silk and crepe, and I have been to one where I was the chief and only mourner. Some have been in full sunlight, others in a driving rain, and at least one required a pickaxe to break the frozen soil. Yet, among the many, I still vividly recall the funeral of Catherine Eddowes.

I did not attend the burials of Mary Nichols or Annie Chapman, but I understood they were sparsely attended. Unfortunates tend to shed relatives like a dog does its winter coat, and there are few upright citizens willing to be seen publicly grieving for a known prostitute. Eddowes's funeral, on the other hand, was a circus. When Cyrus Barker and I arrived the following Monday, the streets were lined with people outside the Golden Lane Coroner Center, and some had let upper rooms nearby to look out upon the spectacle. One would have thought Kate Eddowes a member of one of London's premier families.

The funeral was to be at Ilford Cemetery, which I must admit was shocking to me. Apparently, Eddowes was to be buried in hallowed ground, in spite of her occupation. Someone, some benefactor, had not only put up the money for a proper funeral, he must have also pulled a few legal strings. She was brought out by City Police pallbearers in a coffin of polished elm with oak moldings, and lain in a glass-sided hearse. A beautiful wreath of white lilies was placed on the coffin. Behind was a mourning carriage carrying four of Catherine Eddowes's sisters. Whatever they had thought of her life, when she was sleeping rough and giving herself to men for mere pennies, they were there when she was the toast of Whitechapel. Also there was John Kelly, her common-law husband. He was fiftyish, with short, spiky hair and a collar too tight for his neck. If anything he was cowed by the sisters he traveled with and seemed to keep to himself.

"Drunk," Barker said to me.

"Kelly?"

"The crowd. Part of it, anyway. There was a wake last night in many of the public houses. Many stayed up all night."

I looked closer. Some of the men had donned morning coats and crepe-lined top hats, but they had been put on hastily over their normal clothes. The women had fetched bird-covered hats and bonnets from closets, and knit shawls, but had not polished their shoes. Some of the clothes they wore seemed theatrical, as if pinched from a costumer, and much was mismatched, as if it were the best they could do at short notice. Jenkins had coordinated with Mac to have our mourning apparel brought to our rooms. I felt over-dressed, but I had promised myself that I would be there and prepared.

"Don't begrudge them, lad," Barker said, as if divining my thoughts. "They have their own ways of mourning here in the 'Chapel."

A third vehicle came up behind the coach. It was a brougham for members of the press. The reporter Bulling was there, his face red with drink, and not the only one, too.

At a signal, the front carriage driver gave a click of his tongue and the lead horses tossed their black-plumed heads and began to pull. The procession gave a ragged cheer and began to move. We walked with the crowd, since we were not a part of the City Police, represented by Superintendent Foster and Inspector McWilliams. A body of constables kept order merely by their presence and the solemnity of the occasion.

The route to the City of London Cemetery was by way of Great Easter Street, Commercial Street, Whitechapel and Mile End Roads, until it reached Ilford. The crowd were old and young alike, including babies bawling in their mothers' arms. Some had known Kate, most had not, but were paying their respects, and some had come simply out of curiosity. I looked about and wondered if the Whitechapel Killer himself was here. One would think he could not stay away from this display of his own handiwork.

"They must be joking," Barker rumbled, breaking into my reverie.

"What now?"

"Look ahead."

I did. There was a wall of constables stretching across the street. Scotland Yard men. Would there be an altercation here, between the Yard and the City men? No, as we approached, the Met came forward while the City retreated, staying within the City limits. They would not cross over and see the woman to her grave, and neither would the constables from nearby "G" Division step into their territory.

"Stupid," I said.

"'Call no man fool,'" Barker quoted from the Psalms. "Once you start, you will never stop."

As we passed the white chapel of St. Mary Matfelon Church, the crowd swelled as the mourners waiting there mingled momentarily with the participants. Those who had come to pay their respects here gave the procession a gravitas it greatly needed. Some of the women were actually crying, and I suspected they were Eddowes's true sisters, those of her profession that had been with her every day, commiserating with her struggles and few momentary pleasures. I saw one of the constables reach out with a gloved hand, and pat a weeping woman on the shoulder. There, unheeded by anyone but me, was one of Scotland Yard's finest moments.

It was a long walk, snaking through the entire district that the Ripper prowled, and many walked in pinched and broken shoes, though no one complained. It was an event people would remember in their old age. "Was you there at Old Kate's funeral? That was something worth seeing, was it not?"

When we finally reached Ilford and Forest Gate, there were hundreds more mourners already waiting at the cemetery for our arrival. It was a crush. The two crowds merged and without the presence of the police there might have been chaos.

"Shall we observe at a distance, Thomas, or do you feel the need to be graveside?"

Just then a man carelessly clipped my ear with an elbow.

"At a distance would be fine," I said.

We let the procession continue to the Church of England portion of the cemetery, which was full of falling leaves, reminding me of the changing seasons. A breeze blew through the cemetery, sending leaves cartwheeling over everything. It seemed very apropos. The dead leaves would soon cover the dead woman's grave.

A chaplain in his long surplice read a ten-minute speech, not quite eulogy, nor yet sermon, either. What does one say over the coffin of an unfortunate? One cannot act as if she was virtuous, but on the other hand, only the most hard-hearted of clergymen would dare say anything derogatory in front of this crowd.

"Who's paying for all this?" I finally asked my employer.

"The City officials have waived the fees for her burial. The rest was donated by a local churchman."

"'Ashes to ashes, dust to dust,'" I heard the chaplain's voice travel on the wind with the dancing leaves.

"God rest her soul," Barker added.

"'Flights of angels, sing thee to thy rest,'" I said to myself.

# CHAPTER TWENTY-FOUR

Scotland Yard is famous for its staunchness, its gravity, and the seriousness with which it handles every complaint. Without question, it is the best police force in the world. That motion having been put forward and seconded, there is occasionally an atmosphere as if they were a group of boys at play. One must understand that there were no women working there to scrutinize behavior for its gentlemanliness, and though some denizens had crossed the fifty-year threshold and were in their dotage, the median age was about twenty-five.

We were in the Records Room on the morning of the second of October, looking over the latest arrest records in connection with the case, when somewhere in the hallways a voice called out, "Oy!" Aside from being a beloved Yiddish term of surprise, it is often used in the Yard, its meaning being a combination of "Stop what you are doing," "Come to my aid," and "You've got to see this!" It is the vocal equivalent of the police whistle.

Barker and I debated whether to go to the aid of whoever made the call. After all, there was a beehive of constables there ready to handle any emergency. Then a few ran down the hall past our door. Immediately, we were on our feet. A prisoner had tried to escape, I thought, or a fight between suspects or witnesses had broken out; those were the only reasons I could conceive on the spur of the moment. By the time we reached the door, more officers shot past, and I realized something of sufficient magnitude had occurred that it was siphoning men down the hall. Just because the Guv and I were new did not mean we would be caught flat-footed. We sprinted down the now congested hallway. Men were jostling to get ahead of us, but the Guv has a way of swinging his elbows as he runs that make him a danger to one's eyes and throat. Most gave way.

We turned into the main hall of "A" Division, expecting to find a riot in progress, but instead, everyone inside the building was funneling out the front door. Had a bomb threat been made? Was Barker right that the populace wouldn't stand for the Yard's methods and had come to protest? No, everyone running out the door was turning right toward the Embankment and following after the man in front of him. We could but do likewise.

Reaching the corner of Great Scotland Yard and Northumberland Street, we passed through a makeshift barrier and into the geometric grid of bricks and blocks that formed the skeleton of the New Scotland Yard building. Designed by Norman Shaw, it was intended to replace the poky and disorganized halls of the old building with order and ample space for all possible future needs. What it lacked in space beside the river and Great Scotland Yard Wharf, it would make up for in height. I understood it would be five stories tall. When finished, it would dwarf all the buildings nearby, but that was still a year or two to come. We ran among the brickbats and pallets trying not to trip, and to avoid puddles which had formed in the sandy soil. It slowed my progress, because I knew this group of philosophers would jeer and laugh at the first man who tripped and fell.

Ahead, most of the residents of Scotland Yard had settled in a ring around a half-built structure, taking turns stepping down into a recently finished basement. We waited our turn, and when we finally reached the room squeezed in, having no idea what to expect.

The small, unfinished cellar was packed with men standing shoulder to shoulder, lit by a single dark lantern in the middle. We shuffled forward until we could see. There was a bundle on the floor, originally swathed in black cloth and rope, but now lying exposed. It was a torso; pale, naked, headless, and limbless. A female torso.

The Ripper had left us a present on our very own doorstep, just to prove to us and the whole world that he could do it and get away with it. If Barker weren't there, and him such a Puritan, I'd have let out a few curses in frustration.

The victim appeared to have been young and well formed and the skin so pale as to remind me of a mermaid. The limbs had been sawn with some degree of precision. As we watched, one of the chief inspectors came out with a length of canvas and covered the body in preparation to carry it to a hand litter left behind in the street. We watched in fascination as he tried to lift it. It slipped out of his hands and struck the ground with a squelching sound that rather made me queasy. Two attempted it next, and found it no easier to grasp than the one. Finally, a third joined in and rolled the partial body into a makeshift sling held by the others. Some of the men were assigned to examine every inch of ground from the old building to the water for clues.

The sight made us angry. One of the officers roared and beat upon the walls in his wrath. The walls were suddenly too close, and we were buffeted about. Everyone was yelling and cursing at once and trying to get to the entrance. Eventually, we pushed our way out into the sunshine and the cool, salty air. Men lit cigarettes and pipes and tried to calm their nerves. Some had recourse to hip flasks, though it was not yet noon. We stared into the inky river.

"This case," I said. "This case—"

"I know," the Guv replied. Neither of us finished the thought.

"We always seem to be behind."

"Aye. We are not acting, but reacting. We must find some way to get ahead of him."

"The newspapermen shall think it is Christmas. This is the worst possible thing to have happened to the Yard."

"There's nae more to see here, Thomas. Let us return to our desk."

I turned and began to walk back to Great Scotland Yard Street. The thought in my head was unless the murderer was found, Jack the Ripper or no, New Scotland Yard would be built on an unsolved-crime site. I'm sure the irony was not lost on the Guv, either.

"An arm was found farther down the river earlier this week, in Pimlico," he told me. "I'll bet it belonged to this poor woman."

"What a horrible way to die," I cried.

"I have little doubt she was dismembered afterward, lad."

"Still, cut into pieces and tossed into the Thames, and the main part left here as a warning."

"Her soul went to heaven at the first instant. The rest is just unfeeling clay. As for the warning, granted, it was a bold move to leave a corpse here on Scotland Yard soil, but it was a convenient place to hide a body. Depriving a person of his or her life takes but a moment and can be done in the heat of anger, but disposing of a body is always the most difficult part."

"You're saying that woman was killed for whatever reason, and the body left as an afterthought, rather than that she was deliberately killed and left as a warning? Why?"

"He cut off her head to make her unable to be identified."

"It's probably floating in Bayswater right now, waiting to be found," I said.

"If he is as clever as he is daring, he'll have destroyed the features somehow, to prevent recognition."

"You're certain this is not the work of the Whitechapel Killer?"

"It's not his method. This fellow has not sliced the abdomen or removed her organs, and so far the Whitechapel Killer has not attempted to remove limbs from his victims."

"But two women-killers at the same time, that's a coincidence, and you don't believe in coincidences."

"I do not. Generally, it means one has not considered all the factors. In this case, a fellow is getting rid of a body a piece at a time. The limbs are not that difficult, but the torso itself is more so. Why not bedevil Scotland Yard, already chasing after a hobgoblin, by placing it in the construction site and blaming it on the Ripper? He is the perfect scapegoat."

"You called him 'the Ripper,' sir."

"Did I? Damn and blast. You see how easy it is to fix a label on someone? Deucedly hard to get rid of it afterward."

"Suppose there are two killers, sir, and they are working together. This is an example of the second's work coming to the fore."

"The Whitechapel Killer does not strike me as a social fellow. He is secretive and silent, in spite of these false letters to the press. If there were a second killer, and this is his work, then more likely he is mimicking the first and need not actually know him. He was inspired by the Whitechapel Killer's success to try this himself. It is quite a strong message, is it not? You are powerless, and I can even set a murdered citizen at your very door, within your own walls. If a talented reporter gets hold of it, he can have every woman in London feel as if she narrowly escaped death, from the simplest char to Her Majesty. Perhaps especially Her Majesty."

"The murder is bad enough. I mean, it is terrible and the dismemberment. But the obliteration of all identity must be the worst of all. If she is not identified, she'll go to her grave unmourned and unknown. Meanwhile, her parents, or perhaps even her husband, shall wonder forever if she is alive somewhere, and has left voluntarily. It's sickening!"

"'Tis, indeed," Barker rumbled.

"And naked," I went on. "A further indignity. He spared her nothing. One would think Evil can go no further."

"Thomas, you must not allow yourself to become emotionally tangled in this case. It can break you like a matchstick. Practice emotional detachment, as much as is possible. Do not allow this to overshadow the case we are already investigating. That has precedence over this one."

"And if they are working together?"

"Then I believe we shall uncover proof of that connection."

We returned to our chairs around Barker's desk.

"I hope so. We have to get this fellow. It would be terrible if he were never caught. It would damage the reputation of the Yard forever."

"Then between us we must see that that doesn't happen."

"Ahem."

We looked up. A sergeant was standing in the doorway. "You gonna make a fresh pot or jaw all day?"

I jumped to my feet and hustled down the hall. All Scotland Yard investigation runs upon a never-ending supply of black pekoe tea, strong and hot. If the Opium Wars with China proved anything, it is that the entire country runs upon it.

Returning to the kitchen, I emptied the pot, pumped the water, added the tea leaves, and lit the hob. When the tea was finally brewed, I found Barker at my elbow.

"Let us get out of here. Question someone, even if we've questioned them a half-dozen times already. Talk to people. Anything to get away from this blighted street."

"Gladly," I said.

I felt hemmed in by the walls and hallways of the old building. We seized our hats and passed through those halls again until we stepped out in the street. Eagerly, we passed through the front gate and hailed a cab. We pulled out into Whitehall traffic. It felt as if we were escaping.

There were other occupations that did not require one to view dead and bloated bodies on a weekly basis. One went to an office, filled out forms and created paperwork, and at some point prescribed by one's duties, one went home and didn't think about work anymore. One kissed one's wife and lifted one's children into the air, because, of course, one was safe to marry because one was not shot at or stabbed or frequently beaten up. We saved London one person at a time, but the city regarded us not. Then we took it personally when an individual slipped through our fingers and wound up wrapped in a roll of dark wool, without a head or limbs.

"Tell me it is early days, and we shall get this fellow."

"It is, and we shall."

"Where are we going?"

"Ho's. He might have some gleaning we can use."

Ho was Barker's closest friend, a monosyllabic Chinaman who was first mate aboard the *Osprey*. Now he ran a tearoom in Limehouse. He also traded information. We now had a new piece he might trade for something we could use.

When we arrived at his tearoom, through a clandestine tunnel beneath the Thames, I munched on doughy rolls while my employer conversed with the Chinaman in Cantonese. Ho is bald, save for a thick queue, and has long, weighted earlobes. At one point he was a Buddhist monk, but he looked more like a pirate than a monk.

"Two inspectors came in here last week," Ho said, switching to English. "Discussed with each other whether there was a demand for female organs among medical students. A specimen in a jar could go for as much as five pounds sterling."

"That's a month's wages down Whitechapel way."

"It would not work as a going concern, however," Barker pointed out. "Even murder among the drabs of the East End, the lowest level of society, draws the attention of the community and Scotland Yard. You'll have to do better than that."

Just then our food arrived. Sweet and sour pork, snail dumplings, and fried rice. I had been queasy an hour before when the body was found, but my appetite had returned. The living must go on.

"Two City police discussing the case here said it must be the work of a foreign sailor. The bodies are found close to Dockland. The other gave the opinion that Asians have strange rituals involving human sacrifice. I charged him double."

"Oh, come now. Is that the best you can do?" Barker asked, biting off half a dumpling.

Ho crossed his bare arms, which look flabby, but are actually well muscled. He was speculating over which tidbit to pass on to his friend.

"Two men came in last night, late. Mentioned a person named Lusk."

"Lusk? Aye?"

"They discussed how to make an example out of the Jews, to 'run them off.' One said they must burn the synagogue. The other said if they attack the silver merchants they can loot their shops."

"So," I said, "on one hand, we have the Whitechapel murders as a way to make money selling female organs to hospitals. On the other, we have them killing unfortunates in order to blame the Jews so they can loot their prosperous stores."

"Man said Lusk did not approve."

"They must be members of the Mile End Vigilance Society," Barker said.

"If anyone had the organization to make an attempt on the Jews, it would be they," I said. "I must say I am surprised Lusk would not go for it."

"Just because he runs a vigilance group does not ipso facto make him a thief and an opportunist. It is possible that he only wants the women at Whitechapel to be safe. Someone there should."

"Are we even?" Ho asked.

Barker picked up a small cup of tea with his thick fingers and downed it, deep in thought.

"Three fact for one," Ho reminded him.

Barker slapped the stout table. "Done. Consider us even. Come, lad."

As we walked into the tunnel under the river, I stopped, as I often did, and listened to the sound of the Thames moving over-head. I knew not by what alchemy it didn't all come crashing in to flood the tunnel.

"I suppose somewhere on the river there is a head and some limbs bobbing," the Guv remarked.

"First you make me eat snail dumplings and now you discuss floating limbs," I complained.

"I'm the one who ate the snail dumplings," Barker said.

# CHAPTER TWENTY-FIVE

Barker and I were getting ready to go into the station the following morning, when there was a knock upon the door. A message was handed to my employer and he shut it again, reading it. He frowned and handed it to me.

"We're to report to Leman Street as soon as possible," he said.

"Another killing?" I asked, reaching for my shoes.

"I think not. More likely some sort of inspection. The constable who delivered the note was spotless. Fresh collars and cuffs. Let's wear our best shoes this morning."

We broke our fast on buttered toast and tea downstairs, then walked briskly to the corner of Commercial and Leman Street. A crowd had already formed and at least a dozen constables stood about looking anxious. It was nearly seven in the morning and a light mist was falling.

"Who is that?" I asked Barker, pointing to an officious-looking person talking to reporters. He seemed familiar, like I had seen an engraving of his face in the newspapers. A minor royal, perhaps?

"That is Henry Matthews, the Home secretary," my employer stated.

"The one who hired Munro after he resigned from Scotland Yard?"

"The same."

"Has the commissioner been sacked?"

"Your guess is as good as mine. You have a brain. Pray, draw your own conclusions."

Just then, DCI Frederick Abberline stepped out of the station. The next we knew we were being introduced to Matthews. The Home secretary did not seem overimpressed by us, but I assume nothing short of pulling the Ripper from a hat in darbies would have satisfied him.

"Where is Warren with that blasted dog?" Matthews asked.

"I'm sure he'll be along directly," Abberline assured him.

We stood about for twenty minutes or more. Some of the crowd moved on to their occupations, or left out of boredom. There was nothing to see but a squad of constables looking uncomfortable.

Finally, Commissioner Warren arrived, with a man leading a sleepy-looking but wiry bloodhound. His hide looked like brown velvet, and his eyes were heavily hooded, but his manner was businesslike. He was ready to be set loose on something.

"The commissioner had a field trial two nights ago in Hampstead Heath, after it was closed," Abberline explained to us. "He himself acted as bait. The hound tracked him successfully to a thicket. There is to be another trial this morning to see how he fares in the streets of Whitechapel."

"Will the gentlemen of the press come forward," the commissioner of police asked.

Certain men in the crowd detached themselves from doorways and conversations and came closer to where Warren and the jowly hound stood. One of them, Bulling, actually reached out and patted the dog.

Warren gave a short speech. I took it down verbatim for Barker's benefit, but there is no need to repeat it all here. The gist was that no detective, no matter how educated or insightful, was a match for a bloodhound with a keen nose. He described in great detail how he had come up with the thought of a hound himself to track down the Whitechapel Killer, how he had found a trainer, got permission to use Hampstead Heath to test his theories, and how Barnaby, that is, the dog, had proven an unqualified success. The entire speech was highly insulting to the Criminal Investigation Department, who, with Abberline as the only exception, had thrown in their support to Munro. The suggestion was that if Scotland Yard were reduced to Warren and one dog, he would function without them very well, thank you.

"Should this test prove successful, I can imagine a canine division of hounds and handlers, brought to bear against the thieves and murderers of the East End."

"There you go," Abberline muttered to Barker. "In one sentence, he has insulted the entire Metropolitan Police and half of London."

Then Matthews, who must have had hearing as good as the Guv's, spoke up. "But he has done so with great authority and self-assurance."

Warren pulled a handkerchief from his pocket with a flourish, holding it aloft, then wiped his hands and neck with it, covering it with his scent. He handed the linen to the dog's handler and turned to the crowd.

"I now go in the guise of a criminal, to see if I can outsmart Barnaby's expert nose."

He turned and marched through the crowd. When I last saw him he had stepped into an alleyway on the Commercial Road and was gone.

After a few minutes to let the quarry escape, the handler went down on one knee and put the cloth to the bloodhound's muzzle, who took in the odor eagerly. He charged off on the lead, followed by the handler, and the reporters and the crowd that remained.

"I'll stay here," Matthews said. "Contrary to modern opinion, I have no wish to watch the man publicly humiliate himself."

Likewise, Abberline appeared too dignified to follow after a dog, but he had no difficulty sending us. We did not trot, but walked swiftly at the tail of the line.

"Cobblestones are a far different surface from a grassy trail," Barker remarked. "I'm not sure how long they can retain a scent."

"This isn't the West End, where there is a crossing sweeper on every corner," I said. "The streets are spattered with night soil and awash in horse urine."

"There are fish carts and butcher shops, sausage factories and meat pie shops. Blood drips from carts and flows into gutters. It isn't like Hampstead Heath at all."

"True."

"Even now people are walking across the trail of Warren's shoes, carrying the scent away. There are hundreds of thousands of people going about their daily lives."

"But think if it works," I said. "Suppose the Whitechapel Killer kills again, and we get this little fellow there in time to get a fresh scent."

"Aye, but that's quite an 'if.' The dog would have to be sent for the second the murder was found. If 'twere in the middle of the night, there might be a chance to catch the killer, but if the murder was discovered after five o'clock in the morning, the trail would be obliterated within an hour or so, I should think. Not that I claim to be an expert on bloodhounds, of course."

"Is there some significance to the fact that the murders seem to occur very late in the night, sometimes three or four o'clock? Who is about at that time of night, other than insomniacs?"

"Sailors returning from their revels, men who have come to White-chapel for a night of debauchery. Then there are factory workers. Many take an overnight shift to meet the demand for steel or other goods. The truth is there are many occupations in the East End that require working overnight. One forgets that while the commerce occurs in the West End, the manufacturing occurs in the East."

"Then there is the good old-fashioned lunatic. Do you suppose he is really affected by the moon?"

"I hadn't consulted the lunar cycle, but I imagine it has already been dismissed. The Yard is nothing but thorough. If he went by a particular pattern, we'd have been alerted to it by now."

"You hope," I said.

"You believe someone would still hold back information on us at this late date?" Barker said.

"Scotland Yard is definitely taking sides these days, and it's important which side one chooses."

"I refuse to engage in such childish notions."

"That's your side, sir, and it is an exceedingly small one."

"You think I should play politics?"

"No, but Matthews seems to think this is Warren's last hurrah. And while we have been brought in by Anderson, once Munro is in office again, I suspect he'll have no use for us."

"Perhaps," Barker conceded.

"Sir, this was intended to be a temporary assignment, anyway, was it not? You do plan to open the agency again."

"I hope the Whitechapel Killer shall be caught soon, lad, but I cannot give you a date when we shall be able to open our doors again. This investigation could extend into the new year."

"If it does, sir, I hope we will be staying somewhere more permanent than the Frying Pan."

"I'll take it into consideration."

The hound ahead of us suddenly bayed and we all quickened our steps. He was still on the trail. We passed through an alleyway or two and then suddenly we heard celebrating ahead. Coming into a courtyard, we found the bloodhound on two legs with his paws on the chest of Charles Warren, who was patting him vigorously. We joined in the applause.

"It was a nice little trick," I said. "The trail was no more than minutes old and no one had time to cross it and confuse the dog. The commissioner's got his publicity, which I'll admit, Scotland Yard needs at the moment."

Flushed with the pride of success, Warren gave another brief speech on the modernity of police methods, no stone left unturned, and that sort of thing. In the middle of the speech, Barker moved through the crowd and spoke to the dog's handler. They shook hands and I suspected a pound note was passed along. Barker made his way back to where I stood just as the brief speech ended. There was more applause, but some dared to boo him, as well. Though this was the East End, the crowd was smart enough to realize they had been gulled. In fact, I imagine they were less likely to be taken in than their western neighbors.

"See a man about a dog?" I asked.

"Aye, he's agreed to come with us to the last two murder sites, Dutfield's Yard and Mitre Square. We'll test whether Barnaby can pick up the actual scent. I want Swanson and Abberline informed, but not the commissioner. I'm sure they are here. Search for them and tell them I want to see them."

There was no great hurry. Charles Warren was being photographed with the dog, and every photographer wanted their own picture of Barnaby. Apparently, nothing sells newspapers like a canine hero, even if the heroics were staged for public benefit. I pushed my way through the crowd, and spotted Swanson's elephantine shape first. He was standing on a low wall a head above the crowd, looking down on them. Did he hope to see the Ripper there, and how would he know him? By his own eyes?

"Sir!"

"Yes, Constable Llewelyn?"

"Inspector Barker would like to see you for a few minutes. He has procured the services of the dog and would like to test his nose against the actual murder scenes."

"I won't miss that," he said, his eyes still scanning the crowd. He had the eyes of an eagle. They were searching for his prey and when he found it, he would pounce quickly and without mercy.

Next, I looked for Abberline. He had a normal build and was less noticeable in a crowd. It took me several minutes, but I finally found him issuing a warning act to that rascal Lusk and some of his men. I had no doubt they had supplied the boos during the commissioner's speech. Did the man have an occupation or was he using his trumped-up position to extort money from local businesses?

One doesn't go up to a detective chief inspector, ideally. One steps up behind the man, to the left, and looks away until one is noticed. Sometimes this may take a while.

"What is it, Constable?" he snapped, as Lusk disappeared into the crowd.

I gave the same information that I'd given to Swanson, without the same result.

"Is the press in on this?" he asked. "I won't have the commissioner humiliated."

Loyal to the end, I thought.

"No, sir, just the four of us and Barnaby, of course."

"All right, then."

About a half hour later the crowd had dissipated, and photographers had stopped fouling the air with magnesium sulphate. We met the dog and his trainer, and began heading north.

"We'll have to be careful, going into the City territory again," Swanson remarked.

"Just some men out taking a dog for a walk," Barker said.

"Three of whom happen to be Scotland Yard inspectors," Abberline added.

"Everyone must have an occupation. We live by the sweat of our brow."

"Save your Bible quoting for another time, Barker."

When we reached Mitre Square, all of us could have found the exact spot where Catherine Eddowes's body had been found. As it turned out, we didn't have to. Someone had recently poured fresh blood there. I reckoned it had been there a day or two. It was brownish black.

"S'truth!" Abberline said. "Those blighted tour guides have contaminated the scene."

"Pig's blood, I reckon," Swanson said. "Easily available in this part of town. Among the Gentiles, at least."

"Let us give the dog a try," Barker said.

The handler came forward with the animal and it put its nose to the blood-soaked ground and let it sniff for all it was worth. Immediately, it turned and followed an invisible path to the front entrance. We followed after, expectantly. It was difficult not to, in spite of the odds. It was also more exciting being in the lead, at the head, rather than the tail.

Barnaby started quickly and headed into Duke Street. He went a few hundred yards before slowing to a trot. He began to sniff to the left and right, to double back and go again. Eventually, he stopped in the middle of the road.

"He's lost it," Abberline said, cursing.

"Hurry him along a bit and see if he picks up the scent again!" Swanson suggested.

We led him a hundred feet or so, but he only snuffled here and there, looking for a scent.

"Take him back to the last place he smelled anything," I said.

"No," Swanson insisted. "We should go forward to just beyond the next street and see if he locates the trail again."

"But suppose the Ripper turned in the next street? We should backtrack and start all over again, only more slowly."

"I suppose we could try another victim's trail—" I began.

"Gentlemen!" Barker growled over all of us. "I believe we must accept the fact that the trail has gone cold. It has rained several times since the double murders. The scent has likely washed away."

In spite of everything, we'd had our hopes dashed. Abberline made a few choice remarks not worth repeating.

"Thank you, Jarvis," Barker said to the handler. "A canny beast you have there. Too bad he cannot work miracles."

Barker bent and scratched the bloodhound under its floppy ear. It was glad of the attention.

"Good boy, Barnaby. Mind, sir, that he gets a hearty meal when you get home."

"At least he made the commissioner happy," Swanson said.

"There is an ABC in the next street," the Guv said. "I'll buy us each a cup of tea, then we can take a couple of hansoms back to 'A' Division."

The last I saw of Barnaby, he was going by in a cab a few moments later, wagging his long tail and enjoying the ride.

"So much for the canine squad," Abberline quipped over his tea. "At least our boots are safe."

# CHAPTER TWENTY-SIX

I was in the offices of Scotland Yard that afternoon, pinning photographs and sketches of the victims and suspects to a large cork
board under the Guv's direction, hoping we could come up with
some conclusions we hadn't found before. Barker was being, if not
downright finicky, then exact.

"No, no," he said. "Take them all down and put up the large
ordinance map of Whitechapel."

"Right," I said, exercising the patience I was getting so good at.

"Then put the photograph of each victim over the location
where their bodies were found."

I took a handful of map pins and soon had all four photographs
pinned in their locations.

"Got it."

"What have you got in your hand?" Barker asked.

"The photograph of Martha Tabrum, whose throat had been cut
earlier this year."

"Is she a genuine victim of the Whitechapel Killer?"

"I was waiting for you to tell me, sir. Some inspectors have speculated that he was practicing his craft, preparing for what would come later."

"Then why give up for six months after he'd had a taste of killing? It was successful, after all."

"If he was in fact the same killer as the one who slaughtered the other women. Then there's the torso found in New Scotland Yard. To be frank, I didn't know what to do with this sickening photograph."

"There's no need to hang it, lad. It's a different killer entirely and not in our jurisdiction."

"What do you mean?" I cried. "It happened right under our very nose."

"There are only two ways for the body to have been moved to the New Scotland Yard site: either it was carried in under the scrutiny of the guard, which I find difficult to believe, or it arrived by boat on the river. I believe that is a case for the Thames River Police. Scotland Yard will quibble, it being right in their own yard, but this is obviously a river case, since two of the missing limbs have been recovered there. I imagine the other missing limbs shall be found soon."

"And the head?"

"No, not the head. It's not difficult to bury a head, but a body is another matter. If the head is found, the victim could be identified and eventually tied to the killer. Of course, I'm speaking of a thinking criminal. If he is not, having disposed of a young woman for whatever foolish reason, he might have been equally foolish enough to throw the head into the Thames."

Barker was interrupted by someone speaking very loudly in the lobby. We stopped our conversation and listened.

"That voice sounds familiar to me," I said.

"Let us see who it is and what he wants," Barker suggested.

We walked down the corridor to the lobby. A man was arguing with the desk sergeant. He was demanding to see the commissioner, but Meadows was trying to assure him an inspector could answer all his problems. It was George Lusk, the head of the Mile End Vigilance Committee, the one who had tried to drive us off his patch.

"What seems to be the problem?" Barker asked.

For once, Lusk looked glad to see him, but he might merely have been glad to see a familiar face.

"Push," he said. "I've had a communication from the Ripper himself!"

"What's in the package?" my employer asked. Then I noticed a small box on the counter in front of Meadows. He seemed to be avoiding it as much as possible.

"Some sort of organ. Might be a bit of liver or kidney, I reckon."

Barker crossed and lifted the lid of the pasteboard box, which was wrapped in paper but had already been opened. He peered inside, pulled a pencil from his pocket, and used it to poke about at the object.

"It's part of a kidney. Probably human, by the size." He lifted the box to his nose and sniffed it. Right then, I decided not to have another kidney pie for at least a year or two. "Not fresh, but not preserved in spirits, either. As I recall, Catherine Eddowes was missing part of a kidney. Mr. Lusk, I suspect you have just won your audience with the commissioner. Sergeant Meadows, send word to DCIs Swanson and Abberline that there has been a new development in the case."

"Yes, sir."

"Come with me, Lusk."

"Have there been any changes in Whitechapel that you've noticed, Mr. Lusk?" Barker asked as they began to climb the staircase, the box tucked under my employer's arm. As I approached it, the box gave off a rancid odor, like spoiled meat. Exactly like spoiled meat.

"No changes, save that the Jews are having a time of it lately. By the way, I hope there's no ill will regarding our little disagreement the other week. I didn't know you were with the Yard. As you can see, we turn over any information we come across."

"It's your mansion, Mr. Lusk. You run it as you see fit."

Lusk visibly relaxed. "That's what we like about you, Push. You're fair-minded."

"Are the Jews continuing to have messages written about them?"

"They are. Someone's scribbling warnings all over the district. Everyone's talking about some sort of Jewish conspiracy."

We reached the commissioner's office. We were stopped by Warren's secretary, but when Lusk wordlessly held out the letter in his hand, he understood that something of importance had occurred. He stepped into his office, and in a moment Warren himself came to the door with Swanson in tow.

"Come in, gentlemen," he said. "What is your name, sir?"

"I am George Lusk, of the Mile End Vigilance Committee, Commissioner."

"May I see the note? How did you receive it?"

"It came to my home."

"Did you open it there?" Warren asked.

"I'm not a fool. It could be just about anything. I opened it in an alleyway outside of the office."

"When did you get it?"

"About an hour ago."

Commissioner Warren tapped the box with a fingernail. "Is this what it claims to be?"

"As near as I can tell, yes, sir," Barker replied.

Warren took the box, raised the lid and peered inside.

"S'truth," he said. "Do you suppose it is Eddowes's?"

"Not for certain. We'd have to get a surgeon to put the two pieces together, but Catherine Eddowes has already been interred."

"If it comes to that, she can be uninterred."

"After all the pomp and ceremony?" Swanson asked.

"The public need not know. Perhaps Dr. Brown took extensive notes, however, and can confirm or deny this bit of kidney without the need to see the body again. More likely it is a calf or pig's kidney, or a specimen from a medical establishment."

"The handwriting does not look the same as the first," Swanson said, and began to read the postal card out to us.

*From Hell*
*Mr. Lusk*
*Sor*

"Sor?" I asked.

"Do not interrupt," Barker said. "Continue."

*I send you half of the kidne I took from one women prasarved it*
*for you tother piece I fried and ate it was very nise I may send you*
*the bloody knif that took it out if you only wate a whil longer*
*Signed*
*Catch me when you can*
*Mishter Lusk*

"Addressed to?" Barker asked.

"Mr. Lusk, Head Vigilance Committee, Alderney-Street."

"He can spell 'vigilance' and 'committee,' but not 'nice' or 'mister,' " I noted.

"I am of the opinion that this letter was written by an educated man attempting to sound less literate for our benefit," Warren said.

"We'll examine the two cards together, sir," Abberline said.

The commissioner pointed at the box. "See that the specimen is examined. Take it to Golden Lane."

"We could find a closer medical man to examine the kidney," Abberline pointed out.

"No," Warren said. "I want Dr. Brown, the one who performed the postmortem on Catherine Eddowes."

"Yes, sir," I said, looking over at Barker. He nodded.

I moved down the halls of Scotland Yard, with all eyes on the box I held in my hands. I took it outside, and summoned a hansom in Whitehall Street, then took it into Whitechapel.

My thoughts were a jumble. It seemed to me that the two letters were not the work of the same man. The first was in red ink, the second in black. The first called himself "Jack the Ripper;" the second ended with a taunt, but was unsigned. Both inconsistently butchered the Queen's English. Barker claimed that any letters were fake and that the killer may be illiterate, but I was not as sure. The author of the second letter had an actual kidney, which would be very difficult to lay hands upon. Perhaps the real killer had been spurred to write after the first one, but if so, why not come up with a name for himself? It was all a puzzle.

Once in Whitechapel, I handed the box into Dr. Brown's eager fingers.

"Scotland Yard believes it could be the other half of Catherine Eddowes's kidney?" he asked.

"Yes, sir."

"We shall see."

He put sixpence into my hand, sixpence to partially defray the cost of the cab. Sixpence for my troubles. The rest would eventually be coming out of Anderson's pocket.

What if the box really did contain the other half of Catherine Eddowes's kidney? Then it truly was sent by the Ripper, and he wrote the threatening letters which had London in a panic. *What if Barker is wrong?* I asked myself. I relied on Cyrus Barker's opinions. It was unthinkable that he could be groping blindly in the dark like the rest of us.

# CHAPTER TWENTY-SEVEN

One evening when our shift at Scotland Yard Headquarters was finished, we went along Whitehall to the familiar narrow lane of Craig's Court and stepped into our offices. Jeremy Jenkins was gone for the day, having quitted our chambers promptly at five-thirty for the Rising Sun, but when I had turned on the electric lights, there was something waiting on Barker's desk: two large leather-bound commonplace books, side by side. Barker came around the edge of the mahogany desk and opened one.

The first contained articles from the *Times* and other reliable newspapers. Carefully pasted within were commentaries by statesmen and matter-of-fact accounts of what had occurred. The second contained illustrations from the *Police Gazette* and similar publications, speculations from often anonymous columnists of a lurid and imaginative nature, and comments from everyday citizens and the like. Barker settled into his chair and pulled the first book toward him. I took the second one to my desk, sitting in my comfortable old seat, and began to peruse Jenkins's handiwork.

One would think that having seen what we had seen and done what we had done over the past weeks, we would be weary of the case. We were, make no mistake. However, we were also driven to bring it to an end, and any step might bring him across our paths. Later, inspectors and constables would mention Jack the Ripper as a matter of course, but those of us who participated in the case were loath to speak his name. It seemed tempting fate merely to mention those three words.

I couldn't say what the Guv was reading but mine bordered on sheer hysteria. The Empire and every institution within it was crumbling because one man chose to kill four unfortunates in an insignificant part of the capital.

Everyone had a theory. It was the poor, the sailors, the Chinese, the Jews. It was lascars or secret societies, the Russians or the French, the Germans or the Irish. Anyone, of course, but a wholesome, clean-limbed Englishman. It was the foreign-looking fellow that lived down the street. We lived in a nation that offered itself as a haven for communists, socialists, and anarchists, but the citizenry looked likely to change its mind.

Barker spoke up, as if divining my thoughts. "If these newspaper accounts are to be believed, all London is terrified."

"Not just London," I said. "Here are responses from Scotland, France, and even America. Everyone seems to be holding their breath, waiting for us to catch the fellow."

"Then we cannot afford to make a mistake."

"Every woman feels unsafe, and every man seems angry and frustrated that he has not personally caught him."

"With the wonders of the modern steam engine, the killer might be hundreds of miles away in only a few hours, and could return the next day. He hasn't, I suspect, but he could. The possibility frightens everyone."

"The deeds and the letters seem almost demonic."

"Man requires no inspiration for hellishness, Thomas. He can be plenty evil on his own."

"What stops him, do you suppose? I mean, why does he not kill every night? Heaven forbid, of course, but you understand my question."

"I do," Barker admitted, "but I have no answer for you yet. I wish I did."

"A pity. I had a dozen other questions behind that one."

"Such as?"

"Is he married? Where does he live? Does he have an ordinary life in the day and hunt at night?"

"Is that all?"

"Far from it. Could there be something wrong with him, physically, which makes him do it? Has he had scraps with the law or is he otherwise a law-abiding citizen?"

"So many questions," Barker said.

"And so few answers. Do you think him a Jew?"

"No religion is proof against madmen. Not even Christianity."

"Some would say—"

"Let us not concern ourselves with what some would say," Barker said with a sniff.

I could name the number of times on two hands that I ran out the door or down the street at Barker's heels without the slightest idea where we were going or what we would find when we got there. In his mind, I suppose, I need merely be assured that he knew what he was about, and that I was just the assistant. Besides, I would probably have opinions, which would merely get in the way, or suggestions, such as taking a cab. After dinner at the Frying Pan, we were leaving the restaurant when a street Arab seized Barker's sleeve and whispered in his ear. He turned without preamble and began to run.

"Where are we headed?" I yelled after I had managed to get within earshot of my employer.

"The Drake!" he bellowed over his shoulder, and widened the gap between us again.

This was what he had been talking about when he suggested I memorize these streets. It was to know what was ahead of us, to anticipate which way an adversary might go, and the quickest way to hold him off or how to get to an address from where we were. It was the ability to think clearly and decisively on one's feet. The Drake Club was in Halifax Street, six streets away.

Something had happened there. What could it be? Was the Duke of Clarence there with his tutor? Had Stephen revealed who he was and attacked someone with a knife? One thing was certain. If I didn't hurry to catch up with my employer, I might be too late.

When I reached the old mansion that held the Drake Club, Barker was thumping on the door, which apparently was locked. Looking inside, I saw only a little light from within, far different from the brilliantly lit atmosphere of our former visit. I caught up with him just as the door opened and followed him inside.

Save for the butler who greeted us, the ground floor was deserted. It was a shambles. Furniture was overturned, vases smashed on the floor, pillows ripped open and sofas slashed. The carpet was covered in brown glass, stuffing, strewn flowers, and pampas grass. The butler was grim.

"Is the Countess in?" Barker asked.

"I'm not sure he is receiving visitors, sir."

"He sent for me," my employer replied, handing him the note.

"Very well. Come with me."

We followed him up the stair. The bannister had been broken. I assumed someone had gone over it to put it in such a ramshackle condition. When I was first brought here my eyes were assaulted by the strange admixture of fabric and objects brought together hap-hazardly. Now I was concerned that such an interesting arrangement had been destroyed. What had happened here this evening?

The butler led us into Inslip's room. He was sitting on a sofa in a pajama suit of pale silk which was marred with spatters of blood. He held a handkerchief to his nose and there was a purple bruise under one eye that looked recent. He turned his head and gazed at us out of the uninjured eye.

"Who did this?" Barker asked.

"Inspector Littlechild," he said.

My employer stopped to survey the room with his fists pressed into his hips. It was as badly demolished as the lobby had been. An orange tabby limped among the broken crockery and jumped onto the sofa beside its master.

"Were arrests made?"

"Oh, yes. I was able to get some of our clientele out the back door and away, while that monster and his pack of wolves tore my par-lor into pieces."

"Who was arrested, then?"

"All my beautiful young fillies."

"Your stable? All of them?"

It took me a minute to realize he was discussing the young, attractive men I had seen in the hall on our last visit.

"As far as I could tell. One or two of them might have been out of the building."

"Was it a regular raid?"

"Darling, don't browbeat me. I couldn't stand it at the moment. It was Littlechild and a squad of constables. That's all I know. I assume it was sanctioned by Scotland Yard."

"How did you manage to get released so quickly?"

"I have a very good solicitor. He's working on getting my girls freed. I hope for everyone's sake he succeeds, because if this goes to trial they will roll over like puppies wanting their tummies rubbed. They may look pretty and stupid, but they can recognize names."

"Names?"

"Oh, big names, Push, dear. Powerful men have powerful appetites. Government officials, admirals, clergy."

"That would not be good. I assume your father is hard at work this evening."

"He's probably bawling out Commissioner Warren as we speak. Littlechild will be fortunate if he is a dogcatcher by morning."

"I feel partially responsible for this, Henry. You see, I took over Littlechild's duties with the royal family. He must have felt he had to do something to put himself back in their good graces, such as closing down the establishment that corrupted the royal heir."

"'Corrupted' him," Inslip said. "I'm sure we didn't show him anything here he wasn't already familiar with."

"Will you be all right?"

"Oh, you know me, Cyrus. I'm almost used to this sort of thing by now. We may move but we won't go away. Gives me a chance to redecorate. The West Side next time, I think. Chelsea or Fitzrovia. Someplace posh. I'll miss Jack, you know. He's made the district interesting, but it's probably for the best if we keep our heads down for a little while."

"Mr. Barker and I are sorry we could not have been on hand when your property was damaged," I said.

"So, your lad does have a voice," the Duchess said. "Thank you,

Mr. Llewelyn. We're like cats, you know. We always land on our feet. More of Daddy's fortune will be spent, but he doesn't mind. Oh, he'll grouse, of course, but he has long since given up the notion that I can change my spots."

Just then a table gave way under the weight of a lamp and they fell to the ground with a clatter. We all stared at it, including the cat, which Inslip was stroking.

"I'm being a bad host," he went on. "They confiscated all the good cigars and the whisky, but I don't believe they found the wine cellar. I could have Pigeon bring up some champagne."

"None for us, thank you. Don't open a bottle on our account."

Our host pulled the cat up into his lap and held it. I speculated that he was completely overwrought, frightened and angry, but was doing his best to appear composed. Everything he had built had been destroyed.

"What have you been charged with?" Barker asked.

"Running a bawdy house, but they cannot possibly prove it. You see, this is really just a club. I rented rooms a few streets away for accommodations, shall we say? The Yard doesn't know about them yet. The first thing I did when I got back was to cancel the lease. There is nothing to connect me with it on paper."

"Clever, I'll grant you that."

"It is trial and error here. I am responsible for my people."

"So, what services did the Drake Club offer?" I asked.

"We had a grill, dining room, and smoking lounge. We offered drinks and had a game room for billiards and whist. Another room had a small stage for performances—*tableaux vivants* and the like, often bawdy, but then this was a private club. The real purpose, however, was to show men that there were others like them here in London. We introduced them one to another, encouraged them to mingle. It was not my intent to run a bawdy house."

"You will build again, I am sure," Barker murmured.

"I will. I intend to. For tonight, however, I shall mourn the Drake Club, and plot deviltries against Inspector Littlechild. He will regret what he did here tonight for the rest of his life."

Barker reached forward and scratched the cat's forehead. It stretched its neck out for the attention.

"We shall take our leave, then."

"If you see Philippa soon, give her my love."

We made our way gingerly down the staircase, and the butler saw us out.

"That's the second time he mentioned Mrs. Ashleigh," I said to the Guv. "How does he know her?"

"He is her cousin. His father, the Earl of Sanditon, is in the House of Lords, and on the Board of Commission for Scotland Yard. I suppose we should probably call the Countess 'His Lordship,' but he eschews such titles."

"My word," I said. "Did Littlechild know he was assaulting a peer?"

"Probably not. He was trying to improve his relationship with the royal family by destroying a temptation to the Duke of Clarence."

We wandered through the streets deep in thought.

"The way he spoke, he acted as if men who are only interested in other men are like an ethnic minority, like the Jews or Chinese."

He did not respond. We walked along, me with my hands in my pockets, which Barker doesn't like, and he with his clasped behind him. I shook my head.

"You have a problem?"

"I do. I know such things exist, in boarding schools and such, but I was not aware it was on such a scale. Are the men who visited the Drake Club married or bachelors?"

"Both, I assume."

"So they are hiding their private interests?"

"Of course. They are illegal and condemned by the church. But as Henry said, one cannot change one's spots. They did not visit the Drake Club out of some need for excitement, as one goes on a night of gambling and carousing. They go to meet others of their kind and feel as if they are not alone."

"That must be wretched for them," I said.

"It is," Barker admitted. "For some time, I searched the scriptures for such passages as might apply. In the end, I decided it wasn't my place to tell another human being how to live his life."

"I see."

"Within reason, of course. Do take your hands out of your pockets, Mr. Llewelyn."

# CHAPTER TWENTY-EIGHT

The following morning, the seventeenth of October, we were to return to the palace. So far we had twice been unable to see or speak to Mr. James K. Stephen, and my employer felt he could neither confirm nor deny a connection to the so-called Ripper without a conversation with him. Sir Henry Ponsonby was able to get us an appointment during one of their tutorials.

"Didn't Sir Henry say the duke was twenty-four?" I asked as our cab neared Buckingham Palace. "That's an advanced age to require a tutor."

"I gather His Highness is a lackadaisical student, and I'm certain there must be a great deal of preparation if he is to eventually become king."

"I wonder that they don't sack the fellow, Stephen. Men have been sacked for less. Do you suppose the duke has any say in the matter?"

"Let us withhold judgment on that score until we've spoken to Stephen, shall we?"

I don't know what I was expecting when James Stephen entered the room, but the man himself was a surprise. He was tall, broad shouldered, handsome in a square-jawed, athletic way. He had a head of blond curls a matinee idol would envy, and brown skin from lying in the sun. His eyes were blue, and when he spoke it was in an Old Etonian drawl.

"What can I do for you, gentlemen?"

"Mr. Stephen, we are working for Scotland Yard on the White-chapel case."

Stephen sat down on a divan as if the palace belonged to him. "I assume you want to know where I was on the night of the last murders," he said.

"No, sir. We know very well where you were that evening. You were at the Drake Club."

"I don't know what you're talking about. I was here that evening."

"I could provide the name of the man, or rather the boy, with whom you spent the evening."

"That's a damnable lie, and slanderous, Mr.—"

"Barker," the Guv said. "Cyrus Barker."

"I shall remember that, Mr. Barker. My father is a chief justice."

My employer smiled tolerantly. "I know that, Mr. Stephen. In fact, there is very little about you that I do not know. For example, I know you prefer a cocktail made from champagne and stout, and you have cigarettes made for you especially from Astley's."

"Obviously, you've been talking to the staff at the Drake," Stephen said. "What exactly is it that you want?"

"Let me see if I understand this correctly, sir. You were hired as the Duke of Clarence's tutor, based upon your excellent student record. Since then, you and His Highness have become . . . close."

"Be careful," the tutor warned.

"I shall. The royal family has not been told of your friendship, because if they had, you would be sacked. They would forbid you from ever seeing the heir again. However, were that the case, you might reveal to the press not only your relationship, but also the fact that many on the staff here at Buckingham Palace share the same tastes you do. It would cause a major scandal. Therefore, Sir Henry is on the horns of a dilemma."

"Look, Barker, what do you want? I must get back to my lesson."

"Discretion, Mr. Stephen. I want discretion. You know the Drake has an unsavory reputation, yet you took His Highness there more than once. The press might not write about it yet, but they have eyes and ears and they stay up late if there is a story to write about."

Stephen looked down and I saw a resigned smile on his lips. He shook his head.

"You don't understand," he said. "I did take Eddy to the Drake once, to show him what it was like. Unfortunately, he liked it. I'm not responsible for every decision he makes. He does as he pleases. My control over him is limited."

"I understand His Highness is all but engaged to be married," I spoke up. "How does he feel about that?"

"We've talked about it extensively. While he has no interest in Princess Alix, he understands his duties as the heir to the British throne. He is willing to go through with them provided the princess agrees to give him certain liberties and separate rooms. I think she will. She appears to be a docile little thing. Goodness knows Eddy won't be the first English monarch with an interest in men."

"Sir Henry might have other ideas about the matter."

"Poor Ponsy. I'm afraid we've given him a hard time of it. I wouldn't envy him having to tell Prince Albert, who has bagged more ingénues than a Sandringham hunting party, that his son, the product of his loins, is a poof."

"You really cannot control him?" Barker asked.

"I'm trying. You must understand. When a young man has certain feelings and believes he is the only one in the world to have them, and then he discovers there are others like him, he wants, he needs to speak with them, to share company with them, and learn from them. He wants to have the freedom to be himself."

"Does he want to be the royal heir?"

"Not especially. I think Eddy loves his grandmother, but after she passes on and his father, a known womanizer, is on the throne, perhaps morals will ease and he might step down from his duties."

"You said he was willing to undertake his duties," Barker said.

"Yes, I did. And he is, but you cannot blame him for hoping it might not come to that. He's confused right now. Who wouldn't be in his situation? But I know Eddy better than anyone in the world. He'll do the right thing."

Barker sat farther back in the seat, but not all the way. We were in Buckingham Palace, after all.

"Have you and the duke been traveling around Whitechapel?"

"Oh, rather, yes. He's needed to get out of the palace."

"So, you've been to the Drake. Where else?"

"There are one or two other establishments, not as nice as the Drake. Public houses where gentlemen alone are welcome. We've been to a few music halls that are daring. And, of course, we've just driven around. His Highness is very interested in the Ripper case. We've been to all the spots where the women were found."

"In what sort of vehicle have you been traveling?"

"A closed coach."

"What of the royal seal on the sides?"

"Don't take us for total fools, Barker. We covered them."

"And what did you wear on these excursions?"

"Evening kit, of course. Capes and top hats. We are gentlemen."

Now it was Barker's turn to shake his head. I began to speculate myself. If the people of Whitechapel saw a strange coach with all its emblems covered, and a flamboyantly dressed gentleman in the same areas as Jack the Ripper, it would be a small matter for them to believe them one and the same. The Ripper was like a hermit crab, gluing bits of legend to his shell. Suddenly, the killer is an aristocrat, who does his killing in a coach and wears a cape and topper. Jack is a toff.

I was thinking of my next question when a door opened and a young man strolled in.

"James, I finished my essay . . . Oh."

Barker and I rose automatically. It was the correct thing to do in the presence of the Duke of Clarence. He was in his shirtsleeves and a silvery waistcoat with a cobalt blue tie fastened with a large pearl. He was of slight build, with pomaded brown hair, a small waxed mustache, and eyes like fried eggs. They were impossibly white with pale blue irises. The only other man I had ever seen with eyes like that was Oscar Wilde.

"Your Highness, these gentlemen are from Scotland Yard."

Those eyes, so placid, seemed to harden and catch fire. "Oh, really? And what do they want?"

"They were concerned that with our recent visits to Whitechapel, we might place ourselves in danger."

"There is a good deal of unrest there at the moment, Your Highness," Barker said. "A band of vigilantes has taken over the area."

"Someone threw eggs and vegetables at our carriage on our last visit. Do you recall that, James?"

"Of course. They claim they are starving there, yet they throw enough for a good meal at a passing carriage."

"So, tell me, Mr.—"

"Inspector Barker, sir."

"Tell me, Inspector Barker, how is the Ripper investigation coming along?"

"Well enough, Your Highness. We certainly have enough men on it at the moment."

"Are there any promising leads? That is the proper phrase, is it not?"

"It is. I understand you and Mr. Stephen have become quite the sleuthhounds."

"We have driven around the East End on a few occasions, yes," the duke said. "Have you heard that my father once walked about the East End dressed as a workman to see how the lower classes live?"

"I had not, Your Highness. That is very forward thinking of him."

"Is it not? James tells me that Siddhartha Buddha did the same thing."

"So I understand."

"You know the Buddha?"

"I grew up in China, sir."

"You're not the common chappie I would expect from Scotland Yard."

"I am a special inspector, Your Highness, brought in by the new assistant commissioner, Robert Anderson."

"The more the merrier, eh?"

"I have experience tracking men."

"Why are you here, perchance?"

"He came to ask me about the vehicle we were traveling in," Stephen told him.

"I was not speaking to you, James. I was speaking to the inspector," the duke said.

That must have hurt, I thought. Now I understood what he meant when he said he could not control the duke.

"We wanted to be certain that the coach we saw in Whitechapel was yours. There are many who claim this killer commutes from the West End."

"Are we suspects?"

"Well, sir, sometimes it is difficult to separate the fox from the hounds."

"How so?" the Duke of Clarence asked.

It occurred to me then that one wrong word from Barker's lips and we would be off this case and in serious trouble. I looked at him, wondering what he would say next, but then I never could guess what he'd say next.

"The easiest way to find the killer is to eliminate as many people as possible. In the beginning, everyone is a suspect. Your being in the area now and then made both of you 'persons of interest,' but having satisfied my concerns, I feel safe to say that neither of you are the man we are looking for."

"Were we suspects, then?"

"Yes, Your Highness, you were."

The heir broke into a smile. "Good! Excellent! I'd like to think I had done something to concern Scotland Yard at least once in my life. I've spent most of it trying unsuccessfully to impress my father and grandmother. Let them worry for a while."

"We've had Sir Henry worried," Stephen said.

"Old Ponsy would worry if there was a crack in my morning egg. He worries about all sorts of things that he cannot control."

*And you're certainly one of them*, I thought.

"You are taking your time in tracking down the fellow," the duke went on.

"Tell me, Your Highness," Barker said. "You've had the advantage of seeing all there is to see. Is there any person, or type of persons, or any place you think might be of interest to Scotland Yard?"

"There is," he said, as if glad to tell us where we'd gone wrong. "The sailors. They carry knives, they frequent prostitutes, and they are often foreign and hot-tempered."

"Because you have suggested it, I promise I shall look into the matter thoroughly. I'll relay the message to 'A' Division and see if we can't investigate them."

The royal's soft-boiled eyes glittered. "Really?"

"Of course. As you say, the two of you have investigated the matter. We take your opinion seriously."

The duke looked stunned. He looked as if no one had taken his opinion seriously in his entire life. For all I knew, no one had. "Thank you."

"We must get back to our lessons," Stephen said.

We all rose.

"It was a pleasure to meet you, sir," my employer said.

The prince nodded and left. Stephen put his hands on his knees and pushed himself into a standing position. He raised an eyebrow as if to say, "You see what I have to deal with?"

"Can you gentlemen see your way out?"

"We can."

"Do you really intend to look into the matter of the sailors?"

"We have plenty of constables milling about in the East End. It would not hurt to investigate the docks more thoroughly."

"Thank you. Am I still a suspect?"

"You are and shall remain one until this killer is caught. If you are not guilty, you've nothing to worry about."

"Ah."

"James!" the duke called.

"Coming!" the tutor replied, and with a final glance our way, hurried to the door.

"What now?" I asked the Guv.

"We report to Sir Henry that the duke and his tutor are no longer viable suspects in the case."

"But you just told Stephen he is still a suspect."

"Just because someone has an alibi doesn't mean I don't suspect them. Alibis can occasionally be got round."

"Can anyone at the Drake Club be trusted, as far as being able to claim Stephen was there at a certain time?"

"Aye. Pigeon."

"Pigeon?"

"The butler. Henry Inslip occasionally refers to him as his conscience. He's an old retainer of the family. Honest to a fault. Not that one could find fault with honesty."

# CHAPTER TWENTY-NINE

A fter we returned from the palace, Cyrus Barker led me back to the Frying Pan again without so much as a word, and ordered a shepherd's pie and some chips to be washed down with bitter. The pie was very good, or maybe I was just tired and hungry.

"You look in a proper mood. What are you thinking?" I asked.

In answer, Barker tugged a small, ripped envelope from his pocket and handed it to me. I could almost see his eyes glittering behind his spectacles. It was a common envelope, but no penny stamp was affixed to it. It had not been posted. Had it been delivered by messenger, perhaps? I pulled out a piece of foolscap and regarded the letter, which had been written in red ink.

*Dear Push,*
*here you have thrown in your lot with Scotland Yard. Don't rightly care what bloodhounds nip at my heels I'm having too much fun ripping whores. I'll get another one before first snow. don't count yourself smarter than a common peeler*

*Catch-me-if-you-can.*
*P.S. Try the kidne pie Ha ha*

Carefully, I put it back in the envelope and returned it to the Guv. "Where did this come from?"

"It was shoved under the door of our room overnight. Do you think you can dissect the letter for me?"

I would rather have sat back and ordered another pint, but I knew that wasn't going to happen. I suppressed a sigh and took the letter out of the envelope again and stared at it. Taking a final swallow of my tepid ale, I wiped my mouth and began to speak.

"First of all, he knew who you are, and that you were staying here. I suppose that's not surprising the way word travels around here. Also, we have not gone out of our way to disguise our presence in the area. There has to be some curiosity about us, as Mr. Lusk and his vigilantes knew all about us. I would speculate that this makes our work more difficult, since he will be able to recognize us, while we won't recognize him."

"Continue," Barker said.

"He's not afraid of you, which means he's either as good as he thinks he is, or else very stupid. Or he's trying to put up a brave front and convince himself. The fact that he's addressing you is a sign you have attracted his attention, for all his claims."

"Mmph."

"The 'ripping whores,' the 'catch-me-if-you-can,' those are cadged from a previous letter. This one hasn't called himself Jack the Ripper, either. The mention of the kidney pie is his way of saying he was here at some point, eating and drinking while we were walking Whitechapel. He intends to demoralize us by claiming he was under our very noses."

"To some degree," Barker said. "Nearly all correspondence between criminals and their hunters is bravura. He is boasting that I cannot catch him. Or rather, that I cannot catch the Whitechapel Killer, for whoever wrote this is patently not him."

"On what evidence do you base this?"

"Logic," Barker said. "A syllogism: most people in Whitechapel are illiterate, the Whitechapel Killer lives in Whitechapel, therefore the Whitechapel Killer is illiterate, and therefore cannot have written that note."

"What of this?" I asked. "The Whitechapel Killer is literate, only Jewish people in Whitechapel are literate, therefore the Whitechapel Killer is Jewish."

"Do you believe the killer is Jewish?" the Guv asked.

"On the one hand I agree he lives here in the area, as you have maintained, but he must be very savvy in order to have survived so long as a free man. He is intelligent, even educated. Where else can such a person be found in the East End besides the Jewish quarter?"

"It runs counter to my theory, but I do not dislike it," Barker admitted.

"Did I get it right?"

"I'm sorry, but this is not an agricultural fair. You do not win a blue ribbon for occasionally deducing a plausible idea."

"Double or nothing."

"Rascal," he said, and swatted at me with his hat. I dodged from the would-be blow.

"As a matter of fact, I cannot claim the Ripper is Jewish until I've reached a few conclusions," I stated.

"Such as?"

"Are the Jews covering up for him? I have a difficult time believing a man can inflict such damage all by himself. People have friends, relations. Whitechapel is densely populated. Surely someone will spot him eventually. Or already has."

"He is taking a terrible risk each time, murdering women for sport, or worse, unless perhaps part of it is the chance of getting caught. He likes danger."

"I wonder if there are odds among the bookies concerning the Ripper, if and when he will strike again."

"I can just about guarantee it," the Guv said.

I pinched the letter between my fingers, feeling the crisp paper. "I imagine they would love to see this."

He took the letter and envelope. "That they never shall."

"Have you shown this to Scotland Yard yet?"

He tucked it back in his pocket. "It's addressed to me. They have several of their own. Besides, it doesn't say 'Jack the Ripper.' It could be from anyone."

"Anyone that 'rips whores' and is being pursued by Scotland Yard."

"Perhaps," he said.

"Do you think the duke or his tutor, or both of them together, is the man for whom we are looking?"

"Frankly, no, I do not. The Duke of Clarence has been in Scotland until yesterday, so Sir Henry has informed me, and Stephen has been watched very closely. He was in the palace during the double event."

"So going there has been a complete waste of time," I cried.

"It was necessary to eliminate them both as suspects."

"So many wasted hours. And visits to the Drake Club. Unnecessary!"

"It's worse than that, Thomas. We have been manipulated from the very beginning. Where do you suppose this came from?"

So saying, Barker reached into his pocket and removed the Royal Command.

"From Robert Anderson."

Barker's mustache spread out in a smile. "Robert has no connection to the palace. Who do you suppose gave it to him?"

"I don't know. Who?"

"One of three men, all of them working on the same side: Inspector Littlechild, the home secretary, or James Munro."

"Then Anderson was working for them!"

"Not necessarily. When it was offered to him he had no reason to assume it was being used against us. He thought it might be helpful. And it has been, to some extent."

"Then why were we given it?"

"To embroil us in this possible royal scandal, which I'm sure Munro has known about for months. To slow us down."

"The duke and Stephen really had nothing to do with the killings?"

"Nothing save the same morbid curiosity you and your friend Zangwill displayed."

I took a gulp of my ale and slammed it down on the table more heavily than I had intended.

"Who else?" I asked. "Who else is working for Munro? Swanson?"

"Of course. He is closely watching his chief suspect, the man Munro believes is the killer."

I snapped my fingers. "It's Druitt. That's the fellow's name."

"Exactly."

"We never saw his file."

"You never did. I may have strolled into his office once when he was out of the building."

"Through a locked door, no doubt."

"There is no locked door for a man with skills, Thomas."

I smiled. "So, what is it with this Druitt fellow?"

"He's a teacher and a barrister, studying for the bar. Almost as brilliant a scholar as Stephen. But there is madness in the family. In Montague Druitt's case it is hereditary. His mother was institutionalized, and his father was a drunkard. This past year he has been subject to bouts of depression and lapses of memory. Not to draw out the story too much, his family believes he is the killer, and he himself suspects it."

"That's it, then. If they have the case in their pocket, we have no way to solve it."

"Not necessarily, lad. He may be convinced he is the Whitechapel Killer, but he hasn't convinced me."

"Why not?" I asked.

"The man has no knowledge of Whitechapel. I suspect the killer has a knowledge of the area that is greater than our own, we who have walked the streets every night. It's how he appears and disappears so quickly."

"Then who is it?"

"Someone we haven't considered well enough. We must start over."

"Back to the beginning."

"Don't sound so dispirited. The beginning is always a good place to start."

"We're back at the beginning, and everyone is in Munro's pocket: Littlechild, Matthews, Swanson, the palace—"

"Bulling."

"The reporter?"

"Who do you think told him we had shut our doors and joined with Scotland Yard?"

"Who else?"

"Lusk. He tried to stop us not long after Bulling was not successful in warning us away."

"I suppose at least half of Scotland Yard would like us to fail to track the killer."

"At least that, Thomas. The rest would rather their own find him, rather than a 'special inspector' and his constable."

"It's just you and me, then," I said.

"Of course."

"Against everybody."

"Aye."

"Marvelous."

"Isn't it? That's the way all our cases are, Thomas. You and me, tracking down our quarry. Truth to tell, I prefer it that way."

# CHAPTER THIRTY

We began our nightly tour of the 'Chapel, and I was glad to say nothing of any import occurred. No one threatened or harassed us, or harassed anyone else, for that matter. No windows were broken in any Jewish establishments that evening. However, when we returned to our rooms, there was a new envelope on the floor, having been slipped under the door, and it was addressed to me.

"Do I get my own letter from the Ripper?" I asked, picking it up.

"It looks to be better paper than mine," the Guv remarked.

I opened it. It was written in a formal hand on buff paper.

"It's just an address. And a time. Two o'clock tomorrow afternoon."

Barker examined the note. "A feminine hand, and an appointment during calling hours."

"What do I do?" I asked.

"Attend, obviously."

"Without you?"

"I don't expect you shall be in any mortal danger."

"I hope not. One never knows with women."

I arrived at number 37 Cornhill Street a trifle early and reconnoitered the area as is my usual habit, but doing my best to calm the butterflies in my stomach. This could be anything or nothing, I knew, from a prospective client to a person with a clue about the killings, but I was certain it was from *Her*. She had recognized me at the Lyceum, and wished to speak to me. Was this her home? It was possible that Asher Cowen, the MP, might have some kind of abode here in his district, among his people. A moment's thought convinced me otherwise. Certainly a woman would not invite a former suitor to her own home. Not in front of the servants. It would be indiscreet.

Not content with my stomach, my heart began to flutter as well. I could see the news in the morning's paper: suitor found dead in front of woman's home, alleged heart attack. No, make that "dies of a broken heart." I pulled my watch from the pocket of my trousers by the chain, a terrible way to treat a timepiece, and checked the time. It was one minute until the hour. Not allowing myself to be early, I waited the full minute, then walked up to a glossy black door set in a prosperous-looking limestone wall and tapped upon the knocker. A few seconds later the door was opened. I held my breath.

A woman stood there holding the door, who looked too young and prosperous to be a servant. I deduced the house belonged to her. She was in her late twenties, with dark hair, olive skin, and sardonic eyes. One eyebrow was raised as she inspected me. I removed my hat.

"I suppose you had better come in," she said.

"I am Thomas Llewelyn."

"I know who you are. And you're not Jewish at all? Remarkable."

"I am part of a plainclothes squad for Scotland Yard," I explained, which was not technically true but was the easiest way to explain it. "Pray forgive the attire."

"When I was asked to host this little rendezvous I was dead set against it, but I was promised you would do nothing that might damage anyone's reputation."

"That is the last thing I should want to do."

"You are well spoken. I shall give you that."

Then a voice came from another room, a voice that made my heart skip a beat. "Ouida, is he here?"

The woman smiled at her friend's impatience. "He is."

"Bring him in, then. Do not interrogate him in the front hall."

"Come along, Mr. Llewelyn. Your Juliet awaits."

I followed her, hearing my footsteps inordinately loud in the hall and noticing the scuffs on the toes of my shoes. Oh, that I had appeared in the best my wardrobe could provide. The hall was well decorated with thick carpets and small paintings on the way. Palm fronds were arranged in a large pot. I entered some sort of parlor and I cannot recall anything there, because my eyes were full of her. She rose as I entered, and nodded toward her friend. We would have our privacy, within reason. There were no doors, and I knew it likely Ouida would stay within earshot.

She had become a woman now, Rebecca Mocatta Cowen. Mrs. Asher Cowen, the wife of a man of substance. Her parents must have been very proud. She had married well and in short order would produce offspring to polish the escutcheon on the family shield.

"Thomas," she murmured.

I felt something like an electric current go right up my spine.

"Pray forgive my attire," I said. "I am working."

"Oh, Thomas, why did you never come to call? I could have got round Mother's objections eventually, you know."

"It wasn't your mother. She was only doing what was best for her family. Rather, it was your father. He was very kind, but I understood it would break his heart for his daughter to marry outside of the faith. I could see that he cared very deeply for you."

"Yes, I'm afraid I am his favorite. You missed all the arguments. Mother sensed you were hovering nearby and set her plans in motion. Asher began courting me within a week. There were histrionics all over the house. I refused to marry him. Mama slapped me, and I went on a hunger binge. I was going to die for love, for love of you, Thomas, if you must know. A girlish fancy. But you never called or came again. I waited and waited, and made Asher wait with me a full six months before I finally agreed to marry him. You were rather cruel, not to mention ungallant."

"Yes," I muttered. "I'm afraid I was."

"I wanted to tell you that. I did nothing to warrant such treatment. Perhaps, I thought, you might explain yourself to me someday, so that I could extinguish the torch I've been carrying and get on with my life. Then I saw you in the theater the other day and I recognized you immediately."

I nodded. I didn't trust my voice.

"We were together five minutes, perhaps ten. You did not kiss me or pledge your troth, yet I dream about our conversation every day."

"As do I," I managed to say. My throat was dry.

Her dark eyes widened. "You do? This is not in jest?"

"I felt as strongly as you, and still feel the same way. Probably, I always shall."

"Five minutes," she said.

"Five minutes."

It was during my first case as Cyrus Barker's assistant. He was trying to introduce me to Jewish culture in order to instill in me the need to protect the Chosen People, and so he hired me as a *shabbes goy* for the Rabbi Mocatta, lighting the candles and fires forbidden to a Jew on the sabbath. No one had expected a spark to ignite between Rebecca and me. She stole down from her room and we had talked. Five minutes, no more. But that is all it takes, I suppose.

"I was warned off," I explained. "Not by your mother or father, but by my employer. My occupation pays very well, but there are inherent risks in this profession. A day or two after our encounter I was in hospital. I've been there three times since. I've been injured a dozen times. Shot, stabbed, beaten. I was blown off a bridge once. This is no occupation for a married man, Rebecca."

"Then why didn't you just change positions?" she asked, just like that, with all her feminine logic behind it. So sensible.

"I don't know if I can explain it. Working for the Guv, for Mr. Barker. It's not just a situation, it is more like a crusade. He only takes cases that genuinely matter. He—we—protected the Jews from a pogrom last time. It's very possible we may do so again over this Ripper business."

"Is it really as dangerous as all that?" she asked.

"The last fellow who had my position died. Murdered, floating in the Thames."

"But surely some other fellow could do the work. My father has connections in the City. I'm sure he could find a suitable position for you, clerking in an office somewhere."

I shook my head. "You don't really know me, Rebecca. I am a widower. That is, I was when you met me. I did eight months in Oxford Prison for theft. I needed to buy her medicine. You're wasting your time and concern on someone who is unworthy of it. Perhaps it would be best if you just forgot about me. It would be better for everyone all around."

Then she came forward, and before I could do anything, she took my hand in hers. They were warm and soothing like the balm of Gilead.

"That I will never do, Thomas. You cannot tell a heart to do anything, don't you know that by now? Mother has tried. Father has tried. Goodness knows, Asher has tried. He heard about my secret heartache. He has tried his best to make me forget you."

We sat down side by side, and I took both her hands in mine.

"Is he a good husband?" I asked. "Is he attentive? Does he love you?"

She squeezed her eyes together and looked away. When she looked back, her jaw was set.

"My marriage is a masquerade," she said. "He acquired me the way one purchases a vase from Japan and puts it high on a shelf to admire. Asher keeps a mistress in Islington and occasionally visits a house for low women. One can smell cheap perfume on his clothes when he returns. He . . . he has an illness our physician is treating him for and we cannot start a family until he is well again. Of course, I stand by his side when he makes speeches and attends dinners. Frankly, they are a bit of a bore, but I must tolerate them so he can rise to whatever position he has set his eye on next. He hopes to be prime minister one day, the first openly Jewish one, he says, since Disraeli was baptized as an Anglican."

"I'm so sorry," I finally said.

"It sounds so terrible, but it's not as bad as that. I'm alone much of the time, with the servants. Sometimes Mama comes to see me, or my sister, or Ouida, who is my closest friend since Amy died. You knew Amy Levy, did you not?"

"Yes. I'm friends with Israel Zangwill, if you recall."

"Oh, that's right. He mentioned your name to me."

I leaned forward and looked at her in earnest. "See here," I said. "If you are in an intolerable situation, you have but to say the word and Barker and I will help you leave. We can put you in the Carlton Hotel for a couple of days, until you decide what you want to do from there."

She laughed. I'd have liked to hear her laughing but not that way. There was a trace of bitterness in it.

"I cannot say I love him, but he is my husband and I should try to make him a proper wife. I don't know what to say, Thomas, save that between us, we've made a horrible mess of things. If somehow it were miraculously repaired, what then? I presume you will not leave your position, nor will you marry me while you work for Mr. Barker."

"You are right. We have made a hash of it. But we do have one tool we can use."

She looked up into my eyes. I could sit beside her and stare into those dark, lusterful orbs for the rest of my life.

"And that is?"

"Cyrus Barker himself. He's awfully good at advice. He's the wisest person I know. He prays over things and thinks them over before reaching a conclusion, which is generally the right one."

"You understand," Rebecca said, "that I cannot leave Asher. He needs me to support him and his career. Whether he is an ideal husband to me, I shall certainly try to be an ideal wife to him."

I took her hand again.

"I would not have it any other way," I said.

Just then, Ouida returned with a tray of tea. It was another example of how the beverage was used in England, to smooth over awkward situations. She sat down across from us, one part friend and three parts chaperone, and began to pour.

"You have a lovely house," I said to my hostess.

"Thank you. Mrs. Cowen tells me you are some kind of detective."

"Private enquiry agent, actually."

"And how does one become a private enquiry agent?"

"Oh, the usual way, you know. I began at university."

"Which one?" she asked. She was sharp, but not disposed to hate me. Not yet, anyway.

"Oxford. Magdalen."

"Did you know Oscar Wilde?"

"He was a senior boy while I was in my first year. We met once or twice. I'm not sure if he'd remember my name."

We talked of this and that, while she probed me the way a surgeon probes, with a sharp scalpel. The patient found it painless enough; anything to sit beside Rebecca for a few more minutes. Finally, she said the words I dreaded to hear.

"It was so nice to have you come."

I stood and bowed gravely. "Thank you for inviting me. One so rarely gets a glimpse into these old houses of the City. Whenever I pass by, I shall remember this afternoon and these beautiful rooms."

I turned and took Rebecca's hand. I could feel it trembling.

"Mrs. Cowen, I am delighted to make your acquaintance again. I shall look forward to speaking with you at a later date. I must be away now. I am sorely busy. It was charming to take tea and renew old acquaintances. Good afternoon, ladies!"

I turned and left the room. Finding my hat in a seat by the front door, I stepped out and resisted the urge to lean against the frame and breathe like a fish that had been thrown onto dry land. What a mess. What a bloody mess.

Had I done something, anything, when Rebecca and I had first met, it might have changed the outcome somehow. But I did nothing, leaving her to struggle along against the machinations of her parents and the odious Mr. Cowen. Very well, he wasn't odious. I didn't know that for a fact. But he was an idiot. A mistress, when the loveliest girl in the world was at his beck and call? Could such a man appreciate her? No, a thousand times, no. The real me, the natural me, the one I had been when I first met Rebecca, might have stolen her away without blinking an eye. However, I had been changed by working with Cyrus Barker. As much as I loved her, she was Cowen's, and I had no right to take her, even if he did not appreciate her. If he beat her or mistreated her outright, certainly, but there seemed limited evidence of it. She had grounds for adultery, but not everyone will make such a claim against their husband, and thereby ruin her own good name. I must give it some thought. Much thought, in fact. That, and I should consult Cyrus Barker about the matter.

Which would be the ideal time? That evening, when we walked Whitechapel together. Provided the Ripper didn't strike again, we would have the entire evening for a full airing of events, past and present, concerning Rebecca Cowen, née Mocatta. If I had the courage.

# CHAPTER THIRTY-ONE

When we returned to Scotland Yard, we learned that Robert Anderson was back from his enforced holiday and was in the building. Knowing that he would have a good amount of work to do, including being brought up to speed by Commissioner Warren himself, Barker thought it prudent to wait until we were called in to see him

"What are you going to say to him?" I asked.

"I haven't decided. I'll see what he has to say to me first."

"And if he doesn't say anything regarding Munro, what then?"

"Then we'll know he has a reason for hiding it, and shall need to uncover it."

"Why not just ask him outright?"

"What?" the Guv asked. "Club him over the head while he reads his mail? We've been friends for several years. I should think he deserves better treatment than that."

"Have it your way, then."

"Oh, I intend to."

After an hour or so, during which Barker studied the latest suspect file, we were finally called into Anderson's office.

"Ah, gentlemen," he said from the depths of his chair.

The color had returned to his cheeks, and though he didn't exactly look five and twenty, he looked a world better than when we saw him last and he had brought us into this case, possibly the biggest in Yard history.

"You are looking well, Robert," Barker said.

"I feel better. When I reached Switzerland, I slept for most of a week. Then I was ravenous and my wife was hard-pressed to feed me, and finally my strength returned and I spent much of the time walking in the cool Alpine air. It restored my health and I believe my spirits, as well. She'll tell you I was a trial as a patient, and frankly, I was. My doctor informs me that had I continued as I was, I'd have collapsed within a fortnight. But what news when I returned!"

"You did not get the newspapers in Switzerland?"

"My wife would not allow them. 'They'll only upset you,' she kept saying. Two more murders by this Whitechapel Killer while I was gone! I had no idea he would continue to attack unfortunates in the East End. Forgive me if you have been asked to do too much. I had anticipated that you would have a dull caseload in my absence, but this! It beats all, as they say."

"It has been very interesting," Barker said.

"And I suppose you have managed to be in the thick of it."

"Well, the lad and I have taken rooms in a public house in the Commercial Road and have patrolled Whitechapel every night."

"More work? I suppose, Mr. Llewelyn, that he has taken advantage and made you work round the clock."

"Frankly, sir, I was keen as Colman's myself to track down the fellow, especially after two in one night. The man's a devil, I tell you."

"Then I'm glad I did not miss his capture while I was in Switzerland. I'd have regretted it for the rest of my professional life. Tell me what you have learned and whom you suspect, Cyrus."

Barker caught him up on events. He is no storyteller and has no ability to embellish beyond the barest facts, but this was the appropriate time for such dry facts, and he told it well enough.

"You are of the considered opinion that neither the duke nor his tutor are responsible for the murders."

"No," Barker stated. "The duke was out of the country when the murders occurred and Mr. Stephen was . . . occupied and accounted for."

"Thank you for sparing me the details," Anderson said.

"If he is not the killer, Mr. Stephen is allowed his privacy."

"As long as he is not breaking any other laws. So, you are back to the beginning, then. The rabbit trail led nowhere."

"Not exactly," Barker corrected. "We have eliminated several suspects, and a few more are under suspicion."

"I am wondering what will happen," the assistant commissioner asked, "if all our suspects are eliminated. Then what shall we do?"

"Track down new ones and start again," Barker replied, as if it were only a matter of common sense.

"I hope you appreciate that heads will roll if this fellow isn't caught. Salisbury's government is hanging by the most gossamer of threads."

"If it were easy, the killer would have been captured by now, Robert. The man works randomly and anonymously. There are few patterns he displays, yet somehow he has managed to frighten the entire population of London, cast himself in the role of a fiend, and made a mockery of our offices."

"You can understand why Warren is not exactly pleased with the state of the investigation. I almost promised him you would bring him to justice."

"It all depends on whether he is working alone or has help. It is possible he is being aided without his neighbors' or relatives' knowledge of what he is doing. This is too big a secret to keep to one man. If he is alone, he is a feral beast and will inevitably be caught. If he has help, it might take longer."

"We haven't got 'longer.' He must be caught soon or something might happen to this country as we know it. Warren has hinted at declaring martial law. What can the Yard do if troops are occupying Whitechapel?"

"Warren does not have that kind of power," Barker said.

"That's what they said about Cromwell."

"Anyway, he wouldn't."

"How do you know? This case is making a desperate man of him. Who knows what he will do, if cornered."

"Robert, you are confusing the prey with the hunter. You're starting to sound like James Munro."

I blinked, I admit. He had mentioned the one name I had expected he would not reveal. Anderson frowned for a moment, then he actually smiled.

"I suppose some have recounted the rumor that he and I are hatching a plot to undermine the Yard."

Barker folded his arms and sat back easily. "Of course. Once you were on the Continent, they could not wait to tell me. They see the two of you as evangelicals, conniving to get Warren sacked. I personally believe that you would no more rather work under one than the other."

"Then no more need be said of the matter," Anderson said.

"Exactly."

"So, tell me, is there anyone you currently suspect?"

"There's someone I am thinking of, but he has an alibi for the murders. I must see if I can break it."

"Then, by all means, bring him in and we'll see if we can break it together."

"That did not work for Pizer."

"But he was a Jew," Anderson pointed out.

"So is this suspect."

"We mustn't go about arresting Jews if we can avoid it. It causes unrest. There are a lot of Jewish anarchists in the East End."

"Are you more concerned with the safety of the Chosen People, or of causing unrest in the East End?" Barker asked.

"Both concern me. I don't want to see them harmed, and I am aware how indebted financially England is to Rothschild and others. As well, I understand that the population finds them very alien and is concerned that so many are arriving here. So far, we have seen no need to prohibit them from coming. I honestly hope it remains that way."

"You might have warned me about Munro's machinations."

"To tell the truth, I was not aware that word had gone out regarding the matter, among the officials of Scotland Yard."

"And where do you stand?" the Guv asked.

"It is an internal matter involving men in higher positions than I. Of course, I was hired from outside Scotland Yard myself, but I can see the sense of officers rising from within. Logic dictates commissioner will eventually be a rank that is earned rather than bestowed. It depended upon the pool of men from which the situation can be drawn."

"I think Mr. Abberline imagined a vast conspiracy of evangelicals, accomplishing diplomatically the overthrow Cromwell was unable to retain."

Anderson actually chuckled, which was a very good sign that his health had returned. "Leave it to the Anglicans to distrust all nonconformists."

"Am I relieved of my duties, Robert? You are returned. I'm sure there are prospective clients waiting for me to open my doors."

"Bide a while, Cyrus, if you would. You've come this far, and know as much as anyone. Both of you. Why not stay until it is done?"

"As you wish," Barker said, without consulting me. I believe he knew how I would feel about the matter. "We have put many days into this case. 'Twould be a great pity to leave it now when we are so close. I should be quite put out if the case were solved tomorrow based upon the information the lad or I had provided."

"So are you? Close, I mean?"

"It has been sheer luck on the Ripper's part that he has not been caught so far. I do not believe his luck can hold out much longer."

# CHAPTER THIRTY-TWO

I don't know how anything gets done in Scotland Yard. There is too much traffic through those weather-beaten halls. It is not a place conducive to thought or ratiocination. There is never any silence. People are chattering all day long, either to witnesses, colleagues, or suspects. Detectives talk through their thought processes, and sometimes those conversations can become heated. Men accuse each other of crimes, large and small, and others protest their innocence of said crimes. It's enough to give a man a thumping headache.

Luckily, the Guv had a well-appointed office just around the corner. At the time he rescued me, I had made my fourth or fifth pot of tea and was dangerously close to running out of digestive biscuits. He came up beside me and took me by the elbow in that way of his that brooks no refusal.

"Let's go back to our chambers, Thomas," he said. "I cannot hear myself think here."

"Gladly," I said, donning my helmet and adjusting the strap on my chin.

In the entrance, I told the desk sergeant that we were out investigating a case and it might be well to find a constable to make more tea soon. Then we walked in rare autumnal sunshine to Barker's chambers. Jenkins looked relieved to see us. Having a room all to oneself has a way of making time drag. His desk was littered with copies of the *Illustrated Police News*. He opened his mouth to say something to me, probably something cutting about my uniform, but the Guv interrupted him. He had the first of his inspirations since leaving "A" Division.

"Have you read about the killings, Jeremy?" he asked.

"Indeed I have, Mr. B. Plenty gruesome it is, too."

"It would have to be to be in that rag," I said.

"This ain't no rag, Mr. L. It's nothing but the gospel truth, so help me!"

"Do you think," Barker broke into our argument, "that you could clip and collect articles pertaining to the Whitechapel murders? You must purchase a few scrapbooks for the purpose. Good ones, I think. Leather bound."

"Of course, sir," Jenkins said. He's a skinny fellow, loose as a scarecrow, with a hawkish nose and black hair.

"I wish he'd had the foresight to collect the issues that have gone through this office in the past few months," I said.

"Got 'em, Mr. B.," our clerk said. "I take them home every night to read to the pater. He does like it when I read to him after supper. Then we discuss the events of the day. He's got a perfect horror of throwing away newspapers. I've got them going back several years."

Part of what Jenkins said was not strictly true. I had met his father on two or three occasions. He was one of the city's best forgers at one time, but that had been when we were fighting in the Crimea. Now he sat, silent and gray, staring at nothing, a victim, I suspected, of dementia. His son refused to admit it, out of respect for his father, perhaps, who at one time shed a larger-than-life shadow. Jenkins implied, even claimed outright, that they engaged in lively conversations, but I suspected that he had been robbed of all speech. The most I had heard from him was a sigh. Barker and I never spoke of it, but we both joined in this fantasy, asking Jenkins how his father was, and what he had been up to recently. It was the least we could do for a man who not only kept our offices running, but had stopped several people who had meant us harm.

"Excellent. Thomas, give Jeremy a tenner. No, two of them. Jeremy, I want you to create the definitive scrapbook on the Whitechapel Killer. Comb the newsstands for articles and opinions on the subject."

"What newspapers, sir?" he asked, a trifle dazed.

"The *Times,* the *Daily News,* the *Dispatch,* the *Standard,* your beloved *Illustrated Police News,* the morning *Post,* the *Jewish Chronicle,* the *Pall Mall Gazette,* the *Star,* and anything else you think might be of interest. Use your own discretion."

He looked like a fellow in deep water who had just been thrown a lifeline. Something to occupy him during the long day until five-thirty and his first pint at the Rising Sun.

"I'm your man. I'll give you my absolute best."

Barker patted him on the shoulder. "One could not ask for more. Now, as for you, Thomas . . ."

I looked over at him. Unlike Jenkins, I had plenty of things to do, from the minute I awoke with the aid of the Guv's boot in my shoulder, to the minute I fell in bed eighteen hours later.

"Yes, sir?" I asked, with a little less enthusiasm than our clerk had shown.

"I want you to collect a list of all lunatic asylums in London and the surrounding boroughs. Include in your list the workhouses, as well, because the insane are often kept in their casual wards."

I had flipped out a fresh notebook and was writing shorthand.

"Got it," I said.

"From that, compile a list of places that accept paupers from the East End. Rule out any from Kensington, for example, which are mostly for the rich, or good old Bethlehem, which is too far away. As I recall, there are several asylums north of the city in Hackney, for example."

"Hackney," I said as I wrote. "Then what, sir?"

"I want you to visit those institutions and get a list of previous or temporary patients that have been released within the past few months."

"I see where you are headed," I said. "The killer has very likely been institutionalized at one time or another. But how am I going to get them to tell me? I'm sure that's private information."

"You have two things going for you, lad. One of them is that uniform. The other is your ability to charm them into giving you information."

"Charm? Me?" I asked.

"Aye. Some of us do not have your talent and education, and must use our fists instead of words."

"I shall do my best, sir."

"Capital."

"And what will you do?" I dared ask.

"I plan to stick at the sides of Inspectors Swanson and Abberline and squeeze them for information, the way one squeezes water from a sponge. I refuse to be pushed to the sidelines in this investigation. We shall push, prod, and make ourselves alternately useful and a nuisance."

"As it happens," I said, "that is what I do best."

"Precisely," Barker replied.

My employer opened his smoking cabinet. It was about the size of a medical cabinet with two doors carved in a design that looked faintly like owls. Inside are drawers for tools, a jar full of his particular blend of tobacco, and a few tins of other brands. Above it, between the finials there, is a rack for his pipes, all of them made of meerschaum. Most are chalk white, but some have been smoked so long they could almost be mistaken for briars. He selected one, stuffed and lit it, then sat himself in his favorite chair in all the earth. Even the ones in his study do not bear that honor. He plopped into it, puffed on his pipe until it was really going well, and began to think. I doubted one could find a killer just by thinking, but then I had my own duties to perform.

There is no greater aid to the private enquiry agent than the *Kelly's Directory*, which lists every business, charity, government office, and landowner in London. I found twenty-five lunatic asylums therein and over thirty workhouses. I dusted off my Hammond typewriting machine and spent close to an hour typing all of the information into it, so Barker could see it all at a glance. Well, two glances, one for each page. Then I worked out which ones were in the East End or nearby and even collated the information by district, so that someone, presumably me, did not have to crisscross the area from one institution to the next. When I was done, the Guv's pipe was put away, but he was still facing forward, unmoving, stonelike, deep in thought. I laid the sheets in front of him and he grunted, pulling them closer.

"What a marvel these new machines are," he murmured. "Have you noticed how illegible the forms are at the Metropolitan Police building? The inspectors' handwriting is atrocious, because the men are uneducated and are not taught proper copperplate. Suppose a man were falsely accused or worse, let go, because of a misspelling or an illegible word!"

To get the full irony, one has to realize that this was Cyrus Barker saying these words, who may in fact have the worst penmanship in all Britain, including Manx, the Orkneys, and the Isle of Wight. A child sedated with opium could manage a better scrawl. However, it got me thinking.

"You know, sir, it would not hurt our reputation to appear organized and professional. What if we sent regular reports to Warren, neatly typed and in a proper folder, explaining what we are doing and have accomplished so far? You said we should be transparent. Of course, we don't have to tell him everything we've done. It would be better than having him order us into his office in a day or two and demand what we've been up to."

Barker sat back in his chair. For all I knew, he had not heard a word I said. Then he leaned forward and thumped the desk with his fist, rattling the glass.

"I like it!" he said. "Do it, by all means. We'll also provide a revised version for Sir Henry Ponsonby. That's good thinking, lad. I knew we needed to get away from the Yard and wipe the cobwebs from our minds."

That was typical. Fresh air and sunshine got the credit for my idea. Had I pulled the teapot from the small kitchen there, perhaps *it* would have come up with the idea.

"I'll get on it, then, sir."

I pulled my notebook from my pocket, put another piece of paper in the Hammond and began to type. This was what I did best.

I can pull a trigger or introduce a fellow to my right jab, but I'm best with ideas. Creating a report that looked authentic, while simultaneously praising our efforts and obfuscating what we didn't want to reveal, takes a certain level of talent. I have acquired few skills in my life, but that was one of them.

So engrossed was I in my work, I have no recollection of what the owner of our chambers did while I wrote. There is a slight memory that he paced the room deep in thought, but perhaps that is merely the likeliest option. He did not slip out, of that I am certain, for he was there when I was done. Perhaps he read one of the hundreds of books the chamber held, though I suspected most were there to impress our clients.

Setting the finished copy in front of my employer, I scuppered back to my chair in case he should find it unsatisfactory. I had placed five sheets of fresh vellum before him, single-spaced. Barker read. He is not a fast reader, but when he is done he has grasped every nuance and can quote back full passages.

He read and I watched. When he reached the final page, he opened his drawer and removed a stylographic pen, which he preferred to a stylus and bottle that might spill ink upon his antiseptic desk. He unscrewed the cover, held the nib down to let the ink flow, and then wrote that signature I'd seen a thousand times in my life. That was it. No corrections. He looked through the lower drawers of his desk and found an envelope the size of the letter without folding it.

"Thomas," he said, "your penmanship is better than mine. Please write 'Commissioner Warren—Private' on the cover."

I did as he asked, using my best orthography. Afterward, he put the signed report in the envelope and tied the loop of string which secured it.

"Now take this to Scotland Yard and hand it in at the front desk. Change out of your uniform and return."

The duties took me about a quarter hour. By the time I returned, Barker and Jenkins were in their hats and coats. Automatically, I checked the time on the watch from my pocket.

"It is but five past five," I said.

"We are shutting down the office early," Barker explained, or didn't.

"Why?"

"Jeremy assures me the Rising Sun serves excellent mussels and porter. Did you have other plans? You could go back to Scotland Yard and boil more tea for an hour, if you prefer."

"No, no," I said. "Mussels and porter are fine."

The Guv passed between us and out the front door. Jenkins and I locked up together.

"Did you put him up to this?" I asked.

"It was Mr. B's idea," Jenkins assured me. "He asked about the mussels. Maybe he just got a bit peckish. I know I am."

"The only dinner you'll graze on is at the bottom of a pint glass."

"Porter is nourishing and healthful. Says so on the adverts."

We caused a minor sensation when Jenkins walked into the public house a half hour ahead of time. It was as if the sun had slipped in its orbit. He had to tell and retell the tale at the fireplace to such friends as were there. The rest would arrive for alternate versions. Meanwhile, the Guv and I dug the mussels out of their shells and washed them down with strong porter. I tried to make a remark about the Walrus and the Carpenter, but it fell on deaf ears. Dining as he was, I suspected Barker was still working, and had been all afternoon. The mussels, like most food, were wasted on him. His mind was in the case already, trying to work out where the Whitechapel Killer might strike next.

"Goulston Street," he muttered.

"What about it?"

"That's where he was last seen. The bloody apron and the message in chalk."

I felt the briny mussel slip down my throat before taking a bitter, hopsy sip of porter.

"What about it?"

"He's just completed a bloody crime, the bloodiest of his career. He's wiping his hands. He throws it down."

"He writes the note."

Barker raised a finger. "That is not yet determined. Such notes are scrawled all over Whitechapel. He may have just dropped the cloth in front of it. But Goulston Street."

"Ghoul Street, more like."

"He's covered in blood, at least his hands are, in spite of the apron. He needs to wash. He's accomplished his objective, even after being interrupted in Elizabeth Stride's murder and being forced to retreat. He's done for the night. I suspect he's on the way home. If one could draw a line from Mitre Square to Goulston Street, I believe one would be heading into the murderer's personal neighborhood."

"You're certain," I said.

"Of course I'm not certain, lad. It is merely a theory I would like to test. And test it we shall, tonight. I suggest more mussels and less porter."

# CHAPTER THIRTY-THREE

The next day I began my tour of the East End asylums. Needless to say, I was not looking forward to it, but then no one came to such places voluntarily. I went in uniform in order to make my visit authoritative, but truth to tell I didn't know what such institutions could or could not reveal about their patients. Promising myself that I would keep my emotions in check, I chose one at random, the Poplar Lunatic Asylum.

First of all, the building was large and brick, and surrounded by a high gate. In fact, that was the standard architecture for each building. There was a porter in a booth at the front, and I explained my purpose. I was waved through. There were benches along the walkway and some patients were outside in the morning sun. They were being watched over by an imposing man who was either a guard or a nurse. A few of the patients attempted to come to me, but were coaxed back to their benches by him. They were a pathetic lot. Most here seemed to have been born with medical conditions in addition to their madness. The patients were docile for the most part, and I suspected they have been given sedatives. Many stared into space, and did not communicate with their neighbors.

Finally, I reached the door and found a sort of clerk in the lobby. Introducing myself, I asked if it was possible to see patient arrival and departure records going back to the summer. The clerk said he would need to speak to the doctor in charge, and I offered to speak to him myself. That would not be necessary, I was assured, and the gentleman disappeared down the hall and returned a few minutes later. A clipboard was handed to me, and I began to go through the loose pages, looking for recent departures. There were two. Most of the patients were coming in. I needed to have the man decipher some of the abbreviations there, and it turned out he was well up on all that occurred there at the asylum. Of the two men, one had been released because he was bedridden and his family took him home to die. The other was being transferred to a facility in Devon. I wrote down the names and pertinent information, and shook the fellow's hand. The entire process had taken less than half an hour.

There was no need to crisscross London a half-dozen times, so I found a workhouse nearby. The people there were not insane, for the most part. They were just destitute. Children played in the cobblestone streets and it was like a small town, only without anything growing nearby. No trees or plants of any kind, it was a town made of brick. The citizens were dispirited, and I would have felt the same were I sentenced to live there. We have but one short life on this planet, and they were spending it imprisoned because of a few debts. Oh, I'm sure some deserved it, being gamblers or spendthrifts, but others were here due to a profligate spouse or father, or they had backed a note for a friend and had all their possessions taken away.

Again, I found someone who understood what happened there, a warder, who was able to inform me that they occasionally took in temporary patients with mental problems as long as they did not cause much of a nuisance. In fact, some came back regularly, when a "fit" was on them and their families could do nothing with them. The workhouse had a barred section for more serious cases, and a guard to watch them. I came away with three names. One was a sailor subject to fits. Another spent half his days at home and the other half in cells, particularly during the full moon. He was a true lunatic. The third was one of the suspects filed in the case, the

Polish Jew, Kosminski. The information corroborated the file we had at Scotland Yard. The visit coincided with one of his manic episodes. I took down the names of the subjects and some notes about each.

And so the morning passed. Each place looked slightly different than the others, but the conditions were mostly the same. Some places were cleaner than others, some were better run, but all were depressing in the extreme. I thanked God for a sound mind. My story would bring tears from a washerwoman's eyes, but it was nothing compared to what these men and women had endured. They had no purpose in life, but were waiting to die. I felt sorry for the families, as well, unable to care for their family member at home with their constant shifts in moods. It was tragic.

Soon, I realized the buildings were all over the area, evenly spaced across the East End, but so anonymous that I could pass under their eaves and never know it. They did not announce themselves frequently. The workhouses might occupy part of an entire street, but they were often tucked away, and the district grew around them. What better place to hide these houses of misery than among so much other misery?

"How did you find your search?" Barker asked when I returned to Scotland Yard.

"A dozen names," I answered. "This is time-consuming, sir."

"Just so," he rumbled. "Take your time. Have you the list?"

I pulled my notebook from my pocket and showed it to him. He took it from me eagerly.

"It is something to investigate while we wait until he strikes again."

"You think the Ripper will commit another murder?"

"Oh, I am sure of it. Why shouldn't he? We are doing a poor job of stopping him. He is committing murder in our very streets and yet we cannot find him. Ah."

"What is it?"

"That fellow, Kosminski again. He lives in Goulston Street."

"That's right."

"Attacked his sister-in-law during one of his episodes. Broken scissors."

"But he was at work during the killings. He is a night watchman at a factory."

"I don't see who would continue to use him as a guard after he was incarcerated in an asylum. There is more to this than meets the eye. Continue to investigate."

"This is a fishing trip," I complained.

"You like to fish. If anything turns up, it becomes due diligence, and you look professional. No one could ask for more. Besides, it gets you away from your duties making tea and delivering messages."

"There's that, I suppose."

"I could get you transferred to walking a beat, if you prefer."

"I'm walking a beat right now, sir, from seven to midnight. Longer, if something happens."

"Then you have no reason to complain."

"I wasn't complaining, sir. 'All things work out for the best in this, the best of all possible worlds.'"

"Whom are you quoting now?"

"The German philosopher Leibniz."

"Well, don't. That's the sort of thing that will get you in trouble here."

"Yes, sir."

"Don't you have duties to perform?"

I sighed and went back to the kitchen and began making a pot of tea. It brought men in from the other offices while it brewed. I opened a fresh tin of biscuits and even Barker came into the hallway. He likes shortbread. Most desserts he finds oversweet, but he was raised on the stuff, handmade by his little Scottish mum until she and his father died in a cholera epidemic in China when he was eleven and he became a street child, disguising his European origins behind a pigtail and a pair of spectacles. I suspected shortbread reminded him of better times.

The tea was just about ready and the various constables and sergeants were chatting in the hall. It all seemed genial enough until it stopped. A man I had never seen before came up beside the Guv, seized his arm, and pressed him face-first against the wall. He had the gall to try to twist my employer's arm behind him. The attacker was perhaps five and forty, with thick side whiskers framing a square face. He looked angry. Barker's chest thumped against the wall. There was a sort of collective moan from the men in the corridor. I knew there would be hell to pay.

Barker twisted and muscled his body until the two of them faced each other, beady eyes to implacable black spectacles. Then suddenly, the Guv unleashed. He seized the man by the waistcoat, and the next I knew, he was spinning him down the corridor. Abruptly, he stopped the fellow's progress just when it looked as if his face was going to smack into the wall. Then he twisted him the other direction, until at the last moment he let go. The man sailed through the air until coming into contact with the floor. He slid along the floor several feet until he passed into an open doorway where he knocked over a chair.

There was a chorus of shouts and laughs from my professional colleagues and for a moment tea was the last thing on anyone's mind. Barker's assailant came charging out of the office covered in the dust he had picked up in the corridor. He took a swing at Barker and connected on the jaw. I saw the Guv's head shift back with the blow. My employer did not seem inclined to punch back. When the chap tried to throw a second blow, the men of the Yard immediately surrounded him and stopped him from trying again. He was herded into another room and Barker back into his. A half-dozen men offered him their handkerchiefs because his lip was bleeding, but he turned them down. I made a cup for each of the combatants, though I was inclined to accidentally spill one in the lap of the one who started it. It was all over as soon as it had begun.

"What was that all about?" I asked the Guv when things had calmed down. "Who was that fellow?"

"It was Littlechild, in charge of the Royal Squad. He is angry because we replaced him in Ponsonby's favor. We gave the royal seccretary an excuse to bar the inspector from the palace."

"You let him hit you. I could have blocked that punch."

"No doubt. It is important to know how to take a punch. And when."

"When?" I asked. "I already know that. The answer is never."

Barker dabbed at the corner of his mouth with his handkerchief.

"He needed to save face. He couldn't be completely trounced in front of his compatriots. Besides, we are guests here. If we humiliated him in public, sympathy would lean in his favor. One good punch on my chin did me no harm, it restored his dignity, and it turned the favor in our direction."

"But we don't even know the man. Why should I care whether or not he feels better?"

"You shouldn't and I don't. However, it matters how the other inspectors feel about our conduct. We are being judged every day. We wouldn't want to undo the good you've done supplying tea and biscuits all around, would we?"

"I suppose not."

"Good."

"But you could have trounced him."

"Easily. Did you see how slow that punch was?"

"You could have had a pipeful while you waited."

Barker chuckled, then winced at the cut on his lip. "Droll. Very droll."

Just then, Abberline rushed in, looking concerned.

"What happened?" he asked.

"A minor altercation," the Guv said.

"What was the cause?"

"Sir Henry barred him from the palace, I assume. The inspector was of the opinion that it was my doing."

"And was it?"

"No. I'm only here temporarily. I have no interest in slicing a piece of the pie for myself."

"Someone said you flipped him about with some of your Asian mumbo jumbo, as if he was a rag doll."

"It was less violent than hitting him. If I'd hit him, he'd still be unconscious."

"You recall what Warren said about staying out of trouble?" Abberline asked.

"That *was* me staying out of trouble. He's not being carted out in a hand litter, bound for Charing Cross Hospital."

"I'll try to keep the commissioner mollified," the detective chief inspector said.

"Thank you, Frederick," Barker said, taking the liberty of using his first name.

"How is the case coming on?"

"We are still hunting leads from six in the morning until midnight, isn't that so, lad?"

"Yes, sir," I responded.

"Are you making any progress?"

"I had PC Llewelyn type up a full report to the commissioner this morning. I'm sure he will make it available soon."

"Hmmm," Abberline said. "I hear you twirled Littlechild around like a baton. Sorry I missed that."

"If you'll call him in for a demonstration, I'll show you how I did it."

"That won't be necessary," Abberline said dryly. "How did things go at the palace yesterday?"

"There were several issues over which Sir Henry was concerned. I convinced him we were taking matters in hand."

"And are we?"

"We are. Aren't we, lad?"

"Of course," I responded.

"There, you see."

"Very well."

Abberline left the room.

I turned to my employer. "About that, sir. We are, aren't we?"

# CHAPTER THIRTY-FOUR

We were walking about the docklands that evening when Barker put a foot on top of a low piling and looked out upon the black waters of one of the basins.

"Thomas," he said, "I am pulling you from your duties at Scotland Yard. Those menial tasks are a waste of your time."

I agreed with him, but wasn't going to admit it.

"What will you have me do instead, sir?"

"I want you to take the position at the Goulston Street mantle factory. Do you recall the notice in the window? We passed it a half hour ago and it is still there."

"Does that mean you think Aaron Kosminski is the Whitechapel Killer?"

"I cannot say for certain, but he is like a persistent itch; an irritant. If we can dismiss him, we can get on with our work."

"I can't guarantee that my skills are good enough to get the position, but it is possible the owner has grown a little desperate."

"Aye, well, he is not the only one."

"This is a devil of a case," I said.

"I suspect whatever mental malady the Whitechapel Killer suffers from is growing steadily worse."

"I have heard of tumors in the brain, sir, which cause a change in behavior."

"At some point, he shall lose his grip on reality and draw attention to himself. We must be placed at the best advantage when that occurs."

Somehow, I had expected that being hired would be more difficult. I had prepared answers to possible questions, explanations for my current circumstances, and was prepared to argue, if necessary, because I wanted to succeed for Barker's sake. All that working into the night had been for naught. He barely glanced at my letters of recommendation. Instead, he had given me a little test that spoke volumes.

"Sew me a buttonhole," Wolfe Kosminski said. Apparently, he was the older brother of Aaron.

A letter from the Archbishop of Canterbury would have meant nothing if I hadn't been able to do it. I couldn't wait to tell Barker I had succeeded on the strength of my sewing skills.

"Not bad. This is where we do our piecing," he said, pointing to some tables where men were rolling out fabric and pinning paper patterns to them. I noticed there were no women working there. I would have thought the seamstresses would outnumber the seamsters, but such was not the case.

"No women work here?" I asked.

"I don't hire women," Wolfe Kosminski said. "I don't much like mixing the sexes on the factory floor. It only leads to unwanted drama and distraction, which causes injury. I have seen it happen before."

He came to a narrow stairway in a corner and called out to the room above.

"There is only one woman here, my wife, Sarah," he explained. "She cares for our child upstairs. Little Herschel is the first Kosminski born in England. I hope my brothers will marry someday and raise more boys so that our name can prosper here."

Kosminski's wife came down the stair then, holding the baby over her shoulder. She seemed rather shy and concerned with her own duties.

"This is Thomas," he said, referring to me. "I have just hired him. I am showing him around."

"You have a handsome baby, Mrs. Kosminski," I told her.

"*Danke,*" she said, carrying her baby back upstairs.

"I speak French, and a very little German," I said. "What language do your shop workers speak?"

"Mostly Yiddish and German. But we all need to learn English, so I hope you can help them to speak and understand it."

"Of course. What shall my hours be?"

"Seven to seven. We lock up promptly at eight."

I suddenly saw the flaw in Barker's plan. I would work twelve hours. There would be no more time to make tea or study files at Scotland Yard, and I would probably be too exhausted to march all over Whitechapel with Barker.

"We close at five on Friday, of course, and are closed on Saturday."

"And Sunday?" I asked.

"Seven to seven, like any other day."

"Of course."

"There is one more part of the position I must explain to you before you begin. Let me take you to the back of the shop and I'll explain as we go."

We began to pass along the tables and I nodded to the workers sewing there who were naturally curious about a new employee. They seemed an unhappy lot, some past their working prime, others nearly children. A sweatshop. That's what this place was, exploiting its workers to make a profit.

"My brother Aaron is the night watchman," he said. "He is troubled mentally, subject to bouts of extreme excitement. He does not talk much, and only to us. He does not like strangers or changes of any kind. He finds change threatening."

As we neared the back, I encountered an odor: pungent, primal, and very potent. I couldn't help but raise a hand to my nose.

"I know," Wolfe Kosminski said. "It is terrible. Aaron refuses to bathe. He is guided by voices in his head, which tell him what to do. Aaron!"

He opened a door. The smell inside made the bile rise in my throat. I saw a young man sitting on a cot, who sat up when we arrived. Our eyes locked for only a second before he looked down and away.

"Aaron, this is Thomas. He starts today."

The younger Kosminski was near my own age, with light brown, greasy hair, the dawn of a mustache on his lip, and wispy side whiskers. His eyes were large and watery. The most remarkable feature was how his skin was stretched tautly upon his face. The man was nearly skeletal. Though possibly a few inches taller than I, I doubted he weighed seven stone. He seemed preternaturally aged; there were commas carved into each cheek by starvation. He pulled up his feet, which were bare and gray with grime, in order to bury his face in his knees.

"Now, now, little brother, that is no way to act toward the new man. Do you remember your English? Say hello to Mr. Llewelyn."

After a moment a sound came out. I could not call it a word. It was like a sigh, a muffled sound that had no obvious origin, and which one could not understand. I had heard such sounds in the asylums I had visited in this case. It was something in between a buzz and a moan.

"No, now, *Bruder,* be nice. Thomas is new here and willing to overlook your nasty habits, but I won't have you being uncivil to him."

Perhaps Wolfe was trying to produce an apology from his relative, but he was not succeeding. Aaron Kosminski turned away and lay down on his bed, which consisted of several burlap sacks and blankets thrown on top of one another. He wore a none-too-clean shirt and braces and an open tweed waistcoat over a pair of baggy trousers.

"We'll leave you then. I'll see you after dinner."

Wolfe led me out of the room and closed the door behind me. I let out a breath and drew in another one, but I was still too close to the source of it.

"To tell you the truth, we almost don't notice the smell anymore— the family members, I mean. We grew up with it. Aaron has always been as you see him."

"He is touched in the head?" I asked.

"Aaron is just Aaron. There is no other way to describe him."

"Forgive me, but are there not places where he could be treated? I mean, with the factory needing to be run, and a new baby. You must be overbusy."

"You cannot imagine. But no, we must look after him ourselves. He is family. I could not imagine him locked up in a cell and mistreated. He is so fragile, you see."

"I hope I did not speak out of turn."

"No, no, of course not. I brought you to see him because I cannot hide it for long. If you wish to turn down the position, I understand. You see now why no women will work here. Sometimes Aaron must be restrained. But he means no harm, you understand."

"I suppose I can take it if I am not seated too close to the back. But why is your brother so thin?"

"He hears the voices and does what they tell him to. They tell him not to eat food prepared by others, only what is left in the street."

"But this is Whitechapel," I argued. "Almost no food is left in the street."

"Precisely. We control him by giving him his walk in the evenings after dinner. He must eat two bites before he can go out: two full bites. Oh, he distresses himself atrociously, but he'll eat a little, or he won't get to go out."

"Go out? You let him out?"

"Oh, yes. He's harmless. We let him out around five. He sleeps during the day, you see, and is awake all night. It is his natural schedule. He returns around seven-thirty. Then we lock him in for the night. That way, he acts as night watchman, but also we know where he is all night."

"What does he do while he is out?" I asked.

"He grazes. That is my little joke, you see. He walks and picks up as much food as he finds on the ground. He's a great walker. He'll go as far as Mile End in one direction, and Cheapside in the other."

"Does he interact with anyone?"

"Not to my knowledge. He doesn't go into any buildings. They'd toss him out because of the smell. Mostly, he just wanders about in his own little world, listening to what the voices tell him."

"How sentient is he? Does he communicate with you?"

"Of course. He understands Yiddish, German, and some English, though he doesn't speak the latter. He cannot read, but when Sarah bought him a primer to learn his letters, I think he was insulted that it was for a child. He gave it back to her immediately."

"It cannot be easy caring for a full-grown adult."

"It isn't, believe me. At times he can be manic, too full of energy. He's harder to control then. For the most part, however, he is docile, like today."

"Poor fellow," I said.

"So, will you accept the position?"

"Yes, I will."

"Good. We could use an extra pair of hands. I'll show you to your table, and one of our workers will instruct you in how to put together a mantle."

"It is difficult?" I asked. "Compared to, say, a coat?"

"If it were not difficult, we would not be able to charge so much for one, but I think you are capable enough of the work. This way."

A mantle, I learned that day, or a mantlelet, as it is sometimes called, is a close-fitting coat for women, generally made of silk, that is longer in the front but gathered in the back to allow a bustle to project outward. The sleeves are either dolman or sling sleeves and are adorned with jet beads or embroidery. They are gilding for such lilies as require it. Younger women may have no need for it, but many who are older have acquired the wherewithal for seed pearls, jet beads, and other ornamentation, working under the assumption that if one cannot be a work of art, one can wear one. I never noticed such a garment before I entered the shop that morning, but I noticed plenty of them afterward.

The owner passed me into the hands of the seamsters, who began to show me the stitches I would need to learn in order to produce the finished product. I still could not believe I was working as a plainclothes police officer. If in my final year in public school I had been able to list a hundred possible occupations for my future that possibility would not have been on it.

As we set to work and I began to build my first mantle, I turned over in my mind what I had learned about Aaron Kosminski, knowing for certain that Cyrus Barker would not care for a single word on the subject of women's mantle making. What was my opinion regarding Kosminski as a possible suspect in the Ripper murders? I had to admit to having serious misgivings. He was so small, while Jack the Ripper was larger than life. The only thing offensive about him was his odor. He would not speak to anyone in the street, not knowing their language, so how could he approach someone like Catherine Eddowes or Long Liz Stride, who would have towered over him? How could he overpower Dark Annie Chapman who was twice his weight? I could not imagine it. Prince Eddy, Stephen, or someone connected to the palace seemed a much more viable candidate than a speechless immigrant who didn't bathe and could not even look one in the eye.

Near noon we were given a short break to use a public lavatory down the street, and to eat lunch. I had none, of course, but Mrs. Kosminski was kind enough to feed me a potted meat sandwich, rather than risk that I might go out to some sort of restaurant or public house and not return. After fifteen minutes we returned to work, which continued until seven o'clock. By that hour, all my fingers had bled from being pierced by needles, my shoulders were shivering from exhaustion, and my feet were cramping from standing so long.

It occurred to me then that I must have the best situation in London, working with Cyrus Barker. While others flogged away at work like this, I was sitting in a well-appointed chamber, reading a newspaper necessary for my position, taking light dictation, and typing the odd letter. All right, so occasionally I was shot at; the thing was, I was paid ten times the salary for less than half the work. It seemed to defy logic. Someone's mathematical calculations were off. Unless, of course, the difference was simply a matter of address. Whitehall was not Whitechapel and never would be.

Aside from my personal revelations, only one thing of any note happened that evening, and that was that Aaron Kosminski went out for his walk. Those poor words do little to describe the actual event. Wolfe knocked at the door of the youngest Kosminski, who came out in a pea jacket and broken hat not in keeping with a family of mantle makers. After eating a few bites, he seemed so excited, he was shaking. Wolfe crossed to the front door and Aaron shot out of it in a pair of stout boots, leaving behind a ghastly breeze of effluvia that we workers did our best to wave away.

A few minutes later, an old woman entered, who proved to be the elder Mrs. Kosminski. The younger came down from the apartment above, greeted her with a kiss, and they spoke together in what I assumed was Yiddish. Then they went upstairs to finish dinner for the brothers who did not take their nourishment in the street. We continued to work.

Near seven o'clock, Aaron returned, looking a good deal calmer, and Wolfe came down from supper. Windows were locked, projects put away, and the tables cleared of anything valuable that might be viewed from an outside window. We were shown to the door.

"You did good work today, Thomas," Wolfe said to me. "I'll see you in the morning at seven."

While agreeing, I calculated in my head. It was a twelve-hour workday. As I stepped outside, and the door closed behind me, I heard the sharp sound of a bolt being drawn on the door. There would be no mantle stealing on these premises tonight.

The workers wandered away one by one. I proceeded down Goulston Street, wondering whether I might find a hansom in Commercial Road who could take me to the Frying Pan. I could not walk more than a few feet.

Then Cyrus Barker stepped into a nimbus of gaslight from an alleyway and gestured to me. I turned and followed him, hoping our destination was not far away. He led me down a narrow court until he stopped at a door and opened it with a key. The muscles in my limbs jumped as I climbed a flight of steps to the first floor. I didn't know where I was, nor was I curious. The Guv led me down a hall to a flat and let me in. A room had been set up with two beds and a table and chairs. There was a fire in the grate, and when I looked down, I recognized the boric acid sprinkled on the floor. While I was working, we had changed residences. There was a cold selection on the table, and some bottles of ale.

Curious, I moved to the window. The room overlooked the Kosminski Mantle Factory. As I looked down through the skylight of the factory, Aaron Kosminski shuffled by under my gaze.

"So," Barker asked. "How was your day?"

# CHAPTER THIRTY-FIVE

I was fortunate that once I began working for the Kosminskis, Barker no longer considered it necessary to march around White-chapel until midnight. Instead, he followed the youngest brother about the district at a discreet distance from the time he left the factory until his return a few hours later, when he was locked in by his brothers for the night.

"What does he do while he is out and about?" I asked over a breakfast of water and day-old bread.

"He lopes about for the most part. He has a quick, hopping step that makes his head bob up and down as he walks. Perhaps he is partially lame but has overcome it. Anyway, he doesn't interact with anyone. Sometimes he just stops as if he had thought of something important, or is receiving instruction from those voices in his head. He may not move for ten minutes, then he'll suddenly lope off again. His eyes dart from side to side, but they do not fix on any person or object for very long. To be truthful, I assumed he would fixate upon a particular female, or females in general, but I saw no sign of it. His eyes followed whatever passed him by. But that wasn't what struck me most."

"Oh, really? What was that?"

"No one looked at him, or paid any attention. It may have something to do with English manners. They studiously avoided looking at someone so malodorous and unpleasant, as if not willing to cause embarrassment. Either that or they have ceased to notice him at all. He comes, he goes, he does not interact with anyone, and he is not in a position of authority like a policeman, so he is a nonentity. He stands there and is not noticed, like a servant in a drawing room."

"Do you suppose anyone knows who he is?"

"I imagine the Jews know. After all, he is one of them. The Kosminskis are respected within their community and perhaps simultaneously pitied, as well, for having an apparent imbecile as a family member."

"Apparent?"

"Aye. We have no real understanding of his intelligence. I really must discover how clever he is. Has he ever had any sort of conversation with his family in front of you?"

"They speak to him, but mostly it's just orders or questions he can answer with a nod or shake of the head. 'Are you hungry? Did you remember your jacket?' Sometimes he responds with a word or two, but I can't make heads or tails of what it is. It may be slurred or he might have an accent or impediment to his speech. It's mostly just mumbles, and it has a peculiar quality, as if it were coming from someone else, the way a music hall ventriloquist throws his voice. It's the strangest thing."

"I feel I must either discover some sign of real intelligence in Mr. Kosminski or pull you from the premises and have us go back to our former routine. I'm starting to be concerned that this is a false lead. I dare not pull any other constables or inspectors into the investigation unless I have more proof. Can you think of some way to get into his room in the factory and toss it without attracting attention to yourself?"

"Not offhand," I admitted. "He's nocturnal. Doesn't get up until two o'clock in the afternoon. He stays in his room for the most part until five o'clock. I would have to get in between five and seven when he returns. The problem is others may be watching, and Wolfe Kosminski passes in and out."

"It would have to be during those two hours. We must imagine some sort of ruse you might employ to get inside."

"If I could stand a sewing dummy in front of the door, I might be able to conceal myself from view for a few moments, but I'd be taking a risk of being caught and sacked. Then we wouldn't have a pair of eyes inside to evaluate whether he's the Ripper or not."

"That might be worth the risk if a quick tossing turns up anything worthwhile."

"What am I looking for, precisely?" I asked.

"Bloody rags. The missing organs of those poor women, preserved or otherwise. The knife he kills with. A bag of some sort."

"But you thought it unlikely he'd carry a bag."

"I was wondering how he lugged those bloody organs home. He couldn't just put a fresh kidney in the pocket of his trousers."

"That's disgusting," I said. "But then, everything about this fellow is disgusting. His room smells like a charnel house. But how shall I get in?"

Barker rubbed his chin. "Rather than following after Mr. Kosminski again, perhaps I could provide the distraction."

"That would certainly work. If you were someone looking for an address or wanting to place an order, that might give me enough time to look for something."

"Excellent. I'll wait until our suspect is safely down the street and away before I arrive. Don't move until you see me pull your notebook from my pocket."

"I will. Tonight, after five? I'll be ready."

It was a long day in anticipation of his arrival. I pulled my sewing dummy rather close to Aaron's malodorous door, where most of the workers were loath to go. Young Aaron came out of his room around three and looked vaguely in my direction without actually looking me in the eye. He was scratching his chest and hair. I'll get fleas, I thought, on top of possibly getting caught. He went upstairs where the family dwelt and came down again at five. Wolfe made him put on his coat and he shot out the door, running in that gangly way of his.

About five minutes later, a familiar figure came looming through the door.

"Is Mr. Wolfe Kosminski on the premises?" the Guv asked in a loud voice.

"I am he," the elder Kosminski stated, as he got up from a table where he was sitting and went to greet the visitor.

"Pleased to make your acquaintance. I'm from the *Clarion Herald*."

"Not another reporter! Out, sir!"

"Hear me out, if you will. We understand your factory was singled out for public humiliation due to a rival's inflammatory article, which we consider to have been racially motivated. It has been said a Jew cannot receive proper treatment in the town. We wondered if you would be willing to tell me how this has affected your business, in terms of sales and in finding willing workers. I don't claim that we can rectify the situation you find yourselves in, but it may stimulate business for you."

"I suppose I could answer some questions for you, yes," Wolfe Kosminski replied.

Barker reached into his inside pocket and retrieved my notebook. I looked about me. All the workers in the room were focused on his arrival. I stepped back toward the forbidden door.

I squeezed too quickly into the space and forgot to hold my breath. The odor assaulted me. My eyes watered and I resisted my body's attempt to gag. My stomach somersaulted and tried to contort. To keep from making a sound I was forced to jam my handkerchief into my mouth. Slowly, my eyes cleared.

The room was rectangular, built against the back wall as a kind of lumber room. It was perhaps ten feet long, but only six feet wide. A bed was there, covered in large sacking with a pillow and a blanket. No white sheets had ever touched this bed. The pillow was blacked where lank, dirty hair lay for hours each night. There was a small desk with a mismatched chair of cane, worn thin and broken. On top of the desk was a collection of objects arranged in a rough circle: the limb of a child's doll; a pencil stub; a penknife with no blade; a foreign coin, possibly Swiss; a piece of rope. I need not go on. They were items picked up from the gutter, things even the people here had no use for. Perhaps the voices had told him to pick them up. The interesting thing was the arrangement. Everything had been placed just so, forming a circle, but evenly spaced. It was a kind of altar.

On the floor by the desk were wires and red paper, the raw materials for making paper flowers, a minor industry in the East End. The paper was covered in dust. The Kosminskis must have tried to force some work out of their youngest, but he would not or could not oblige. I did not envy Wolfe Kosminski trying to deal with this recalcitrant brother.

A coat hung on a broken coat rack, by a deerstalker hat. I felt in the pockets on either side, but they were empty. Nothing. Nothing so far. Where might he hide something? The man owned practically nothing.

I patted the bed from one side to the other, looking for the knife or something completely disgusting. An old folding screen stood against the back wall, but a quick glance showed there was nothing on the floor behind it. In the far corner I encountered something hard and square. It was the last thing I expected to find. A book. A rather large book. I pulled it from where it was concealed, in the corner under the mattress by the pillow. I pulled it open, and glanced down. Turned the pages, and glanced again. I was late. Closing it carefully, I stowed it away again and arranged the pillow, then I stopped and backed away, taking in one last visual sweep of the area. Quietly, I eased the door open and slipped out.

"Mr. Kosminski, I feel you have been ill-used. It is not right that one Jewish factory should be subject to persecution while the Gentile businesses beside it receive no such abuse. We shall make an issue of it, sir, I promise you. This cannot go on. Do you know that several kosher shops have had bricks thrown through their windows this very week? But come, sir. I see you must be about your business, and I must be about mine. Be sure to see my article in the *Clarion Herald* this week. Good day, sir!"

No sooner did I get out the door than I fell into a fit of coughing. My stomach was trying to crawl out of my throat. The next I knew, Wolfe Kosminski was slapping me on the back.

"Are you unwell, Mr. Llewelyn? You look nearly green."

"I'm sorry, Mr. Kosminski. I fear I have been working too close to a certain room. My wish was that I could grow accustomed to it, but the flesh is weak."

"It does you credit for trying. This mantle is coming along well. You will soon be making them all by yourself, I think."

Acting as if I had no other wish than to make mantles for fashionable women for the rest of my life had become second nature by now. When had I become such a liar? I told him anything to make him go away so I could finish coughing up my spleen.

There were still two hours to go before I could return and tell Barker my news. They dragged even worse than the ones that had trickled minute by minute to five o'clock. But then, that is private enquiry work. Long stretches of boredom punctuated by intense minutes of pain and disgust.

Finally, Aaron returned to his nightly incarceration, looking manic and flushed. I signed Wolfe's ledger logging the time. I said good-bye and walked out the door, down Goulston Street, and into an alleyway that led into Cambrian Street, where I let myself into our rented flat. I ascended the stair.

Barker was in his perch, looking down onto the skylight windows of the factory. The smoke from his pipe circled his head. He turned on his stool and looked at me.

"Well?" he asked.

"No organs, no knife, not so much as a bloody rag."

"Blast!" he barked.

"But there was a book hidden under his bed. A German anatomy book."

"An anatomy book?"

"I don't know if he can read, but his filthy fingermarks were all over the illustrations, and they were so dog-eared as to be almost falling out."

# CHAPTER THIRTY-SIX

We now have enough," Barker announced that evening, standing across from the factory in Goulston Street, "to suggest that Scotland Yard give us a constable or two to watch Aaron Kosminski."

"I'd have thought that a certainty," I said.

"Not necessarily. The evidence you found, while damning, is circumstantial. He owns a book on anatomy. So do most doctors. He is of diminished mental capacity, though he may possess a cleverness we haven't seen so far. He attacked his sister-in-law with scissors."

"You know, that doesn't make sense at first glance. His record at the workhouse said he was trained as a hairdresser, but no one would train someone who spent his days staring at the wall, muttering to himself."

"What are you driving at?" Barker asked.

"I suspect that he's been declining mentally ever since he left Poland. At eighteen, he might have been neat and orderly, reasonable and able to speak. Since coming here, however, his mental faculties have given way and he has become violently insane."

"That might be difficult to prove without questioning his family, but if it is true, what would it prove?"

"It's the timing, sir. At one time he may have had no thought of killing anyone. Then one day he did and he may have ruminated on it without doing anything about it. But finally, in August, he gave in to it. There has to be a logical progression of his sinking into madness."

"Unless there was a catalyst," Barker said. "A trigger."

"You mean his sister-in-law?"

"Aye. They came here, three bachelors. Then one of them gets married to a local girl. Soon she is with child. Now it could go either way. He might hate the changes of having first one stranger in his life and then a little one, or he might have developed stirrings, longings for her."

"It's possible his illness may have retarded the onset of puberty," I said. "Perhaps he found himself having all these confused feelings and desires. She won't give him what he wants, so he attacks her in anger."

"But when he returns from his time in the workhouse he sees women nearby that could gratify his sudden needs. He's not a normal twenty-five-year-old, however, so instead of having the traditional rite of passage of boys, he cuts her throat."

"Why?"

"Who knows the answer to that? Because he's mad. Perhaps she belittled him. Perhaps they all did. Unfortunates are not known for their discretion. She told him he smelled. She called him a scarecrow. Or perhaps she refused him because he was a Jew, or insane, or because he won't or can't talk, or because he stares. There are a hundred reasons at least. These women are bold as brass. They won't spare the feelings of a man like that. If she got him angry enough, he might cut her throat without hardly realizing he's done it."

"That's good reasoning. You see, we must have a convincing argument for Swanson and Abberline. We have to know who, what, when, why, and how. A story, like you just came up with, whether all the facts are true or not, may help to convince them. It is not necessary that they believe he is the only suspect. In fact, if they do, we may be pushed to the side. We just want to convince them that he is a possible suspect. Let us go down to 'H' Division and see what we can do."

I was tired after my long day, and famished, but I wasn't going to argue with my employer. Having discussed it thoroughly, he did not seem inclined to talk, so we marched down Commercial Street and made our way to Leman Street. Our luck held there. Swanson had just arrived in order to confer with Abberline. I thought Swanson might be easier to convince of the two. Abberline seemed likely to prefer his own theories.

"Gentlemen, might we have a word?" Barker asked.

The two chief inspectors were seated at a table scarred with tea rings. They looked up at us.

"What can we do for you, Barker?" Abberline asked.

"I promised Mr. Anderson that I would not withhold material from you and I intend to keep my promise. Mr. Llewelyn and I, having established alibis for the various suspects connected to the royal family, have looked elsewhere. We've been tracking a suspect for whom there is already a file, and we came upon some new evidence this afternoon."

Both of them sat up, Swanson looking hopeful, while I saw doubt on Abberline's bewhiskered face.

"Does this suspect have a name?"

"Kosminski. Aaron Kosminski."

The chief inspectors looked at each other as if they both tried to pull the name from their memory. They must have had hundreds of suspects by now.

"Fellow attacked his sister, didn't he?" Swanson asked, after a moment.

"That's right," Abberline said, snapping his fingers. "He'd been put in the workhouse while she was giving birth. Not much more than a youth. The smelly one!"

"What put you on to him?" Swanson asked.

"His family's mantle factory is in Goulston Street, where the commissioner wiped away the message."

" 'The Juwes are the ones who will not be blamed for nothing,' "
Abberline quoted. "You think someone was trying to tell us something?"

"Perhaps. We realized the only alibi he had was that he was
locked up at night. No one was actively watching him, you see. If
there were some way for him to get out and return, he would have
no alibi and would be close to several if not all of the murders.
Therefore, I got Mr. Llewelyn a situation in the factory."

"That's more important than tea in 'A' Division?" Abberline
asked.

"Regrettably, yes. Tell them what you found, Thomas."

"This young Kosminski fellow, Aaron, has a small room on the
premises. I thought it worthwhile to see if there was anything
he had concealed there, some proof that he was Jack the Ripper. I
believe I found it."

Both Swanson and Abberline moved to the edge of their chairs.
The latter was not going to let it go without comment.

"Well, out with it! What did you find?"

"An anatomy book, well thumbed. Printed in German. You'll
recall he speaks almost no English."

"Can the fellow even read?" Swanson asked.

"It had diagrams, sir. Anatomical drawings of female reproduc-
tive organs. Well looked at, if you know what I mean. There were
dirty fingermarks all over it."

Both of the inspectors tried to speak at once. Swanson broke into
a gap-toothed grin and even Abberline had a wry smile.

"We know there is not enough evidence to convict him based
upon the presence of a book," the Guv said. "However, I have secured rooms on the first floor across the street, which have a fine
view of the factory. But we are just two men. If we had a constable
or two to watch the factory overnight, they might be able to see if
he goes in and out."

"If he takes one step out into the street, we've got him," Donald
Swanson said.

"Where does he go?" Abberline asked.

"Anywhere and everywhere. Mostly north of Commercial Street.

Within six or seven streets of his home in any direction, if one could call it a home."

"Tell us about the family again. There is a brother in charge of the factory, isn't there?"

"Wolfe," I said. "And another brother, Isaac."

"Have you questioned them?"

"Not yet. I was preserving my incognito."

"We can question them again at the right time."

"Does he still reek?" Abberline asked.

"Like nothing I've ever smelled before," I said. "It's horrible."

"When does he leave the premises?"

"They let him free around five every day. He sleeps most of the day away. I suspect he is completely nocturnal."

"A real lunatic, eh?" Abberline said. "He does everything but bay at the moon."

"One's heart must go out to the brothers who must tend to such a fellow."

"Sorry," Abberline said. "I'm already sharing a piece for every girl he cut up. I've run clean out of sympathy for him."

"You'll get your two men and not constables," Swanson said. "I want two plainclothes detectives, seasoned veterans. You won't mind sharing your room with a couple of officers, will you?"

"No, sir," Barker replied.

"Good work."

Abberline would not leave it at that. "No royal involvement in the case, then?"

"Both suspects at the palace have iron-clad alibis."

"You're sure? Buck House has a reputation for leaking like a sieve."

"New safeguards have been put in place to make certain no one could enter or leave."

"A shame. The duke is out of our hands, but I'd like to see Stephen prosecuted under the Labouchere Amendment."

"One could not do so without involving the royal family," Barker said.

"Barmy, isn't it? Her Majesty is pushing us for quick action, while her grandson is visiting fancy houses in the Ripper's territory. Someone needs to inform the old girl."

"Would you like the honor?" my employer rumbled.

Abberline put up his hands. "Not I. Sounds like a duty for the royal liaison."

"It is being managed discreetly. Sir Henry Ponsonby will inform His Highness, the Prince of Wales. At some point the prime minister will be involved."

"Something must be done," Abberline continued. "Not about the prince, I mean this Ripper fellow. He's making us all look like idiots. Look, I don't care what your politics or your religion are. I don't care how you feel about the commissioner or Munro or even Anderson. It's all moot if the Yard is discredited to the point that we become a laughingstock. If the chaps above us are locked in a political struggle, I say we all work together to stop the Ripper for the good of the Yard. Donald here has a subject he's watching closely as well, a fellow named Druitt. I was hunting an American named Tumblety for a while, who was in London collecting female organs in specimen jars, but he was on his way to America when the double event occurred."

"I agree we should work together," Barker said. "What of you, Donald?"

Swanson sat back in his chair and crossed his arms.

"I know what has been said around here, or at least implied," he said, his Scots accent coming out under pressure. "I have not been impeding the investigation in order to force Commissioner Warren to resign. That is a dangerous game which could end with no survivors. For a month, I have believed that the killer is a highly intelligent person that has been sending us on a goose chase, but maybe I'm wrong. Maybe he is a lunatic working randomly. We have Druitt in the East End, subject to lapses in memory, and now we have this Kosminski laddie, little more than a teen, who owns a book of anatomy which cannot be admissible in court."

"That's the problem!" Abberline cried. "If this were France, we could arrest them both, search their rooms, and find all the evidence we need to convict them. The laws of this country require that we be open and aboveboard, and find the proof before we arrest them. It's not enough that we know for a fact that one is the Ripper."

"In Scottish courts, it would be considered not proven," Barker agreed.

"Could you imagine the fury of the English public if Jack the Ripper walked out of the Old Bailey a free man?" Swanson asked.

"We cannot let that happen," Frederick Abberline said. "Facts. Evidence. We need blood samples and a weapon. Perhaps another bit of torn apron. Kosminski is mad. Perhaps he has a box full of souvenirs under the floorboards of his room."

I thought of the altar he had made from found objects.

"Are you saying I should go back into that room, sir?" I asked.

"Something should be done."

"For now," the Guv said, "let us agree to work together and to monitor both subjects very closely. If a chance avails itself, we shall try to get into Mr. Kosminski's room again."

Barker may have said "we," but I knew better. When the time came it would be me in Kosminski's charnal house, searching for evidence.

# CHAPTER THIRTY-SEVEN

October gave way to November. In Whitehall, people added long coats and scarves to their attire. In Whitechapel, they huddled in doorways out of the wind, and scurried to their destinations. Guy Fawkes Day was approaching, and Christmas was beginning its long but inevitable arrival.

We had received two presents already, in the persons of detectives Hoskins and Worth, of the CID. They arrived each night around ten and stayed until six in the morning. They watched Aaron Kosminski intently through the skylight and windows of the factory while Barker and I slept. They were quiet and professional. They brought sandwiches and a jug of coffee to get them through the night. We could not have performed our duties successfully without them.

One evening they had arrived as usual and we had bedded down for the night. I was still working at the mantle factory, trying to find a new way to break in to Aaron's bedroom to search for evidence. The lamps were out, but a fire was making a feeble attempt to warm the room.

Barker's paw of a hand was suddenly on my shoulder. He had lit a candle. I pushed myself up onto my elbows and shook my head to clear it.

"What has happened?" I asked.

"They have not seen Kosminski in an hour. I know there are portions of the room we cannot view, but he is constantly moving. At some point he should have passed under the skylight or by a window. He does not or cannot read and he slept through most of the day. I don't think he's on the premises."

"How did he get out?" I asked, pulling on my shoes.

"If I knew the answer to that, lad, I would have enough evidence to arrest him."

"It's Mischief Night," I pointed out.

"Did he seem excited when he returned from his evening walk?"

"He did," I admitted. "He was agitated, and there was some color in his cheeks. He mumbled something to his brother about people preparing for the festivities, but of course, I could make no sense of it myself. Wolfe translated for me."

"It bodes ill for the women of Whitechapel. Unfortunately, he could have left anytime during the past hour and might be anywhere within a mile."

"Or he could be somewhere in the building, having one of his cataleptic fits."

"Is that a risk you're willing to take?" he asked.

"Not after what he did to Catherine Eddowes."

The four of us hurried downstairs and into the street, making our way to where the revelers were gathering. We split up there. Nearby a church bell rang eleven times.

"Do you really think Aaron Kosminski is the Whitechapel Killer?" I asked.

Barker nodded. His hands were folded behind him and his head down watching the road ahead of him.

"You know how I feel about coincidence. There could be two lunatics strolling the East End at the moment. It is conceivable, but it is not likely. Not as likely as the possibility that they are one and the same."

"I agree, and every murder is a short walk from the factory."

We approached a bonfire at the corner of Osborn and Old Montague Street. Smoke rose from a fire there that had burned for hours and was being refueled with wood from fences. A Guy Fawkes dummy hung by the neck from a lamppost, swinging in the air. Most of the people there were drunk, but not in a cheerful way. It was a night with no real historical purpose anymore, save that these people trapped here needed to numb their minds to forget their horrible existence in these blighted streets.

"I don't see him," I said, after a few minutes.

"Nor do I, but he's difficult to spot. He has a way of blending in with the background and seems to know these streets better than we do. He has squeezed between buildings I can't fit through. He's a scarecrow."

We pushed along, looking right and left, until we found a second celebration several streets away. The Guy hanging from the night post, dangling over the fire, had a huge Hebrew nose. The crowd was shoving one another, trying to precipitate something.

"I don't like this. This could become a riot very easily."

"Keep looking," the Guv said.

"He could be a mile away by now, or back safe and sound in his bed."

"He could," he admitted. "But I perceived a trifle more urgency this evening, or perhaps it was excitement. He seemed to be enjoying the spectacle."

"Did you follow him openly?"

"No, I went to pains not to be seen. It caused some looks of concern, I can tell you. I had to show my badge to prove what I was about."

A third location, outside a public house, was just breaking up. The fire was smoldering. It was windy and sparks were being snatched up from the embers and carried through the air. That's just what we need, I told myself, a fire in the East End to seal the Ripper's reign.

"I should have brought my coat," I said. I'm awfully good at complaining if the situation requires it. "I know, keep looking."

We turned and plunged into an alley.

"Did you hear something?" Barker suddenly asked. Our progress was halted momentarily. I stopped and listened. Nothing. Nothing. A sigh.

Barker began to trot. I felt the hackles rise on the back of my neck.

The next thing I knew, I was stepping into a puddle of watery blood, and Barker was bending over a figure leaning against a wall.

"The Ripper!" I said.

I looked over my employer's broad shoulder. There was a young woman with a very pale face wrapped in a shawl.

"No, Thomas, she's giving birth."

"I'll get a doctor and a hand litter," I said, turning to leave.

"It's too late for that," he said. "The child's head has already crowned."

"I'll get help, then. You can't deliver a baby by yourself."

"I've done it before. What's your name, girl?"

"Svetlana," the girl whispered.

"Where is your husband?"

"At sea."

"We'll make you as comfortable as we can, and then this baby will come."

He ripped off his long coat and squeezed it between her and the wall. Her face went rigid as a spasm came over her.

"Thomas, I need a lantern and some clean water. I don't care where you get it. Just get it."

"Right," I said.

I turned and ran. In the next street, I found the familiar emblem of the Frying Pan. I hurried inside.

"There's a woman giving birth nearby," I said. "I need a lantern and a bucket of water!"

The barman recognized me but was still reluctant to part with his property.

"I don't know," he said. "We have lamps, but we need them for our customers."

I began putting pound notes on the counter. "Look, I'll pay for them, then I'll return them to you. You'll come out ahead."

"Beryl!" he bellowed to the woman in the back. "A bucket of water!"

"For what?" the cook asked, coming from the back.

"Someone's having a baby!"

The old woman waddled out from the kitchen, her face red from the heat. She blew a white curl out of her eyes and looked at me suspiciously.

"We came up on a young woman in an alleyway, just a street away. I need water and a lantern."

She didn't say a word but went back into the kitchen. I heard water being pumped. In two minutes, she returned.

"Kitchen's closed," she announced to the barman. "You, show me where she is."

She seized a lamp from one of the tables and motioned me out. I offered to carry the water, but she refused. I led her back to the alley and she held the lamp high in the air. I saw more than I bargained for. The baby's head was out, and Barker was slowly turning the little body around.

"That's it," he said. "Now stop pushing. Stop! I want you to pant. Pant for me, Svetlana."

By the light, I saw that the mother was young, still in her teens. It was possible she was unwed, but I wasn't going to stop everything to find out.

"The doctor seems to have this well in hand," the cook said, viewing things with a critical eye. "All over but the final shout, poor dear."

"Do you know her? Does she live nearby?"

"Dunno. H'ain't seen her before. Bad place for a birth, though, in a dark alley on Mischief Night. Baby musta been scared right out of her."

"All right, Svetlana, you're doing very well. Now, I need one more big push," Barker said in a soothing voice. Ten minutes before, he was stalking a killer through the East End, and now he was acting a midwife. "Push!"

The young woman wailed and pushed and suddenly there was a sound in the alleyway, a small cry from the newest citizen of Whitechapel.

"That voice sounds strong enough," the cook said, and she smiled for the first time since I'd met her. She took off her apron and wrapped the baby in it, while Cyrus Barker used his knife to cut the cord.

"We must send for a policeman and a doctor. May we bring them into your kitchen?"

The cook shook her head. "Her afterbirth is coming. I serve food in there. But there's a sheltered courtyard right outside. We'll make her comfortable there."

She held the baby while we helped the mother out of the alley and across to the pub. The infant was making small mewling sounds in the cook's brawny arms. Once the girl was seated on a bench by the back door, the afterbirth came. Barker removed and disposed of it with the same aplomb as he had the birth. Was this one of those abilities he expected an enquiry agent to learn? He washed the baby quickly despite her protests, then wrapped her in a new towel and gave her into the arms of her willing mother. Then he washed his hands in the bucket, soaking the blood out of his cuffs as best he could. Afterward, when a policeman had brought a litter and had taken the girl to the London Hospital, he had a smoke with his traveling pipe on a nearby bench. For once, he looked spent.

"Where did you learn to do that?" I demanded.

"In China. For months, I followed after my martial arts teacher, who was a doctor, acting as his assistant. I learned the rudiments of bone setting, stitching wounds, and of course, birthing. They've served me in good stead."

"I was always herded from the room when my brothers and sisters came," I said. "I never realized it was so painful and bloody."

"'In sorrow thou shalt bring forth children,'" he quoted.

"Do you believe she has a husband at sea?"

Barker shrugged his shoulders. "That could go either way, I suppose. It's out of my hands now. Let's go back to our room. It must be nearing midnight."

"No killing tonight."

"It is early yet. They all happened in the early morning hours. But you have work in the morning."

He rose and began to walk through what passes in Whitechapel for empty streets. Most of the revelers had gone home and the bonfires we passed were smoking ash. I was thinking to myself how nice my pillow would feel.

"I suppose there's no way to patrol the East End so extensively that the killer could not strike," I said.

"No, indeed. I don't think all of the Metropolitan Police Force working together in Whitechapel would be enough. On the other hand, he has survived so far mostly due to chance. No one ever came upon him when he was murdering a woman, though several came upon the body soon afterward. They missed an encounter by minutes. It cannot last. He'll be captured soon, if not by us, by the regular force."

"Do you prefer that we catch him?" I asked.

"Oh, I suppose, but it matters little. It would mean trouble for us, newspaper reporters dogging our steps. The commissioner would not be happy."

"No, I don't believe he would."

We finally reached our rooms and entered, climbing wearily up the stairs. Hoskins and Worth had returned and were keeping vigil again.

"Kosminski's back," Worth stated. "Perhaps he wasn't gone to begin with."

I was growing tired of sleeping rough. I wanted pillowcases and a proper nightshirt, or one of the new Indian pajama sleeping suits that our butler, Mac, fancied. Then I thought of the poor young girl who had just given birth on the cold, hard cobblestones of a bleak Whitechapel alley. Soon, I would be going back to middle-class Newington to my comfortable life. Where would she and her helpless newborn end up? Sitting down, I unlaced and pulled off my boots, then unbuttoned my braces. As humble as it was, the mattress and blanket was good enough for tonight. Barker blew out the candle he had just lit. I lay down on the bed, pulled the blanket around me, and settled my head on the pillow, when suddenly I screamed.

By the time the candle was lit again, I was standing fully on top of my mattress, my hand covered in blood.

"What?" I asked, my heart knocking my rib cage with every beat. "How did—"

"Where?" Barker demanded.

"Under the pillow."

He came around the mattresses and when he reached my pillow, kicked it over. There was a dead rat there, a large one.

"It's been cut open," I said, trying to keep myself from being ill.

"More precisely," the Guv said, looking closer by the light of the candle, "its throat has been cut and its viscera removed. It's a message for you from the Whitechapel Killer, the real one. He knows who you are and what you are trying to do."

"My word," I said.

Barker gave me a grim stare. "At least we know what he was doing tonight."

# CHAPTER THIRTY-EIGHT

Several days later I was at work like any other morning, producing garments with mind-numbing regularity. The only difference was that it was the Jewish Sabbath and I would not have to work as many hours as usual. Wolfe and his brother Isaac were bustling around the factory, seeing that we were about our duties with no slowing of production, while Aaron Kosminski had not yet awoken from his slumbers.

Lunch arrived and I washed down a dry sandwich with some tepid water from the pump. I was almost missing the Frying Pan, when there was a sudden rap on the door and a constable entered. The helmet always makes them look taller.

Wolfe Kosminski put down a jacket he was examining and met the officer at the door. There had been trouble in the past about the long hours he had forced upon his employees to work and he was anxious to avoid such trouble.

"What can I do for you, Constable?" he asked.

"Looking for a Welshman, name of Llewelyn."

All the workers turned and looked at me. I did my best to appear innocent. Privately, I wondered what he was about.

"Mr. Llewelyn is right here, sir. What can we do for you?"

"'Ave you got your papers with you, boy?" he asked.

"No, sir. They are in my room. It's not far. I could go get them, if you like."

"You're not going anywhere without me. We'll get them and take them to 'H' Division."

"But I need him to work!" Wolfe insisted. "What has the fellow done?"

"We just need to see that his papers are in order. Come along, you."

He took my arm and hurried me out the door.

"What is this about?" I demanded.

"Hush," the constable said. "Listen. There's been another murder. Your inspector is at the location right now."

"The Ripper?"

"Number five."

"Where?"

"Miller's Court. You know where that is?"

"I do. It's nearby. What happened?"

"I didn't go into the room, but I got an eyeful from the window. Depraved is what it is."

"What room are you talking about?"

"Sorry, sir, I'm telling it backward. The dollymop—the unfortunate—had a room in Miller's Court. She were a cut above the others. Much younger, better looking. Bit of a stunner, I hear, but she ain't no more. I volunteered to come get you, sir, 'cause I didn't want the others to see me get ill."

"Are you coming with me?"

"Not if I can help it, but he wants you there now. 'Op it!"

I began to run. Miller's Court was a narrow alley to the northeast, not far away, off Dorset Street, but a few streets away from where we slept. The Whitechapel Killer was murdering his latest victim practically within earshot. I felt we were no more a hindrance to him and his plans than a bluebottle fly is to a horse.

Bell Lane became Crispin Street, then I turned into Dorset and came to the entrance to Miller's Court. I stepped to avoid where someone had been ill. The street was packed with people, their expressions ranging from terror to curiosity to downright excitement. The police were shooing people away, far back enough that no one could see in. I passed under a brick arch, and down a narrow alley to a corner room, with windows on two sides. The windows were being guarded by grim-looking constables. There were nearly as many officers as citizens present. I skirted them and came to the front door. The PC there recognized me and waved me through.

"Brace yourself," he murmured.

The room was larger than one would expect for a common prostitute to rent, but then I understand the unfortunate who lived there had been uncommon. Her name, I came to learn, was Mary Kelly, and she was from Dublin. She was blond, and what passed in Whitechapel for beautiful. She could have worked in any West End brothel, or married a rich man, but for some reason, she ended up here. Here in this lowly room, she lost her beauty entirely.

As I said, the room was large, with a bedstead, a table, and chair. There had been an attempt to brighten the place with flowers and cushions. That effect had been spoiled now by all the blood, sprayed and dripping down the walls. The chamber had been a light tan in color, but now it seemed mostly scarlet.

She lay on the bed, almost as if lounging there. She had been boned. The flesh had been stripped from her skeleton as if she were a steer. The bed was drenched in what must have been gallons of blood. She had no face, beyond a pair of staring eyes. Her organs had been removed piecemeal, and stacked in a pile on the nearby nightstand. I assumed her throat had been cut to begin with, but now there was no way to tell. Her dress was lifted, and her limbs posed almost provocatively, but the flesh had been carved from her thighs, leaving only bare bone. Never before or since have I seen a sight more revolting, more pitiable, or more inhumane. I would not even wish such a fate on the very man who did it.

I fell back against the wall by the door frame. I wasn't going to be ill, but I feared passing out.

"Look out there, Constable!" the PC at the door said, touching my shoulder. "That's evidence there."

Looking over my shoulder, I saw blood splatters on the wall, from a distance of eight feet or so. This was no surgeon, performing careful surgery. This blade had been flashing up and down, slinging blood across the room. It had been a frenzy. The victim was Humpty Dumpty; all the surgeons of Charing Cross Hospital could not put her back together again. She had been slashed to mere ribbons of flesh, to pulp, in some places.

The Ripper, whom I felt now fully justified the horrific honorarium, had finally got what he wanted. Not the interruption of the murder of Long Liz Stride and the hurried mutilations of Kate Eddowes. Frenzied as it was, the killer had taken his time with this one. He had hours in which to do his terrible deed without interruption. *How had it happened?* I wondered. But the truth was, I knew. Kosminski must have seen her and followed her, forcing his way in. She would have never allowed such a creature in voluntarily.

I looked at the bed again. In fact, I looked every minute or so. I had a compulsion to look, and to look away, and then eventually to look again. My mind could not accept it. We lived in a society that held women, if not in esteem, at least as creatures that deserved to be treated gently and with polite courtesy. I have seen gentlemen who find the idea of prostitution repugnant nonetheless raise their hats to an unfortunate. If one were to slip and fall, regardless of what she did in the evening, he would help her up again. This fellow, the Ripper, saw them not as human beings, but as corpses awaiting vivisection.

"Ahem," Barker said, coughing into his fist. I looked up at the Guv. So far I had been concentrating on my own emotions. He was as stoical as anyone I had ever met. He had prayed over Eddowes's body, but here there was nothing one could touch without putting one's hand in gore. He sniffed and shook his head. There was a strong odor in the room, the sharp, metallic, iron smell of blood exposed to air, starting to coagulate.

"I need to step outside," I said.

"You ain't the first," the constable at the door muttered. He followed me outside.

There, he reached into his tunic, took out a small cigarette case, and offered me one. Normally, I do not smoke cigarettes. They are made of inferior tobacco. This one I took, and shared a match with the constable. He was another of the older ones, like PC Kirk-wood, who had seen everything. Or almost everything.

"We had one inspector in here that screamed and run out," he told me. "Reckon he was one of her clients."

"That's the worst thing I'll ever see."

"You hope. I have a daughter her age. Dunno your governor, but he's got to help track this devil down. I'll go without sleep and eat standing up, but we've got to catch him. Find some kind of bait and trap him. Anything. I live here. I've got a wife. Sisters. Nieces. If he ain't caught soon, I'll have to move them all out of town after fifteen years on the force. Even bloody Manchester is better than this."

I sucked in the smoke and tried not to cough. At least it was better than the taint of blood.

"How does one even find a clue in there, under all that blood?" I asked.

"He's mental. If he weren't before, he is now. You can't do something like that and be sane afterward."

I put the cigarette in my mouth and put out my hand. "Llewelyn."

"Jerrold," he responded, shaking it.

He reached into his pocket and pulled out a small flask. I took a pull at it. It was Irish whiskey. I passed it back to him surreptitiously, and took another puff of the cigarette. He took a nip and returned it to his pocket.

"If you hear something, I'd appreciate it if you passed the word along. Don't you think it would be tragic if some toff got away with it because he had a barrister with the Queen's Council?"

"What would you do?" I asked.

"Whatever needed to be done. A bunch of us down here have decided it would be best if this didn't go to trial."

I tried not to turn a hair, but secretly I was shocked. But then, I had no sisters and daughters in the East End. If I had, perhaps I would have felt the same. I nodded. There was nothing else to say.

Crushing out the fag end of my cigarette, I tried to go back inside, but a medical examiner was there, dismantling the macabre scene. I stepped back, and heard the clatter of hooves from a vehicle in Dorset Street. Commissioner Warren was coming, with Swanson at his elbow, looking as grim as pallbearers. I stepped back against a wall and tried to look like I wasn't there. Warren passed by and went into that room. Thinking it best to acquaint myself with Miller's Court, I walked to the far end, which was a cul-de-sac. It was nothing but bare, anonymous brick buildings, with doors and covered windows. One wall had been plastered with a poster offering a reward for the capture of Jack the Ripper. When I returned, Barker was standing outside the door.

"What now?" I asked.

"You've got to be back at work."

"I'm not sure I can handle it," I admitted.

"We have to know if young Aaron Kosminski is tucked up in his den."

I put my hand on top of my head. "My God! He could be washing off the evidence this very moment!"

"No, lad, if I know anything about it, he is not cleaning himself at all. The voices forbid it." He put his hand on my shoulder. "You need to get back. We don't want to tip our hand to Wolfe Kosminski that today is different than any other day."

# CHAPTER THIRTY-NINE

I walked through the door of the mantle factory and took my seat at the bench as if what I had just seen had not utterly terrified me. My heart was in my mouth, as the saying goes, and to tell the truth, it wasn't a pleasant feeling. I had to resist the urge to gag. Time and again the sights in that small room would come back to me, all new and vivid and terrible. Something like that stays with a man. Some scars are not physical.

As the door opened, I wondered if I could retain my incognito, or whether I would burst out and inform them I was a police officer come to arrest their brother. *Did they secretly know? Did they suspect?* Then Wolfe Kosminski's face appeared at the door.

"You're back," he said, frowning.

"Yes, sir."

"What did the constable want?"

"Simply to see and verify my papers."

"You're not in any sort of trouble, are you?"

"No, sir, as you can see. They released me immediately, but then they were awfully busy. It looks like there has been another murder."

Wolfe suddenly seized my shoulder. "Where?" he demanded.

"Nearby. Up near Dorset Street, I heard."

"Right, well, it doesn't concern us. You may get back to work. You were gone almost a half hour. Those minutes will be docked from your wages."

"Of course," I said. "I hope it won't disturb Sabbath for your family."

I went back to my seat and picked up a needle and thread, feeling his eyes upon me. He suspected me of something, but of what, precisely? I began to thread the needle, but I was listening for some sort of movement from Aaron's room.

A few minutes later I heard something, one of those barely audible sounds one hears in another room. It was more of a suggestion than a sound, the kind that makes one wonder if one's ears are playing tricks. I'd have given it up if I didn't see that Wolfe heard it, too. He turned his head in answer just an inch. I turned to face Aaron's door and put down my needle.

Then we heard a loud sound from Aaron's room, a booming, metallic noise that made both of us jump. It pulled me toward the door, almost as a magnet is attracted toward metal, but there was something in the way. It was Wolfe Kosminski.

"Mr. Llewelyn," he warned.

He tried to seize me, but I warded him off with a move Barker had taught me, the Butterfly Palm. The hands open together, forming the wings of a butterfly, as they push someone away. To tell the truth, I was amazed I had used it in the middle of an encounter. I had thought the move too flowery to be of much use.

I passed beyond him, still being drawn relentlessly into that room, that horrible charnal house that was Aaron Kosminski's bedroom. I pushed open the door and stepped in. As usual, the wall of foul air met my nose, so that I was forced to press my forearm against it to keep from gagging. The room was empty. No one was there, and yet I'd heard a sound. Two sounds.

Then it came again, this time like a sack of coal being dropped. There was an old screen against a wall, and as I watched, a limb stretched into the room, led by a dirty foot. The limb contorted, and soon a form began to squeeze inch by inch through the opening. It dawned on me then. There was a coal chute there behind the screen, just wide enough for a skeletal figure to squeeze through. I couldn't have done it, but someone determined and obsessed with doing so could have. Someone, of course, like Aaron Kosminski.

Aaron finally drew his head through the small aperture, then turned, spying me for the first time. He was covered in blood. It was in his hair, dried on his skin, and his shirt and the inside of the coat was splattered with it.

"Aaron," I said, but as I spoke, so did his brother Wolfe, who was standing behind me. I turned and looked at the elder Kosminski. His eyes were wide at the sight of his brother, dripping with crimson. He backed away, still staring at him, as he left the room. He had been willing to protect him to a point, but not this creature bathed in blood. He left the room, but I didn't.

"Aaron, how are you?" I asked, trying to calm him down. He was trembling as if he would shatter at any moment.

"Dybbuk," he murmured. It was the only word he ever said to me. It was one of the few Yiddish words I knew. It meant demon. What twisted thoughts were swirling about in his head after slaughtering a young girl that he should call me "demon"?

"It's going to be all right. I'll send for help."

From his pocket, he pulled a pair of scissors. But no, now that I looked at them, I saw it was only half a pair. It had been unscrewed, and he held a half. One very sharp half. Then another part of the puzzle fell into place. He had attacked his sister-in-law with broken scissors. A pair of scissors without their connecting bolt is still broken, is it not? This was the Ripper's blade, a single scissor ground to the sharpness of a scalpel. He jabbed at me and I jumped back.

In a trice he came forward, and the fingers of his left hand seized me by the throat. Even Barker, I believed, did not have the finger strength of that skeletal hand about my windpipe. I tried to break his hold, but as I did so, I saw him cross his arms, preparing to slash my throat deeply from right to left. He hoped to be drenched in blood yet again.

He wouldn't, not if I had something to say about it. He may have fared well against overweight, middle-aged prostitutes, but I was another matter. That's why I jammed my knee where it would do the most good. It made him scream. That's the thing about multiple murderers, I think. They're cowards, and they have a low threshold for their own pain, while loving to inflict it upon others.

He fell back and rolled on the floor howling while I figured what to do next. I was in a room with possibly the most dangerous man on earth, alone, and unarmed. I circled him and absently patted my pockets. One waistcoat pocket held my threaded needles, but the other held something more promising. A small brass tube. My police whistle. I took a breath, brought it to my lips and began to blow.

It echoed in the small room and Aaron clasped his hands over his ears, continuing to howl. Then, without warning, he launched himself off the floor at me. I could not believe how quickly he moved. He was like a gibbon, all sinews and tendons, and shrieking hysteria. He leaped on me and knocked me over onto the bed, and before I had the chance to react, I felt the point of the blade pierce my shirt and slice into my side.

I grunted, and for a moment I lost the breath I was pushing through the whistle. But I still had the needle in my hand. I jabbed it toward his eye. He turned just in time to avoid it, but the needle entered the skin just beside it and was pulled from my weak grip. Blood dribbled from the pin sticking out of his skin, and I took another breath, ignoring the pain of my own wound, and I began blowing again.

There was no way for me to know whether Aaron understood that the whistle would summon the police, or whether he merely could not stand the sound. He began clawing me, and scratching me with his filthy nails, but I seized the wrist which still held the blade slick with my own blood and then we rolled off the bed onto the floor.

He was in a manic state and fighting for his life. But he was clever as well, devilishly clever. He seized the blade from the trapped hand and I gasped as the blade entered between my ribs on the other side.

That was it. The gloves were off. Someone was snarling, and I think it was me. I turned and thumped him hard with the bottom of my fist over the socket of his left eye. His head bounced off the floor. He stopped moving. Pushing myself up off him, I sat back and pulled the whistle from my mouth, panting heavily. My trousers were soaked in blood. Where was a policeman when you needed one? Where was Cyrus Barker? Surely he knew what sort of trouble I might find here.

Out of the corner of my eye I saw movement, and just managed to catch Aaron's wrist before the blade he held in his fist ripped my jugular. We rolled onto the floor again. Aaron's feet were dug into my sides, trying to injure me further with his jagged nails, as with one hand I held his wrist while trying to jam a thumb in his eye. It was the ugliest, dirtiest fight I had ever been in. He was quickly reducing me to the same kind of animal he was in order to survive.

Surely his strength couldn't hold up forever, I thought. How can I best him? For if I didn't best him I would become his final victim. Perhaps I was on the wrong side. If I could get behind him, and wrap myself around him, he couldn't get at me with his makeshift knife.

I had wrestled a good deal in our antagonistics classes, though never with an opponent wielding a blade. I latched onto his forearm and tugged and pushed and kicked and dragged until I was nearly behind him, and then clasped my limbs about his waist. I fell onto the floor and held him as he squirmed to release himself. Then I wrapped my right arm around his neck, squeezing, and inserted the whistle into my mouth again. Finally, I blew for all I was worth and held on as he buckled. He jumped and flailed and screeched over the wail of my regulation Metropolitan Police whistle.

At one point his body was bowed with only his head and his feet on the ground and I was nearly off the ground myself. Both of us were jigging about as he gyrated in a kind of mad fury, a beast captured and cornered. If I could just hold on to him for a few minutes, surely help would come from somewhere.

Then I looked up and there was a dark shape in the doorway. It was Barker in his coat and bowler hat. He bent over slowly and lowered the barrel of a pistol to Aaron Kosminski's forehead. I felt the strength suddenly go out of him.

"Look out!" I cried, as something moved beside him.

Wolfe Kosminski had materialized out of nowhere. He seized Barker's wrist that held the gun. Barker did not hesitate. His elbow swung out horizontally as if it were on a hinge, and it clipped the elder brother on the point of his chin. Wolfe Kosminski dropped like a stone. The Guv's pistol returned to his brother's head.

"Mr. Kosminski," he growled. "My name is Cyrus Barker. I am an inspector from Scotland Yard. You are under arrest."

Then before I knew it, the room was full of constables, and things began to get confused. There was a doctor, and Barker told me not to move, and I think he told me I had done well, but perhaps I just dreamed that part. A handcart was brought and then I was being wheeled down a very bumpy road; the residents were watching me as I went by. That was the last that I can recall.

# CHAPTER FORTY

I awoke sometime later in London Hospital. I was in a casual ward, which I shared with at least two dozen other patients. It was the middle of the night and the gas was low. I remembered I had been stabbed twice. Gingerly, I felt for the heavy bandages about my abdomen. They had been wrapped from my chest to my waist. The wounds had been stitched closed, I assumed. It hurt to move, so I did so as little as possible. Simply lying on a small hill of pillows seemed to be enough for the moment.

My neighbors were asleep. My thoughts were slow. I suspected I had been injected with opium. I had just helped capture Jack the Ripper, I told myself, but it seemed largely academic at that moment. There were no emotions currently attached to the statement. In my condition, it might just as well have happened to someone I did not know.

A nurse came in carrying a candle, making her rounds in semi-darkness. She came along slowly, stopping to study a chart by one patient's bed. Not feeling sleepy, I watched her move about the room. She was a stout woman, with a personality that seemed to brook no nonsense. Not a woman to chaff.

"Awake, are we?" she asked, when she reached my bed.

"Yes, ma'am," I said. My voice came out in a whisper.

"Are you in pain?"

"No."

She lifted my chart. "You were in a fight of some sort. Two stab wounds. Tsk."

"I'm with Scotland Yard. I was in Whitechapel."

"Did you forget you are a man and not a pincushion?"

They are like that, you know, nurses: not satisfied until one is put in one's place. If there was one thing I had learned from my previous visits to hospital it is that it is best not to argue. It only incites them to further discipline.

"Yes, ma'am."

She gave me the gimlet eye, making certain I was not being sarcastic. Actually, I was, but I had not the energy it required. Also, the opium was still working, as if my mind was a chalkboard and I was writing down sentences, but just as quickly a hand was erasing them again.

"Get some sleep, Constable," she said, and moved on. I did not answer because the few words I said had left me exhausted.

For the next hour, I carried on a long soliloquy in my head. I have no recollection of what it was about, merely that I must remember it when I awoke again. It might have been as deep as a cohesive philosophy for the universe, or as common as remembering to look for my notebook in the morning. At some point, I fell asleep again.

The next I knew, it was morning. Sunlight was streaming in from some windows high in the wall. Cyrus Barker was there, looming over me as he had the day before. At least, I hoped it was the day before. Instead of a pistol, he held a bouquet of carnations in his hand. For a moment, I wondered if I were hallucinating.

"For me?" I asked, my voice sounding raspy in my throat.

"They are from Philippa," he explained. "She said she hopes you will be well again soon. But I see these are not the first."

I tried to turn my head, but it barely moved, as if it weren't constructed to move from side to side. There was another bouquet there, of mixed flowers, not large, but tasteful.

"Who is it from?" I asked.

The Guv set down the flowers, then rooted about in the other bouquet for a card.

"Here it is. 'Get well soon. Mrs. A Cowen.'"

Rebecca. *Who had told her?* I wondered. Israel, perhaps? Word travels fast in the East End. It felt good that she had sent them.

"How are you feeling?"

"Thirsty," I said.

He poured water from a pitcher into a tumbler, then lifted my head to drink. Normally when he seizes my head it is to show a pressure point, or the proper method to break a neck.

"I'm having you moved to a private room," he continued.

"Can't I go home, sir?"

"The doctor wants to be sure your wound is knitting and that there is no foreign matter in it."

"Then here is fine enough," I said. "Save the room for someone who needs it. What happened to Kosminski?"

"He has been moved to Colney Hatch, and is being watched carefully. The manic state he exhibited when he killed Mary Kelly and tried to kill you has given way to lethargy. He sits in his cell unmoving for hours. He ignores any conversation or command. He doesn't appear to notice that anyone is in the room, even when he is shaken. I cannot guarantee that his reason, if he ever had any, will return."

"Oh, he had some," I said. "Remember the rat."

"Aye."

"So, it's over?"

"I believe so. The government has decided to keep the matter out of the newspapers, since he was a Jew. They fear there would be riots. Their fears are not groundless, I suspect."

"I was just standing there when he came down through the coal chute, covered in gore."

"And wrestled with him and was stabbed twice in the process."

"I couldn't let him hurt anyone else."

"Well, he won't now, thanks to you. Exemplary work, Mr. Llewelyn."

Normally, he reserved my surname for when I'd done something boneheaded. Exemplary? I was just trying to restrain the fellow until someone got there.

"It was you who deduced the Ripper's identity, sir," I said. Then I realized I had called the killer by that name.

"Aye, in spite of the *Illustrated Police News*'s attempts to sensationalize what were actually just a few murders."

"As I said several weeks ago, sir. They instilled panic in the streets merely to sell newspapers."

I stopped and settled back on my pillows. The conversation was draining me.

"I suppose it is time for some laudanum," he said.

"No, no. I still have some questions. What's going to happen at Scotland Yard?"

"I hear the order has come through for constables to be returned to their regular beats. There will be no more patrolling Whitechapel."

"So they agree that Aaron Kosminski is the Whitechapel Killer?"

Barker nodded. "They do. There is a small chance we are all wrong. There is no way to prove the blood that covered him belonged to Mary Kelly. However, there was no other bloody occurrence yesterday and no obvious way for him to be found covered with blood otherwise. The only way to know for certain is if no more similar murders occur. This conclusion is logical. We went in looking for a madman, and we found one, right on Goulston Street where I expected him to be."

"Occam's razor.

"Precisely."

"Do you suppose Warren is satisfied?"

"Yes and no," my employer said. "He believes Kosminski is the Whitechapel Killer. However, he holds himself responsible for not capturing him sooner, or so Abberline tells me."

"That doesn't make sense," I said. "He's responsible for running the Yard, not finding the killer himself. That was Swanson's and Abberline's duty. And yours, too, I suppose."

"So many letters from the public and articles in the newspapers have been published, pointing to the inefficiency of the Yard, that in order to circumvent a vote of no confidence for the government and for the Metropolitan, in particular, Warren may decide to resign."

"But wouldn't that be exactly what Munro wants? He would be a natural for the position. It would be uncontested."

"Abberline says by Warren taking the blame, a new and better Yard may grow from the ashes, or at least that is what Warren believes."

"But, I—ah!"

Barker frowned and stepped forward. "What is it, Thomas?"

"A pain, sir. A sharp pain in the ribs."

"Your medication has worn off. I shall return in a moment."

I sat back and tried to relax, but I was angry. It wasn't fair. Barker had solved the case on Warren's watch, and he deserved to share in the success therein. To take the blame merely because he hadn't caught the Ripper sooner was simply unfair. At the same time, I had to admire his stamina and resolve. He would eventually take the blame and sail off with it, leaving Scotland Yard to expand in reputation and move into its new buildings. It was like Moses not being able to enter the land of Canaan.

Barker returned with a nurse who wasn't satisfied until she had ladled laudanum down my throat. I hate the licorice flavoring that is used to disguise the taste in patent medicines, but worse than that is nothing to hide the taste of the laudanum at all.

"There you go," she said. She wasn't the same one as the night before, but her bedside manner was no improvement. "That'll start taking effect in a few minutes."

"Thank you, nurse," Barker said, as if he was bestowing blessings from heaven. I'm blowed if the woman didn't begin to simper. I don't understand it, but sometimes he has that effect on women.

"So," I said after she was gone. "Warren may be out soon. Is there a way to keep Munro from getting his position?"

"You don't think he can do the work?"

"I didn't care for the way he went about it," I said.

"That isn't what I asked. Do you think he can do the work?"

"I don't know. I suppose so. He was second in command when Warren took over, and expected to succeed. I suppose he can."

"So do I."

Barker leaned forward and sniffed Rebecca's flowers.

"Hothouse flowers," he said. "Not as much bouquet as naturally grown ones, but nice, all the same. Is that not Rabbi Mocatta's daughter?"

"Yes, sir."

"I was not aware you had retained your relationship."

"We met by chance while I was in Whitechapel."

"And how is Asher Cowen?"

"Right enough, or so I hear. I haven't spoken to him yet."

Barker's blasted eyebrows rose above the edge of his round spectacles.

"I only spoke to her once, and shall probably not be renewing our acquaintance. I presume Israel must have told her I was injured."

"Mmmph," Barker said. Tacit disapproval, with the expectation that I should do better in future.

"We should have thought of the coal chute, sir."

"Aye, Thomas, you are right. There is an incline between Goulston Street and the alley to the east, so that the ground floor of Kosminski's factory becomes the cellar in Aaron's room."

"What is to become of the family, sir? Was Wolfe arrested?"

"Arrested and released. It was rather obvious that this family was suspicious of their brother's involvement in the Whitechapel killings. They did not know about the chute, which was disused, but suspected he might be getting out somehow. If the Yard arrested them, however, it would have to admit in court that Aaron Kosminski is the killer, and they—we—hoped to avoid that at all costs. Not that we told them that. We kept Wolfe and his brother for several hours until they voluntarily signed him over into the custody of Colney Hatch. He will have alienists watching and assessing his mental abilities and condition. Do you know why he smelled so terribly?"

"I assumed it was because he never bathed," I said.

"True, but he had taken the blood of all his victims and smeared them across his chest. That is why he was so fetid."

"My word, that's disgusting! Did you search his room thoroughly? I was wondering if they ever discovered any sign of the organs he carried away with him."

Barker shook his head. "Oh, lad. I hoped you had worked that out. The young man with whom you have been sharing the premises at 27 Goulston Street is a cannibal."

"But I thought it a joke, the Lusk letter and the half a kidney, fried and et. That was written by one of the newspapermen."

"It happens to be true. Perhaps he was not the gentleman everyone expected Jack the Ripper to be, but in terms of being mentally depraved, Aaron Kosminski was everything Grub Street could hope he would be. Of course, they will never know."

I tried to think of that, but it was too much for my worn-out brain to take in just then.

"You're starting to shimmer, sir," I said.

"I imagine that is the laudanum taking effect. I've kept you talking far too long. You must get your rest."

"Have you moved back into Newington, sir?"

"I have, but we're still at Scotland Yard for now."

"Has the doctor given any indication of when I can leave?"

"A few days. No more than a week. We shall take it one day at a time. Now, rest."

By then the room appeared to be teetering, and I thought I was on some large seagoing vessel, a floating hospital, and I fell asleep again.

# CHAPTER FORTY-ONE

A week later, I was finally able to leave the hospital. The doctor had weaned me from the opiates and was reasonably assured that no bit of foreign matter such as a small scrap of shirt had been left inside the wound, which could lead to a fatal infection. Sometimes I think my chief attribute as an enquiry agent is that I heal quickly.

The doctor had ordered another week of bed rest, but I was having none of it. It was time to settle this case and return to our offices. People would be clamoring for Barker's services by now and it would be nice to sort things out and get things back to the way they were, if that was Barker's intent. I put on my uniform, conscious of the fact that it would probably be the final time I wore it.

It was good to be home again, and I would not miss the Frying Pan. Etienne Dummolard was not effusive, but he made a *pain au chocolat* for my breakfast with fresh-pressed coffee. It was no pleasure pulling myself up into the hansom cab that was ordered to our door and I understood how Robert Anderson must have felt the night he hired us. My biggest fear was that one of my wounds might open again or begin to seep blood, and I'd have another week of enforced bed rest. After a couple of days I start to go mad from in-activity, especially if I know Barker is out doing things without me.

Alighting slowly in Great Scotland Yard Street, I pushed through the gate and into the entrance of the main building. No sooner had I entered than I knew things had changed. The desk sergeant looked pleased to see me. In the hall, one of the detectives patted me on the shoulder, and another said "Good work." By the time I reached the small kitchen, it was full of officers wanting to hear the story of how I had captured Aaron Kosminski, also known as Jack the Ripper.

They say that any true account, if told enough, becomes a story. One discards certain facts and retains others. Events are rearranged for the effect they have upon the audience and one attempts to be dramatic or humorous. To tell the truth, I had not been rehearsing my tale beforehand, preferring not to think of the events surround-ing Kosminski's capture. When I told it to Barker during my con-valescence, it had been disjointed and brief. In front of a room full of detectives, however, it had to be coherent. Whether it was or not, they tore it apart, asked questions, combed through facts, and pulled inferences from me I hadn't thought of before. Barker listened and nodded approval.

A phrase from Shakespeare came to me then. It was *Henry V*, unless I miss my guess. This "band of brothers." I didn't know these men well, but we had bonded over the teapot and the search for a multiple murderer. I had been an outsider, but was no longer. Look-ing about the room, I realized I had not been a part of something larger than myself for some time, at least since university. Barker and I were a team, but a very small one. It felt good to be part of a larger entity.

Afterward, the Guv and I were called into Anderson's office.

"This is the man of the hour," he said, shaking my hand.

"Hardly that," I said.

"He's being modest. We have been questioning the Kosminskis and have gotten signed statements from the brothers to the effect that he had the ability to escape on the nights in question when the unfortunates were killed. It isn't much, but it is as close to a confes-sion as we will ever get. The youngest brother is hopelessly mad, and can tell us nothing. We even plied him with questions from an interpreter that speaks Yiddish and German."

"It isn't that he has no brain function," I said. "It is like his mind is in a dream world or he is listening only to the voices in his head. He doesn't seem to care much for the events of the real world."

"I wonder," Barker said, "if given his freedom he would ever kill again. Over a period of a few months he went from cutting a throat to eviscerating a woman. There is no way for him to go any further. Does he begin again, or duplicate the last murder?"

"It is academic. This fellow is never getting out again. He shall be locked away for the rest of his days."

"But there is no plan to announce that Jack the Ripper, or whatever we prefer to call him, has been captured?" I asked.

"No. At some point in the future we may make unofficial mention of it, if the Jews are living in relative safety, but not now. After the Kelly murder, there were several minor attacks upon Jewish businesses. The Kosminskis had a window smashed, though I think it was merely because they were Jewish."

"Was it Warren's decision not to notify the public?" Barker asked.

"His and the prime minister's. The palace and the Home Office were consulted, as well."

"And Warren is to take the blame for not catching the Ripper, when in fact he has," I said. "I suppose Munro must be happy."

"If anything, he is chastened," Anderson said. "Officially, Warren will take the blame, but unofficially, he'll become a martyr. Cato throwing himself upon his sword and all that. Munro will not be able to say anything negative about his predecessor."

"I'm glad to hear it," I told him.

"And what about you two gentlemen? Shall you return to private work, or would you like to continue on for a while? The positions are still open, and while I cannot promise another case so engrossing, there is always interesting work to be done. That torso in New Scotland Yard, for example. We have determined it was not the work of the Ripper. You could concentrate on that murder this very afternoon, if you like."

"I cannot speak for the lad, here," the Guv said. "Any thoughts, Thomas? You decide."

I looked at him askance. Surely he was not really putting the future of the agency into my hands.

"I've certainly found the work interesting, and even stimulating, but I still prefer private work. For one thing, we can pick and choose the cases. The caseload here is relentless."

Barker gave me no indication whether my decision was the right one or not, but by now, I was well accustomed to flailing in the wind.

"I'm sorry to hear that," Anderson said. "I was looking forward to working together with you both. Thank you for coming to my aid when I was ill. You were the only men in London I could trust to take on the task."

"Not at all, Robert," my employer said. "If you need us, remember that we are but one street away."

We stood and shook his hand. Anderson's grip was firm and dry. It was good to see him restored to health. Passing down the stair to the ground floor, we found ourselves in the same passage as the first day. Like a jack-in-the-box, the selfsame sergeant stuck his head into the hallway.

"Another cuppa!" he demanded.

Was I still employed, since I was in uniform? I supposed I could make one final cup.

"Coming, sir. Right away," a voice called from the kitchen. Some poor, luckless fellow was now doomed to make tea here for the rest of the year.

"Don't call me 'sir'! I work for a living!"

"Yes, S-Sergeant."

Barker patted my shoulder and I went to change out of my uniform. Some things don't matter. Whether I actually did apprehend Jack the Ripper, it didn't impress the sergeant in charge of the uniforms and equipment.

"Don't suppose I'll get much use out of a uniform this size," he told me. "I couldn't take it home to the nipper. He's already outgrown it. I suppose I could dress up a dolly."

"Or give it to the Guy," I suggested, referring to the Guy Fawkes dummies that would be burned in effigy.

"Now there's a thought. P'raps I'll save it till next November."

"Sergeant, do you think I could keep the whistle?" I asked. "It got me out of a scrape and has sentimental attachment."

"You take it," he said. "I've got three dozen in a box under the counter."

He reached out and took my hand. "Good luck to you, son."

I pocketed the whistle, then went down the hallway to the Records Room, which PC Kirkwood called his domain.

"The case is over and we're leaving now," I said. "I just wanted to say thank you."

"The pleasure was mine, PC Llewelyn. Or rather, Mr. Llewelyn. If you ever need to look at a file, just let me know, and I'll see if I can get permission to show it to you."

"Thank you. That will be very helpful. I'll see you again soon."

I'm not much for good-byes. They make me uncomfortable. If I could get out of the building quick enough, I wouldn't have to shake another bloody hand. I climbed the stairs, where Barker was waiting for me in the corridor, talking to Abberline and Swanson.

"The inspectors have offered to take us across to the Rising Sun and stand us a pint, Thomas."

"Right. Marvelous," I said. *Damn and blast.*

So, of course, I was forced to recite the entire story again. We sat and ordered pints. Evidently, the rules against drinking on duty didn't apply to detective chief inspectors.

"I can't believe we left Kosminski's record just lying about for you to pick up," Abberline complained.

"It doesn't matter who found him, as long as he was found and stopped," Swanson said.

"Fat lot of good it will do us since we're not to get credit for it," Abberline complained.

"Would you rather," Swanson said, "that the killer's identity be revealed and we have a full riot in Petticoat Lane?"

"I would. Nothing wrong with pounding the skull of a vigilante every now and again."

As a rule, we did not touch alcohol before noon, but currently we were not employed. We'd signed our resignations and would receive our wages in due time, and Barker had not yet restarted the agency. We were a couple of chaps on the dole. I looked over at my employer. That is, my former employer. He was munching on a pickled onion from the bar, seemingly without a care. *How soon before he opened the agency again?* I wondered. He didn't seem in any kind of hurry.

"That must have been a desperate fight, Thomas," Swanson said.

I wasn't aware he knew my first name.

"I wasn't sure whether I was in the right place at the right time, or the wrong time. He attacked me before I could decide."

"It's too bad," Abberline said. "An inch in another direction and you could have drawn a police pension."

"Wish I'd thought of that then."

An ale led to an early lunch of sandwiches sliced from the joint and some chips. The Sun did good chips. Put the Guv next to a couple of inspectors and they could talk methods and cases for hours. It was close to noon before the inevitable shaking of hands, and promises to renew acquaintances soon. At last, we stepped out into Great Scotland Yard Street again and headed for the gate.

He'll expect me to ask whether or not the decision to stay in the Yard or reopen the agency were truly mine to make, I told myself. I decided I wasn't going to bring it up. If anyone should speak of it, it would have to be Cyrus Barker, currently unemployed. No, not unemployed. He was now a gentleman. I was the one who was unemployed. After all, if you've got no agency, you don't need an assistant, do you? He hadn't asked me to be his secretary or his chauffeur in the interim. I was currently without gainful employment, but I had some money saved. It seemed comical to realize that I had become his lodger. I wondered what he would charge for room and board.

We walked down Whitehall Street and as I looked toward Craig's Court, my eyes saw it. *BARKER AGENCY. PRIVATE ENQUIRY AGENTS.* The hoarding was back up. When had he ordered it restored? It had to be before he'd asked me whether we would stay with Scotland Yard or not. The question had been moot. At least we were back in business and I was employed again.

"Hallo, Mr. B," Jenkins said as we entered.

"'Lo, Jeremy, How have you been?"

"Well enough, sir. I believe congratulations are in order."

"Thank you. Please don't ask me to repeat what happened just yet. I'm tired of telling it."

Barker entered without a word, passed through into his chambers, and filled a pipe from the smoking cabinet in the bookcase. Then he sat down in his chair and looked at the post and the newspapers that had arrived that morning.

Suddenly, Jenkins seized my hand, which was resting on his desk. He inclined his head to the front entrance. I frowned. What was he driving at? He moved his eyes toward the door, rather insistently. I took two steps toward the front door and looked back at him. Almost imperceptibly he nodded. I walked to the door, opened it, and stepped out.

I looked up. The hoarding was just the same as it always was. The alley that was Craig's Court looked the same. Then I looked down. Barker's name had been installed in its rightful place. Below it now, there was a second plaque, of bright new brass. It read:

Thomas Llewelyn
Private Enquiry Agent

I knew the Guv would not appreciate any sentiment. Even a thank-you just then would be too much. I would thank him later. As it was, I reentered, nodded to Jenkins, then went in and sat down in my chair. However, I coughed, for emphasis.

Barker's pipe was going and he was slitting envelopes and considering which case to take. If being away a full street to the south had accomplished anything, it had given us a half-dozen or more cases from which to choose. No having to accept just anyone who came in because we weren't busy. My employer put every letter and envelope in the second drawer on his right. He never left anything on top of his desk. Then he picked up the morning edition of the *Times* and flapped it in a way he has that irritates me and he knows it.

Meanwhile, I pulled out my notebook and began to compile my notes. After all, I was employed again and I was expected to work. Barker was reading and I was preparing a final report from the agency for Scotland Yard.

"Asher Cowen," he said.

"Oh, please," I told him. "Do not mention his name to me. I'm tired of hearing it. What has he done now? Is he to be knighted or become the Lord Mayor of London?"

"Neither," Barker said from behind the newspaper. "He dropped dead last night while giving a speech in Stepney."

# AFTERWORD

Aaron Kosminski returned to the workhouse and eventually was admitted to Colney Hatch Lunatic Asylum in 1891. He was transferred to Leavesden Asylum and remained there until his death in 1919. He was never lucid enough to confirm or deny that he was Jack the Ripper.

Robert Anderson was a fixture at Scotland Yard until his retirement. He then wrote a series of books on Christian theology, as well as his memoirs, *The Light Side of My Official Life*. He was knighted in 1901. In his memoirs and in various interviews, he claimed that Jack the Ripper had been caught and that he was a mentally insane Polish Jew.

DCI Donald Swanson had a long and distinguished career at Scotland Yard. In a handwritten memorandum in his own copy of Anderson's book, he confirmed that Kosminski was the killer.

Charles Warren stepped down as commissioner of Scotland Yard shortly after the final killing, taking the public blame for not catching the Ripper. He was knighted for service to the Crown in 1888.

James Munro succeeded Warren as head of Scotland Yard. He was commissioner of Scotland Yard for three years.

DCI Frederick Abberline remained at Scotland Yard for several years. Eventually, he moved to Zurich and took over the European branch of the Pinkerton Detective Agency.

Prince Albert Victor (Eddy) became engaged to Princess Mary of Teck after two unsuccessful courtships, but died of what the royal palace claimed was pneumonia.

James K. Stephen, like his famous cousin, Virginia Woolf, eventually committed suicide. He had been admitted to a mental asylum in Northampton. When Prince Albert Victor died, he went on a hunger strike, dying twenty days later on February 3, 1892.

Inslip opened an establishment in Portland Place called the Hundred Guineas Club. He survived the Cleveland Street Scandal of 1890, which revealed the existence of a homosexual underworld and forced many aristocrats to flee the country.

Thomas Bulling was a reporter for the Central News Syndicate. Robert Anderson and others suspected he was responsible for the "Dear Boss" letter and the invention of the name "Jack the Ripper," in order to sell newspapers.

Israel Zangwill went on to become a famous author and apologist for his people. He invented the phrase "melting pot," and wrote a famous mystery novel, *The Big Bow Mystery*.

# ACKNOWLEDGMENTS

I am fortunate that there are so many individuals and organizations researching Jack the Ripper and publishing their findings in books, articles, and private forums. This book is the result of many years of study, and I am indebted to those who made this search possible.

As always, I wish to thank my agent, Maria Carvainis, and my editor, Keith Kahla. He and his wonderful team convince me that the Barker and Llewelyn books could not be in better hands.

Thanks must also go to my daughters, Caitlin and Heather, who cast a gimlet eye upon my work and provide encouragement. And finally, to my wife, Julie, who types, edits, advises, and occasionally stands firm as the conscience of Cyrus Barker. No one could do it better.